THE PERFECT VICTIM

Al Jackson, traveling salesman, knows that he isn't likely to get any equipment sales in Willow Creek, but he's nursing a hangover and stops here anyway. He's a friendly guy, on the road too long, and can't help flirting with the waitress, Grace. But Willow Creek folks don't take well to outsiders making time with their Grace. So when she is found murdered the next morning, everyone naturally assumes that the foreigner must have had something to do with it. And now Jackson is in jail while the town howls for blood. Only the real murderer knows what happened—and he has no intention of letting the salesman live to see a courtroom.

WINNER TAKE ALL

You've kicked around the world, a soldier of fortune. But nothing prepares you for a man who shows up in your San Francisco hotel claiming to be your twin, with an offer to switch places for ten thousand dollars. Yeah, there's going to be some rough stuff—you've got to settle your twin's gambling debt with some very dubious characters in Reno—but the money looks good, and you're up for it. You get to live the high life for awhile, which is something you could definitely get used to. But you don't figure on lovely Linda. And you sure don't figure on the neat double-cross that saps you right between the ears. Because, my friend, you've been swapped for murder!

James McKimmey Bibliography
(1923-2011)

CRIME NOVELS

The Perfect Victim (1957; expanded from "Riot at Willow Creek," *Cosmopolitan,* 1957)

Winner Take All (1959)

The Satyr (1960)

Cornered! (1960)

24 Hours to Kill (1961)

The Wrong Ones (1961)

The Long Ride (1961; expanded from "The Long Ride," *Cosmopolitan,* 1960)

Squeeze Play (1962)

Run If You're Guilty (1963; expanded from "Death Trap," *Cosmopolitan,* 1962)

Blue Mascara Tears (1965)

A Circle in the Water (1965)

Never Be Caught (3 novelettes, 1966: Never be Caught, And Then She Was Dead, Kill Him Again)

The Hot Fire (1968)

The Man With the Gloved Hand (1972)

JUVENILE FICTION

Buckaroo (1979)

As Benjamin Swift

Playoff (1981)

As Dewey Daniels

The Martindales' Nightmare (1981)

PERFECT VICTIM
— — —
WINNER TAKE ALL
— — —

James McKimmey

Interview with the Author by Allan Guthrie

Stark House Press • Eureka California

PERFECT VICTIM / WINNER TAKE ALL

Published by Stark House Press
1315 H Street
Eureka, CA 95501
griffinskye3@sbcglobal.net
www.starkhousepress.com

ISBN-13: 978-1-944520-28-1

Layout by Mark Shepard, www.shepgraphics.com
Cover design by James Heimer, www.jamesheimer.com

First Stark House Press Edition: December 2017

FIRST EDITION

Interview with James McKimmey
by Allan Guthrie

James McKimmey. Author of seventeen books and more articles and short stories than there are days in the year, James McKimmey is one of the most gifted crime writers of the '50s and '60s. *Cornered, 24 Hours To Kill, Run If You're Guilty, Squeeze Play* — you'll only be disappointed if you don't like fast-paced plots, snappy dialogue, fleshed-out characters or enough tension to snap a bungee cord. Allan Guthrie was lucky enough to speak to James for Noir Originals.

Allan Guthrie: In 1957 *Cosmopolitan* published a shortened version of your first novel under the title "Riot At Willow Creek." In 1958 Dell published the longer version as *The Perfect Victim*. How on earth did you manage to sell a first book so successfully?

James McKimmey: When I was in the Army during WWII, I had a good friend named Herb. We stayed together from Fort Leavenworth, Kansas, all the way to Germany where he was killed in action. Herb was a very wise young man. His advice to me about finding success was, "Surround yourself with good people."

I've had two marriages in my long life, the first to Marty for 47 years and ending only with her death, the second to Starr and heading for a successful decade now. I was fortunate enough that both came my way, giving me those good people I so much needed to find the marital success I've enjoyed.

In the case of my writing, I had to go looking.

When I started out with my writing career, I was living in East Palo Alto on the San Francisco Peninsula. I rented a water tower for $5 a month and wrote in there, concentrating on science-fiction stories and doing Ki-Gor (a spin-off of Tarzan) novelettes for *Jungle Stories* as John Peter Drummond, where I truly learned plotting. But I wanted to break into the so-called slick market with more general fiction, for not only the money, but also to have my work read in large-circulation magazines such as *Saturday Evening Post, Collier's, American*, and other such periodicals then in business.

I'd learned that the most successful freelancers working on the Peninsula then were Samuel W. Taylor, who'd written everything from *Saturday Evening Post* serials to short stories to novels to nonfiction books to movies, and his friend Rutherford Montgomery, one of the most successful juvenile authors ever to come along that literary path. I also learned that Sam was president of the local Authors Guild which met in San Francisco. I joined the Authors Guild and met Sam. And when I learned that Sam was driving Monty to the next meeting as a guest speaker, I suddenly developed car trouble. I phoned Sam and asked if he could drive me to that meeting too.

The night of the meeting I found myself riding in the back seat of an automobile containing Sam and Monty up front. How surrounded by successful people can you get? I rode, listening, and learned more about the writing business I was trying to enter from those two pros conversing than I'd learned in my entire prior life.

I had interested a literary agent about then and sent him several short stories pointed at that larger general market. He'd tried to sell some without success. The two I'd most recently sent he returned without trying to sell them, writing that they weren't good enough even to put on the market. I told Sam about that. He said, "Let's see them." He read the stories and said, "The hell they aren't. Send them to my agent and I'll write him an introduction for you."

I sent them to his agent who sold one to American and the other to *Collier's*.

The Perfect Victim

Now I had the agent. Now I could start writing that first novel. Opportunistic? Well, maybe. But not at anyone's expense. And how much do you want to be a writer anyway? It's how much I wanted to be one.

The new agent was Carl Brandt, of Brandt & Brandt. He had writers ranging from Sinclair Lewis to John P. Marquand. And it was about now when I saw on one of those hour-long TV dramas so popular then a young highly gifted actor playing the part of a character named Buggie, a hip musician-type and the personification of evil. I wrote down the actor's name when the credits rolled. And then the plot of my first novel began shaping itself around a pivotal character named, you guessed it, Buggie.

I tried the idea with Carl Brandt, who said, "Write it." To finance it, I got a job as an expediter in an electronics plant and started writing the book evenings. When it was completed, I sent it to Carl who gave it to his book agent, Lucille Baumgarten, who thought it would work best in paper and sold it immediately to Dell. I quit my job, determined to use the advance money so carefully that I could write full time. Meantime, although I didn't know it, Carl and his son, Carl, Jr., sent a copy of the book to *Cosmopolitan*. Days later they sold the first serial rights to that magazine for twice what the advance had been from Dell. Publication of the *Cosmo* version preceded the Dell.

Just days after the *Cosmo* sale, Marty and I were awakened by the telephone. I got up and answered it. In those days, telegrams were popular. A Western Union clerk read this one to me. I went back to bed and Marty said, "What was that?"

"A telegram."

"What kind of telegram?"

"An invitation to a party."

"What kind of party?"

"A Hollywood party."

"Who's throwing it?"

"*Saturday Evening Post*. It's for all those movie stars they've profiled. I don't know anybody at the Post."

"Where's the party going to be?"

"At the Beverly Hilton Hotel in Beverly Hills next weekend. It's RSVP. I'll send them a telegram we're not going."

"What do you mean we're not going!"

"We can't afford it!"

"What the hell do you mean we can't afford it! You made more on your book these past days than you did all year working in that electronics plant! Get on the phone! RSVP them we're coming! And wire for hotel reservations too!"

"What hotel?"

"The Beverly Hilton Hotel, you idiot!"

The stars at that party included the brightest of the era, including John Wayne, Zsa Zsa Gabor, Jayne Mansfield and Charlton Heston. Carl Brandt had wrangled my invitation from his brother who was on the staff of the *Post*. Carl's personal reward to me for writing that novel.

There's an addendum. A few years later I was in Los Angeles pushing a new book. I told Jay Richards, my Hollywood agent then, about how, in my first novel, I'd patterned Buggie after the young actor I'd seen on TV.

"Who was the young actor?" Jay asked.

"Mark Rydell. I sent him a copy of that first book and explained his influence."

"He's a director now, for *Gunsmoke*. I'll get his number. Phone him up. He'll like hearing from you."

I wasn't at all sure about that, but I phoned. I said, "I'm sure you won't remember me, but I'm Jim McKimmey. And—"

"Jim! Where are you?"

"Here in Hollywood. And—"

"Let's have lunch. Tomorrow okay? Come over to the Desilu Studios and ask for me. About one? And bring your new book. I want to read it."

We had lunch in the commissary at Desilu the next day, the Hollywood party all over again, only more so. I never admired Mark Rydell more, before or after that lunch, no matter how that gifted gentleman later ascended as one of the most important directors of our day.

That's how it happened, selling that first book.

AG: Now that's what I call an answer! Thanks, Jim. Before I ask you about some of the other good people you surrounded yourself with (among them John D. MacDonald and Ray Bradbury), I want to backtrack to a question about the Ki-Gor novelettes you wrote for *Jungle Stories*. This is news to me. How many did you write and over what period of time? Were they based on your own ideas or did you write them to order from outlines? And have you used any other pseudonyms apart from John Peter Drummond?

JM: I don't remember how many Ki-Gor novelettes I wrote for *Jungle Stories*. Only two or three within a year's span, I think. Malcolm Reiss, a great editor with Fiction House, had bought some of my science fiction for *Planet* and asked me if I'd like to do some Ki-Gors. It was income and experience, and I went for it.

I read Hemingway's African adventures as well as Robert Ruark's. I think I got the flora-fauna down okay. I plotted them well enough, I think, and they were my own ideas. But I couldn't make the characters talk right. Malcolm Reiss wrote me and said he liked everything but the dialogue. Malcolm said that Ki-Gor, a product of the jungle, talked a lot like a British aristocrat, which was a bit disconcerting.

I stopped writing them when I sold my first slick short story.

As far as pseudonyms, I also used Turkel Jones. Another was Benjamin Swift, and how that came about was that Joe Gores, one of the few really good writing friends in my life, told me about a guy who was making a good living writing novels designed to assist slow school readers. The guy was Albert Nussbaum, who'd once been on the top ten list of the most wanted criminals in America. He'd been doing time at Leavenworth, had corresponded with Joe about writing from that prison, and had gotten out because Joe Gores stood up at a hearing and convinced a board that Al should be released.

I wrote to Al, who lived in Los Angeles, and introduced myself. In turn, Al gave me the name of his editor at Scholastic which resulted in my selling that publisher *Buckaroo*. Al also introduced me to Pitman to whom I sold *Play-Off*, which was published under the Benjamin Swift pseudonym.

After Al found out I'd been selling to *Good Housekeeping*, I tried to return his favors by suggesting that we collaborate on a short story for the late, great GH fiction editor, Naome Lewis. We decided to use a pseudonym, of course. I can't remember it now – it was something like Mary Truestuff or something similar. We put "HEART" in the title because they liked heart in titles. And we worked out a story, back and forth, and came to a polished product which Al mailed from L.A. under that pseudonym. Back came a wonderful letter from Naome Lewis. We didn't sell it, but it was close. The last I heard from Al, who later died, was a letter written on a cruise boat where he was a guest writer along with none other than John D. MacDonald.

AG: After the sale of *The Perfect Victim* in 1958 you suddenly had the freedom to write full time. How hard did you find it to structure your time? Your output was extremely impressive. By my calculations you'd had ten novels published by the end of 1963! Did you put in your six or seven hours a day come rain or shine, or did you write in bursts? What was your secret?

Winner Take All

JM: I tried to put in six or seven hours a day. But I didn't always do it. And sometimes I put in more hours than that. An example would be *Winner Take All*. I got the idea I could write 5,000 words a day. So I sat down with that goal in mind. And I did it for 10 days in a row, no matter what the hours added up to. That's how long it took to write Winner, 10 days, 50,000 words. I read it through once and edited it that much. I then asked Marty, my wife then, if she would type it onto bond. I didn't want to look at it again. She did. It sold immediately. Anthony Boucher gave it a fine review. I wrote The Satyr next and completed that one in 17 days. But I could never do those two things again.

I think the real and only secret involved in writing and selling at any sort of prolific rate is having an actively buying market for your product. During that interval to which you're referring, there was still a good paperback original market. But as in all aspects of life, conditions changed. Dell stopped publishing the kind of books I'd been writing. In fact, by that time, they'd bought *The Hot Fire* and didn't publish it within the usual time frame they had those before it. Later, they decided to publish the book. And, because of the good contract my agent had drawn up, they had to buy it from me all over again.

It's quite simple, really. Any writer has got to have a market for his wares. I suppose if a writer is good enough, there's usually a market somewhere for what he or she has written. But I think it's possible that there are some really fine manuscripts out there that aren't published simply because there's no good market for them. Time can change that, of course. But if it takes too much time, how long can any writer live?

AG: You don't write detective novels, focusing instead on the viewpoint of the ordinary man, the victim, and, often, the criminal — on many occasions pre-dating the contemporary thriller by using multiple viewpoints in the same novel. What was it that drew you towards this particular (and, to my mind, fascinating) branch of crime/mystery writing?

JM: When I began writing *The Perfect Victim*, I didn't think that I was writing anything in the crime/mystery genre. I just had this basic idea and overall plan for a novel. When I'd finished, I realized that the book could be in that general category. There was a murder, after all. After it sold to Dell and then to *Cosmopolitan*, I knew the effort was definitely in the crime/mystery arena. So I didn't go there on purpose, I just naturally happened to get there.

Where the multiple viewpoints came from I definitely remember. During that phase when I was writing for Fiction House, which is to say *Planet* and *Jungle Stories*, my editor was the legendary Malcolm Reis. He was a marvel. It was for him that I started writing the longer-length stories. I was using a single viewpoint and I was having trouble. Malcolm wrote me a letter of advice that has remained with me to this moment. He said, "Think in terms of your longer stories being movies. Move that camera around so that you're getting different points of view." I began to think in those terms and was astonished to find that it made all the difference for me. And it was primarily using that technique in my novel-writing that produced whatever that branch of crime/mystery writing most of my books might represent.

AG: Which of your Dell novels generated the most income for you? Deservedly so? Was there any talk of movie adaptations?

JM: The Dell novel that generated the most income for me was the first one, *The Perfect Victim*. It did so because it also was sold to *Cosmopolitan*, had good foreign sales and also was optioned twice as a movie. The first option was to Stanley Frazen who also optioned one of John D. MacDonald's books. As John wrote to me at the time, "I hope you realize that we are now in a most curious relationship. If the movie Frazen is making from *Soft Touch*, which for some reason which passeth all understanding they have retitled *Deadlock*, makes any money for Frazen, then he will very probably pick up your option." Frazen didn't pick up the option. But the book was again optioned when Paramount story editors Joe Goldberg and John Boswell optioned all of my paperbacks for films. Although that option was renewed, none of the books were made into a movie.

The longer efforts that generated the most income were the short novels, or novellas, I wrote for *Good Housekeeping*, a Hearst publication like *Cosmo*. There were only three as I recall – a new editor-in-chief replaced the original novellas with second-rights condensed romance novels, which obviated the opportunity to do more of them. You understand that the dollar was worth more then. My price was in five figures. And so we could live a year on one sale of one novella to *GH*. Add a short story here and there, and we could live very comfortably. We had a big camper-truck at the time, and I would go out daily somewhere in these Sierra mountains, usually by a beautiful stream, and write so many words of one of those novellas. The reward, over and beyond the doing and the monetary reward, was eventually seeing the work in a magazine with about five million readers. It was the time of any commercial writer's life and surely the time of mine.

If there was a personal favorite of any of those longer efforts, I guess it was *The Perfect Victim*. I liked that story, and it opened up so much for me.

AG: You mentioned John D. MacDonald again, and I promised I'd ask you to elaborate. Among other things, the John D. MacDonald quote ("This man [McKimmey] can manipulate tension and character in ways that are beginning to alarm me") that appears on the back cover of your novel, *24 Hours To Kill*, inspired me to write an article ("James McKimmey: the Man Who Alarmed John D. MacDonald") on the way you build tension in *Run If You're Guilty*. Just how much of an influence was he?

JM: The MacDonald influence has been, I guess, rather huge. But I would also like to include Ray Bradbury in this answer because, dissimilar as they were, both were very big writing heroes to me. Both gave me a tremendous amount of time, attention and encouragement. Both became extraordinarily successful. Ray is still the hero to me he always was. I was enormously impressed by his work. I still am. But that has been a different influence than John's. Ray writes on pure instinct. He taught me to rely on that much more than I might have otherwise. But most of us just can't approach writing exactly as Ray does for the simple reason that he, in my opinion, is a genius. What he has done, and how he has done it, is not what the rest of us can do. I believe that Ray has a very good concept of who he is as a writer and what he has accomplished. But I don't think that he truly recognizes the fact that he is genius. Which, all by itself, makes him one of the nicest geniuses who has ever come down the literary trail. That's what I think about Ray Bradbury.

John MacDonald, on the other hand, was a highly industrious man with very good intelligence, who could think his way along his career with great good judgment and taught himself to write as well as he did by writing. And I could better relate to that in terms of trying to do likewise. Early in my career, the late, great mystery critic and science-fiction editor, Anthony Boucher, rejected one of my short stories with the notation that I was writing as good Bradbury fiction as Bradbury wrote on a bad day. I had to take stock.

Then came my interest in John D. The same Anthony Boucher later reviewed one of my Dell novels, the one with MacDonald's quote, stating that I was using the ways (my emphasis) of MacDonald by then, but not aping the style as I had that of Ray Bradbury. I got over attempting to write exactly like Mr. Bradbury, but I don't think I ever quite got over using the ways of Mr. Macdonald, which is to say that I wanted to write entertaining fiction with as much sense of place as existed in reality, do it for as many readers as possible and get paid as much as I could for doing it. I never remotely approached John's readership or, certainly, his earnings. But the desire to do it was always there.

And there is where heroes and followers part ways. The hero does it. The follower only tries to do it. One cannot successfully imitate genius. Which is why there is only one Ray Bradbury. But can you successfully, and truly, imitate a writer such as John D. MacDonald? I don't think so. I don't believe he was a genius. But he had a combination of qualities including a desire and ability to work harder than anyone else in the world that made him the unique writer he became. Most of us don't want to work as hard as he did as a way of professional life. I didn't. But if I had, I still wouldn't have accomplished precisely what he did because his traits as a writer were unique to him.

I see nothing wrong whatever in having heroes. They can give you what you need when you need it. But eventually certain of their capabilities entirely outweigh yours. What happens then is that you start depending more and more upon your own capabilities, those unique to you. That's when you become the entity that is honestly what you are.

But those earlier heroes leave their marks so that what you eventually become includes a part of what they were. I was very fortunate to have had two men such as John D. MacDonald and Ray Bradbury as the principal heroes of my life. Whatever qualities I might have as a writer, as opposed to the deficiencies, which I definitely own as well, those two surely helped develop. I've been extraordinarily lucky to have had them in my life.

(originally appeared in *Noir Originals,* February 2004; reprinted in *Paperback Parade*, issue 63, May 2005)

Allan Guthrie is a Scottish literary agent, author and editor of crime fiction. He has authored four hardboiled novels—*Two-Way Split, Kiss Her Goodbye, Hard Man, Savage Night* and *Slammer*—plus several novellas, for which he has been short-listed for the CWA Debut Dagger Award as well as nominated for an Edgar Award. He also helped launch the first digital-only Scottish publisher, Blasted Heath. Guthrie lives in Edinburgh.

PERFECT VICTIM

— — —

James McKimmey

Author's Note

The music of Shorty Rogers is mentioned within the text of this novel, and I have taken license to place this progressive jazz within a juke box of a coffee shop, which is perhaps an unlikely place for it. I have done so because this music, in my mind, represents the best background for the impending violence of the story.

If the geographical setting of the story seems familiar to some, that is the end of familiarities. A geographical setting which actually exists was used for this story, in order to achieve better reality. But actual people are not represented here.

—J.M.

1

People gathered quickly and everyone wanted to go upstairs and look, but in the end only five people saw the body lying in the room on the second floor of the Willow Creek Hotel.

Sheriff Grove Beaman stared down while his deputy, Doug Havery, knelt beside the body and said, "Grace is as dead as she could get."

George Cary stood at the doorway with Lola Hale, the hotel's owner. George was the editor of the *Willow Creek Standard*, but he was not thinking like a newspaperman at that moment—he was thinking only that despite the blood clotting the thick auburn hair and the odd staring of her eyes, Grace Amons was somehow just as beautiful as ever.

Later Hugh Seltz, the coroner and local undertaker, arrived; and there was quite a crowd waiting on the street when they brought the body down the stairs. Everyone stared and clucked, because in all the history of Willow Creek nothing like this had ever happened, and already a deep hatred and anger had begun to grow. Nobody but two people actually knew who was responsible for Grace's death, and of course they weren't talking about it.

But Jack Noble, George Cary's linotype operator, later put into words exactly what the town thought. In the office of the *Willow Creek Standard*, he removed his rimless glasses, blew his nose and said to George Cary, "I always liked Grace. I really did."

"I guess we all did, Jack."

"Dirty, rotten thing to happen to her, George. I'll tell you that. I'd like to have about five minutes alone with that sonofabitch who did it."

"Whoever it was," George said.

"There isn't any doubt about that, is there?" Jack asked angrily.

"Who? Who the hell are you talking about?"

"That stranger. That salesman. That rotten bastard of a raping salesman!"

There was a conviction in Jack Noble's voice that would have made one of those persons in town who knew exactly how Grace had died smile in the coolness of his intellectual satisfaction; but that did not matter because Jack Noble, like most of Willow Creek, cared only about one thing:

"... That rotten bastard of a raping salesman!"

But that was on Tuesday.

It was on Monday when the stranger, the salesman, drove into town.

2

Ahead, beyond a concrete viaduct that crossed over a slim willow-lined creek, the sign read: *Willow Creek, Population 1500*. It was in sight now, a dusty old village with a skyline no higher than the water tower on the north and the grain elevator on the south. The stranger thought, "I'll bet this burg is as lively as a Baptist Church on Monday morning."

He sighed, inspecting the flat, browned, Midwestern fields blazing under the high summer sun. His flashy brown tropical suit was wilting fast, and he could feel the sweat soaking into his straw hat with its large yellow band. Still, despite a bleak attitude and a hangover that was only beginning to diminish, his perpetual, habit-formed, ingratiating smile did not disappear.

His name was Al Jackson, home-based at Omaha, and traveling representative for Farm Equipment, Incorporated. He made an average yearly income of fifty-one hundred dollars, which was obtained by boosting his minimum guarantee with a healthy padding of his expense account; and admitted only three quarters of it to his farm-bred wife. His favorite pastime, next to liquor, cigars, stud poker and dirty jokes, was convention smokers where the girls really took their clothes off.

He'd started late that morning, feeling lousy with his hangover, and he was just hoping to God that he could find a decent hotel and some decent grub. They were all hick towns down here, and he bet himself he would have one sweet hell of a time selling a dime's worth of equipment around here. These farmers had never got on their feet since the drought, and if the company would only let him have a territory like Lou Walters got over there in eastern Iowa and western Illinois, why it would all be different....

And while Al Jackson drove slowly toward the centrally grouped main places of business of Willow Creek, sniffing with distaste the aroma blown by a hot breeze from the livestock pavilion behind the movie house and wondering why he never had any luck in this world, George Cary, publisher of the triweekly *Willow Creek Standard*, sat at the counter of the Willow Creek Hotel Coffee Shop, quietly enjoying another typical noontime meal.

It was cool in the coffee shop, and somehow detached from the old grayness of the rest of the town. The chrome and white leather of the booths seemed new and fresh, and the music of Shorty Rogers was, at that moment, playing from the jukebox at the end of the room.

There were, at this noon hour, six other people in the shop beside

George Cary.

To his right, at the counter, sat Joe King, lessee of the Conoco gasoline station on the east edge of town. To his left was Willy Turner, sometimes unemployed but now a general employee of the grain elevator. Behind the counter was Grace Amons, the waitress, her full figure showing well beneath a blue nylon uniform. And coming in from the kitchen, carrying a case of Seven-Up, was muscular seventeen-year-old Chuck Beaman, son of the sheriff, winner of Willow Creek High letters in baseball, football, track and basketball, and reported by the state's sport writers as being the best potential back the Big Seven would see in years.

Behind George, seated in a booth, was Roger Cook, son of the vice-president of Willow Creek's Community Bank, nineteen years old and summer vacationing between his freshman and sophomore years at the University two hundred and fifty miles away. Across from him was his summer guest and fraternity brother, last year's pledge captain in the Sigma Beta house, a twenty-one-year-old resident of Hollywood, California, where his father, a former native son of the Midwest, was engaged in the motion picture industry—William R. Alstair's son, Buggie.

It was a typical, matter-of-fact noon hour for George Cary, and it was this typical matter-of-fact quality that George had come to accept and even like.

Twenty-three years ago, when George was twenty-two, just graduated from the University and newly arrived in Willow Creek, the town had seemed an ordinary, rather dull Midwestern village—a temporary compromise for something much better in the future.

But now, with the settling of years, Willow Creek and its daily activity had become something else; there was in it, now, a decided contentment, a feeling of surety due to its absolute predictability, a steady, reliable comfort, in fact that helped fortify the shell George had built slowly and dedicatedly around himself ever since the shock of losing Julia in that automobile accident fifteen years ago. He had been driving at the time, and still hadn't quite forgiven himself, although the police said the other driver was equally at fault.

There were unescapable moments of regret, of course—when he remembered the intensity of his youth when he'd plunged into his journalism studies at the University, even making Phi Beta Kappa, ablaze with the ambition of becoming the best journalist in the world, and realized that now at forty-five he'd done nothing whatever to materialize those dreams.

Yet he was able to soften the regret. It was a simple matter of compressing the emotions into a quiet, mature control.

Much the same way, in fact, that he tempered his emotions when he looked at Grace Amons in her blue nylon uniform.

It was a fact that there was a universal quality of sexual attraction about Grace that few men would not experience, and George was not one of the exceptions—even though, since the loss of Julia, he had determined to remain chaste in the manner of a man who had been irrevocably in love with his wife.

Still, sitting here at the counter, watching the movement of Grace—a lithe attractive movement, unconscious and inherently honest—he thought as he had thought on a dozen different occasions, that raising hell with Grace in bed would indeed be a pleasurable way of interrupting the routine of his life in Willow Creek. He would certainly have been the last man in the world not to have understood the attention given Grace by every male in the room.

Willy Turner, for example—a stocky youth of twenty-four with bull shoulders and thick black eyebrows beneath a short forehead—was hunching forward over the counter, small black eyes alight, and saying, "What's new, Grace?"

"I found a horse in my bathtub this morning, Willy."

"Oh, yeah?" And then, after taking time to think up a proper answer: "I ain't a horse, but I wouldn't mind waking up in your bathtub, Grace."

"Oh, cut it out, Willy."

There was about Grace such an honesty that even such an obvious inference as Willy had just made was handled with casual good will.

Joe King, the service station operator, called, "Hey, Grace. How about that ham on white?"

"Okay, take it easy, Joe," Grace said, and then to Willy Turner, who had gripped her hand as she stood in front of him, "What'll you have, lover-boy?"

"You really want to know?" Willy asked, suddenly grinning.

"I've got an idea, only I'm fresh out," she said. "What else will do?"

"I might settle for a hamburger."

"You'll have to," Grace said.

George went on with his sandwich, amused. He could see in the large mirror behind the counter the reflection of the rest of the coffee shop. Roger Cook was sitting in a booth with that friend of his from the University.

Looking at Roger was a perfect way of realizing how much time had gone by. It had seemed only a year or two ago when Roger, a thin pale-faced boy with narrow shoulders, had walked the street with a kite in his hand. And now here he was probably six feet tall and with that startling baritone voice.

Just then George's reflections were broken by the entrance of the stranger in Willow Creek, the salesman, Al Jackson.

In the mirror George watched Al Jackson swagger across the room to sit at the counter.

"Well, well!" he said to Grace in a rasping, brassy voice. "Hello, beautiful, where you been all my life?"

Grace dropped a menu in front of him. "Right here in Willow Creek, mister, just waiting for you."

The man laughed loudly. "Well, I'm glad you waited, honey, because you and I are going to make some real beautiful music together."

"With you it'll be pretty corny music, I'll bet. What'll you have?"

"Wheat cakes, sweetheart, a side order of ham, and some best home-cooked coffee."

The man looked around, his eyes trying to include everyone.

"Wow! This heat! How do you stand it?"

The room was absolutely silent. There was, George detected, actual tension—it had been the stranger's entrance, in itself an intrusion into the Willow Creek privacy, and it had also been the man's cocky and intimate manner with Grace, a privilege that was believed reserved for Willow Creek's own. Joe King's eyes flickered toward the stranger then back to his sandwich, a look of irritation on his face. Willy Turner appeared genuinely angry.

But the stranger seemed to notice none of this. "Say, my name's Al Jackson. I represent Farm Equipment, Incorporated. First time I've ever been in this particular part of the state. Going to get around the countryside for the next three or four days."

George at last nodded faintly, and with this, the salesman said eagerly, "Say, is this town dry or what? I didn't see a bar whole way in."

"Partially dry," George said. "You can get package liquor at either of the drugstores. Beer at the pool hall."

"Well," Al Jackson said, "that's better than nothing."

Grace brought the man his late breakfast, and the room remained silent, except for the clinking of silverware. Joe King finished first and walked out with one final distrustful look at the salesman. Willy Turner stood up, glaring at the man who did not look up, then walked heavily out of the shop, large shoulders bunched.

George followed him, spoke to Lola Hale in the lobby, and strolled down the sun-drenched sidewalk, thinking that he wanted to talk to Amanda White in her notions store about her new ad.

It was an old habit, talking business with Amanda White, another of the series of comfortable things he did, day in and day out—but he couldn't say life was always dull. Even the entry of a stranger into Willow Creek created a definite change. He watched Willy Turner climb into the brand new Oldsmobile that was, George knew, the property of Curt Black who ran the grain elevator and was Willy's current employer. Willy made the car leap suddenly down the street with an angry acceleration that made the tires scream. George shook his head, wondering what exactly was going on in Willy's mind right now....

And Willy, as he gunned the car down the street, hunched over the wheel and swore. He'd sure as hell tell Curt to get the word out to the farmers so that creep wouldn't sell a dime's worth of the junk he said he handled. Damn him anyway, talking to Grace that way!

And then, thinking back to Grace, Willy's anger subsided somewhat as he remembered just how Grace had looked behind the counter that morning.

A pulse began beating in Willy's neck, and he gripped the wheel even tighter. Damn, he would like to get to Grace! She couldn't hold out forever, and then, by God, it would really be something!

Willy drove on, mind spinning through a whirl of mental orgies, and by the time he rolled the car up in front of the grain elevator, his face was dripping sweat, and his hands, when he removed them from the steering wheel, were trembling....

3

With business in the coffee shop lulling, Grace came around the counter and walked over to the booth where Roger Cook and Buggie Alstair were sitting.

"Hello, fellas," she said. "Sorry I kept you waiting, but you know how those guys are at noon."

"We just wanted Cokes," Roger Cook said.

"That's what I thought, Roger," Grace said to him politely. "That's why I waited until things had slowed up. How are you anyway, Roger?"

Roger smiled. He was nineteen. He'd finished his first year at the University. He was certainly a man in every physical sense, especially in his surprisingly baritone voice. And yet childhood—a fairly protected childhood, at that—was not so far behind that it was entirely easy to shed the self-consciousness of adolescence. It was a troublesome period when Roger himself was not quite certain every minute just which he was, man or boy; although here close to Grace, he felt all the emotions of a mature man.

"I'm fine, Grace," he said, and was glad that he'd lost much of his former shyness—but then who could remain shy after that first year as a pledge in the Sigma Beta house?

"And how are you," Grace said, "is it Buggie?"

"Buggie it is." Roger's friend smiled confidently. "Just fine, Grace. How are things with you?"

"You know," Grace shrugged. "Same old thing."

"Sure," Buggie nodded sympathetically. "I know."

"Plain Cokes, fellas?" Grace asked.

"Just plain," Roger said.

As Grace walked away, Buggie studied her movement carefully, a half smile on his lips; and Roger also gave one long if more guarded examination. Then Buggie turned back to Roger.

"Now don't tell me you've never fooled around with that, Rog?"

"Who said I haven't?" Roger grinned. "Did I say that?"

"Well, have you?" Buggie asked. "How was it, man?"

Roger shrugged, still grinning. "How do you think it was? You're looking straight at her."

He wasn't kidding Buggie, he knew. He was not even intending to. But he was feeling good, enjoying Buggie's stay, and enjoying talking this way, especially when Grace Amons was the chief topic. He'd never thought when he'd first pledged Sigma Beta and known Buggie only as the whip over the pledges, that he would ever enjoy being around Buggie. Yet everything was coming off just fine, and he was still a little proud that Buggie, who after all was a pretty big man on the campus, had come home with him.

Grace returned with their Cokes. "There you are, boys," she said, and walked away with the same generous movement.

Buggie, smiling and relaxed, pushed a coin into the jukebox selector on the wall beside him. The music of Shorty Rogers returned to the interior of the Willow Creek Hotel Coffee Shop. "I go for that Rogers, man," Buggie said, "but I'm surprised to find his records in a burg like this. Some salesman must have had a good line."

"Yeah, well, we're not such hicks, you know," Roger said. "And the man's music has a good beat. He puts a kick in it."

"Real wild," Buggie said. "Did you ever see *The Wild One*, Rog?" He was drumming his fingers against the table.

"I didn't see it," Roger said. "Was it good?"

"It was wild, man. It had Brando in it. One of his early movies. He rides a motorcycle. Real nowhere with anything but just getting his kicks. I think they used this Rogers to work on the music. Anyway, the music made everything right. My old man met him once at a party."

"He did?"

Buggie nodded, growing more reflective, and for an instant Roger thought he saw a shadow going over Buggie's eyes. But then, quickly, Buggie was smiling once again, eyes bright and alert. "Say, what was that guy's name who was in here—that big guy with the shoulders and no neck. Looked like a damn pig."

"Willy Turner?" Roger asked.

"Willy Turner," Buggie repeated, shaking his head. "I'll bet that boy's real wild. Did you see his face when that cornball of a salesman over there tried to go to work on Grace?"

Roger nodded. "He's kind of wild, all right. I mean, there were a lot of people around here a few years ago who thought maybe he wasn't right or something, but he's not so bad now."

"Why? What did he do?"

"Well, one time he cut this pregnant dog up."

"He what?"

"Doug Berry, he's got a farm south of town, came up along the creek and found Willy and this dog Willy'd hung up by the legs. Willy'd cut the dog down the front and taken out the unborn pups and smashed them all against a tree trunk."

Buggie suddenly started laughing. "You're kidding! He did that?"

"He did," Roger said.

"What the hell did he do that for?"

"He said he just wanted to see what the pups looked like."

"My God, what a crazy sonofabitch. Real wild, man!"

Roger nodded reflectively. In a way, now, what Willy had done seemed crazy enough to be funny. But it wasn't funny then. It was a long time ago, but Roger remembered well enough that he'd been pretty frightened of Willy in those days.

But those days were over. Everything was on a different level now. He had little to do with Willy, and Willy had little to do with him. Roger wanted things to stay that way.

"How about the rest of those people?" Buggie said. "How about the guy with the white hair? What's his interest in this fair metropolis?"

"You mean George Cary? He publishes the *Willow Creek Standard.*"

"The local crusader, huh?"

"I don't know if you'd call him that," Roger said. "What would you crusade for in Willow Creek anyway?"

"Yeah," Buggie said, nodding, half smiling. "What the hell would you crusade for in Willow Creek anyway? Do you really like this town, Rog?"

"Like it?" Roger asked. "I don't know. I never thought about it, I guess. You grow up in a place, you get attached to it. It's not Hollywood, I'll admit; but then," he added, grinning, "it's got Grace Amons."

"Yeah," Buggie said, turning his eyes toward the counter.

"You know," he added, looking curiously at Roger, "I think you're crapping me about ever having gotten close to that. I really do, Roger."

"What makes you think that, Buggie?" Roger asked.

"I might even go so far as to say I'm fairly damned certain that you're a virgin, Rog, old man."

"Go to hell," Roger laughed.

"My God," Buggie said, "imagine staying a virgin with something like Grace living in the same town."

"It can be done," Roger said. "It isn't just one big happy bedroom in Willow Creek, you know."

Buggie nodded faintly, his gaze returning once more to the activities of Grace behind the counter. "Now tell the truth, Roger. Have you tried? I mean, the honest-to-God truth. Have you?"

"Hell, yes," Roger said. "I told you. It wasn't a try. I did it. Right in the middle of the lobby of the movie house. There were six people watching at the time. She beat me to the deck, as a matter of fact, and the word got to my folks, and we had a family celebration. They were crazy about me and Grace getting together that way!"

"All right. I'm serious. It could be done, you know."

"It has been, as a matter of fact." That was the truth, Roger knew; and so was his sarcasm when he'd intimated his family would be crazy about his getting together with Grace, especially his mother. All she had to do was look at Grace, and her day was ruined.

"Yeah, but not by you, old man." Buggie straightened suddenly. "Why don't we try it?"

"Try it?" Roger asked.

"Why not? What have we got to lose?"

"Hell, that's all I need. To get the word out that I'm fooling around with Grace."

"No, now look," Buggie said. "*You* don't worry about that, do you?"

"My feelings don't always represent those of my loving parents."

"Do you care that much about what they think, Roger?"

"It isn't just that," Roger said. "Only this is a small town, Buggie. Things are different here. You can't get away with certain things. Sometimes you may not even want to."

"Roger," Buggie said, smiling pleasantly, "I thought you were a big boy now."

"Knock it off, Buggie," Roger said irritatedly.

"So forget it," Buggie said, shrugging.

"Forget what? You talk about trying to make Grace, only that's all we've done. Talking about it is different from doing it."

"All right," Buggie said, "do you want to try it?"

Roger hesitated, then said, "Sure. Okay. But I still don't see any action."

"Well, you're about to," Buggie said, but just then the salesman pushed his plate away, stood up and put on his straw hat.

"Well," Al Jackson said to Grace, "how about it, beautiful? How about you and me waking this burg up tonight?"

"I'd love to," Grace said, "but I've got to sit up with my poor mother."

"Yeah. Oh, sure," the salesman said, "only if you get bored, you know where to find me. Right here in the hotel."

"Gee," Grace said, "that's just wonderful."

"Okay, beautiful. You're missing the time of your life."

The salesman walked out, and Roger said, "He got a hell of a long way, didn't he?"

"No class, no style," Buggie said, smiling. "Watch this, old man. This is how we do it at Hollywood and Vine. Oh, Grace ..."

4

George Cary walked on to Amanda White's shop, a quiet store full of the endless things that women of Willow Creek bought to make and repair their own clothing. At the far end of the room was the small cubbyhole which was Amanda's office.

"Amanda?" George called.

"In here, George," Amanda answered from the office.

George felt a sudden quickening, the thing he'd felt for quite some time now whenever he saw Amanda. There was no explaining the feeling. Amanda was a handsome woman, he supposed, with her clean-angled face and thick, carefully groomed black hair. Yet it was something else, too, a sort of comfortable relaxed feeling when they were together.

"Just thought I'd check with you about that ad I'll be running. I'm putting it on page one with the bank ad."

"I leave it up to you, George."

Amanda had never married, George knew, and yet there was nothing particularly old-maidish about her. She was, he guessed, about thirty-seven or thirty-eight; but he could not imagine that anyone ever had or ever would molest Amanda.

"How about a cigarette, Amanda?"

Amanda smiled, showing white even teeth. "I think I will at that, George. Close the curtain a little tighter, will you?"

Amanda did not smoke in public. At first George had wondered at her extreme caution, but finally he had agreed with her that probably it was best for business. Smoking by women was no longer a novelty in Willow Creek, but Amanda White smoking would have been, and as Amanda said, she would lose at least ten good lady customers if she did so publicly.

George lit her cigarette, then one for himself. "A whole lot of excitement in Willow Creek today," he said, smiling. "A stranger in town. He stopped in at the hotel coffee shop."

Amanda nodded. "I'm sorry I missed it. Who was he?"

"A salesman. I don't know any more about him."

"It sounds interesting," Amanda said.

George could not help but enjoy Amanda's reaction. A stranger in town actually did interest her.

Just then there was the tinkle of the bell as the front door was opened. Amanda started to snuff out her cigarette, but George, looking through the curtains, said, "It's just Grove, Amanda."

"In here, Grove," George called; and a moment later, Sheriff Grove Beaman, a tall, wide-shouldered man wearing a light blue suit, entered the small office. He had an athletic grace, and the power in his body was evident at sight. His face was an older duplicate of his son's, Chuck Beaman.

"Sinning again, Amanda?"

Amanda laughed. "I've got to have some vice, you know."

Sheriff Beaman grinned, the weather lines fanning from his blue eyes. Then he turned to George. "Saw you come in here, George. You eaten?"

"Yes, I have, Grove. Thanks anyway. What's new in the sheriff's office?"

Sheriff Beaman shrugged. "You know nothing ever goes wrong in Willow Creek, George."

George nodded. "I know."

"Well, if you won't eat with me, George, I'll be on my way."

"Next time," George said. "Take it easy, Grove."

When Sheriff Beaman had gone George said, "Well, I'd better be getting back to the shop, Amanda. I hope you like the new ad."

"I'm sure I will, George."

"Say," George said impulsively, "how about walking downtown to-gether tomorrow?" Amanda's house was just three blocks from his own.

"Walk, George? Why, I think that's a very nice idea."

"Fine. I'll see you then, Amanda. Don't work too hard. And don't get caught smoking."

He laughed, putting his hand lightly on her shoulder, and then walked out briskly, feeling secure and pleased with his world, small as it was.

Amanda paused, looking at her cigarette, still feeling his touch. Then she ground the cigarette out, a tremble going through her.

In the coffee shop, Grace had responded to Buggie's calling out her name by coming around the counter once more.

"Grace," Buggie said, holding up a dollar bill, "would you mind changing this?"

"Sure," Grace said leisurely, coming up to their booth. "What do you want?"

Buggie smiled softly, and Roger studied his easy, confident manner.

"Quarters, Grace."

Grace returned the change from a pocket of her blue uniform, letting her hand brush Buggie's.

Buggie put a quarter in the selector and leaned back, smiling. "You pick out the records, Grace."

Grace cocked her head, then bent forward. "Um—let's see."

Leaning forward had made the top of Grace's uniform drape open, and Roger looked at the upper part of her breasts. He felt suddenly very warm.

Grace turned and looked at him. "What do you like, Roger?"

Roger licked his lips and shrugged. "It's up to you, Grace."

"Something slow and hot?" Grace asked.

"Right," Buggie answered. "Something slow and hot, Grace."

She punched three selections, and once more Roger could see inside her uniform. She turned her head again, catching him, but her eyes were steady and friendly.

She straightened and began moving her shoulders with the music. She was leaning close against the table so that the edge pressed across her thighs.

"Grace," Buggie said, "I really wish my dad could see you. He's in the picture business, you know."

"So I've heard."

"He'd have you in front of the cameras in ten seconds."

"So how many girls have you told that to, Buggie?"

Buggie grinned. "Not a one before you, Grace."

All three of them laughed, but Roger could, see that Grace was pleased.

"Listen, Grace," Buggie said, "we've been thinking."

"No kidding?"

Buggie kept smiling. "We've been thinking things are pretty dull right now, and we wondered if you had any ideas?"

"Ideas?" Grace said. "I thought a pair like you two would be just full of ideas."

"Well, now, Grace," Buggie said, "we are. But we're not certain they match up with yours."

Again, Grace cocked her head and moved her shoulders with the music. She looked very calm, almost sleepy, but inside she was feeling a rising excitement. Ideas, he had said. And she was getting some....

5

At first, this morning, Grace had not even remembered her visit to old Doc Granger's office.

She had awakened slowly in her room on the second floor of the hotel, delighting in that fuzzy area between sleep and consciousness, feeling very cozy and snug.

It was a nice room; really much better, in fact, than the one she'd had at home on the farm.

The bed was large and comfortable, and although one window overlooked the alley and the iron fire escape which ran along the outside of the building, two others faced the front where you could watch whatever activity there was on the street below. There was a nice soft upholstered chair and a floor lamp for reading movie magazines, and a very nice vanity with a big mirror where Grace had stuck her pictures of Tab Hunter and Rock Hudson and Montgomery Clift

She knew, of course, that she was due in the coffee shop in only minutes, but Grace was pleasantly irresponsible—a condition Lola Hale generally overlooked because Grace's presence behind the coffee counter kept business brisk. And so she lay there contentedly, unclothed, even the single sheet kicked away.

And just then there had been a soft tap at her door. "Grace?"

Grace pouted full lips and sighed sleepily. "Oh, Chuck?"

"Can I come in, Grace?"

"No."

"Oh, come on, Grace!"

Grace sighed again and pulled the sheet up around her. "Door's un-locked," she said.

The door opened instantly and Chuck Beaman came in, grinning.

"Of all the times!" Grace said, pouting but obviously not angry.

"Ah, Grace," Chuck said, and he closed the door behind him and came over and sat down on the bed.

Grace looked at his tanned, freshly scrubbed face, his light-brown crew-cut hair. The heavy jobs Lola had given him this summer had added mus-cle upon muscle. His fresh white T-shirt was tight across his chest and shoulders, and his Levi trousers bulged with steel thighs. "You look just exactly like Susan Hayward right now, Grace."

"Oh, get out."

"I mean it, Grace. Just exactly."

"Oh, nuts," Grace said, but her pout changed to a smile. "And stop that."

"Ah, Grace."

"Chuck! I'll be late getting downstairs."

"No, you won't," he said huskily.

"Chuck, I will too. Stop that."

"You won't be," Chuck said.

But Grace knew very well she was going to be late that morning.

Still, later, she didn't hurry dressing, and she really tried to think more about what Doc Granger had told her about being pregnant.

She hadn't been surprised. She knew what was what about those things, and she should have been more careful, she guessed. Still, what was done was done, and she was pregnant, all right. And that was a problem.

Of course, she didn't know whose baby it was. Maybe it was Chuck Beaman's, but maybe it wasn't. Still, she'd thought, Chuck Beaman would be best. She liked him well enough and he was a lot of fun. But she was not sure just how to go about it. She'd thought about it all morn-ing, trying to figure out the best way, so that she would be sure to wind up married and all....

But now, here in the coffee shop, standing before Roger Cook and Bug-gie Alstair, a whole new pattern of thought had suddenly opened up for her, and she just wished that she were smarter so that she could think more clearly.

This boy, Buggie, was kind of cute at that. He wasn't corny like most everybody else, and she felt a kind of excitement at the way he went at it.

Moreover, he was from Hollywood, actually, and his father was some kind of big shot out there and had a lot of money.

But Grace was not positive about just how far she would get. After all, she was a little over two months pregnant already, and she would have to claim that the baby was premature or whatever you called it. Maybe it would work, but then maybe it wouldn't. Buggie was cute all right, but he was smart, too. There was something about him that made you know that it would be pretty hard to put anything over on him.

Well, then, Roger Cook.

Now he was something altogether different, and somehow Grace felt better about that idea. After all, she'd known Roger for a long time; and she'd been aware for that long a time that she attracted Roger. That had always pleased her, made her feel kind of honored somehow, because Roger was different, actually. He was more, well, refined. Mr. Cook, Roger's father, was the same way—so tall and dignified, kind of like Roger. And important too, being vice-president in the bank.

Of course, Roger's mother didn't like her, Grace knew that. Mrs. Cook always seemed to kind of look down her nose at all that joking and stuff all the fellows did when they were around Grace, as though it kind of made her sick or something.

But now—well, maybe that would help everything actually. Maybe Grace wouldn't have to marry anyone at all. Mr. and Mrs. Cook were pretty well off, and couldn't you just see their faces if she were to walk up to them and say, "Mr. and Mrs. Cook, I'm pregnant. Your son is the father."

All of a sudden everything seemed very clear. If she could just fix it right, why, it would all be so simple. Mr. and Mrs. Cook might offer her a very great amount of money to leave town and keep Roger out of it. And she would, and have the baby, and then she could keep right on going. Maybe she could get to Hollywood after all, on her own, free and clear.

But it all depended on Roger. She was pretty certain, though, that she could count on him....

"Well, Grace?" Buggie said. "Have you got any ideas?"

"I always like to have a little fun," she said.

Buggie grinned. "So do we, Grace. Why don't we just have it together?"

Grace cocked her head and ran the tip of her right forefinger lightly over the table top. "Are you asking for a date?"

"Why, sure we are, Grace," Buggie said. "Aren't we, Roger?"

Roger hesitated, then said quickly, "Oh, sure! You bet we are, Grace!"

Grace looked at Roger squarely. "All right."

"Well, gee," Buggie said—Roger was amazed at the way Buggie could adjust his approach to match the situation—"that's just fine, Grace! What do you want to do?"

"There really isn't much to do, is there?" She pursed her lips. "Why don't you boys just come up to my room tonight? Two-twenty-two. About seven-thirty?" She lowered her voice slightly. "If you could bring a bottle, it wouldn't hurt anything, would it?"

"It wouldn't hurt anything at all, Grace," Buggie said.

Just then the tall, wide-shouldered Sheriff Beaman walked into the coffee shop. He glanced around, then waved heartily at the booth where Buggie and Roger sat.

"Hello, boys. How are you, Grace?"

Buggie nodded politely and Roger said, "Hello, Sheriff Beaman."

Grace returned to the counter, and Buggie grinned at Roger. "You see, Roger? Nothing to it."

6

It was blazing hot in Willow Creek when Roger and Buggie, in Buggie's new Ford convertible, drove away from the hotel.

Six blocks later, they met an old Cadillac. Roger waved; and the man in the Cadillac, an elderly man smoking a pipe, waved back.

"Who was that?" Buggie asked.

"Old Doc Granger."

Buggie grinned. "No kidding? Old Doc Granger?"

Roger nodded. "He's the family doctor around here."

Buggie kept grinning.

"What's so funny, Buggie?"

Buggie shrugged. "I don't know. It just figures, that's all. Old Doc Granger. I mean, it just figures."

Old Doc Granger was feeling good. As soon as he got home and picked up his luggage and fishing equipment, he would be on his way to the first rest he'd taken in years.

He was used to work. He was used to Willow Creek. He didn't mind either one because his life was wrapped up in both. Like that Cook boy he'd just waved to. Along with dozens and dozens of other Willow Creek residents he'd brought the boy into the world. He was proud of that, and he felt a little closer to them than he might had he chosen to practice in a large city.

Of course, there were the bad parts too. Like people you'd known for thirty years dying and your not being able to do anything about it and feeling just as bad as those in the family. And then there were other things. Like Grace Amons turning up pregnant.

Doc shook his head. She was a nice girl, really, a girl with strong emotions who followed those emotions in a way that was, to her, very honest.

Well, regardless, now he was going fishing, and Doctor Clements would have all the headaches for a few days. He would see Grace when he got back and maybe try to make her understand that she'd better finally settle down. But right now he was going to forget everything. Right now he was going fishing.

Roger Cook lived in a large white frame house at the west edge of town. It was a comfortable house, with a solid, substantial look, and Roger had, except for his one year in college, lived in it all his life.

It seemed, being home this summer, that things should be just the way they always had been; and yet he realized that things had changed. For one thing, as he and Buggie came into the house and were met warmly and enthusiastically by his mother—quite a pretty woman with only the faintest traces of gray showing in her deep-brown hair—he no longer felt quite the same way about her devoted attentions. It was not that he didn't appreciate his mother, it was just that he found himself uncomfortable in the wake of her obvious affection.

Mrs. Cook was telling them to come in and sit down at the dining room table, and Roger was somewhat embarrassed because she was insisting that both of them drink a nice glass of tomato juice though, as he told her, they had just had a Coke in the coffee shop.

"Now, here. Tomato juice is good for you. Do you boys eat enough at school, Buggie?"

Roger caught a peculiar smirk on Buggie's face; but then, just as though the look had been an illusion, Buggie sat down and smiled—the way he'd smiled at Roger after the fraternity initiation had ended and he'd congratulated Roger for becoming an active of Sigma Beta, a kind of transformation that had really amazed Roger.

"Yes, ma'am," Buggie said, "we eat very well."

Once at school, Roger remembered, he and Bob Kent had sneaked out of the fraternity house at eleven o'clock at night—a privilege not allowed pledges—and gone down to Milt's Malt Shop for a hamburger. Buggie had been the active who passed by and saw them through the front window. He'd just glanced at them and smiled a little. But when Roger and

Bob Kent got back to the house, Buggie was waiting for them. They each got ten boards, administered by Buggie himself. Those blows had felt like the cuts of a knife, and Roger still remembered that look on Buggie's face.

But Buggie could be extremely pleasant, just as he was now, sitting at the table with Roger and his mother, poised and smiling.

"Well, I'm just glad you boys eat well," Mrs. Cook was saying, "because I do worry about Roger."

"Don't you worry about Roger, Mrs. Cook. We've got a fine group in our fraternity. We all get along swell."

Mrs. Cook beamed. "I'm so pleased, Buggie. And I'm so pleased that Roger brought you home this summer. It's so wonderful having you boys home with me!" Then she stood up. "Now you'll have to excuse me. I've got to get things started in the kitchen. Are you sure, Buggie, that you're enjoying yourself?"

"Why, yes, ma'am," Buggie said, "I'm really enjoying myself."

And Mrs. Cook said, "Well, that's just wonderful," and hurried off to the kitchen.

For a moment there was silence; then Buggie, looking across the table, said, "Drink your tomato juice, Roger."

In a way Buggie really was enjoying himself. This town killed him, it really did. But it was better than going home. Not that Buggie disliked the Old Man. That wasn't it exactly. It was just the way he was. The Old Man was always busy at the studio. It wasn't that he was so important really—he actually wasn't, although he made a pretty good living all right. He just was kind of tied up all the time, acting as though he were important, as though he had a lot of talent or something, instead of being someone who'd gotten into the production end of the studio when it had been pretty easy to get into the motion picture business. And when he did have some free time, like at night, well, the Old Man knew how to find the right kind of girls to eat up that time, too.

Not that Buggie blamed the Old Man for all that fooling around, not after *she* left him. The Old Man had a perfect right to do anything he wanted after that. As a matter of fact, Buggie liked the way the Old Man went about that business of women. "Love 'em and leave 'em, that's the way to treat 'em," the Old Man had told Buggie. And Buggie had known the Old Man was right ever since that time he'd come home and found *her* with that guy.

She didn't know Buggie'd caught her, because he was very quiet and careful, but he had, nevertheless; and later, when the Old Man had come home, Buggie lay on his bed in his room, which was right next to theirs, and he heard all of it. *She* wouldn't let the Old Man touch her, even though the Old Man begged her—and after what *she'd* been doing earlier. That was the first time in years that Buggie had cried, and it was the last time. It didn't even bother him when *she* finally left for good and didn't even ask for Buggie's custody.

Well, now he didn't feel at all like he did then. He hadn't heard anything about *her* for a long time, and he didn't care. He didn't even care whether or not he ever saw the Old Man again either. It was simply that he just didn't care.

At first Buggie hadn't wanted to come to the University. The Old Man had insisted on it, though, because he'd gone there, and threatened to cut out with the money; and, well, there hadn't been any choice.

But it hadn't been so bad; in fact, it had been a lot better than staying at home around the Old Man. Of course, the first year wasn't much good, with all that hazing and stuff. But Buggie figured that if the Old Man had taken it, he could take it better. And then, after that, he'd been on the other side; and that wasn't bad at all. On top of it, he'd gotten a lot of kicks out of beating the Old Man's record. The Old Man had said he was smart in school, smarter than anyone else in the fraternity; only Buggie had beaten the Old Man sideways and backward. Without trying, Buggie had a straight A average, and nobody else in the fraternity— practically nobody else in school—had done that well.

And then he'd developed an interest in people like he'd never had before. He liked to see what made them work, like looking through a microscope and watching them on a slide.

Like with Roger Cook. He'd never met anyone quite like Roger before. Now that Willy Turner, there was somebody else. Buggie knew Willy's type.

But Roger—the way his parents kept him bottled up, trying to protect him so much—why, it was damned near every week that either Roger's mother or both Mr. and Mrs. Cook went driving over to the University, just to see him. Buggie really couldn't understand anybody's parents doing that.

Well, that was why, after Roger had been initiated and the hazing was over, Buggie had decided to be friendly with Roger. Just to examine Roger a little more and see what made him tick, what with his parents and coming from a little dump like this. And that was why, when Roger asked him to spend a few weeks with him at home in Willow Creek, Buggie had accepted.

It had worked out pretty good—at least it was better than going home. Somehow, it was just as good to be in Willow Creek as anywhere else. Better, in fact, because now he'd taken an interest in the town itself.

Buggie had never seen anything like it. Just a little poke of a town in the middle of nowhere. Hot and dry and small, really small. Honest to God, the people stared at you every time you went down the street. Now it wasn't so bad, because everyone knew he was a friend of the Cooks. But at first, they had looked at him like he was something from Mars. And not in a friendly way either, but like they would just as soon have shot him for putting his nose in their town. It was a laugh.

Buggie was making a real study. Letting everything go into his head. Comparing all of it with the books he'd read. Still, he'd been here three weeks now, and things had been pretty quiet. It was okay. It wasn't bad. But every once in a while Buggie wanted desperately for something to happen. Anything. Anything that would put some spark into things. It wasn't a feeling that he could figure out exactly. It was just a need that grew on him, and lately it had been growing on him more and more.

7

After an early dinner Mr. Cook, a tall, pleasant-looking man with iron-gray hair and a lean, Lincolnesque face, said he would have to do some more work at the bank that evening, and Mrs. Cook announced that she was going to attend the weekly meeting of the Willow Creek Sewing Circle at Mrs. Sam Boseley's house. Buggie and Roger went up to Roger's room.

It was a corner room with two exposures, and so there was a very slight breeze going through it now although the heat was still intense. The walls were paneled in knotty pine, and there was a double bunk, and all through the room were Roger's possessions collected during his nineteen years. His tennis racket hung on a wall. A model airplane hung from the ceiling. Roger had always felt a comfortable security here.

Buggie had dropped on his back on the lower bunk, and Roger sat in the maple chair he'd owned for ten years.

"Buggie," he said slowly, "I've been thinking. Maybe we'd better forget it."

Buggie turned his head and looked at Roger in surprise. "You mean Grace?"

"Yeah."

"Roger," Buggie said, "you must be crazy."

"I just don't think we ought to do it," Roger insisted. "I don't think we *can* do it."

"Roger," Buggie said, "don't talk about how we can't do it. Just tell me where we're going to get hold of that liquor. She said bring a bottle, and that's what we're going to do. Shall we go downtown and buy it?"

"Listen, Buggie," Roger said, "you don't understand. I mean you just can't do certain things in Willow Creek. Hell, if we were back at the University, why, I'd beat you over there. I really would. But this is crazy. If my parents knew—"

"Why don't you forget your parents for once?" Buggie asked. "Just think about that liquor. Your old man's got some stuff in the cabinet downstairs. I saw it."

There was downstairs, as a matter of fact, a bottle a brandy, a bottle of apricot wine, a small bottle of crème de menthe, and a fifth of domestic port, as yet unopened—a liquor supply rarely touched.

"Listen, Buggie, even if we went over there, we couldn't take any of that. My God—"

"Why not? You don't want to go buy it like any normal civilized human being in any other town in the United States. So we get it out of your old man's cupboard. There's a bottle of brandy in there. We just take it and go, man. Your old man will never notice. We'll put the bottle back."

"Buggie," Roger said insistently, "we couldn't do that."

"Well, we're going to," Buggie said. "I know a girl like this. She wants liquor, she's got to have liquor. We're not going up there without it."

"I don't think we're going up there at all," Roger said.

Buggie sat up suddenly. "You don't think we're going up there? The hell we're not! What's the matter? Everybody else is playing around with this dame. Why not us? What the hell is so awful about that?"

"Buggie, listen," Roger said, "you don't understand. We *can't* go over—"

"The hell we can't!" Buggie said, standing up. "I get us all lined up and you give me that crap that we can't! God Almighty, are you crazy?"

"Take it easy, Buggie," Roger pleaded. "She'll hear you!"

Buggie's face was a mask of anger, his hands were clenched at his sides. He glared at Roger, and then, suddenly, his face softened and his hands unclenched.

"Oh, now look, Rog," he said, his voice suddenly quiet and polite, "I'm sorry. I guess I'm just not used to a town like this."

"That's all right, Buggie. Hell, I just wish it wasn't this way myself. I mean—"

"Rog," Buggie said, "it's all right. What the hell, anyway." He strolled back to the bunk and lay on his back, lacing his fingers behind his head.

"It's just one more woman, anyway."

Roger looked up, then down. "That's right."

"But, you know," Buggie said carefully, "it's kind of a shame, at that. I mean not going up there and seeing Grace. What she couldn't teach you, you know?"

Roger nodded. "She gets around, all right."

"Man," Buggie said softly.

"It would have been something, when you think about it," Roger said. "I mean just to see what would happen. You know."

"I know, brother."

Roger opened and closed a hand, a sliver of excitement going through him. "But I don't see how we could have done it."

Buggie turned casually on his side. "I don't either, Rog. I mean, I understand how it is—how you wouldn't want to get caught."

"That's the whole trouble," Roger said.

Buggie was silent for a moment, then he said slowly, "You know, I'll bet we could get into Grace's room without getting caught. I'll bet we could just drive downtown and walk down the alley back of the hotel and when nobody's looking, just go up there."

"Without anybody seeing us?"

"Why not? I'll bet we could do it."

Roger shook his head. "I don't know, Buggie."

"Well, look," Buggie said. "We'll forget about the liquor, see? I mean, what the hell. The idea is just to maybe sneak up there and stay a little while and that's it. See?"

Roger was thinking about what Buggie had just said, and he was thinking about how Grace had looked earlier in the day. That sliver of excitement inside him began to grow.

Just then Mrs. Cook's voice came up from below.

"My goodness, you boys'll swelter up there. Why don't you come on down and have a nice glass of iced tea with me before I leave?"

Buggie looked at his watch, then swung himself off the bunk and grinned pleasantly at Roger. "Listen, Roger, it's only six-fifteen. Why don't we go down and have some iced tea, and you think about it, and then if you want to, why, we'll just do it."

"Well—"

"Boys?" Mrs. Cook called.

Buggie lifted his voice. "We'll be right down, Mrs. Cook." Then he turned to Roger, still grinning. "You know, all this reminds me of Buzz Curry—did you hear that story he told about that girl he picked up in Damon's Lunch that time after finals?"

Roger shook his head, and now he returned Buggie's grin. "No, I don't think so, Buggie."

"Well, you know Buzz. Anyway, he took this girl home. She had her own apartment, see? And they had this bottle of whisky. Well, Buzz talked her into playing strip poker, and ..."

8

At a little before seven-thirty Roger and Buggie casually walked down the alley between the rear of the theater and the livestock pavilion, then ducked into the back entrance of the Willow Creek Hotel. They caught one glimpse of iron-haired Lola Hale at the desk, but she had her back turned. Sam Aikens, the cook, called from the coffee shop, "Going to the show tonight, Lola?" And Lola called back, "Well it's Monday night, isn't it, Sam?"

Then they were upstairs and knocking on Grace's door.

"Come in," Grace said, opening the door. "My God, you look like a couple of escaped convicts. What's going on?"

Then they were inside finally, the door closed behind them.

Buggie grinned. "We had a race up the stairs."

Grace shook her head. "The energy of youth!"

"That's what we've got, Grace," Buggie said. "We've got more energy than we know what to do with."

For the first time Roger relaxed a little and grinned at Grace. Grace smiled back and said, "I'm glad you came, Roger."

It was a slight thing, Grace smiling that way at Roger, as though, suddenly, Buggie were not in the room; but it was enough to drain the good feeling out of Buggie instantly. Once again, all the irritations of being in this junky little burg came back into him. He crossed the room, sprawled in the large chair and said:

"We didn't bring the booze, Grace, on account of the fact that Roger didn't want to buy any. I understand they sell it in the drugstores here, but apparently nobody is supposed to walk in and buy it. As a matter of fact, Roger's old man has got some booze in his cupboard, but what he does with it is keep it there in that cupboard all the ever-loving time, and nobody's supposed to touch that either. It's kind of confusing, isn't it, Grace?"

Roger and Grace only looked confused, so he said:

"So what the hell anyway. So we don't have any liquor."

And then, quickly, Grace said, "I've got a little. I'm sure of it." She opened her bureau and brought out a pint bottle of whisky, half full. "Sure. We can have this." She smiled at Buggie. "All right?"

The irritation flickered away and Buggie smiled back. "Sure, Grace. That's just fine."

"Take the load off your feet, Roger," Grace said, "while I fix the drinks. Sit over there on the bed."

And while Roger sat down and Grace arranged three glasses on the top of the bureau, she tried to organize her thoughts as carefully as she was able.

She'd seen the tension on Roger's face when they arrived, and she knew exactly why. A visit like this for Roger was risky. Grace felt no defiance about that; it was just something that she understood quite clearly. Yet he did look more relaxed now, although Grace couldn't tell. She might not, she thought, get another chance with Roger.

And thinking that left her disturbed once more. She had never schemed before in her life, and that was exactly what she was doing now. That had bothered her earlier, in the afternoon, when she was in the coffee shop with just that salesman at the counter.

Then it had been just everything—knowing she was trying to trick Roger into something, when all along she really liked him a whole lot. And then thinking about the fact, as though she were actually realizing the full implication of it for the first time, that she was going to have a *baby*.

Her feelings got all mixed up, and when that salesman had gotten fresh with her again, why, she'd done something she never would have done before—she threw a glass of water straight into his face.

Joe King, who'd been coming in, rushed right over, and Lola, who'd seen what had happened from the lobby, hurried in too. They told the salesman he'd better watch his step and then talked to Grace, trying to make her feel better, Lola even telling her to take the rest of the after-noon off. But all Grace had been able to do was cry all the way up to her room, then lie down on her bed and cry until she couldn't cry any more.

She just couldn't stop feeling funny about everything, and she even did that crazy thing of getting up suddenly and undressing and showering, scrubbing herself until her skin actually hurt, just as though it were the most important thing in the world.

Then Chuck Beaman had knocked on the door, and there she was with nothing but a towel in her hands. Still, she told Chuck to come in any-way. It made two tears roll down her cheeks, but she did it; and then she was with Chuck all over again....

But now, she realized, she couldn't get all mixed up any more. Now she had to do things right.

She turned and handed Buggie and Roger their drinks, then she moved to Buggie and sat down on his lap. "There's a shortage of chairs, but maybe this is all right. All right, Buggie?" She stretched her legs toward Roger, still sitting on the bed. "You can hold these, Roger."

Roger for the first time noticed exactly how Grace looked. She was wearing a simple white dress printed with yellow flowers, and her legs were bare. Roger could not see how there could really be very much underneath that dress but Grace, and when he shyly put one hand around a shapely calf, he felt the excitement leap inside him.

"Well, here's to it," Grace said, holding up her glass.

"Here's to it, all right," Buggie said, then tasted the straight whisky. Roger, he noticed, took an over-sized gulp, eyes watering, then grinned like a damn stupid calf. Buggie put a hand lightly on Grace's thigh, feeling good at least that she'd chosen his lap, and said, looking up at the mirror where Grace kept her pictures of the movie stars, "Are those your favorites, Grace?"

She nodded:

"Well, you're our favorite, Grace. Isn't that a fact, Roger?"

"That's a fact, Buggie," Roger said, his blood drumming through his veins. This was not the first drink he'd had in his life; he had, in fact, gotten pretty woozy on Sigma Beta's Purple Poison the night of Homecoming. But still he was not used to liquor, and in his nervousness he'd drunk almost all the whisky Grace had put in his glass. He could feel its effects already. There was the faintest *sh* sound to his s's now. But the whole fact was that he really didn't give a damn. "That's a hell of an absolute fact," he said, and the only thing wrong with the moment was that he was afraid he might have to excuse himself, and he didn't care much for letting go of Grace's calf.

"Grace," Buggie was saying, "I've seen a lot of movie stars—as a matter of fact I know a lot of them personally. But they just don't compare with you."

"Oh, that old line again," Grace said.

"It's really not a line. It's the truth. Why, you're beautiful, Grace."

"Oh, listen to him."

"Isn't that a fact, Roger?"

"Why, that is a fact," Roger said positively. "Why, you bet that's a fact!"

"And look at those legs," Buggie said. "Look at her legs, Roger."

Roger held Grace's leg up a little. "Why, I never saw more beautiful legs in my life, Grace."

Grace giggled a little, and Buggie grinned. And then Roger could wait no longer. He ruefully disengaged his hands from Grace's leg and said, "Excuse me, everybody, will you?"

When Roger had disappeared into the bathroom, Buggie kissed Grace, just as she knew he would.

And then Grace decided to try something, not sure at all that it would work.

She whispered, "Listen, Buggie. Roger's a little tight, isn't he?"

"I guess he is." Buggie grinned.

"Buggie," Grace said intimately, "three's kind of a crowd, isn't it?"

Buggie looked at her carefully, a bit surprised. "Why, I guess it is at that, Grace."

"I mean sometimes you can't have as much fun with three around, and I really did want to have some fun, Buggie. But Roger—he's not like you, Buggie. I mean, you've been around and all. But, gee, Buggie. I mean with Roger and all—"

Buggie was really pleased. Somehow, right from the beginning, he'd felt that Grace was more attracted to Roger than she was to him. Otherwise he would have come up here alone. But now she was telling him that she wanted to be alone with him.

"Well, Grace," he said, "why don't we just get rid of Roger?"

Grace pursed her lips worriedly. "Buggie, you never know about somebody like Roger. I mean, I know. They're kind of quiet, you know? But then they have a couple of drinks, and they're not like you thought at all. I don't want any trouble. And besides I feel kind of—well, sorry for him, I guess. I mean, maybe if I just had a few minutes alone with him. I mean, he expects something to happen. And that way he'll be satisfied. Would you mind, Buggie? Then, if you wanted to ... well, you know—"

Buggie's good humor was gone once more. "So you want me to take off, right?"

"Well, you know, Buggie. I just mean—" She motioned her hands awkwardly. "You know, Buggie."

"Yeah," he said, "I know exactly. So I don't feel like taking off, Grace. So I feel like staying right where I am."

He started to kiss her once more, but Grace stood up and moved away, just as Roger reappeared from the bathroom. Buggie's face tightened in anger, and the foolish, happy look on Roger's face, as he sat down on the bed once again, only intensified that anger.

Grace stood nervously by the bureau. "Gee, I just wish we had more liquor, that's all I wish."

Buggie grinned viciously. "Why don't all three of us walk down to the drugstore, buy a quart and drink it out of the bottle on the way back?"

Roger laughed, but Grace put her hands tightly together. Then she said, brightening, "I know where we can get some. In Lola's room. She's got several bottles. She went to the movies tonight. She wouldn't miss it. Her room is at the end of the hall."

"Gee, that's great, Grace," Buggie said. "That's just fine."

"It's room two-forty-six, Buggie. Right at the end of the hall. She's got a cabinet. Right by the window. Do you want to get it, Buggie?"

"Grace," Buggie said, grinning, "I'm all tired out, actually. I just want to sit right here and look at you. Roger, you run along and get it, will you?"

Roger was silent for a moment, then he said, "Oh—all right."

"And be careful," Buggie said. "You don't want anyone to see you, you know."

Roger stood up, flushing slightly; and Buggie looked at Grace, noticing the faint signs of anger showing in her eyes. Buggie had made up his mind. He was going to get to her, all right, and tonight. And if she got really good and angry, why, it would be even better.

"Okay," Buggie said to Roger, "take off."

Roger went to the door and opened it slowly, trying, Buggie knew, to make it seem that he was not as worried about being discovered in the hotel as he really was.

"Take your time coming back," Buggie said.

And then it came to Grace suddenly. "Maybe I'd better go with you, Roger."

Buggie felt his grin disappear. This bitch, he thought. This lousy bitch!

"You relax like you said you wanted to, Buggie," Grace said. "We'll be right back."

And then they were gone, and Buggie sat there, feeling the tightness in his middle, feeling the anger make his head throb....

In Lola's room Grace got a fifth of bourbon from Lola's cupboard while Roger, relieved that they had managed the length of the hall undetected, watched, smiling happily. He started to open the door to return to Grace's room, but Grace put a hand over his.

"I'm not in such a hurry, are you, Roger?"

"Me?" Roger said. "Oh, I'm not in any hurry. Not me." Grace uncapped the bottle. "Do you mind a girl who'd drink from the bottle, Roger?"

Roger motioned his hands. "Holy smoke. Not me, Grace." He watched Grace lift the bottle and drink from it in an abandon that turned the excitement in his stomach to a hard knot. She handed him the bottle then and he lifted it, letting another drink splash down his throat.

"That Buggie is a riot, isn't he?" Roger said. "He gets on a kick, you know? You never know how Buggie is going to be."

"I've forgotten all about Buggie," Grace said, and Roger realized that she was only inches away from him, her back against the door. "I'm just thinking about you, Roger."

Roger grinned. "You'd better watch what you say, Grace. You could get in trouble talking that way."

"Maybe I'm not afraid of trouble. Maybe I like some trouble now and then. What do you mean by trouble, Roger?"

"Well," Roger said, blinking a little. "You know, Grace. You know what I mean."

"Come over here, Roger," Grace said, snapping the lock on Lola's door and walking to the bed. "Come over and sit down, Roger."

Roger stood there, surprised for a moment, then he said, "Well, sure, Grace!" He sat down beside her on the bed.

"Roger," Grace said, "don't you know how much I've always liked you?"

"Is that a fact, Grace? Well, I've always liked you. Do you know that? That's the damned truth. Do you mind if I kiss you, Grace?"

"I don't think you ought to ask," Grace said. "I think you should just go ahead. You can do anything you want to do, Roger."

"Holy smoke," Roger said, and then he kissed her, feeling very warm and wonderful.

Grace slid a hand gently behind his neck, tilting her lips up to him once more. This time he kissed her for a very long time, eagerly accepting the way she wanted to do it, and feeling his heart banging inside him.

"Gee, Roger," Grace said, "why did you wait so long to get around to this?"

"I don't know," Roger said honestly. "That's a fact, Grace!"

And then he felt her hand moving inside his shirt. "Roger, it's true what I told you. You can do anything you want to do."

"Is that a fact?" Roger whispered. "Do you really mean that, Grace?"

"Sure, I do," Grace whispered back. "What do you want to do, Roger?"

Roger knew well enough what he wanted to do, but he wasn't certain if he would know just how to go about it.

In the end that didn't matter, however, because Grace did.

9

They had been gone twenty minutes, twenty-five minutes, and Buggie stood and paced the room, hands knotted. Thirty minutes. He swore silently and steadily. And then they finally came back, and Buggie looked at Roger's face and then at Grace's, and he knew.

Buggie controlled himself, watching Grace uncap the bottle and pour the drinks, not even looking at Roger now.

"Here you are, Buggie," Grace said. She met Buggie's eyes steadily, and Buggie realized it was a cool, defiant look now.

Then Grace gave Roger his glass, picked up her own and leaned back against the bureau.

Buggie said, "Do you want to come over here and sit on my lap, Grace?"

"It's too hot, isn't it, Buggie?"

"Yes," Buggie said, "it's pretty damn hot."

The room was silent then except for a hot evening breeze rustling the drawn blinds.

"Excuse me," Buggie said abruptly, and he stood up and walked into the bathroom. There, door closed, he looked at his face in the mirror, rubbing a hand angrily across his cheek. He turned, leaning back against the sink, eyes half closed, a deep frown between his eyes, and then, suddenly, he half opened the door and said, "Roger, come here a minute, won't you?"

Roger appeared, and he closed the door behind them. "What is it, Buggie?"

Buggie whispered. "You got her in there, didn't you?"

"Got her?" Roger whispered back.

"Cut the act," Buggie said. "So you got her. All right. So fine. So admit it."

Roger gestured self-consciously. "What the hell, Buggie."

"Yeah, what the hell! So what kind of a deal is this? This is quite a party. It's so one-sided it's giving me a pain. It's like I ask you to Hollywood and take some broad upstairs and leave you sitting down below on the davenport. Some sport, huh, Rog, old man?"

"Listen, Buggie—"

"All right. So what the hell. I mean, so she puts out. So it figured. I just want to know one thing. Is this something you've tied up for yourself or what?"

"No, Buggie," Roger said, shaking his head. "You know better than that."

"So all right. Maybe we look at it like fraternity brothers then, which we happen to be. You want to hog the whole bit, tell me. I want to know. It's good to find out about a guy."

"Listen, Buggie," Roger said, "I know maybe it seems like—"

"I don't give a damn about what anything seems like," Buggie said. "I just want to know if we're going to spread this thing out."

"Spread it out?"

"Don't be dumb. I want to know—do you want to take off now and spread the joy around a little?"

Roger, Buggie saw, no longer looked very happy. He looked, in fact, pretty damn grim. There was a faint hue of red in his face.

"Okay, Buggie," he said finally. "Sure."

Buggie grinned. "So okay. She's a cheap chick, man, but what the hell! Right, man?"

"I'll take off," Roger said, opening the door and returning to Grace's room.

Grace, Buggie saw, was looking at Roger intently. "Look, Grace," Roger said. "I've got to go."

"You do?" Grace said, and Buggie could see alarm going into her eyes. "I mean, you fellows have to go?"

"Just Roger," Buggie smiled.

"But why, Roger?"

Roger looked at her, meeting her eyes, and Buggie could see something else—he could see that Roger was hurt. My God, Buggie thought.

"I just can't stay," Roger said. "Some other time, Grace."

"Roger, listen—"

"He just can't stay," Buggie said. "And that's a fact, Grace."

Roger hesitated a moment longer, and then he started for the door. "So long, Grace."

"Roger—"

But Roger was opening the door, stopping, trying once more to hide the fact that he didn't want to be caught leaving the room; then suddenly he stepped back, closing the door gently.

"What's the matter?" Buggie asked irritatedly.

"Nothing," Roger said, half angry.

"Well?" Buggie looked at him. "Is there somebody out there, is that it?" But it became obvious there was, because now they could hear the murmur of voices on the other side of the door. Buggie groaned inwardly. "The point is, Grace," he said in a stage whisper, "Rog doesn't like getting caught coming out of a girl's hotel room."

Roger flashed an angry look at Buggie.

"It's all right, Roger," Grace said. "I understand. You can just stay until they leave out there."

Buggie, tensing inside, looked at the window facing the alley. He walked over to it, looking out through the side of the drawn shade at the fire escape. He turned to Roger.

"Why don't you take the fire escape, Roger?"

Roger's face had reddened now. "I don't have to sneak down the fire escape."

"I know that," Buggie said. "You just don't like being caught in Grace's room. Take the fire escape, Rog, old man. Grace understands. She just said so."

Roger paused while Grace looked at him imploringly, and then he walked to the window. "I'll see you," he said mumbling the words so that they were barely audible. His face was burning.

Buggie snapped off the floor lamp and pulled the shade. "So long, Roger."

Roger climbed out to the fire escape, glancing once at Grace, and Buggie saw Grace turn suddenly away, eyes moist.

Roger listened to the shade being pulled behind him, and then began making his way down the fire escape steps. He felt his face continue to burn. Damn it anyway! What the hell was the matter with him, getting mad like that? Maybe it was the liquor. He could feel it, all right. But whatever it was, he'd made a fool of himself.

So he knew what Grace was like—she'd sure proved that in Lola's room. But that didn't change the fact that it had been the first time for him, with anybody. And he'd been pretty certain that it was something special with Grace too. And somehow he'd felt that he shouldn't have run out like that, that Grace really did want him to stay.

Well, he'd fouled it up now. He'd seen the look on her face when he'd moved to the fire escape. Damn it, damn it—And then they came around the corner when Roger was a fourth of the way down the escape—a youth and a girl. They stopped right beneath him, the girl standing back against the building, the youth moving close to her, kissing her.

Roger froze.

In the room Buggie turned on the light and grinned at Grace.

"Well, Grace, here we are. All alone at last!"

"Buggie," Grace said, "I really don't feel so hot. That's the truth, Buggie."

"Well, gee, Grace," Buggie said. "I'm sorry. I really am."

"Maybe," Grace said, "some other time."

"Maybe," Buggie said, "right now, huh?"

"Buggie, it's the truth. I really don't feel good."

"And like I said, Grace, I'm really sorry to hear it." Buggie had crossed to her now and put his arms around her waist.

"Buggie, some other time," Grace said. "In just another night or so, and—"

"Come on, Grace, let's quit wasting time, shall we?"

"Buggie, no."

"Why not?"

"Buggie, I really mean it. No."

"And damn it, I say yes!"

The anger exploded inside of him. It got into his blood and swept through him so that he couldn't see.

"Buggie, please. No!"

She started to scream, and he got a hand over her mouth, feeling her squirm wildly. It was all going haywire inside him, everything. "You bitch," he whispered. "You bitch!"

She got his hand away from her mouth for one second, starting the scream, and then he struck her, knocking her across the room, following her, shoving her hard toward the wall. She bounced against the wall, mouth starting to open again.

At that moment Roger came back in through the window. "What the hell—" he whispered.

But Buggie was lunging at Grace again, twisting her before she could get out more than a gasp, then shoving her once more, hard.

She stumbled backward, hands clawing, and then she was falling, striking the bureau with the back of her head and crumpling to the floor.

Buggie started for her again, but Roger was on him, stopping him. The anger in Buggie suddenly quieted. He stood there, motionless, staring down at the inert form of Grace.

"My God, Buggie—"

"She's just knocked out," Buggie said fiercely, "that's all."

"What happened?" Roger said, still grasping Buggie's arm. "What the hell happened?"

Buggie shook Roger's hand away. "Never mind!" He walked across the room and knelt beside her. Then he saw it. Her eyes. The lids were not completely shut. There was just the faintest opening of them, but enough to see her eyes staring ahead, sightlessly. He straightened and stepped back all in the same motion.

"Buggie," Roger said, moving forward, "we'd better—"

"Don't touch her," Buggie snapped. "She's dead."

10

Roger froze, staring at Grace. "Dead?"

Buggie grabbed Roger's arm, spinning him. "Now you listen to me. You listen to everything I tell you. Because if you don't, so help me, Roger, I'll kill you. What are you doing here anyway?"

"There was a couple down below in the alley, so I started back up. Then I heard that scuffling—"

"Did they see you? Did they hear anything?"

"I don't know. I don't think so. Listen, Buggie—"

"Well, damn it, they better not have!"

"Will you tell me what happened, for God's sake?"

"We just got into a scuffle. That's all. Then she fell and hit her head on the bureau. It was an accident. You saw it—" Buggie's eyes were narrow and bright. "Switch off the lamp and look down outside."

"Buggie—"

"Do it!"

Roger walked to the window, switching off the lamp, then looking down. He turned, switching the lamp on again. "They're still down there, but I don't think they heard anything."

Buggie wiped a hand across his mouth. "All right. Take care of the glasses."

"The glasses?"

"We've got to get out of here. We've got to clean up everything."

"Listen, Buggie. Now wait a minute. We can't do that. She's dead!" If Roger had been a little drunk before, he was not now.

"All right," Buggie said, turning to Roger, his voice a rasping whisper, "she's dead. So what do you want to do? Put your head out that window and call the whole town in? Do you want to do that? Nobody knows we're here. Nobody is going to know we were ever here. You listen to some crapping sense, Rog, old sport. You listen to me when I tell you to take those glasses and clean them up and hurry!"

Roger picked up the three glasses, took them to the bathroom, and washed each one carefully, feeling, strangely, that it was someone else's motion doing this, not his.

"Dry them and don't touch them again," Buggie said. "What else have we touched?"

Roger shook his head. "I don't know," he said woodenly.

"Now you understand one thing," Buggie said, moving a hand forward, grasping Roger's shirt. "We're getting out of here! We're not getting caught. You understand that, don't you, Roger?"

"Yes," Roger said shortly. "Yes, I understand that. Take your hand off my shirt!"

Buggie's hand snapped away. "Let the rest go. We've got to take off. You can't tell when—" He closed his mouth, staring at the window. "We can't get out by that fire escape. We've got to go down the hall. That's the only way. And if somebody sees us—" He looked angrily at the body on the floor.

Roger stood there silently. He did not look at Grace at all.

"Let's go," Buggie said.

They moved to the door, and Buggie carefully opened it a crack. "All right. Now!"

He swung the door open and stepped outside. Roger followed. The door shut silently behind them; they moved down the hall.

They passed a half dozen doors, then reached the stairway. Buggie stopped once, glancing at Roger, and motioned him on.

They went down the steps, trying to place each step lightly, and then they reached the first landing and came around the corner of the partition.

Leaning against the banister in front of them was the salesman, Al Jackson.

"Well, hello, there!" he said loudly. "Well, hello!"

Roger felt something lurch in his stomach as he and Buggie stood there motionless.

Jackson leaned forward clumsily and grabbed Buggie's arm. "Well, what do you say there, hey? How's it go, huh?"

The man's eyes, Roger saw, were glazed. He smelled of alcohol.

Buggie shook the man's hand from his arm, then said to Roger tightly, "Let's move."

They went down the steps fast, noticing that the register desk in the lobby was empty.

Behind them the salesman called, "Hey, there!"

They reached the alley, looking toward the bottom of the fire escape. The boy and girl were no longer there. They ran then, into the blackness behind the buildings—down, to the opposite end of the alley, then onto the sidewalk.

"Easy, now," Buggie said. "Walk naturally now."

The street was deserted as they got into Buggie's car parked near the front of the sales pavilion. Buggie leaned back, smiling.

"Well, we made it! What do you think of that, Rog, old man?"

"That salesman—"

"Drunk. Blind drunk."

Roger started to speak once more, then, looking at Buggie's face, he felt a cold, peculiar feeling running through him. He rubbed a shaking hand across his face, shuddering a little. "My God, Buggie, she's dead. Grace is dead—!"

"But we're out of there," Buggie said, still smiling, driving away in the direction of Roger's house.

"What the hell's the matter with you? She's dead, don't you understand that?"

"Yeah," Buggie said, nodding, driving along slowly. "Yeah, she's dead, all right. Only we didn't get caught up there. We've got a chance now. Only we've got to be careful. We didn't cover everything, you know."

Roger shook his head. "You just don't get it. She's dead!"

But Buggie was not listening. Something was moving through him, a feeling of exultation, a kind of release from the tension that had been building inside him. Now there was something going on. Something real. And it built the excitement in him, made him wholly alive again. Dead she was, and they were in trouble, real trouble. They hadn't cleaned that room up properly. There were fingerprints. That damned salesman, drunk or not, had seen them. No, they weren't out of trouble at all. And yet that did not diminish that feeling of rising excitement in Buggie. The realization of exactly what had happened and exactly what might happen only made his brain whirl more quickly, more accurately. Grace was dead; only nobody knew how she died, and they weren't going to either. Not while he could think this clearly. By God, he thought, something has finally happened. And that need which had been growing on him had suddenly found relief, like the sudden quenching of a terrible thirst....

As Buggie drove toward Roger's house, the salesman continued his drunken climb of the steps in the Willow Creek Hotel until, finally, he made the second-floor hallway. There, leaning against a wall to steady himself and humming happily, he clumsily pulled a box of small cigars from his shirt, dropped the box, then, after great effort, retrieved it and got a cigar out. He stared at the cellophane-covered object for a moment, shoved the box back into his pocket, and looked slyly down the hall. Oh, he'd seen her come out of that room earlier that afternoon, all right. Oh, he'd watched that behind of hers wiggle all the way down the hall, all right.

He staggered down the hall until he stopped in front of the door la-beled 222. Oh, you're something, all right, he thought. You are really something, beautiful!

He opened the door, moving forward, almost falling once more, and then looked around the lamp-lit room. A blackness spilled in front of his eyes, and he caught himself by putting one hand on the head of the bed. Everything was sure as hell swimming. He straightened, saying, "Hey, beautiful! Where the hell are you?" He grinned and started to put the cellophane-wrapped cigar in his mouth. "Where are you, old kid?" he said, and then stumbled, his eyes still not moving down to see the still body on the floor on the other side of the bed. "Ah, you ain't here, huh? Ah, that's a shame, beautiful. You and me, we could have made some music, all right, all right."

Once more he swayed into the bed, dropping the cigar to the floor, and then fumbled his way out of the room into the silent hall. He zigzagged up the stairs to the third floor, and then he was inside his own room, dropping crosswise across the bed, snoring loudly.

The lights of the Cook house were on when Buggie parked his car in the wide driveway beside the house. Buggie looked at Roger sitting mo-tionless in the car.

"All right," he said. "Come on."

"I don't feel like going in there, for God's sake," Roger said. His head was aching now, a heavy, banging ache.

"All right," Buggie said. "You forget what you feel like doing and what you don't. We're in a pile of trouble, buster, and we'd better be careful. We've got to act absolutely as though nothing has happened. Do you un-derstand that?"

"I don't want to face them. I want time to think. What's the matter with you, anyway? Don't you know she's dead back there—?"

"Don't I know she's dead back there?" Buggie mimicked. "You're damn right I know she's dead! And that's why I'm telling you to straighten up. We're going in there, and you're going to act as though nothing has happened. Do you get that through your head?"

Roger shook his head stubbornly. "I don't want to face them."

"Well, you're going to, and that's an absolute fact. Now where have we been?"

Roger sat silently, muscles flickering along his cheeks.

"Did you hear me?" Buggie said. "Where have we been?"

"Downtown. We went for a drive."

"All right. Where?"

"The river. We went to the river, and then came back and walked around a little downtown."

"Right," Buggie said. "Now you're getting with it. Let's go." They went in through the back porch into the kitchen, and just then Mr. Cook's voice rang out. "Is that you, boys? We're in here in the living room. Come in, won't you?"

Roger stood frozen, shaking his head. "I won't face them, that's all."

"The hell you won't," Buggie whispered. "Now get going."

Teeth together, Roger walked out of the kitchen.

"Say, we're all here together now," his father said happily, meeting them in the dining room. "I just haven't had a proper chance to talk to you boys. Do you notice that it's cooled off a little?"

Buggie, Roger saw, smiled broadly, nodding very politely. "Why, so it has, sir. It's a relief, isn't it? It's been quite warm."

"Too warm for me. Come on in the living room. Do you have a little time to spare for the old folks? What have you been doing anyway?"

"We just drove around a bit," Buggie said brightly. "We drove down to the river and then walked downtown a little. That's about it."

"Well, fine," Mr. Cook said. "Say, I've got a rather good idea. A little unusual around here, I'll admit. But how would you boys like to have just a little sip of wine with Mother and me? How about that, dear?" he called to Mrs. Cook, seated in the living room. "Don't you think it's about time we all had a drink of that port I got last year?"

Roger gripped his hands, keeping his face turned from his father; the liquor he'd already drunk was bitter inside him now, its effects dulled to nothing, but he was certain his father could detect it through his eyes, through the odor of it on his breath. But his father seemed to be detecting nothing at all.

"Why," Mrs. Cook called back, laughing prettily, "I think it is time. Only just a little bit for me, Father."

Mr. Cook got out the bottle from the cupboard. "The fact of the matter is, Buggie, this is a bit of an occasion. The three of us have never enjoyed a drink together before. But I think now is the time."

At any other time, Roger would have appreciated this moment—somehow he had never thought it would be possible to enjoy a drink of any kind with his parents. But now here was the opportunity, and he couldn't enjoy anything. All he could do was think about Grace lying up there. Any minute now, somebody would find her, and....

"There, Roger," Mr. Cook said. "You carry a glass to your mother and take one for yourself. Buggie, here."

"Thank you, sir," Buggie said graciously, as Roger handed a glass to his mother in the living room.

"Dear," Mrs. Cook said to Roger, "your eyes look so funny."

"It's riding in the convertible," Buggie offered quickly. "It always does that."

"Well," Mr. Cook said, as they seated themselves, "cheers, everybody."

Roger sipped his drink grimly, then sat there, hand gripped around the glass. He wanted only to get this over and get upstairs where he could really think about what had happened.

"Well, Buggie," Mr. Cook said, "how do you like it here in the small town?"

"Just fine, sir," Buggie said, and Roger stared at Buggie in a kind of fascination at the calm, comfortable way Buggie was handling himself. "I really am enjoying myself, sir."

"Well, Buggie," Mr. Cook went on, "we want you to feel right at home. I've just been worried that you might find it a little dull."

"Not at all, sir," Buggie said. "I wouldn't say that things have been the least bit dull, sir."

"Well, you're a fine boy, Buggie," Mr. Cook said. "A lot of fellows your age seem to feel they have to get pretty wild to have any fun, and I guess knowing that, well, that's why Alice and I are grateful that you and Roger can enjoy yourselves like you're doing."

"Well, we certainly have been finding plenty to do, all right. Haven't we, Roger?"

Roger nodded, his nerves jumping inside him. "Oh, we have, all right."

"Well, that's just fine," Mr. Cook said, and he'd drunk almost all of his port. "It proves you've got a lot of sense and maturity, Buggie, to see anything here when you're used to something entirely different."

"Well, sir," Buggie said, body relaxed, eyes brightly alert, "it seems to me that people are pretty much the same anywhere."

Mr. Cook nodded positively. "You're right, Buggie. That's it entirely. Now I haven't been to your home, Hollywood, and I haven't met any of the picture people I know your father associates with. But I have been to Chicago and once to New York, and I would say that, basically, people are the same everywhere."

"Yes, sir," Buggie said.

"The only difference," Mr. Cook said, "is the place itself. Do you follow me, Buggie?"

"I think so, sir, but I'd like to hear more."

Roger sat there stiffly, unable to take his eyes off Buggie.

"Well," Mr. Cook said, leaning back comfortably, "you can't deny that the place itself has got to determine quite a bit how people go at things. And places differ because of the inherent purpose of each place. I mean, take Hollywood, for instance. Now I don't know much about it, I'll admit. But I think you can take it for granted that the purpose of Hollywood revolves around the motion picture business."

"Yes, sir," Buggie said.

"That, then, determines that place's purpose, and that purpose is what creates the only difference between the people there and the people here, and that is, actually, only a superficial difference—don't you see?"

"I think so, sir."

"Well, then, take Willow Creek on the other hand. Willow Creek is the center of this particular agricultural area. That is its purpose, and no more. We all function around the wheat and the corn and the cattle and the hogs. Our bank wouldn't exist if it weren't for all these fields you see around here, all the livestock. Everything in this little town of ours exists for that. And that's why everything is the way it is. The ways of cities are not needed here. Oh, maybe a handful of us might like things a bit different, but we're the minority, and we're bound by the group. The farmers are the nucleus, and all of us here in Willow Creek exist because of the farmer."

"You certainly put it well, Mr. Cook," Buggie said.

Mr. Cook smiled and looked down at the empty glass in his hand. "Well, Buggie, I've had a lot of time to think about it. I mean, I've generalized about this, but it all has a very specific application to each of us."

"How do you mean, sir?"

"Well, I mean we're bound, each of us, to the traditions of Willow Creek. I mean there is no room for any real break from those traditions."

"Could you be a little more specific, sir?"

"Well, like our conduct, for instance. Conduct is very important in Willow Creek, Buggie. I don't know precisely where the laws of our conduct started or just precisely who started them. But they exist, nevertheless, and we've got to follow them to the letter."

"I guess that's kind of a bad thing, sir," Buggie said.

"Not necessarily, Buggie. At least, I don't think so. Who was it—Chesterton?—who said he would rather believe in the undistinguished multitudes who are a contributing part of society than in any special single opposer of tradition who views from the outside? Well, something like that anyway."

Mr. Cook smiled rather apologetically.

"In other words," he continued, "tradition comes from the multitudes.

A reaction against tradition usually comes from a single opposer. To defy tradition, you usually have to do it alone. One man against the world."

"Well, isn't that how progress is made?" Buggie asked. "Isn't it always that one violator who points the way, who starts out what might eventually become tradition?"

Mr. Cook nodded. "I think you're right, Buggie. Multitudes don't like change. Only a strong individual can advocate change. But one thing you can say for multitudes. On the whole they make fewer mistakes than the individual in revolt—after all, what they stand for has been tested by time. The loner's opinion may be nothing more than a whim—sometimes a madman's whim, at that."

Buggie sipped at his drink politely. "Well, I certainly enjoy hearing your opinions, Mr. Cook."

Mr. Cook shrugged. "I just wanted to try to explain a little bit about why we are the way we are, Buggie. I don't know that I've done it very well. It's just—well, somehow tradition has been established here in Willow Creek, and we live by it. I don't really know what value any change would be here. I mean, real change. Whatever it is we are, whatever it is we do—well, it has worked for a long time now. It ought to go on working all right."

Mr. Cook started to lift his glass, then noticed it was empty. He straightened, smiling. "Well, I just wanted to say, Buggie, that if we appear a little stiff, a little restricted—there's a reason for it. Alice, Roger, myself—we're a part of Willow Creek, and we have to respect it. Moreover, we have to respect the exact part we play in Willow Creek's social structure. I can't do what, say, Joe Neely does. Joe Neely gets drunk every Saturday night, and I can't do that—even if I wanted to. And that is why I think Mother, and I had better retire now, before I pour us all another drink."

Mr. Cook laughed, and Mrs. Cook and Buggie laughed with him; and Roger was very certain that his father would never have poured another drink, under any circumstance.

In Roger's room, five minutes later, Roger gripped his hands into fists, sweat pouring down his face. "How could you sit there and talk like nothing had happened?"

Buggie lay flat on his back on one of the bunks, eyes reflective. "Take it easy, Roger, old sport," he said softly.

"Damn it, they could find her right this minute, and what then? We never should have run out, do you know that? Hell, it was just an accident, wasn't it?"

"That's what it was, Roger. Just an accident."

"All right. We could have told them that."

"That's right," Buggie said. "But it's too late now, man. Besides," he said, turning his head, a faint smile on his lips, "you just heard your father spout off—how would it be if the whole damned town knew we'd been up there fooling around with Grace? I mean, man, aside from the fact that she's dead and the explanations we'd have to make for a little thing like that—"

"I don't get it," Roger whispered furiously. "You act so clinical or something about it—"

And then suddenly Buggie swung his legs around, sitting straight up, eyes blazing. "Now you shut up for one little second, Roger, baby. I'm sick of listening to you quacking like a stupid duck. You listen for once and get it through that thick skull of yours. We're in deep trouble, brother. Grace is dead, right. She's lying up there in that room. Dead. And what the hell do you think is going to happen when they find her? They're going to ask questions, aren't they? They're going to want to know how she died, why, and who killed her. And we know all the answers, because you and I were up in her room. Remember that, Roger, baby. You and I. Not just Buggie Alstair, but both of us, and I'll bring you into it so fast it'll make your pinhead whirl. As a matter of fact, I'll lay it right in your lap. You didn't go running into the street and start sounding off the minute it happened, did you, old man? And they'll want to know why not, Rog, baby. So in other words, if I'm in trouble, you're in trouble—because I'm going to carry you right along wherever I go. Do you see, Rog? And so you start listening to me if you want to keep out of this mess, and you start shutting your mouth, do you understand? Somebody's got to figure out just what we're going to do, and that somebody is Buggie Alstair, do you get that? I want some goddamn quiet now, so I can do that thinking. So shut up your lip and leave me the hell alone, will you? Knock it off, in other words. Do you follow that, Roger, baby?"

Roger started to answer, then did not. He whirled and stared out the window at the silent, warm night. The breeze really was cooler this evening, blowing in nicely, and moving Roger's model airplane on the end of its wire. But Roger did not notice, and the sweat did not stop pouring down his face....

11

It was morning again, and George Cary had just put on a fresh white linen suit and walked into his kitchen to see if the coffee was ready. His was a better-than-average Willow Creek home, a white frame house with yellow sills and a nice hedge in front. George could have afforded a larger, newer home; but since Julia died, there really was no need for it.

George took a roll from the breadbox and carried it with a steaming cup of coffee to the blue and white breakfast nook where he could, as usual, look through the north window at the two elms and the cottonwood and the cherry trees. The sight had become very familiar now, after twenty years; and yet there were times like this morning when George wondered at his presence here.

He'd been born in the shadow of the University, not of wealthy parents, but of conscientious parents who had given him the taste for learning. At eighteen he'd entered the College of Journalism on a scholarship, paying the balance of his expenses by working nights as an office boy in the daily newspaper. He was an excellent student; and when he'd been elected to Phi Beta Kappa, John Riley, who was then dean of the college, said, "There have been some good journalists in this world, and there will be some more. George Cary will be one of them." Now George wondered all over again why the prediction had not come true.

Well, he thought, it could have been Julia. He'd met Julia during his junior year; and the summer before his graduation, he'd spent a week visiting her family here in Willow Creek. She'd been freshly beautiful and intelligent, not only a queen of the Kappa Alpha Theta house, but of the entire University. Yes, he thought, maybe it had been Julia—or maybe a combination of things all revolving around her.

If he and Julia hadn't married right after his graduation, he might, he thought, have simply bummed his way to some other part of the country—New York, San Francisco—or perhaps even abroad; and in time he might have gotten the kind of job he wanted. But he and Julia did marry right away, and the kinds of jobs he could get right away, even though they offered eventual opportunity, did not pay enough money to support Julia in the way he wanted to support her.

And so they had come to Julia's home, Willow Creek, because Harry and Mary Shields, Julia's parents, wanted them to; and George had purchased the *Willow Creek Standard*—then no more than a semimonthly with a small job press—and purchased it with money borrowed from Harry Shields.

Well, he remembered, that had been a fair, unfavored business deal, except for the fact that from nobody else but Harry Shields, the area's most successful lawyer, could he have borrowed the sum necessary to buy the *Standard*. He'd expanded, and made enough profit to improve and increase the equipment and paid every bit of the loan back, with interest, and done so in a very short time.

He'd done well by Julia and proved that he was a good businessman as well as a potentially good journalist, but that was just where everything had stopped. He'd continued on, of course, a pride to the community, certainly nothing to be ashamed of. But somewhere near the beginning he'd planned to make all of this temporary, a period in which to mark time for Julia; in a little while he'd planned to go on to do what he'd intended in the first place.

But he hadn't gone on. Somehow it just had never happened.

Again, was it Julia? he wondered. Partly, he knew. Because Julia was an only child and because she was extraordinarily close to her parents, somehow he could never bring himself to force her away from Willow Creek. And yet it hadn't been Julia completely. Even after the automobile accident, which had instantly killed her and her parents, he'd still remained, because living in Willow Creek was pleasant and slow and a good deal more comfortable than picking up and starting all over somewhere else.

And then George stood up quickly, suddenly remembering that this morning he was to walk downtown with Amanda White.

She was waiting for him at her door and came down to meet him on the walk when he appeared. She looked fresh and somehow a little younger. There was a high tone of color about her cheeks, he noticed.

"Morning, Amanda. It's a pleasant, peaceful morning, isn't it?"

And several minutes later, when they reached the edge of the business district—that was when George saw Lola Hale walk away from the doorway of her hotel, face peculiarly stiff and white, eyes oddly veiled. They stopped beside her, and Lola blinked at George, then said, simply, "Grace."

"Lola," Amanda said, "what's the matter?"

"Grace is dead," Lola said in an odd monotone.

"Dead!" George said.

"Yes," Lola said, looking at them, the shock still clear in her eyes. "Grace is dead.... Somebody killed her."

The news had come first to Sheriff Beaman. Lola, when she'd noticed Grace's door ajar that morning, had decided to look inside. She'd seen Grace, stared at her, and then she'd run downstairs and telephoned Sheriff Beaman. Sheriff Beaman had dressed hurriedly and was now driving up to the hotel as George and Amanda stared unbelievingly at Lola Hale.

In a way, George thought, the whole thing seemed unreal. He watched Sheriff Beaman shove himself from his car and come striding toward the hotel, shoulders bunched, formidable-looking in his determination—and yet Sheriff Beaman had not really looked like a professional policeman to George, but rather just Grove Beaman, his friend.

As Sheriff Beaman passed, he said, "Come on, George. You've got a right up there as a newspaperman." And that, strangely, had surprised George, because until that moment when Sheriff Beaman said it, he had not even thought about being a newspaperman.

George touched Amanda's hand briefly, saying, "I've got to go, Amanda."

Then, Lola Hale beside him, he followed Sheriff Beaman and Doug Havery—Sheriff Beaman's single deputy who had just arrived—upstairs to the second floor.

At the entrance to Grace's room everyone stopped, staring inside. George could see just a part of Grace's legs. He noticed Lola stretch forward, looking once more, then move back quickly to lean against the opposite wall of the hallway.

The sheriff and Doug Havery had entered Grace's room, and George stepped to the doorway and waited, watching Sheriff Beaman move around Grace while Doug Havery leaned down and plucked an object from the floor.

"What's that?" Sheriff Beaman said.

Doug Havery handed him the small cellophane-wrapped cigar.

Sheriff Beaman's mouth compressed grimly and he swore softly. George, staring at the cigar, frowned, then returned his stare to Doug Havery who was now kneeling beside Grace's body.

Sheriff Beaman, thrusting the cigar inside his coat pocket, said to his deputy, "Couldn't you get hold of Doc Granger?"

"Gone," Doug said. "Went fishing."

"A hell of a time for him to go fishing!"

"Well," Doug Havery said, straightening, "we could call Doc Clements, only I don't see no need for that. She's as dead as she could get. It's Hugh's job now. He's the coroner anyhow."

"Yeah," Sheriff Beaman said, and George was surprised, as he suspected Sheriff Beaman was, to remember that there actually was a county coroner who also happened to be Willow Creek's undertaker.

Sheriff Beaman turned. "George, run down and telephone Hugh, will you?"

And George did, waiting downstairs until Hugh Seltz, a small man with a face marked by an early attack of smallpox, arrived in his black hearse.

George, feeling an odd sensation of sickness run through him, left abruptly and walked down the sidewalk to his office.

He was sitting in the swivel chair behind his desk, rubbing a palm over his eyes, when Jack Noble, his tall, thin linotype operator, appeared a few moments later and said, "I saw her when they carried her out, George."

"Yes," George said quietly.

Jack Noble wore rimless glasses and he took them off and then blew his nose. "I always liked Grace. I really did."

"I guess we all did, Jack."

"Dirty rotten thing to happen to her, George. I'll tell you that. I'd like to have about five minutes alone with that sonofabitch who did it."

"Whoever it was," George said.

"There isn't any doubt about that, is there?" Jack asked angrily. "There can't be any goddamn doubt about that at all, can there?"

George looked up at Jack, frowning once more, and at the same time realized just exactly how little he'd done that a good newspaperman should have done. He'd walked away, hadn't waited to find out anything more at all.

"Comes in here and gets himself drunk," Jack said. "Thinks he can get away with anything!" Once more Jack blew his nose, then wiped a forearm across his eyes angrily. "Well, this'll be the last thing he'll get away with!"

"Who are you talking about?" George demanded.

"Didn't you hear, George? They found that cigar up there with Grace. There's only one man who'd smoke that kind of cigar—little teeny kind of cigar no man'd smoke except somebody like him! Mike Denton says he almost never sells that kind of cigar. He says he would lay his bottom dollar on it that he didn't sell a box of those things to anybody else but that guy! They've got him right now. Yanked him right out of his hotel room, still half drunk and all, and slapped him right in the sheriff's car."

"Who, Jack?" George said angrily. "Who the hell are you talking about?"

"That stranger. That salesman. That rotten bastard of a raping salesman!"

12

It was nine twenty-five Tuesday morning when Buggie and Roger learned that the salesman, Al Jackson, had been arrested on suspicion of having murdered Grace Amons. It was thirty minutes later when the word came that Al Jackson had told Sheriff Beaman that he remembered nothing whatever about what had happened after seven o'clock the evening before.

Before that Mrs. Cook had been on the telephone constantly, and Roger and Buggie remained up in Roger's room, the morning sun beating down on the roof, bringing the room to a steaming heat.

Now, Buggie was pacing excitedly, hands gripped tightly at his sides, mouth smiling, eyes sharp and alive.

"Damn, we've got it made! We've absolutely got it made! That Jackson doesn't remember a thing. Do you realize what that means, Rog, old man? Do you?"

Roger stood at the window, unable to look at the expression on Buggie's face. He hadn't slept all night. His head ached. His whole body ached.

"What are you made of, anyway?" he said to Buggie, his voice hoarse.

"We have just been gotten off the hook!" Buggie said, continuing to pace. "That crapping salesman has just hung himself up there in our place! He doesn't remember a thing, man! What do you think of that?"

Roger spun around. "He had nothing to do with her death. And we know it! Damn it, he's innocent. What are we going to do about it?"

Buggie did not answer. He simply laughed.

Roger wiped a hand across his lips, and found his hand was trembling. "All right! You listen to this. This is where we draw the line. I don't give a damn what happens. I don't give a damn what they do to us, or what anybody thinks! They're going to get the straight story, do you hear that?"

Buggie stopped pacing, his eyes on Roger, small crinkles running away from the corners. "Yes," he said quietly, I hear that, Rog, old man."

Roger stood there, glaring at him.

"So move then," Buggie said. "So walk out of this room and down those steps and sound off. And do you know what will happen then? I'll tell them it was you who knocked Grace around. How does that sound? And you think they wouldn't believe that? Remember, old man, I'm just a nice, innocent friend of yours on vacation. Your mother and father think the world of me. They really do. I haven't got an enemy in town.

But you, Rog, you're a member of one of the first families in this dump, and I'll lay odds there's more than one hick around here who'd like to see the eminent Mr. Cook's son put a smear on the family coat of arms. Right, Rog? Am I right? Raped, they said she was. Raped by you, maybe?"

"You're crazy!" Roger whispered hoarsely.

"Sure! And you think they couldn't prove who raped her? They can make tests, you know. They can find out." That was a lie, and Buggie knew it, but it was a nice touch and he could tell by Roger's eyes that Roger was convinced. He grinned at Roger.

"So go ahead and do it, Rog, old man. Tell them exactly what happened. Try it. Go, man."

Seconds ticked by slowly; and then, the trembling going deep inside him, Roger turned back to the window, one hand gripping a sill until he felt blood coming from underneath a fingernail. Behind him, he heard the soft laughter of Buggie Alstair.

On the lower bunk of his cell in the county jail, Albert Jackson sat and rubbed his hands together nervously. He really couldn't get things straight yet. His head hurt, and he'd been sick twice already; but it wasn't the hangover, it was this that had happened to him.

Footsteps sounded in the corridor, and Jackson stood up anxiously.

Sheriff Beaman, followed by Doug Havery, stopped outside the cell. Sheriff Beaman unlocked the door, and they both stepped inside, staring at Jackson. Jackson motioned pleadingly with his hands.

"Fellows," he said, "you've gone and made a big mistake. That's the truth."

"Sit down," Sheriff Beaman said.

"But, you've got to listen—"

"Sit down!"

Jackson sat down. "Fellows, listen—"

Sheriff Beaman's mouth was tight. "Jackson, you were in enough trouble, but you're in more now."

Jackson shook his head uncomprehendingly.

"Our coroner," Sheriff Beaman said. "He's found out something that we don't like at all. We really don't, Jackson."

"What are you talking about?" Jackson said, and his voice, he knew, was going out of control. It kept going shrill in the middle of a sentence.

"Grace was raped," Sheriff Beaman said.

Jackson kept staring at the sheriff, wiping a shaking hand across his forehead.

"It was bad before," Sheriff Beaman told him, "but it's worse now. Do you want to start telling us the truth, Jackson?"

"I've told you the truth, Sheriff. The honest-to-God truth. I had a little too much to drink, that's all. Just too much and I kind of blacked out. Only I wouldn't 've done anything like that. Why do you think I would've done anything like that?"

Doug Havery moved back against the bars of the door and folded his arms in front of his chest. Sheriff Beaman was standing so that the late morning sunlight coming in from the single barred window shone against his face and defined his features harshly.

"Have you ever been in trouble before, Jackson?"

"No."

"Jail record?"

"No!"

"It won't do you any good to lie to me, you understand that, don't you?"

"I'm not lying to you, Sheriff. You've got to understand that!"

"Jackson, we know you were trying to fool around with Grace. She had to toss a glass of water in your face to cool you off. And we found that cigar in her room. We know you bought that kind of cigar right in town, Jackson. You bought it from Mike Denton in the pool hall. It doesn't take any brains to figure out what happened. You got yourself tanked up, then went up there to Grace's room and did what you did."

"Sheriff, listen," Jackson pleaded. "That couldn't be true. I wouldn't 've done anything like that in a million years!"

Sheriff Beaman squared his shoulders. "We're going to let you think about it, Jackson. We're not going to get rough with you at all. You just sit in here and think about it, and pretty soon we'll be back. Then maybe you'll start telling us the truth."

"Sheriff," Jackson said, I've been telling the truth—!"

But Sheriff Beaman and Doug Havery had gone. Jackson collapsed on the bunk, pressing the heels of his palms against his eyes.

It was a hell of a note, he told himself. It was the lousiest note of all.

And wouldn't it be him, Al Jackson, who got into this trouble? It was always like this. You want to see how bad luck goes? Look for Al Jackson, and you'll see!

He pulled himself up and staggered over to the small barred window, looking out across the courthouse lawn. What was he doing here? Willow Creek! And his being accused of murdering and raping that waitress!

Despite the heat, Jackson shivered. He felt lost and alone, and yet he didn't want to get hold of Myra—he couldn't do that. He just couldn't.

He stumbled slowly back to the bunk and fell down on it once more. Boy, he could see how Myra would take this. She'd believe him like that sheriff and that deputy did!

Well, maybe he had that coming, all right. Only when it came right down to it, he didn't see why. Sure he fooled around a little. But he didn't see where Myra had such a big bitch about it anyway. When she got pregnant he didn't have to marry her. No, sir. Who would have told him he had to, he wondered?

No, by God, he married her of his own free will, and she should have been pretty grateful for it, and if he fooled around a little after, what kick did she have coming anyway? He did *her* the favor, didn't he?

So now she'd started wanting him to settle down and quit fooling around. And that was gratitude for you. Especially the way she was holding the kid up to him, knowing he really did like the boy.

And now there was this, and Al Jackson felt a cold chill run along his spine. It came to him, the whole impact of it, and he realized that he could lose everything with this.

He tried to think, to make his brain work cold and clear. He ought to have help, he knew that. He ought to have a lawyer to keep them from propping him up like a sitting duck this way. Only he didn't want to call in a lawyer—not yet. Because the less he made of it right now, he thought, the better the chances were that it might blow over and they'd figure out how wrong they were and let him go. And then maybe the word wouldn't get back to Myra.

Quite suddenly he felt tears blurring his eyes, but he really couldn't help it. It always went wrong, every time. Take his record with the company. All right, he'd played around a little with that farmer's wife outside of Omaha. So the dumb farmer had reported him, and he'd had a sweet time explaining to the company that it was the farmer's imagination. So now there was this, and if the company found out about it, that was the end of Al Jackson with the company.

Yes, sir, he thought, this was the way it was every time. Some had it good, some had it bad; and so how did Al Jackson have it? Every lousy, stinking time....

When, later that morning, Roger and Buggie finally left Roger's room and walked downstairs, Roger hoped that they could get out of the house, free and clear, with no more than a word to his mother.

But just as he and Buggie reached the bottom of the stairway, Mrs. Cook called to them from the living room.

It was Mrs. Boseley, perspiring in a wilting organdy dress, stopping in, and Mrs. Cook had always insisted that Roger stop to chat awhile with any of the friends or neighbors who dropped in.

And so now they were in the living room, and Mrs. Boseley was resuming in her nasal monotone, "Sam got just a peek of her when they brought her out. Stars, the way she looked, Sam said!"

Mrs. Boseley made a clucking kind of sound, shaking her head, and Roger felt his nerves going raw inside him.

"Stars," Mrs. Boseley said, "Sam said she had the most awful look you ever saw on a body's face—like when she died, she'd just been through something terrible."

Roger glanced at Buggie, but the only indication that Buggie made in reaction to Mrs. Boseley's words was the flicker of a small muscle along his jaw.

"Well," Mrs. Boseley said, "it's a terrible thing, and I haven't felt like this since Hanna died. Poor Hanna, so young and all, just like Grace— only I think it was even better for Hanna, even with cancer and all. I feel just awful!"

Roger's mother sitting quietly, her hands in her lap, said, "I feel awful too, Jennie."

"Poor Grace," Mrs. Boseley said, "dead and all now, and we'll have to be thinking about her funeral—did you think about that, Alice? Somebody'll have to, what with Grace's pa dying of kidney trouble like that last year. We girls in the sewing club ought to get together and talk to Reverend Pritchard."

"We'll do that, Jennie," Mrs. Cook said.

"Stars," Mrs. Boseley said, "I'll have to have something new to wear. I've got just the one black dress, but that was almost worn out at Hanna's funeral. You never know if there'll be another funeral right the next week anyway. Stars, it's awful!"

It was then that Roger noticed Buggie straightening a fraction, his eyes more attentive as he watched Mrs. Boseley.

"Well," Mrs. Boseley said, "I guess we all know that Grace was Grace and maybe not all we'd hoped for. She had her faults, I guess, but, stars, don't we all?"

Mrs. Cook nodded. "I guess we all do, in our own way."

"But I guess," Mrs. Boseley said, "the Good Lord is the one to decide about such things, not us."

"Yes," Mrs. Cook said, "you're right."

"I do know one thing," Mrs. Boseley said. "It isn't just the Good Lord who can say as to what kind of man it is who would do a thing like was done to Grace!"

Mrs. Cook had raised her head decisively, as though willing to face realities too, no matter how difficult. "That's right, Jennie."

Roger glanced once more at Buggie, who, clearing his throat politely, his eyes on Mrs. Boseley, carefully said, "Ma'am, I just want to say that I thought Grace was a very nice girl, from what I saw of her, and it seems a terrible thing to me that anything like happened to her *could* have happened to her. I beg your pardon," Buggie went on to both Mrs. Boseley and Mrs. Cook, "but I want to say that while I didn't know Grace like people here in Willow Creek do, I saw her enough to know that nobody ought to stand for what happened. I just hope that whoever did it gets punished, that's all!"

And just then, Roger, mouth going dry, heard his mother begin to cry. He turned to look at her, and watched her dab at her eyes with her handkerchief.

"Now, Alice," Mrs. Boseley said, "we're all upset. You just go ahead and cry. It's the best thing sometimes."

Mrs. Cook shook her head, sniffling. "It's just—" Mrs. Cook dabbed at her eyes once more. "Poor Grace! She was such a sweet girl, really. I always did like her so much."

13

At a little past twelve-thirty George Cary left his newspaper office and looked into the hotel coffee shop. When he didn't see Sheriff Beaman there he walked back down the street and over to the Hiller Café.

It was a small café with only a counter and two small tables, but business was brisk right now, with an extra half dozen men standing at the far right end of the counter around Sheriff Grove Beaman.

George waited behind the group, listening to the questions and comments about Grace pouring from the men, listening to the abrupt definitive answers from Sheriff Beaman as he bent his wide shoulders over the counter and finished a large portion of hot roast beef.

And then Sheriff Beaman noticed George. "Why, hello, George. Going to eat?"

"No, I'm not, Grove."

"Want to see me, George?"

"Are you going back to the courthouse?"

"Right now."

"I'll walk along with you," George said.

The sheriff nodded, picked up a final half slice of bread and wiped up the gravy remaining in his plate, finishing it with one bite. Then he pushed through the men ringed around him and made his way out of the café with George.

"Hell of a day," Sheriff Beaman said.

"I can imagine," George said.

"People wanting to know this, wanting to know that."

George was silent, moving along with the large sheriff, keeping pace with the other man's swift, charging strides.

"Well, George," the sheriff said, "it's a hell of a thing to happen, I'll tell you that."

"Nothing like this has ever happened before, has it?"

"Not that I can remember, and I can remember everything that's happened in Willow Creek since I was born. Got business at the courthouse, George?"

"I want to pick up the legal notices for tomorrow's paper." George looked at his friend, looked at the tanned, smooth-planed face. "What do you think, Grove?"

"Think?"

"Of what happened to Grace?"

The sheriff shrugged. "She was knocked around and raped and she died. Didn't you hear about her being raped?"

"I heard."

"Rape and homicide. Simple as that."

George frowned; some inner annoyance had begun in him, something that was more diverting than the entire tragedy of learning about Grace and seeing her dead.

"You're holding the salesman," George said. "You think he's really guilty."

The sheriff looked suddenly at George, frowning a little. "I think he ought to be held."

"I've got to put the newspaper out tomorrow," George said. "I'll be writing about this."

And then the sheriff grinned. "Hell, yes. Sure you will. I'd forgotten. I get so used to the personal items I forgot you'd want to write a story about this. Do you know what you're going to say, George?"

"That's why I'm talking to you, Grove," George said. "I want to find out just how things are."

Again Sheriff Beaman shrugged. "You know most everything that's happened, George. I suppose most everybody does, but they'll like to read about it again in the paper."

"What do you think happened exactly, Grove?"

"Well, we know that this Jackson had been trying to fool around with Grace. He started that just as soon as he came to town, and then yesterday afternoon Grace had to toss a glass of water in his face for getting fresh. Later on Jackson hung around the pool hall and got himself pretty well beered up—Hank Porter said he was carrying a pint of whisky, drinking that in between, in the can. I think then he left the pool hall, went back to the hotel, and busted into Grace's room. You know the rest. We found two bottles in the room, one of them was an empty whisky pint. We found that cigar of his in the room. Mike Denton sold him a box of that kind, and he says he can't remember selling them to anybody else for the last day or so."

"What does Jackson say?"

"He admits he got liquored up. Says he blacked out. Says he doesn't remember anything. But he says he couldn't have done it. What would he say?"

They were nearing the courthouse now, and the annoyance was growing in George.

"Look, Grove. Aside from that cigar, what proof have you got that it's Jackson?"

The sheriff's head swung around. "Proof?"

"I mean have you found anything else in the room? Those bottles: are you certain they tie up with Jackson? Any absolutely definite evidence?"

The sheriff's eyes suddenly thinned a little; his face tightened a little. "I'm telling you what I want to tell you, George. You know that. What I don't tell you, maybe I've got a reason for. You want to go along with me on this, George. I don't tell you how to run your newspaper, do I?"

"Grove, I'm not trying to tell you anything. I'm just trying to find out what the actual facts are. I want to write an intelligent story on this. I want to put in what I can in the way of facts."

Now the sheriff smiled, but it was not, George noticed, a good-humored smile. "Like I said, George, I don't tell you how to run your newspaper, but the folks just want to hear about Grace and what happened to her. I'll give you all the facts when I'm ready. You just let me do this my own way, all right? The folks in this county have elected me for two terms already. I think they know I'll handle everything all right."

They were walking up the broad sidewalk toward the south entrance of the courthouse now, and coming down the worn courthouse steps was Chuck Beaman.

"Why, hello, Chuck," Sheriff Beaman said.

George nodded to the large T-shirted youth. "Hello, Chuck."

"Dad," Chuck replied. "George. Dad, there's a fellow from the *Helsey Tribune* waiting in your office. He's going to write a story for the *Tribune* and then send it out to the wire service, he says."

Sheriff Beaman grinned. "Well, what do you know?"

Chuck walked back toward the courthouse with them, and George noticed that the boy had an unusually preoccupied look.

"Grove," George said, "I wonder if I could see Jackson? I'd like to talk to him for a little bit."

"Now, why would you want to do that, George?"

George's annoyance suddenly became an angry irritation, which he had to compress forcefully. It was irritating to him that Grove Beaman would not understand that he was the newspaperman in Willow Creek and so had a right to know exactly what was going on. And George realized that he was jealous of this man from Helsey who would write this story for the *Helsey Daily Tribune* and then release it out over the wires. The story would be given good space in the *Omaha World Herald* and some of the other nearer metropolitan dailies.

"I'd just like to talk to Jackson for a little bit," George repeated stubbornly.

The sheriff shrugged half angrily, and said, "All right, George. You tell Doug. He'll let you in."

"Thank you, Grove," and George walked on into the inside of the courthouse as Sheriff Beaman and his son went quickly ahead of him.

14

It was after lunch when Roger and Buggie sat down in the poolroom.

Roger had not wanted to come here, but Buggie, face and eyes alive with a peculiar intensity ever since that exposure to Mrs. Boseley, had insisted. "Not the pool hall, damn it," Roger had objected. "I want a beer," Buggie had said, "so why not the pool hall? That's where you buy a beer, isn't it? What the hell's the matter with the pool hall?"

And so they were in the dark pool hall, sitting beside a round spindle-legged table with a marbleized top. Buggie was smiling. "That Mrs. Boseley," he said, wagging his head. "Honest to God, she killed me."

Roger's mouth tightened. "She's an old friend of the family."

"She may be," Buggie said, "but she's also a ghoul."

"A what?"

"A ghoul, man. You know. She gets her kicks from people dying."

"You're crazy!"

"No, man, I'm not. I mean, this is a kick to her. Somebody's got kidney trouble. Somebody's dying of cancer. This is a kick, you know? Give her a good long dismal funeral, and she's got it made. Stretch out a corpse, and it's like living, man ..."

"Oh, for God's sake—" Roger began angrily.

"How many more of these have you got in town, Rog? Maybe half the town? Maybe three quarters? Maybe the whole bunch?"

"You don't know what you're talking about!" Roger whispered tensely.

"Oh, man, that's where you're wrong. I do know what I'm talking about...."

And then Mike Denton, the owner and bartender, came around the semi-occupied bar wearing his faded apron. He was a thin man with veined cheeks who always smelled just a little bit of alcohol. His dog, a yellow and brown mixture of a dozen breeds, followed him.

"Well!" he said. "What the hell are you doing in here, Roger? Just about the first time you've been in here, isn't it?"

"Yes," Roger said uncomfortably, "I think it is."

"Well, now," Denton said, "this is an occasion, by God. Roger Cook here in the pool hall! What'll you have? It's on me."

"A Coke, Mr. Denton," Roger said grimly.

"Hell, yes." And then Denton turned to Buggie. "You're the kid staying with Roger—from the University, that right?"

"That's right," Buggie said. "Buggie Alstair, Mr. Denton." He put out his hand politely and shook hands with Denton.

"Coke for you too?"

"Beer, if you please," Buggie said.

"Well, by God," Denton said, looking at Roger. "How old are you now, Roger?"

"Nineteen."

"Nineteen! Damn it, I'm getting old. Let's see, you must have been about seven or eight when I got Bingo here, just a pup." Denton leaned down and patted the dog. "He's twelve years old. He's a little lame, but he's all right. Well, what the hell do you know, Roger, you coming right in here today. Does your pop know it?"

"Well—"

Denton laughed. "He will. Well, one Coke, one beer. You boys relax and enjoy yourselves."

When Denton had brought the beer and Coke and returned to the bar, Roger sat silently, right hand opening and closing. Billiard balls clicked, Denton banged freshly opened beer bottles on the wet wood of the bar, and over the din came the drift of voices:

"Ain't anything too bad for that salesman ..."

"Dirty slime ..."

"Ought to be hung ..."

"Let's get out of here," Roger said tightly.

"Relax," Buggie said, "just relax, old man."

"How the hell can you—?" Anger froze Roger's words. He kept banging his fist down on the table. "Buggie, let's get out of here."

But Buggie only slouched back against his chair, eyes half closing as he absently watched the billiard players. "We're in a hell of a spot, do you know that?" he said at last.

"Damn it," Roger said, "keep your voice down!"

"But for the grace of a stupid cornball of a salesman, we'd be in so deep you couldn't pull us out with a truck. Thank God for the stupid cornball of a salesman, huh, Rog?"

"Shut up!" Roger whispered. "I keep thinking about him in that cell.... Damn it, he's not guilty! We know that!"

Buggie leaned forward now, smiling, resting his elbows on the table. "That's right, old man. We know that. But nobody else does. How about it, Rog? Have you changed your mind? Do you want to sound off now? How about you getting up on the table here and making a short revealing speech? Tell the world, old man. Tell them the salesman's not guilty."

Roger's face had reddened. "You're so damned sure about it, aren't you? You figure I don't have the guts, don't you?"

Buggie examined Roger steadily for a full four seconds, then he said, smiling, "Relax, huh, Roger?"

Roger shook his head. "That man is innocent!"

Buggie's smile evaporated. "Oh, you think he is, huh? You really think so, huh? So how did that cigar get in Grace's room then?"

"I don't know," Roger said grimly.

"Innocent! The only damn reason he's innocent is because Grace was dead when he got there. You saw him—blind drunk. Where did he go after we saw him? Straight to Grace's room. And why? What did he do after he got there? How do we know what he did? They say she was raped. So you'd gotten to her, remember I know that, old sport. But maybe this damn salesman saw her lying there, and then—"

Roger's stomach rolled over, and he gripped his hands against the edge of the table. "Just shut up!" he whispered.

"All right, all right. But just remember you and I don't know what that drunk had on his mind. When you get to feeling sorry for him, think about that a couple of times. It's him or us, do you get that?"

Roger shook his head again.

"Let me just put it this way, Roger, old sport. You're in this thing up to your neck, right along with Buggie Alstair. You make one single mistake and you've had it. We've been lucky so far. You'd better not crowd the luck. How do you really know that nobody saw us around that hotel? Are you sure of that?"

Roger was grimly silent now.

"You're not sure, are you, any more than I am. Maybe they just haven't put two and two together yet, because the whole thing's on that salesman. But if you make one little slip, you could bring this thing down on our heads. How much real evidence have they got against that jerk? One lousy cigar that they can't even prove for sure belonged to Jackson. That's all that's between us and the noose, Rog, old man, and if a noose gets in sight I won't go alone, you can be sure of that. You're in just as deep as I am."

Buggie grinned wickedly at Roger.

"You just don't forget who tumbled her, Rog, baby. It wasn't Buggie Alstair. And you'd better keep thinking about that. And you'd better keep thinking about how we're going to keep that salesman on the string, huh? We've got to plan that out, buddy, and carefully, because the minute he gets off the string, we have had it. Right, Rog, old man?"

Roger opened and closed his mouth, knuckles white over the table, but he said nothing. Not a word.

And then three men burst into the pool hall, moving heavily, thick shoes jarring the floor, moving back along the bar until they reached the table beside Roger and Buggie, where they sat down.

Roger looked at them—Curt Black, Bud Hinkle, Willy Turner. They looked back at him impersonally, as if too preoccupied even to think about the unusualness of his being here.

"You boys close up today?" Denton asked them, coming around the bar with his yellow and brown dog.

"Yeah," Willy Turner said. "We closed up, all right. Didn't we, Curt?"

"Yeah," Curt said. "That's right. We closed up."

"Didn't know it was a holiday," Denton said casually.

All he got, Roger saw, was a hard look from each of the men. These three Roger particularly disliked. Willy Turner, an old and ugly story. Curt Black, large and rangy with his confident, unsmiling face. Bud Hinkle, who with Willy worked for Curt—a lean-muscled youth with crooked teeth which he showed in a perpetual grin. Each of them drank from the beer bottles, long swigging drinks. Roger turned to Buggie, starting to speak, but Buggie, with a meaningful motion of his hand, silenced

Roger. Buggie, Roger saw, was looking closely at the trio beside them.

"All right," Willy said, "tell it again. Just what happened."

Bud Hinkle leaned his long arms against the table, drooping his head as he prepared to listen to a story he already knew; and Curt, a muscle moving along the side of his mouth, said, "Lola found her first thing this morning. Up in her room at the hotel there."

Willy nodded, face grim, and Roger realized that somehow Willy seemed today like he had been years ago.

"So then," Curt went on, "Lola, she called Sheriff Beaman, and he went up with Doug Havery and George Cary, and they knew she was dead all right, head all bashed in and the like. That's when they found that bastard's cigar!"

Roger made a movement to stand up, but a hand snapped forward under the table, grabbing his arm. Buggie looked at Roger with hard, angry eyes, then gradually his hand pulled away, and Roger stayed where he was.

"Then what?" Willy said.

"They took her down the stairs and got her in Hugh Seltz's ambulance and took her off to the mortuary."

"By God," Willy said angrily. "Grace dead!"

"Dead, all right, and raped," Curt said.

Willy finished his beer with one swing of his bottle and swore.

"How'd they know?" Bud Hinkle said, lifting his head. "I mean she was raped?"

"You know how they knew," Curt said. "Hugh Seltz found out when he examined her."

"I mean," Bud said, "how'd he do it, to find out?"

"He found out," Curt said. "That's enough."

"Sonofabitch," Willy said, shaking his head; and then he yelled, "Mike, more beer."

Mike Denton came around the bar with three fresh beers, his dog lumbering dutifully behind.

"Don't that dog ever get tired of following you, Mike?" Bud Hinkle asked.

"No, sir," Mike said proudly. "Not in all the years I've had him."

"Mike," Curt asked, "you got any news?"

"You mean about Grace? Just that they got this guy locked up."

Then Roger saw Buggie was moving his chair around, facing himself toward the other table.

"Has he said anything yet, this fellow?" Buggie asked. The eyes of the three men at the other table brushed over Buggie impersonally.

"Well?" Curt asked Denton.

Denton shrugged. "I guess he's admitted getting drunk, all right. They say he said he doesn't remember what happened."

Once more Willy was swearing in a dull, steady monotone. "He was in here last night, wasn't he?" Curt asked.

"Yeah," Denton said.

"Was he drunk?"

Again Denton shrugged. "Couldn't say. He said he had a bottle in his coat, and he was mixing that up with the beer back in the john. I wasn't watching him all the time. But I didn't see a bottle on him. And I don't see how he could get drunk on the beer I sold him. Maybe four or five was all. Not enough to black out on. Still, they say there was a couple of bottles found in Grace's room."

"Good alibi, that's all," Willy said. "Say you're too drunk to remember anything, and then maybe they'll take it easier with you."

"Well, maybe," Buggie said, leaning forward earnestly, "maybe he really was drunk like he says, but if he was, the rest of it doesn't make sense."

"What's your name anyway?" Curt said.

"Buggie Alstair. I'm a friend of Roger's here. We go to school together."

"Yeah, I know all that," Curt said. "I just didn't know your name. How do you mean the rest of it doesn't make sense?"

"Well," Buggie said, and Roger, blood drumming, saw that all four of the men were looking at Buggie with interest. "I mean the way I understand it, Grace wasn't found until this morning, and if this salesman was drunk and doesn't remember anything that happened, he must have been pretty wild, but"—he spread his hands—"nobody heard anything, not a thing."

"Yeah," Willy said, "nobody heard a thing."

"I mean," Buggie went on, "if he was that drunk, why didn't somebody hear him? Grace would have screamed or something, wouldn't she? I mean, if he stumbled into her room drunk?"

"So what happened then?" Curt asked.

"Well," Buggie said, his voice still earnest and polite, "who knows? But I think if that salesman is guilty, he wasn't drunk. I think he just got Grace to let him into her room somehow, and then—"

"That sonofabitch," Willy breathed. "That dirty—"

"I'd say he was dumb," Curt said, "figuring he could get away with a thing like that. He should have been miles out of here. He should have headed out of this town and out of this state and kept right on going."

There was a moment of silence as everyone thought about what had been said, and then Buggie cleared his throat, and said, "I don't know much about these things, but in school we've had some courses on psychology, and I've read quite a little about ... well, like some people are different from the rest of us. Maybe that's the case with this salesman."

"What do you mean, different?" Willy asked.

"Well, I mean some guys get a quirk in them—they get psychotic—"

"Which?" Willy asked.

"I mean," Buggie said, "they're not normal."

"How do you mean, not normal?" Curt asked.

"Well, they look at things different, they get a kick out of things differently from the rest of us."

There was a sudden quiet, and Roger realized that Curt and Bud and Willy were watching Buggie with extreme attentiveness, waiting for him to go on. At any other time, Roger thought, they would hate him for talking about something he'd learned in college.

"You see, there're some guys," Buggie said, "who get a kick out of, say, hurting people, you know?"

"Yeah," Bud Hinkle said, "I heard of them. Like they take a whip and whip somebody and get their kicks that way."

"That's right," Buggie said, "that's what I mean. They're not normal."

"They're nuts, huh?" Bud Hinkle said.

"In a way," Buggie said, "I guess they are at that. I mean, there's a quirk in them somewhere, some little thing that makes them that way—although it takes more than that, I think."

"What do you mean?" Willy asked.

"Well, I mean there're all kinds of people in this world, but you couldn't say that just because most of them have some little quirk in them, that's why they are what they are."

Buggie waited, and when there was no response to what he'd just said, he tried again, "What I mean, let's say some guy commits a sex crime."

Willy put his fist down on the table in front of him. "Like with Grace."

"Well, any guy that commits any sex crime. Let's say that he beats up a girl first—"

"Yeah?" Bud Hinkle said.

"Why does he do it?"

"He's nuts, that's what," Bud Hinkle said, and Roger watched Willy's face darken, the small pinched eyes narrow.

"Like I said, in a way," Buggie agreed. "This quirk they've got, that gives them a thrill out of it."

"Damn," said Bud Hinkle brightly. "It does, no kidding?"

"It's this quirk," Buggie explained. "And they let it get control of them because they're weak, see?"

"No," Curt said. "I don't see what you're talking about now."

"Well," Buggie went on, "this quirk is small, you see? A guy could cover it up in his mind if he wanted to, maybe forget it eventually, and maybe, finally, it would be the same as though he didn't have it. Only instead of covering it up, getting control of it, a guy could also be weak— he lets it grow, see? And pretty soon, you have this guy beating up a girl and then the rest of it."

Bud Hinkle gulped a swallow of beer from his bottle and shook his head unbelievingly. "Boy, I don't understand somebody like that. I really don't."

Buggie shook his head along with Bud Hinkle. "They're the bad ones, the ones like that."

"Yeah?" Curt asked.

"I mean," Buggie said, "they're the really bad ones. They're like—well, like animals. They get that way, see? And it's their own fault."

Roger was watching Willy's fists tightening even more.

"Look," Buggie said, "they're, say, like that dog there."

"Now cut that out," Mike Denton said; he'd been listening silently until now. "Don't compare no sex fiend with my dog!"

"Look," Bud Hinkle said happily, "I'll bet old Bingo's been around plenty in his day, Mike. I'll bet—"

"I don't want no sex fiend compared to Bingo, that's all," Denton said humorlessly and stoutly.

"I just mean," Buggie said, "that when you've got an animal, you've got an animal. And that's what the sort of person we've been talking about is—an animal."

"Just like that goddamned yellow dog there," Willy said darkly.

"Watch your language," Denton warned. "You watch the way you talk about that dog, Willy."

Willy had hunched forward, breathing heavily, his large barrel chest moving in and out over his doubled hands. "Just like that damned yellow dog, no better than that, by God!"

"Willy," Denton said, his voice rising, "I don't keep many rules here, but this is one, do you hear? I don't want my dog talked about that way."

"Dirty sex fiend! A dirty animal, no different from that goddamned yellow dog! Killing Grace, dirtying her up—"

Suddenly Willy shoved himself up with his fists, knocking his chair backward and kicking Denton's dog.

A stifled cry caught in Denton's throat as the dog yelped loudly. Willy started after the dog again, but Denton threw himself at him, swinging his fists, the swinging futile because of his wild fury.

And at the same time Curt was on his feet, grabbing Willy, stopping him.

"What's the matter with you, Willy?" Curt yelled. "That dog hasn't hurt anybody."

Willy blinked as though coming back to reality, then shook Curt's arm away, pushing Denton off easily. Denton started to come back at him, but Curt said, "Let him alone, Mike. Just let him alone."

"What business has he got doing a thing like that?" Denton said. "Damn him, what business has he got to do a dirty thing like that?" He moved back, kneeling, cradling the whimpering dog in his arms. "Did he hurt you, Bingo?"

Willy, eyes dark and preoccupied, was walking toward the door, and Curt and Bud Hinkle, glancing at each other and shaking their heads, followed.

"Poor old Bingo," Denton said, and then he looked up and yelled after the departing trio, "Goddamn you, don't you ever come in here again, do you hear?" And then he turned to Buggie and Roger. "You too, damn you! Get out of here and fast, by God, before I go get a gun and run you out of here."

Roger stumbled to his feet and looked at Buggie, realizing then that Buggie had been watching him intently, a half smile on his lips.

"Let's go, Roger," Buggie said quietly, and they walked out into the sunshine.

They walked silently down the street toward Buggie's convertible, and Roger looked neither right nor left. They climbed into Buggie's car, and Buggie, behind the wheel, leaned back, eyes bright and thoughtful. "That Willy," he said, laughing softly. "Goddamn, that Willy! Don't you see it, Roger? Willy's the answer to everything. ..."

15

That night George was still seated behind his desk in his newspaper office. He hadn't eaten supper in his customary way at the hotel, but had asked Lola Hale to send Sam Aikens over with just a sandwich and a carton of coffee. The coffee had long cooled, barely touched.

Two things were gnawing at his brain, two unanswerable facts that kept prying into his mind again and again, no matter how he instinctively defended against them.

The first had to do with the salesman, Albert Jackson; the second revolved around the fact that he was still aware of being a newspaperman.

In a way, after his visit with Jackson, George had wished that he had not insisted to Sheriff Grove Beaman that he get a chance to talk to Jackson.

Actually, the talk had gone well. Once George had explained that he owned the local newspaper and that whatever story he wrote would be limited to the community, Jackson had gotten over his reluctance to say anything. Jackson had become extremely talkative, and all George had had to do was ask an occasional, quiet question, and Jackson continued to pour his heart out.

And the trouble was George believed Jackson.

He stood up, shaking his head angrily, pacing.

A girl is dead, he thought. They have found a logical suspect. It is Grove Beaman's business, not mine.

But the unrest continued. How do you get locked in this way, he thought. How do you start out just being in a town and then get to the point where you belong to it? And where had the future become the past? Where had what was going to be become what had never been? A journalist, George thought. An honest-to-God newspaperman. And what am I now?

He paused, looking back at his shop with thin eyes. The mats and the rollers and the slugs. A man and type and ink and paper—a press to print with. Print what?

George tightened his mouth. They expected to read what they wanted to read. Don't anger them. Don't faintly annoy or irritate them....

Suddenly he turned and sat down behind his typewriter and began to type. Head thrust forward, shoulders bunched, he wrote slowly at first and then more quickly as though he were making up for a great deal of lost time. And in a way he was.

16

The next morning Sheriff Beaman entered his office on the second floor of the courthouse, a feeling of uneasiness and a half anger gnawing inside him.

For a moment, entering the office dulled that gnawing because of the things Sheriff Grove Beaman loved in this world, his office was high on the list. It was a kind of temple, a shrine, which, when he came into it, eased his troubles.

But when he had removed his jacket and placed his large body in his swivel chair, the irritation started again. It was like the feeling he got when he allowed his mind to wonder ahead to the next election and imagined how it would be if he should lose; when he remembered how it had been before he became sheriff, trying unsuccessfully to run that farm, then having to be a gas station attendant.

Earlier that morning Ted Vernie, in the eager manner he had assumed ever since he'd come out of law school at State and got himself elected County Attorney, had come barging into the sheriff's home just as if they couldn't have met in the courthouse, wanting to talk everything over before the sheriff had even had time to sit down to breakfast.

Well, Vernie could blab all morning long—this thing wasn't in his hands yet. All right, it was Vernie's job to indict Jackson on murder and rape charges if it looked as though Jackson were really guilty. But Vernie could take his time with it and wait until Sheriff Beaman told him it was time to indict or not to indict and like it. All those questions about what had he done when the body had been discovered ... What the hell did Vernie know about it anyway? ("You take my word for it, Grove, whether you like it or not—if I'm going to prosecute this man, I mean to convict him. If you indicate to a community like this that a man is guilty, they want to see him hang, and that's what's going to happen to him if I prosecute him. Now what have I got to prosecute him with, Grove? What have you done to make sure this man's guilty, if he is guilty? You found that cigar. All right. There were a couple of bottles up there, somebody said, only they were thrown away when you let Lola have the room cleaned. Why the hell did you let Lola have the room cleaned? Where are the fingerprints? Where are—?") And Vernie had even started to talk about elections, and at a time like this.

The sheriff hunched his shoulders, the anger going through him all over again as he remembered. He stood up, yanking his great bulk out of the swivel chair, and walked over to one of the south windows, looking out over the town.

He stared out that window, stared long and hard at the town warming to the morning sun. And then he turned and went back to his chair at his desk. All right, he thought, face stern, body straight and hard. He had a murder on his hands, the first murder in the history of the county. All right. He wasn't going to get shaken up over some fancy-pants kid coming around and spouting off his thimbleful of knowledge, telling him he'd better produce evidence. He had enough evidence in his mind to *know* there wasn't any doubt about who was guilty, and that was enough. He'd just made one mistake so far, and that was the whole trouble. He'd been too soft, bending over backward in order to look impartial. Well, that was over. They wanted a sheriff when they put their cross on the ballot, and by God, they had themselves a sheriff! Are you going to bring in the state police? Vernie had wanted to know. Sheriff Grove Beaman pulled out a cigar from his shirt pocket and ripped off the cellophane. He bit a tip off the cigar, half tearing it off, and then spit the tobacco in a wastebasket beside him. State police! …

It was nine thirty-seven when Sheriff Beaman bit the tip off his cigar, approximately five hours before the first copy of that day's freshly printed *Willow Creek Standard* would be read (among others by Joe Hooker, who was eighty-nine and retired on a soldier's pension and who always walked to the office of the *Standard* to get his copy rather than pick it up in his post-office box like most everyone else). And it was just a little after ten o'clock when Buggie, Roger beside him, drove his convertible around to Miller Street and parked behind the jail which attached to the north end of the courthouse building.

He leaned forward, resting his hands lightly on the steering wheel, looking across the green lawn toward the jail with its gray stone exterior and barred windows.

"How many cells?"

"What?" Roger asked.

"I said how many cells are there in there? Didn't you tell me you'd gone through that jail?"

"Yes, but—"

"How many cells?"

"Three, I think."

"Where are they?"

"Where are they?"

"Describe them, for God's sake," Buggie snapped, but inside he was not angry, not irritated—something had slowly happened to him during these past hours, and it was a little like getting the first fine glow of being a bit drunk.

"There're three cells, that's all," Roger said, frowning. "Three cells in a row with bars in front and those barred windows in back, like you see."

"You mean all the cells are on this side, along this wall of the jail?"

Roger nodded, and Buggie half smiled.

"Why do you want to know anyway?"

"Never mind why I want to know," Buggie said, "just answer the questions and the rest of the time keep your mouth shut."

He knew, really, that he ought not to ride Roger any more than he had to, but right now that exhilarating feeling was too much, and he had to let things go the way they had to go, the words came the way they had to come. That salesman, that poor bastard right behind one of those barred windows, maybe even staring out at them this very minute.

He saw her then, the little girl coming down the walk, skipping every fourth or fifth step, swinging a jump rope in her left hand, and the idea came to Buggie all at once, just as clear and sharply defined as though he'd thought about it for a week.

"Who is she?" Buggie asked. "That little girl, just coming down the block."

Roger frowned, then said, "Clyde Brown's little girl, I guess. Why?"

Without answering, Buggie watched the little girl come down the sidewalk, bouncing up, with a quick kick, then strolling almost aimlessly, wandering over the sidewalk in childish abandon.

Buggie looked across the street at the row of frame houses. At the far end of the block, a woman was sweeping the walk leading up to her front porch. Buggie looked back toward the approaching child.

"Roger," he said sharply, "I want you to get out of the car and go over toward the jail. I want you to hurry. Do you understand me?"

"Do what? What the hell—why?"

"From now on," Buggie said, anger in his voice, "you do what you're told if you want to save your neck, do you understand me?"

A muscle in Roger's cheek jumped, and he licked his lips.

"Now take off," Buggie said, "and when you get over there, see if you can catch sight of Jackson. If you can, wave at me. Do you understand? Move!"

Face flushing, Roger climbed out of the convertible and trotted across the grass toward the jail. Buggie watched him move, then turned his eyes back to the little girl. She had stopped to unwind her jump rope now, and had begun jumping, moving forward again.

Buggie looked back to Roger, who neared the back side of the jail, paused, and then turned and waved to Buggie. Buggie leaped out of the car and ran toward the little girl.

The little girl now was even with the jail, and Buggie, as he ran toward her, shouted, "Come on, Roger, let him alone! Just let him alone!"

At the same time, he looked along the street, toward the woman sweeping her walk, seeing her lift her head and turn toward them.

And then Buggie was beside the little girl who stopped in surprise at the sound of Buggie's voice, staring at him.

"Look, little girl," he said loudly, "you just don't pay any attention to that man in there!"

"Huh?" the little girl said.

"Look, honey," Buggie said, his voice still loud, echoing down the block, "just come on, across the street!"

He took the child's hand, and the little girl instinctively jerked her hand away.

"Now that's all right," Buggie said. "He scared you, didn't he?" Then he looked up at Roger, who was approaching.

"Roger," Buggie said, "do you know her? Maybe she'll go along with you. Take her across the street, so if he tries that again she won't hear it."

"Hear it?" Roger said, and the blood drained from his face as he stared at Buggie.

Buggie looked beyond him down the block, and now the woman who had been sweeping had put down her broom and was coming down the sidewalk swiftly.

Buggie clamped his hand unobtrusively but tightly around Roger's left arm. "*Take her across the street*," he whispered tensely.

Roger turned to the little girl. "You know me, don't you?" he asked her, still not certain what Buggie was up to.

The little girl nodded.

"Come on then. Let's go across the street."

The three of them crossed the street just as the woman from the end of the block arrived. "What's the matter? I heard you yelling—"

"I'm sorry," Buggie said. "I guess it just made us mad, that's all."

"What made you mad?"

Buggie kneeled beside the little girl. "Look, honey, you just forget about it. He shouldn't have talked to you. If it frightened you—well, we'll get you home to your mother."

"What happened anyway?" the woman asked.

Buggie stood up, looking grimly at the woman. "That guy, that guy in the jail over there—he was talking to her. It just got us, that's all. I don't blame Roger for running over there." He looked at Roger. "Take it easy, Roger. You can't do anything about it."

"You mean that salesman?" the woman asked.

Buggie nodded.

"What was he talking to her for?"

Buggie looked at her straight in the eyes. "He was trying to talk her into coming over to the cell window."

"He was *what?*"

"Yes, ma'am," Buggie said. "It was the way he was doing it, his voice and all." He pressed his lips together, glancing across the street toward the jail. "They ought to put a guy like that in a strait jacket, that's what I say! Trying to—" He stopped and looked at the white-faced Roger. "Roger, now just calm down. You can't do anything about it. Let's just get this little girl home."

17

It was just about the time Al Jackson was expecting his noon meal when Sheriff Grove Beaman unlocked the cell and stepped inside. Jackson was sitting on his bunk. He started to get up, then decided not to. He smiled tentatively at the sheriff, searching the large man's face for some sign of what was to come.

Sheriff Beaman leaned back against the bars of the cell door, hands hanging at his sides. His eyes flickered over Jackson, his face immobile.

"What have you got to say, Jackson?"

"Me? Say?" Jackson grinned sadly. "I'd like to get out of here, Sheriff. I'll say that, all right."

"What for? To try to fool around with some other little kid?"

Jackson's sad grin remained, but his eyes were not smiling. "I don't follow that, Sheriff."

"That was a dumb thing to do, Jackson. You know how dumb that was, don't you?"

Jackson shook his head once more. "What was dumb, Sheriff?" His voice was rising on him again, and he tried to keep control of it. It was the way the sheriff was looking at him, the tone of the sheriff's voice.

"Two boys heard it and saw it. You know that."

"Two boys?" And Jackson thought back to the occurrence earlier when he'd been staring out of the window of his cell. There was that cute little girl skipping down the sidewalk, and the next second this one kid running across the lawn toward his cell window, and another one yelling something that he hadn't understood. Then both boys leading that little girl across the street while that woman was hurrying up, all of them looking across at the jail....

"What did you say to her, Jackson?" the sheriff said.

"Say to her?" Jackson said, expecting anything now.

"What did you say to the little girl?"

Jackson licked his lips. Oh, why was it always this way? What did he say to the little girl? Was everything going crazy?

"Look, Sheriff, I didn't say anything to any little girl. I saw a little girl out there on the sidewalk, and I saw those kids get out of their car. But

I didn't say anything. Not a word!"

"Jackson," Sheriff Beaman said, "have you ever had any mental trouble?"

"Mental trouble?" Jackson said, his voice rising. "Me?"

"No," the sheriff said, "I don't think you ever have, by God. I think you're just as dumb and stupid as they come. I think you're a degenerate too, Jackson. Do you hear that?"

Sheriff Beaman's face had flushed now, and Jackson could see the hate in the large man's eyes.

"Jackson," the sheriff said, "I'm done playing with you. Do you understand that? This last thing does it. I promise you—"

It happened just then—the rock crashed through the upper glass of the barred window, banging against a bar, ricocheting and striking Jackson's forehead just above the left eyebrow.

Without moving, without looking out the window to see the rapidly moving Oldsmobile go down the street with a burst of exhaust, the sheriff stared down at the wide-eyed Jackson, watching the blood start on Jackson's forehead and spill down the side of his face; and it was a moment when Sheriff Beaman knew a sudden, exhilarating sense of relief. This man in front of him, who only a second before had seemed such a challenge and threat, was going to be destroyed. And Sheriff Grove Beaman was going to be safe.

18

The coffee shop of the hotel was the last place Roger wanted to go that afternoon, but Buggie had insisted, and Roger had not even tried to argue against it. In fact, he was not trying to argue against anything right now; he was just sitting there in the booth across from Buggie, staring down at the Coke Sibyl Broncher (who had replaced Grace) had brought, and not saying anything at all.

The moments went by slowly in the quiet of the afternoon lull. Once Roger looked up enough to notice that Buggie had not touched his Coke but was sitting there staring through the front windows at the occasional passer-by outside, his face a mask. Then suddenly Buggie waved toward the door and called, "Hi, there!"

Roger turned and watched Willy Turner cross the room toward them.

"Sit down," Buggie said enthusiastically.

Willy nodded shortly and sat down beside Roger. Roger instinctively moved away slightly.

"How're you, Cook?" Willy said to Roger without looking at him.

Roger answered stiffly, "All right, Willy."

"What's your name again?" Willy asked Buggie.

"Buggie. Buggie Alstair."

"Yeah. Where'd you get the name?"

"I don't know," Buggie said, smiling. "Somebody tagged me with it somewhere. I don't remember who it was. You're Willy Turner."

"Yeah." Willy looked up at thin, dark Sibyl Broncher, and said, "Give me a Coke, Sibyl."

"What kind, Willy?"

"I don't give a damn. I'd rather have a beer."

"We don't have any, Willy. You know that."

"I know that. So give me a Coke, like I asked."

"A plain Coke?" Sibyl said.

"Make it a beer Coke, Sibyl," Willy said.

"Okay, Willy," Sibyl sighed. "You sure make it tough."

"Yeah," Willy said, "I sure do."

A moment later, Sibyl brought Willy's plain Coke, and in the time it took her to bring it, nobody, Roger noticed, had said another word. Willy sat there looking out toward the coffee shop. There was something about the way Willy was looking and acting that kept making Roger go cold inside.

Buggie, on the other hand, had lost some of his preoccupied look; now he was sitting a little straighter, more tense, watching the silent Willy closely.

Willy finally lifted his glass, tasted the Coke, and brought it down with a bang. He sniffed. "So what happened? I saw you guys in here and that's what I come in here for—to find out what happened with that salesman and that little girl."

Buggie shrugged, then told the story, embellishing it even more, finishing, "... and that was when Roger got mad and jumped out of the car and ran up there."

"Roger here did, huh? Yelling, I heard. Swearing at that guy. Is that right, Roger?" Roger moved a hand dully.

Willy was silent then, and Buggie was silent with him. Roger sat motionless. Sibyl Broncher was back wiping the counter. Verne Haybrider had just seated himself and was opening a newly released copy of the *Willow Creek Standard*. Chuck Beaman reappeared with another case of pop.

Willy looked up. "Do you know what I did? After I heard about that salesman and the little girl?"

"No," Buggie said, examining Willy carefully, "what did you do, Willy?"

"I went up to Curt, this guy I work for, you know? The guy who was with me in the pool hall, him and Hinkle? And I said, 'You let me drive that Olds, huh, Curt?' And I took that Olds and drove it up to the jail, and I took this rock, see? A big old rock. And I threw it in the window where that salesman is, and it busted him in the head, and he bled all over hell! What do you think of that?"

Willy was laughing a little, a kind of choking laughter.

"Willy," Buggie said admiringly, "you're really something, all right. You've got a lot of guts."

"Yeah," Willy said, sobering. "Well, you ask anybody around here, and they'll tell you I can be tough, all right."

"I'm not arguing about that, Willy."

"And it ain't just me that's mad," Willy said darkly. "This whole town is mad, see?"

Buggie leaned back, shrugging carelessly. "Maybe this town is mad, maybe it isn't."

"What are you talking about?" Willy exploded. "They're so mad they're about to go over to that jail and rip those doors down and drag that guy out of there and hang him up by the neck on some tree!"

Buggie smiled, shaking his head. "You don't really believe that, Willy."

Willy stared at Buggie in disbelief, then leaned forward menacingly. "Why? You don't think they've got enough reason?"

"Willy, did I say that? I'm just talking about the way things really are."

"You look!" Willy said. "You take a guy and have him come into a town like this and do what he done, and we don't like it. We don't!"

"Sure. Only you aren't the whole town, Willy."

Willy frowned. "What do you mean?"

Buggie straightened a little. "Well, I'm not saying that salesman shouldn't be dragged out of there and hung up. I'm just saying that everybody isn't like you, Willy. I mean they just don't have your guts. They'll probably let it blow over, see? I'm not saying that's the way it ought to be, but that's probably the way it will be. First thing you know, some smart lawyer'll come in here and get this guy off—"

"After what he's done?" Willy said incredulously.

Buggie spread his hands. "That's the way it goes, Willy, unless—" He shrugged once more.

"Unless what?" Willy demanded.

"Unless somebody kind of takes things in hand. I mean, somebody with guts. Somebody who can do some leading."

"Leading?" Willy asked, frowning.

And then Verne Haybrider at the counter readjusted his copy of the *Standard* with a loud rustle and said, "Queer way for George Cary to be talking."

"How's that?" Sibyl asked.

"Well, here, I'll read it, '... and so because of only one fragment of evidence, evidence that could only remotely be considered adequate enough to condemn a man to a cell, Albert Jackson finds himself locked up behind bars for the crime of raping and murdering Grace Amons ...'" Verne Haybrider's voice hummed on.

And Willy, blinking, suddenly turned back to Buggie. "What's he trying to say, that George Cary?"

Buggie grinned tightly. "I said some smart lawyer. I should have said some smart newspaperman."

"What are you talking about?" Willy said, his voice rising. "What's that George Cary trying to say?"

"He's saying the salesman isn't guilty."

Willy blinked again, then swore viciously.

"Look, Buggie," Roger cut in desperately, "Maybe we ought to get going—"

"Willy," Buggie said, "do you see what I mean now?"

"What does that Cary want to side in with that salesman for?" Willy said. "He oughtn't to be allowed to get away with that!"

"Well," Buggie said, lowering his voice, "why let him, Willy?"

"Why let him?"

"Look, Willy," Buggie said, leaning forward, "you know what I said about this town maybe needing some leading? Well, maybe you're the one, Willy."

"Me?"

"Why not? And maybe this is a good time to start."

"Start what?" Willy asked, voice rising. "Start pulling that animal out of there, and—"

"Now take it easy, Willy," Buggie said softly. "Just listen for a minute and I'll tell you...."

That night, shortly after ten o'clock, George Cary locked up his shop and walked home. It was a beautiful night—clear sky, bright stars, a faint breeze that made the leaves of the trees whisper and cooled the face against the still-prevailing heat of daylight.

And what a day! George did not regret a moment of it. The reaction to his editorial had been almost instantaneous and just as he had thought it would be, including the angry telephone call from Sheriff Beaman and the indirect threat from Lou Collins, who managed the Fineway Clothing Company, that Lou would remove his advertising if George kept on with that line of bilge in the paper. But there had been reaction, and he'd shaken them up a little.

And tomorrow, he thought, walking along, breathing deeply of the night air—tomorrow it would be time to try again. He would arrive early at the shop, fresh and with a clarity of thought....

George Cary slept deeply and dreamlessly that night, and when he returned to his shop the next morning there was a spring in his step. He got out of his suit jacket, loosened his tie, and placed a new sheet of paper in his typewriter; then he stood up and smacked a fist against a palm.

He walked with exuberance, the sense of power and satisfaction building inside him. And it was only when he reached the back part of the shop, barely looking, barely noticing at first, that he saw what had happened.

The back door was ajar, the wood along the lock splintered and gouged with the obvious marks of something very like a crowbar. Then he saw the shiny, silver, coin-like drops of lead dotting the floor from the pot where the lead was melted to the large press and the linotype machine. He looked first at the press, then at the linotype. He looked at the mechanisms of each, at the hardened gobs of lead that had been poured from the ladle of the melting pot straight into the heart of each machine, making them useless.

Then the banner made of press paper, hung across the ceiling with its large slashing letters of red ink:

RAPIST LOVER!

19

The incredible ugliness of it, the childish brutality of it, made George feel for a moment that he had still not awakened that morning, that this was a dream; but then awareness of what had happened became reality, and the anger inside him began. He whirled and walked to the telephone.

A few moments later Sheriff Beaman's sleep-logged voice sounded gruffly over the phone. "Yes?"

"Grove, this is George."

"What's the matter, George?"

"Grove, they've ruined my press and my linotype."

"Who has, George?"

"I don't know. I just came in and found it. They heated up the metal pot and poured lead into the machinery."

There was silence on the other end of the wire, and George said, "Did you hear me, Grove?"

"Yes, I heard you, George."

"They broke in the back door," George said. "Pried the door open."

"That's too bad, George."

"I didn't hear you."

The sheriff's voice repeated, louder, "That's too bad, George."

"Are you coming down, Grove?"

"I'll be there."

"When, Grove?"

"When I can make it, George. I'll get there when I can."

"There's a lot of damage here."

"Yes," Sheriff Beaman said, "it sounds like it."

"Grove," George said, his voice sounding more tense, "I'll tell you frankly, you don't sound very upset about this."

"I just woke up, George."

"Are you awake now?"

"Now, listen, George, I can understand you're excited. Now take it easy. It isn't going to help to get all excited."

"I think you're right, Grove. But you don't sound altogether worried about what's happened here. I think you should be."

"You seem to have a lot of criticism lately, George."

"I don't think that's the point. I—"

"You listen to me, George," the sheriff said, "you wrote an editorial and published it yesterday. Do you remember that?"

"Of course I remember that! That's why—"

"That's why this happened," the sheriff finished. "Didn't you think something like this might happen?"

"I thought I lived in a civilized town, that's—what I thought!"

"People are people, George. You ought to know that. You aren't dumb. You're a Phi Beta Kappa, aren't you? You ought to know that much, or don't they teach people to Phi Beta Kappas!"

George tried to control himself. "Look, Grove," he said, forcing himself to speak quietly, "are you going to get down here pretty soon?"

"Pretty soon, George."

"All right," George said. "Thank you, Grove."

He replaced the telephone slowly and carefully, and then he stood there, hands clenched. They can't stop me, he thought. They're not going to stop me. Somehow, I'll write and print the truth.

The mimeograph machine, he thought—he could use that. Get out some sort of paper anyway, and hammer the truth at them. He started toward the back where he kept the machine, and then he stopped. No. A childish thing to do, really. They wouldn't react. It would be a joke. How then to make them see what had happened here, what was happening this very instant?

Talk, he thought. Appeal first to those you think will listen. If you're a lone wolf in Willow Creek, you're lost. Get somebody with you. Get as many as you can.

The heat was already crowding into the shop, coming with the sun through the front windows. George took out his handkerchief, wiped his brow and then his hands. He replaced his handkerchief and walked toward the door as another kind of heat rose rapidly inside him.

Later that morning, at eleven-seventeen, Grace was buried in the cemetery just south of town. It was a rather brief ceremony, once the body had been taken to the burial grounds, but as good a ceremony, everyone agreed, as had ever been held in Willow Creek. Reverend Pritchard, in fact, went straight through to the last words without stumbling at all, which was unusual.

It was a hard morning, however, for Sheriff Beaman, and now, in the early afternoon, he could not rid himself of that earlier disquiet and anger. He sat in his chair in his office, unmoving, remembering how George Cary's telephone call had awakened him from a dream in which he was performing his sheriff's duties in peace, without all of this having happened. The phone call had dissolved that dream, and what George had told him had only complicated things more. Sheriff Beaman didn't care much for complications.

He swung his chair a little, looking out a window, watching a blue jay dive down to alight on the stone sill, and he kept remembering the nearly inaudible but real anger in George's voice. George was being a damn fool, Sheriff Beaman thought, but knowledge of that did not help the situation. George was opposing him now and Sheriff Beaman did not want any opposition at all. Well, he supposed he could have gone downtown and looked in at the damage in George's shop, but he hadn't. George should have expected trouble anyway, and when he got it Sheriff Beaman did not see why he should come crying to him for help. All right, it was true George wasn't crying. He hadn't telephoned Sheriff Beaman again. The early morning telephone call had been the last word between them. But the sheriff knew that he had not helped anything by turning his back on George Cary. What George could do to stir up any more opposition, Sheriff Beaman didn't know. What in hell *could* he do? Nobody had liked that editorial. And as far as the vandalism, well, what was George going to do about that? Sheriff Beaman knew who was probably responsible after that rock incident in Jackson's cell. But was George, if he found out who had done the damage, going to go out looking for Willy Turner and punish Willy with his own hands? Sheriff Beaman smiled a little, thinking of that, feeling a little better.

And just then there was a short rap at the door. "Come in," the sheriff snapped.

The door opened, Sheriff Beaman saw his son and his grimace disappeared.

"Chuck! Come in, son."

"Are you busy, Pop?"

"I'm never too busy for you, Chuck. Not working today?"

"I worked this morning. It's a little slow right now at the hotel."

Sheriff Beaman knew that because Lola had told him that she was refusing a room to anyone she didn't know. Let them go on to some other town, she'd said. I don't care if it's costing me money, I don't want anything else to happen—not until we see that dirty no-good punished, and punished the right way.

"Sit down, son," Sheriff Beaman said. "You look upset. What's the matter?"

Chuck sat down and looked at his hands. "It's just everything that's been going on, I guess."

"Yes, I know," Sheriff Beaman said. It's got everyone upset. But why shouldn't it? These things don't happen every day."

Chuck nodded, still looking down. I guess I liked Grace quite a lot, all right."

"Hell, yes, son. Who didn't? I liked her too!"

"Pop ..."

"What is it, son?"

"Pop, what's going to happen to this Jackson?"

Sheriff Beaman frowned. "Why?"

"I was just wondering. I mean, you really think he's guilty, don't you, Pop?"

"I haven't said that."

"But you do think so, don't you?"

"It's my job to arrest the people I think *might* be guilty."

Chuck shrugged. "Everyone thinks he's guilty. Not just you, Pop."

"Everyone except George Cary."

Chuck looked up and nodded. "Everyone except George. That's right. And that's why I've been thinking about talking to you ever since I read what he said in the paper."

"What he said in the paper was damn fool nonsense," Sheriff Beaman said, his voice rising.

"I don't know," Chuck said.

Sheriff Beaman glared at his son, and then suddenly he smiled. "Son, I've always told you that you've got a soft spot in your heart for people. I've told you that ever since you were a baby, and it's true. You can never see the bad side of anyone. This salesman or George Cary. Neither of them."

"Pop, George has always been a friend of yours."

"George is still a friend of mine. But I have a job to do. I've got to do that job, and if George is off base, well, I've got to call a spade a spade."

Chuck was silent.

"Chuck, listen," Sheriff Beaman said, "do you think the things George implied are true? If you do, then you must think I'm a pretty bad sheriff—that I can't handle this job—"

"Pop, it's not that at all! It's just that—well, you don't know the whole story."

The room was silent as Sheriff Beaman stared at his son. "How's that, son?"

Chuck shifted slightly in his chair. "Pop, Hugh Seltz thought Grace was raped."

"That's right."

"Pop, look, I'd been seeing Grace."

"Seeing her?"

"Well, look, Pop. We've always been honest with each other. I mean I was more than seeing her."

Sheriff Beaman stood up and walked to the window and looked out. His large hands hung at his sides.

"So that's what I'm trying to tell you, Pop. I was with Grace earlier the day she died."

The sheriff closed his hands and opened them. "You slept with her."

Chuck rubbed a hand across his face. "Yeah, I did, Pop. I should have told you sooner, only—"

Sheriff Beaman turned around and put up a hand. "No, now it's all right. I can understand why you wouldn't like to tell me a personal thing like this. But I'm glad you have. Now, Chuck, do you understand what this evidence business was Hugh Seltz is talking about?"

"Yes, sir."

"And you ... I mean, you think—"

"I think he maybe made a mistake about Grace being raped. She maybe wasn't raped, and everybody in town thinks she was. That's why they're mad, Pop."

"Now hold it a minute, son."

"Pop, you've got to understand what's going on in town. This whole place is boiling. And all because they think Grace was raped. That's not fair to that salesman, Pop. Not if—"

"All right, son! You slept with Grace the day she was killed. All right. Now what does that mean? It means you slept with her, that's all. And that wasn't what killed her, was it?"

"No, but—"

"What killed her was getting beat up! That's what killed her! Not you sleeping with her or her getting raped!"

"But maybe she wasn't raped, Pop. Maybe—"

"What's the difference, Chuck? It doesn't make any difference whether she was or not. She was killed, wasn't she?"

"Pop, it makes a difference to the town. You know that."

"I don't know that!"

"Pop," Chuck said, leaning forward, putting his hands against his face, "I just had to tell you this."

"Sure you did, son. I'm proud that you did."

"I couldn't let it go on that way, without telling the truth, Pop."

"You've always been like that, Chuck. I'm proud of you for it."

"Pop, what's going to happen now? People have to know, don't they?"

"Now, Chuck," Sheriff Beaman said, "you're a little confused, I think. Now, why would they have to know? I don't see why a private, personal matter like this ought to be known by anybody but just the two of us, Chuck. I really don't."

"But, Pop, it's the way people are thinking—"

"Chuck," the sheriff said, holding his voice down, making it soft and understanding, "you keep worrying about what people are thinking. I don't think that's the point at all. It's what actually happens that counts. It's what I do about it. It's what happens later in court—"

"But how about in court, Pop?"

"That's a ways off, son."

Chuck was silent for several moments, then he said, "Pop, do you really think nobody ought to know about this right now?"

"You've told me. I think that's enough for right now, Chuck."

"You think I ought to wait until the trial? I mean, you don't think it would make any difference to people? In the way they look at things right now?"

"Chuck," Sheriff Beaman said, "I can't worry about what people are thinking. I'm the sheriff. I've jailed the man I think is guilty of killing Grace. He's in jail and that's all there is to it."

Chuck nodded thoughtfully, then said, "Pop, maybe I'll wait until the trial then."

"I think you're deciding it the right way, son. And I admire you. I really do."

"Pop, would it really hurt anything, my telling what I've told you? I mean would it hurt your being re-elected and maybe my scholarship at the University?"

The sheriff smiled sadly. "It's hard to say, son. You just never can tell."

"I wouldn't want to hurt you, Pop."

"That's all right, son. I'd rather you did the thing you think you have to do."

"It isn't so much the scholarship. I mean, I want to go to school and play ball and all. I really do, Pop. But that doesn't mean as much to me as not hurting you."

"You've never hurt me, Chuck," Sheriff Beaman said. "And you never will."

"Pop, why don't I think about it some more, and then when the trial comes, then maybe we could talk about it again."

"Son," Sheriff Beaman said, "I think that's a very wise way to go at it."

Chuck sat there for a moment longer, and then he stood up and smiled. "Well, so long, Pop."

"So long, Chuck."

After Chuck had left, the sheriff sat down slowly, his smile fading. He'd raised Chuck to be a good kid. If he'd failed to realize that until now, he certainly was finally aware of it. Chuck was honest and he did what his conscience told him to do. What would he do? Sheriff Beaman took out a cigar and lit it and noticed that his hands were trembling. He'll talk, Sheriff Beaman thought, if he thinks he has to....

The sheriff stood up suddenly, walked around the desk and swung open the door. "Oh, Chuck."

Chuck stopped and turned halfway down the hall. "Come here,

Chuck."

"What's the matter, Pop?" Chuck said, returning.

"Chuck," Sheriff Beaman said, "it just occurred to me. All summer you've been wanting to go on over to the University and look around the campus and have a talk with Coach Braintree, isn't that right?"

"Well, sure, Pop, but—"

"Son," Sheriff Beaman said, "that's what you told me you really wanted to do. Stay around for three or four days and get the feel of the campus, isn't that right?"

"That's right, sure, but I expected to do that just before school starts this fall, not this summer. I mean, I won't have enough money until—"

"Son, would you like to do that right now?"

"Right now?"

"Get yourself a nice hotel room and kind of bum around and take a look at the Athletic Building and all. I'll bet anything Coach Braintree is right in town there, and he'd sure like to see you."

"But, Pop, that'll take money!"

Sheriff Beaman smiled. "Son, this is a little surprise I've been planning for you. I thought later would be the time, but now I think it would be good for you to get away just a little while right now."

"But, Pop, it'll take quite a bit of money if I stay that long."

"Don't you want to go, Chuck? Wouldn't it be kind of nice to get the feel of things right now and then you'd know what to expect? And I mean about everything. Chuck, you're young. You don't want to let things bother you. This was all a pretty terrible thing, wasn't it? Son, I wouldn't let any of this bother you too much. It wouldn't be good for you. We're all men, aren't we? You and I. Like any decent fellow worth his salt. Chuck, if I were you I'd look around and find myself a couple of nice dates while you're there."

"Well, sure, Pop, but—"

"Son, now listen," Sheriff Beaman said, removing his cigar from his mouth, "I didn't do as well as I thought I might have with that little graduation present, that watch, I bought you. But your old Pop had some other plans. Now you go home and you tell your mother you're going to take that trip and she'll give you a check and you can cash it at the bank on your way out. And, son, you take the car."

"Take the car?"

"That's right, son. And don't worry about a thing. I'll even phone Lola for you and tell her you won't be around for three or four days. How's that?"

"Pop," Chuck said, "I don't know what to say!"

"Don't say a thing, son. Just be careful, but have yourself a high old time. All right?"

"All right," Chuck said. "Okay!"

20

At mid-afternoon Buggie and Roger walked toward downtown Willow Creek. Buggie had never felt better in his life. He could feel the good spring in his step, and the air, hot and dry as it was, felt good in his lungs.

"You think you've got everything controlled, don't you?" Roger said.

"You think I haven't?" Buggie said, smiling.

"I could stop everything," Roger said.

"Why don't you? Your head would look real nice in a noose."

They dropped it then, and Buggie walked along, thoroughly content. God, it was going perfectly. Absolutely perfectly. This town, this town! he thought. It was absolutely unbelievable. You gave them a germ and they sat down in bed with the disease in ten seconds. They were waiting for it, ready and waiting for it!

And that Willy! What a dumb, vicious, mean character he was. Perfect! Absolutely perfect! He was big and strong and loud-mouthed, and that made him perfect, and yet—in essence—he was just like the rest of them. Through him, you got the absolute narrowness of them, like looking through glass and seeing the minds of the entire bunch all wrapped up in one. Narrow and biased and with the intelligence of a backward child. They didn't even hate like ordinary people. They didn't hate Negroes because they didn't know any Negroes. They didn't hate Jews because they didn't know any Jews. All they hated was an outsider, someone who was not one of them and who was tainted with the peculiar, preferably something to do with sex. By God, Buggie thought, they even hated sex in an odd backhanded manner. They produced like a bunch of rabbits, but they looked up in the sky and acted like it wasn't going on. Grace, by God, would have been willing to bed down with any dozen guys if they had played it right, and this town knew that. But all of a sudden they were up to here in hate for the guy who'd raped her—and that guy, Buggie thought happily, was no more than a figment of their pitifully warped imaginations.

Buggie held his head high, striding along, a faint smile remaining on his lips, and then he noticed that the north doors of the livestock pavilion were open.

"What are they doing over there?" he asked Roger.

"Tomorrow's sale day."

"What's in there?" Buggie demanded.

"A sale ring. A bunch of seats around it."

"Let's go over," Buggie said, a flicker of excited interest showing in his eyes.

After talking to Fred Mailer, the druggist, George Cary left the drugstore and walked down the street to the bank. He paused outside the old sandstone building, reading the gold letters which were overlaid on the broad front window: *Willow Creek Community Bank—Reserve $200,000.*

Well, he could talk to Sam Perry, he knew, and he also knew it wouldn't do any good. He could talk to Wilson Perry too. But that wouldn't do any good either. The only one here he could really try to convince, he knew, was John Cook—maybe, in fact, John Cook was the one he should have started with in the first place. John was intelligent, reasonably broad-minded—as broad-minded, George thought, as any of the rest of them in this town.

He walked inside, and a moment later was shown into a rather small but neat and dignified office.

"Well, George," Mr. Cook said, standing up behind his mahogany desk.

George smiled wearily. "This is the nicest reception I've had all day, John."

"I can't believe that. Sit down, George."

George sat down, sighing, and Mr. Cook extended a pack of cigarettes toward him.

"Here, George. Light up. You look exhausted."

"Thanks. I am exhausted."

"Now what's all this about?" Mr. Cook said, leaning back.

"John," George said, "you're much too nice, and I can see through it. We don't generally need to be so damned polite to each other."

Mr. Cook smiled and shrugged. "Well—"

"You know I'm on a campaign, don't you?"

"I read your editorial yesterday, if that's what you mean."

"Did you like it?"

"Do you want the truth? Yes, I liked it."

"Good." George inhaled his cigarette gratefully, letting his body relax. "But you don't think it was very wise."

"Do you?"

"I can show you some mined machinery that proves, in one sense, it wasn't. But in another sense, it was."

"How's that, George?"

"I'm clean with my conscience."

Mr. Cook's expression sobered. He looked away from George and rubbed his chin slowly with his knuckles.

"I'm getting experienced," George said. "I've talked to at least twenty people today, and I've poured my guts out to every one of them. I still haven't got anywhere, but at least I'm learning how to get to the point fast."

"Okay, George. Give it to me bluntly."

"This town is about ready to explode."

"George, how can you be sure of a thing like that? How do you know you're not—"

"Go out, John. Look. Listen. There're people on every corner downtown, in every store. You listen, John, and you'll know. You look, and you'll know."

Mr. Cook motioned impatiently. "Is this *your* business, George? Is it mine?"

"It's the sheriff's business, is that what you're going to tell me?"

"Yes. Of course."

"And I'll tell you what I told twenty other people who said the same thing. This is our business. Everyone's business. Because each of us is a part of this town. If something isn't done, there's going to be blood on this town, bad blood, the stinking kind of blood, and every one of us is going to be responsible, not just Sheriff Grove Beaman."

"But, George, Sheriff Beaman—"

"Sheriff Beaman is no more responsible than we are—you or me or anyone in this town. Do you know why? Because a murder has been committed in this town, and Sheriff Beaman no more knows how to handle a murder than you or I do. This isn't his fault. I'm not saying that. I'm just simply saying that he isn't capable for this, and nobody expected him to be when they elected him. Do you see what I'm talking about, John?"

"I'll be frank, George. I think you're overdramatizing."

"You think anything you want, John. But I'm not doing anything but telling the truth. I don't blame Grove. I don't blame anyone. But I'm telling you that something had better be done. We've got a blind man leading a blind community, and we can't trust that unless we expect to see this town turn itself into a mob. And they will mob, John. I'm telling you. They'll mob and they'll kill. And why? Because they don't know what they're doing. Because they're all filled up with hate and vengeance."

"Listen, George—"

"You listen, John. I want you to listen. You particularly, because you're about my last hope. If you listen, maybe we can get somewhere. John, everyone in this town is afraid, just as Sheriff Beaman is afraid. And what are we afraid of? We're afraid of ourselves."

"You're talking nonsense, George."

"That's the one thing you know I'm not talking, John. You know I'm talking the truth. We're all a part of this community—each one of us is—and yet because we're a part of it and depend on it for our survival, we're afraid to offend it, afraid not to be loyal to the way it thinks as a whole, afraid even to do the right thing by it for fear it won't like it. And do you know what this is, John?"

"I don't know what anything is you're talking about."

"It's worshiping a beast, that's what it is," George went on. "There's the beast in all of us, John. You know that and I know it. And it's the beast in us that's causing this town to turn mean and bloodthirsty, enough to want to wipe out a man whether he's guilty or innocent."

"But you really mean to say you don't think that salesman is guilty?" Mr. Cook demanded.

"I don't mean to say anything about whether he's guilty or not!" George said, his voice growing louder. "I only mean to say we don't know if he's guilty. No proper effort has yet been made to find out. There's been no trial, and there won't be any if this isn't stopped pretty soon. Guilty or innocent, Jackson is going to be dead, and dead at the hands of every one of us!"

Mr. Cook shook his head. "I told you, George, you're overdramatizing."

George wiped a hand back through his hair. "John, you know I'm right, don't you? And you know that if you'll only admit that, we've got a partial chance. A lot of people respect you in this town, John. If you'll just get on my side, then some other people will. I know it."

Mr. Cook was silent, apparently thinking it over, and George leaned forward more eagerly.

"Look, John—you don't know how important it is for you to say that you think Al Jackson might just *possibly* be innocent, that *perhaps* somebody else might have done this. You don't have to say you think he's absolutely innocent. I don't even think that myself. John, if you do it, somebody else will get up enough nerve to do it, and maybe this thing can be swung off course."

"George," Mr. Cook said at last, slowly, uncomfortably, "I do wish I could listen to you some more, I honestly do. But right now I'm busy, very busy, and—"

George straightened a little. "John, I know what it means. Don't you think I know that? This is a community bank. All right. I know that. You depend on the community for your business. But—"

"George," Mr. Cook said, "I really am busy—"

George stood up suddenly. "All right! Go to hell!" He turned, strode to the door, and walked slowly out of the office and through the bank, feeling heavy and tired. He walked out into the sunlight, blinking against the glare, and then he looked up and a lurch of new hope went through him. He watched the old Cadillac move down the street, the dust of the highway coating its finish. Doc Granger was leaning forward over the steering wheel of his car, coming back from a good deal of relaxed fishing to his pleasant, relaxed practice. Or at least so he thought....

21

After they had walked into the sales pavilion, Buggie had stood for a long time staring at the interior of this barnlike building with the look of a crude amphitheater. Its show ring and gradually rising benches circled the ring except at one edge, where the high platform of the auctioneer rested.

"What is it like on sale day?" he asked Roger. "Have you ever seen one?"

"Yes," Roger said. "It's like sale day."

"Would you be kind enough to describe it, for God's sake?" Buggie snapped.

Roger knotted and unknotted his hands. "They bring the cattle and the hogs in from the farms and then they put so many in the ring and the auctioneer starts the bids and that's all there is to it."

Buggie shoved his hands in his pockets and stood there silently, eyes half closed, then said, "Let's go."

They drove south out of town on the road leading to the river until they crossed the bridge.

They traveled a quarter of a mile further, and then Buggie swung the car to the left, moving down a twisting dirt road, the gray shale rising to their right, the muddy river ambling slowly to their left. A moment later, Roger saw the Oldsmobile parked ahead, just under a clump of trees out of sight from the highway behind. At their sound, Willy climbed out of the Oldsmobile, Buggie pulled to a stop, and Roger, looking at Willy, felt as though a cold hand had caught hold of him inside.

"Get in the back seat," Buggie said, and Roger did.

"What the hells the matter with coming out in the open?" Willy said. "Why hide around like this? I ain't scared of anybody."

"Willy," Buggie said, smiling engagingly, "get in. And quit bitching, why don't you? How'd you get the Oldsmobile?"

"I told Curt I was taking it, is how I got it."

Buggie laughed softly.

"Listen," Willy said, "this guy Cary. I don't think he's had enough yet. I didn't figure it was enough in the first place, pouring that metal around. We should have done something else—busted up the furniture and like that. Do you know what he's been doing today? Going around talking to everybody and trying to get them to side in with him. He's a rapist lover, all right. That's what he is, a rapist lover."

Willy, Roger knew, liked to use that phrase, because it was one he wouldn't have known if Buggie hadn't told him. He kept using it over and over.

"Now take it easy," Buggie said.

"Yeah, well, he gets me," Willy said. "He really does."

"We're doing all right," Buggie said.

"Yeah, well, I'm going to teach him a lesson. That's what I'm going to do."

"You are, huh?"

"You're damned right. Do you know what's going to happen to that rapist lover tonight? Do you?"

"You tell me, Willy."

"He's going to get some working over, that's what. I already decided. Me and Bud Hinkle, we're going to work that rapist lover over something good, all right!"

"Right," Buggie said agreeably, "and then what happens?"

"He'll remember not to be no rapist lover from here on, that's what'll happen!"

"How about the sheriff, Willy?"

"What about the sheriff?"

"What will he do if you beat up this Cary?"

"What's he done so far, I want to know? I busted that salesman in the head with a rock. I ruint that Cary's equipment. What's he done? I met him on the street this afternoon, and he said, 'Hello, Willy, how are you?' "

"Willy," Buggie said smiling, "you just don't take time to figure things out, do you?"

"What's the matter?" Willy asked belligerently.

"Nothing," Buggie said. "Not yet. You haven't beat up this Cary yet, and that's why nothing's the matter."

"You know, Alstair," Willy said, "you get me mad sometimes with that smart-aleck talk of yours. I mean, the way you say something, you know? You think you're smart, don't you? You think you're something big-time or something, coming in here from Hollywood and all that. Well, don't you forget who you are. You don't belong here any more than that salesman, and I wouldn't forget it if I was you!"

Roger watched Buggie eyeing Willy coolly, and the clutching inside Roger's stomach became tighter.

"Are you finished?" Buggie asked Willy.

"Why? You want to hear more?"

Buggie smiled once more, very faintly. "I'll tell you this, Willy. You can get people scared of you. You're tough, Willy. You really are. But we'd better get one thing straight. I'm not afraid of you. Do you understand that, Willy?"

"Listen," Willy said, his voice rising excitedly, "what is that supposed to mean? Are you starting something? Are you? Because if you are—"

"I just told you one thing, just to get it straight. I told you I'm not afraid of you. I just want you to understand that."

"I got a good notion to work you over, Alstair, just to smarten up that mouth of yours. I got a good notion—"

"You do," Buggie said, "and you'll never see that salesman hang. Do you know that?"

"What are you talking about?"

"I'm talking about the way you go into things, Willy. I'm talking about the way you never think anything out. You start a thing with me, right here in my car. Why? Are you nuts or something? I'm not that salesman, buddy. Did you forget that? You want to remember who I am. I'm willing to help you, Willy. I really am. Because I want to see justice done too, whether this is my own town or not. Now, you, Willy, you apparently don't want to do anything right. You apparently want to louse everything up."

"I asked you what you were talking about." Willy said.

"I'm talking about beating up George Cary. Are you nuts? How far do you think you can stretch things anyway? What's the matter with you?"

"Nothing's the matter with me, but something's going to be the matter with you if you don't start taking straight."

"All right. Let's say you knock this Cary around tonight. What then? Twice now the sheriff hasn't done anything about you. And he knows who threw that rock. He knows you pretty sure enough fixed Cary's equipment. But what has he done, Willy?"

"Nothing!" Willy said proudly.

"And why not?"

"Because he's scared of me, that's why not!"

Buggie put his hands up to his forehead and groaned. "Do you really think that?"

"What do you mean, do I really think that? Hell, yes. I know it."

Buggie groaned again, and then brought his hands down and said, "Now, listen, Willy. You listen and try to get it straight. I'll tell you why the sheriff hasn't tried to touch you yet—because he doesn't want to, not because he's afraid of you."

"What're you talking about?"

"Look—what happens if you beat up this Cary?"

"Sheriff Beaman won't do anything about it, I'll tell you that," Willy said, suddenly grinning.

"Willy," Buggie said, "get with it. The hell he won't. I know you, Willy. You and Hinkle would start beating on that guy and you'd damn near kill him."

"Good enough for him."

"Maybe," Buggie said, "but he hasn't done anything wrong in the eyes of the law. He just printed an editorial. We've got a free press in this country. He just went around today and tried to get people to see things his way. We've still got freedom of speech, Willy. So what happens if you beat him up? You'd force the sheriff's hand, that's what you'd do."

"Crap," Willy said.

"I'm telling you the truth. That's too much. Everybody else has sat still for the other stuff, but some of them—not all of them, I'll admit—but some of them would start bitching. They'd start getting scared, maybe, figuring they could get hurt too if everyone gets too excited. No, Willy, I'm telling you—that sheriff would have to take you in and then where would you be?"

"He wouldn't take me in," Willy said.

"He wouldn't, huh? You think he wouldn't? Have you got something that would stop him if he wanted to, Willy? He'd bring you in, man, if he had to do it with machine guns. He'd *have* to, Willy."

"I'd like to see that," Willy exploded bravely. "I really would!"

"Why, Willy? What good would it do? What the hell do you want to do it that way for? You wouldn't be any good in jail, would you? What could you do then about seeing that that bastard salesman is paid off for what he did to Grace?"

"He couldn't take me in," Willy insisted.

"Willy, aside from that, what's the point in lousing things up when everything is going fine? You're doing a great job, Willy, so far. I just wouldn't want to see you louse everything up."

"I ain't going to louse nothing up."

"Well, then listen to me," Buggie said. "Will you do that?"

"I don't have to listen to you," Willy said.

"I know that. But what's the harm in it? I've got a couple of ideas I think you'll like, Willy."

"I'm sick of ideas," Willy said. "I want that salesman to get it, that's what I want!"

"Hell," Buggie said, "that's what we all want. Only why not listen to what I've got in mind, Willy?"

"I want to get that bastard," Willy said tightly.

"All right," Buggie said. "You will."

"Quick."

"How about tomorrow?" Buggie's eyes were bright, and Roger felt the hand inside him clutching again and again.

"Tomorrow?" Willy said.

Buggie nodded. If you want to listen to me, Willy, I say tomorrow."

"You mean that?"

"I mean it."

"Well, go ahead and spit it out, Alstair."

Buggie smiled. "All right, Willy. I will."

22

After he'd gotten his car, George drove to Doc Granger's house and found that Doc had been there and gone, so he drove back downtown and found Doc just taking off his jacket in his office above the Willow Creek Bakery.

"Doc," George said, "I'm glad you're back."

"Why, hello, George. How are you? You're glad I'm back. I'm not. The fishing was beautiful. What's the matter? Feeling bad?"

"Yes," George said, "I am."

Doc unbuttoned his vest. "Well, now what's the matter, George? You appear healthy enough, just a little nervous, maybe. You ought to slow down a little, George."

"What's the matter with me is the matter with this whole town. Haven't you talked to anybody yet?"

"No. About what, George?"

"You haven't heard what happened?"

"George, I couldn't care less. I just wish I were back fishing."

"Doc," George said, "Grace Amons is dead."

Doc was opening his black bag and he stopped and straightened and rubbed his hands against his opened vest. "Dead?"

"It happened the day you left. Doc, there's a man sitting in jail right now who's supposed to have murdered and raped her, and—"

"Now wait a minute, George. What the hell are you talking about?"

George took a breath. "Doc, you're the last chance. People like you in Willow Creek. I'm not saying Jackson's innocent. I'm not saying that at all, but—"

"George, sit down," Doc ordered. "Will you do that, please?"

George motioned with his hands, and then he sat down. "I'm sorry, Doc. I'm not making sense."

"You sure as hell aren't. Now tell it to me slowly. What the hell do you mean, Grace was murdered and raped?"

George carefully told Doc everything that had happened.

"My God," Doc said softly.

"There's going to be a riot in this town, Doc. I'm telling you facts."

Doc rubbed a hand across his left cheek. His mouth set grimly. "Damn, I leave this town for five minutes and everything goes haywire. I can't believe it!"

"Well," George said, "it's true. Doc, we've got to—"

Doc shook his head stubbornly. "Just let me get used to it, George. I want to look around and talk to people. I want to talk to Grove. Hell, this is Willow Creek!"

"That's right," George said grimly, "this is Willow Creek, all right."

"Let me talk to you later, George. Come up to my office this evening, will you? I've got to understand this better than I do now."

George nodded reluctantly. "All right, Doc."

When George left Doc's office, he stopped at the newspaper shop, intending to lock up for the day. He had noticed the yellow convertible parked outside, but he was surprised when he walked in and found Buggie Alstair seated in the swivel chair behind the desk.

The boy stood up instantly, a smile on his mouth. "The door was unlocked, so I just walked in. I hope I wasn't intruding, sir."

"No," George said, "of course not. Can I help you?"

"As a matter of fact, I just dropped in. I was looking at your machinery back there. That's a shame, isn't it?"

"Yes," George said, "it is."

The boy walked around the desk, extending his hand. "My name's Buggie Alstair, sir. I'm staying with the Cooks. Roger and I are fraternity brothers at the University. I know you're Mr. Cary."

George shook hands with him. "Glad to know you, Buggie."

"If you're busy, sir, why just go ahead with whatever you were planning to do. I just stopped in, as I said."

George nodded, faintly puzzled. "I have been busy today. I'm not right now. Anything on your mind in particular?"

"No, sir," Buggie said quickly. "Not at all, sir. I just heard that you'd gone to the University. I understand that you made Phi Beta Kappa, sir."

"Yes," George said. "But that was a long time ago."

"I have pretty good hopes of being selected, Mr. Cary," Buggie said. "I was just interested, that's all."

"Well, that's fine," George said, and quite suddenly he wanted to talk to this young man, to relieve the tensions of the past hours. He had to kill some time somehow, and perhaps this would take his mind off things. "Sit down over there, Buggie. How are your grades?"

"I've been very lucky, sir," Buggie said. "I have a ninety-five per cent average."

George whistled. "That's fine, son!"

Buggie smiled modestly. "I don't know. I'm taking a purely liberal arts program. I sometimes feel that if I'd approached something more scientific, the challenge would have been greater and consequently more satisfying."

"It all depends on what you want to be. What are you shooting for, Buggie?"

Buggie spread his hands. "I don't know, sir. I think I'll find it when the time comes."

"Well," George said slowly, "maybe you're going at things the right way, Buggie. I'd intended to become a good newspaperman." He motioned at the shop. "You see how it turned out."

"You're in the newspaper business."

"In a manner of speaking. Or let's say I was before my equipment was ruined."

"Yes," Buggie said softly. And then he went on brightly, "You know, sir, I wasn't entirely sure about what kind of vacation I might enjoy, coming home with Roger—I was more or less certain that things might be just a little dull. But it certainly hasn't turned out that way. Things have been pretty lively here in Willow Creek."

"Yes," George nodded. "A damn shame."

"Well, but is it, sir?"

"I don't follow you, Buggie."

"Oh, I don't mean it's a good thing that Grace is dead. I don't mean that at all. I just mean that because something has finally happened here in Willow Creek, maybe it's a good thing—to kind of see what you've got here, how the temper of things goes, what the people are really like."

"Well," George said, "it's difficult to be so clinical about it. If you don't have a stake in this community, then I suppose it is easier. But you can't get the true picture that way."

"Well, sir, what is the true picture anyway?"

George shook his head. "I don't know, son. I really don't." And then he looked up interestedly. "What's your impression, Buggie? You've got the advantage of objectivity, to look at this town and see what's happening to it because of Grace's death? What do you think?"

"Well, sir," Buggie said, smiling, "I think you've got a picture of ignorance here."

"Ignorance?"

"Sure. The kind of ignorance they had at Salem when they burned the witches, sir. The kind of ignorance they had in Germany when Hitler gave them Jews to hate to divert them from the real issue. The kind of ignorance people who kick Negroes grow into to compensate for failure and poverty."

George shook his head slowly. "Things aren't quite that simple, Buggie. It's too easy to analyze with quick judgments that way."

"Why is it, sir? It's true, what I'm saying."

"Buggie," George said, "it's always a temptation to judge by outer surfaces. Especially when you're on unfamiliar ground, when you're not directly involved."

Buggie lit a cigarette slowly, sprawling just a little in his chair.

"Your premise, I take it, sir, is that one has to have a stake in the thing in order to understand it. Is that right? To understand the problems of a Jew, you've got to be a Jew. To understand the problems of a Negro, you've got to be a Negro. To understand the problems in this town, you've got to be a native of Willow Creek."

"Yes," George said. "That's more or less what I mean."

Buggie inhaled his cigarette, waited a moment, then said, "Well, let's just stick to Willow Creek. Let's say we've got a problem in Willow Creek right now."

"Yes," George said, his voice flattening a bit, "I'll admit we've got a problem in Willow Creek."

"The problem is stupidity, isn't it? I've got no stake in anybody here. I really don't give a damn, sir, whether or not Willow Creek dries up and blows off the map. So I can see what you've got here. And so it's like standing off on a hill and watching two trains meeting each other on the same track. You know there's going to be a collision, and yet it doesn't matter because you're not on either one of those trains. Do you see what I mean by that example? I've got a Catholic friend, and it was the way he tried to explain God to me. He said God sees life the same way. God usually doesn't do anything about those trains smashing up, and yet He knows because of His position on the hill that they're going to."

It was, somehow, as though a faint draft had come across the room and blown against George's neck, chilling him.

"You're not trying to compare yourself with God, are you, Buggie?" he said softly.

Buggie shook his head, smiling. "Not at all, sir. The example I used is not precisely correct—not as things stand."

"I don't follow you," George said slowly.

"I've got the view," Buggie said, "but I'm far enough down the hill to have access to the switches, too. What. I mean, I can make damn sure the trains are on the right track."

Now that chill against George's neck had penetrated inside of him, getting to him deep inside.

"Do you want to explain that, Buggie?"

Buggie looked at the tip of his shortening cigarette.

"I wonder, sir," he said, "how it would impress you if I were to say that I've been pulling certain switches in Willow Creek?"

"It would depend," George said, everything tightening inside him, "on what exactly you meant by that."

"What I mean, sir, is that a short time ago I told a nice elderly lady that I thought that a town like this should make certain that the man who killed Grace should be punished."

George shook his head, uncomprehending, but sensing.

"Nothing wrong in that, sir? Is there?"

"Why don't you go on?"

"Yes, sir. I told the same thing to a gentleman here in town whose name, I think, is Willy Turner. I simply extended my views, so to speak."

"So to speak," George said softly.

"Mr. Turner also, along with a couple of his friends, seemed interested in my analysis of a sexual maniac. I was glad to extend my views on that, too."

"Yes," George said, "and what else?"

"I also expressed certain views on your editorial about Grace's murder. I expressed what, if I were of the opinion of someone, say, like Mr.

Willy Turner, I would do about it—not that I am of the view of Willy Turner; that would be nearly impossible, wouldn't it?—I simply mean, if I were of that view, what I would do about it."

"Like pouring melted lead into a press?" George asked, ice in his voice.

Buggie spread his hands, that everlastingly sardonic, insulting smile on his lips. "You can make up your own mind about that, sir. I don't say I did that, but you can use your own judgment. You can use your own judgment, too, about whether or not I was telling the truth when I said that salesman tried to entice that little girl over to his cell window—"

George stood up, jolting his desk with his knees, feeling the pain of the impact. "*You sonofabitch,*" he whispered.

Buggie laughed softly.

"You come in here and tell me that you've personally done these things? That you're, in effect, responsible even for the wrecking of my equipment? By God, I'll—" His hands were moving for the telephone.

"You'll what, sir?" Buggie asked politely. "Call the sheriff? What good would that do, I wonder? You don't expect me to admit to anyone else what I've told you, do you?"

George shook his head in disbelief. "What the hell are you made of?"

"Why don't you sit down, sir?" Buggie asked gently. "Relax, sir."

George stared at him in white anger for a moment, and then he sat down slowly.

"What does Roger have to do with this?" he asked, controlling his voice.

Buggie shrugged. "He helps out."

"But under your direction, I take it," George said.

"We've all got a free will, haven't we?"

George drew a heavy breath. "Now, listen. I don't know why you told me this—what pleasure you get out of it—but you're not going to get away with it, I'll promise you that. I'll go to Roger's father—"

Buggie was shaking his head pleasantly. "No, sir, I don't think you will. I've been checking. You've been to quite a few people today already. You're not going to get anywhere. As I told you, sir, this is just between you and me. To anyone else, sir, I'm like a clam. I just thought you'd be interested in just how stupid this town can be. I could tell you more, as a matter of fact. I could—"

And then Buggie spoke no more. He remained sprawled easily in his chair, leaning sideways to squash out his cigarette in an ash tray on George's desk, staring at the red embers dying.

"Go ahead," George said intently, staring at him. "Go on with what you were going to say."

"Was I going to say anything more?" Buggie asked, straightening. I don't think so, sir."

"Unbelievable," George whispered. "But you'll get no farther with it."

"I think you're wrong, sir. I'll get just as far as these people want to go. And they're a bloody-minded little group, aren't they?"

George wiped the back of his hand across his face. "Get out of here!"

"Yes, sir. Anything you say, sir."

Buggie stood up slowly, carelessly.

"It was a nice chat, sir. It's always a pleasure to talk to someone with intelligence. Good-by, sir."

The boy sauntered to the door.

"You won't get away with this," George said tightly, but Buggie had already gone, closing the door politely behind him, and George knew that he couldn't do a thing about what Buggie had told him or about whatever else it was that Buggie planned to do. He felt sick, deep in the bottom of his stomach, but he couldn't do anything about that either....

23

At four o'clock that afternoon dark clouds formed, shutting out the hot sun, and the air turned still as death; and at five it rained, a quick burst of downpour. The rain stopped then and the dark clouds disbanded, leaving a yellowing sky, streaked by the dropping sun. After that Willow Creek sweated with a steamy oppressive heat.

At six-thirty George walked into Doc Granger's office. "You've found out for yourself, haven't you?" George said, sitting down opposite Doc.

Doc shook his head sadly. "It's nearly impossible to believe, and yet I know it's true."

"Doc, I just heard something that sent chills right into my bones. A boy came to me. A young kid of twenty or twenty-one, a school friend of Roger Cook's. Do you know what he's been doing, Doc? He's been purposely inciting this town!"

"He's *what?*"

George nodded. "It's true." Then he recounted his interview with Buggie.

"Fantastic," Doc whispered.

"But true, just the same. And we can't do anything about it."

Doc brought his head up, angrily. "Just for a thrill, he's doing this! And this town is stupid enough to be led into it."

"That's right, Doc," George said tiredly.

Doc got up suddenly, angrily. "They've all gone mad. They're all acting like animals! And all the while, some sadistic runt of a kid is—"

George smiled ruefully. "That's what I told John Cook. That it was the animal, the beast in us, that was doing this. But it's natural, I think—"

"Natural?" Doc snorted. "Hell, no, at least not for civilized people. We don't live like animals and we're not supposed to act like them."

George watched Doc, silently.

"It's mixed up," Doc said. "It's all mixed up. Half of it is honest-to-God resentment, but the rest of it is a strange mixture of a basic instinct to repay an eye for an eye, and a terrible innocence."

"Innocence?" George repeated.

"Yes, of course," Doc said. "Innocence! What could be more naïve, more innocent than a community like this? We live in a vacuum from anything but this, this world the size of a pinhead, and ruled—what are we ruled by? A bunch of foolish codes and rules, established in the first place out of innocence and ignorance and built upon by more of the same.

"Do you know what it's like when a pregnant wife comes in here, George? Do you know what happens ninety-nine times out of a hundred? I'll tell you what happens. I get sick at heart for a society that recognizes the existence of a life beneath a belly, but fails to recognize the method by which life was begun there.

"This is what's the matter now, George. All their lives, most of these people have been taught that a function as natural to mankind as breathing pure air is something that ought to be hidden behind the nearest barn, to be snickered at and hinted at, but never recognized openly. And do you know what that does, George? It attaches something dirty, something foul to an act as noble as procreating human life. It makes idiots out of people, so help me it does, and in this case, dangerous idiots.

"This is the real trouble, George. To Grace's death they've attached all their back-of-the-barn viewpoint, inflamed now by all the hate it's created inside them. Because all their lives, they've felt and believed that the impulse in them that makes them want to get into bed in pairs and carry on life's functions is something to be hidden and sneered at—because of that, they've identified themselves with the man they think raped Grace and hated him for the animal they feel in themselves. And all the time they're playing into this kid's hands, who just wants to—" Doc stopped, unable to go on.

Then, slamming open a cabinet, Doc reached inside and got out a bottle of whisky.

"In all the time I've practiced, George, I've kept a bottle in here to offer it whenever it seemed right, but I've never once taken a drink in here myself. I'm going to right now. Do you want to join me?"

"Yes," George said, "I do."

George watched Doc pour two water glasses half full, and they each tasted the whisky.

"Doc," George said, "they're going to try to kill that salesman and pretty quickly."

Doc nodded. "I think you're right," he said softly.

24

George was not a drinker. He never had been. Yet, when he'd gotten home late that night after a half dozen drinks with Doc, he went to the kitchen where he kept a single three-quarters full bottle of bonded bourbon and poured another drink, a water glass one-fourth full. He sat down at the kitchen table and surveyed the liquid for a moment, and then he'd downed it with a single lift of the glass.

He was quiet for a number of minutes, and then quite suddenly he rose, jarring the table, and walked across the room to the telephone. After a moment, Amanda White's sleepy voice came on the line.

"I wakened you, didn't I?" George said.

"Yes. It's—two-thirty, isn't it? That's you, isn't it, George?"

"Yes, it's me," George said. "It's I. I'm sorry to be calling at this time. I've been drinking a little, Amanda."

"Are, you all right, George?"

"Yes, I'm fine. Do you mind being wakened?"

"No," Amanda said. "Not at all, George."

"Amanda," George said, "I think I'd like to come over there."

There was a moment of silence, and then Amanda said, "Of course, George."

George hung up without saying any more, got the bottle from the kitchen, and walked down the street toward Amanda White's house, tripping once but regaining his balance.

Amanda opened her door as soon as his foot struck the first step of the front porch.

"Come in, George."

"This is quite a hell of a note," George said a little too loudly, and then he said in a whisper, "I suppose one of the damn neighbors woke up and is watching."

"Never mind," Amanda said. "Come in the living room."

"I've brought a bottle," George said, following her and sitting down heavily on a couch.

"So I see."

George looked at the bottle in his hand. "I don't suppose you drink out of the bottle, Amanda?"

"I never made a habit of it," Amanda said. "Do you want me to take it and fix a drink in a glass for you?"

George looked at her. "Sure, Amanda. If you please. That would be very nice indeed. Do you want to have one with me? I'm a little ahead of you though."

"I think I will have a drink with you, George."

George grinned, and then he seemed to focus on her for the first time since he'd entered the house. It was strange, but she somehow did not look quite as he'd expected her to. She was wearing a nicer negligee than he'd thought she might wear—he'd thought she might wear a flannel robe on an occasion like this. And her hair was quite neat, neither in pin curls nor let down in pigtails; he'd always thought probably she wore her hair in pigtails when she went to bed.

"I think I'm fairly drunk, on the whole, Amanda. If you want me to leave, I'll leave. You don't have to have a drink with me."

"I want to have a drink with you, George," she said, taking the bottle and disappearing to the kitchen.

George, in the silence of the room, felt the first surprise of finding himself in Amanda White's house. He did not know, now, why he'd come; he had never been in this house before, had not, in fact, ever thought seriously about coming here that he could recall.

Amanda returned with two glasses.

"Is it all right with water?" she asked. "That's all I had."

"Quite all right," George said, taking his glass and tasting the drink, then holding the glass up apologetically. "Sorry. I should have waited for you. Sit down, Amanda. Sit down right here."

Amanda sat down beside him on the sofa, lifting her glass too.

"Here's to a swell little town," George said..

Amanda, her eyes searching George's, nodded faintly; and they each drank.

"Here's to one of the greatest little towns in the old United States," George said, and he realized that already he had downed half the drink. "You mix a good drink, Amanda. You surprise me."

"Thank you, George. I'm glad I surprise you."

"It's all right," George said. "Don't mention it. I'm pretty drunk, all right."

Amanda nodded. "That's all right, George. You're very upset, aren't you?"

"Me?" George said. "No, not me. Everything's just fine."

"If you want to talk about anything, George, I would be happy to listen."

"Amanda," George said, "I made a habit a long time ago never to talk business at home. Julia—" He stopped, then shrugged. "You don't, I imagine, want to hear about Julia. That was a long time ago, wasn't it?"

"Yes, George, but it's up to you."

"No, I don't want to talk. I—"

He shrugged once more, smiling grimly, and then he leaned back, head resting against the back of the couch. "Why don't you talk, Amanda?"

"I don't feel much like talking either, George."

He turned his head, looking at her. She smiled at him, and he looked along the gentle line of her cheek, at her lips, down the curve of her throat. He moved his eyes down, over the swell of her breasts beneath the negligee, over the solid breadth of her hips. A feeling came into him, hard and demanding, and he tried to move his mind against it.

"I know what you're thinking, George," she said softly.

He met her eyes, absorbing the look in them. He put his hand over her right hip, waiting. She brought her hand up behind his neck, drawing his face toward hers. She returned his kiss with a deliberate, exploring passion.

"Sorry," he whispered.

"Why?"

He waited a moment, realizing her reply. And then he untied the cord of the negligee, sweeping it open.

"Amanda—" he began.

"Never mind," she whispered tensely. "Don't talk any more, George."

Dawn was coming when at last he spoke again:

"You're not sorry?" he said.

"Of course not, George. Don't think that for a minute. It's not true."

"You look different now. Your eyes—"

"I've covered my feelings for a long time. It's like suddenly opening a shade to light. I'm not used to it. You know all about me now, George. I've nothing more to hide from you. Didn't you ever guess?"

George shook his head. "No, Amanda, I—"

"George," she said quickly, "were you disappointed? Was it what you wanted?"

"Yes," he said, "it was, Amanda."

"That's fine," she said, her eyes alight. "I'm glad, George. You see—the hell of it is I've been in love with you for a terribly long time, and you didn't know it."

"No," George said, "I didn't."

"But don't worry," she said, touching his lips with her finger softly, bending forward and kissing his forehead, "there're no strings attached. Do you understand that? I've lived alone a long time, long enough to love and love only in my mind, my heart. You're free, George. You can knock on my door whenever you want, and I'll be waiting. But you can walk away again, too."

"Amanda, listen—"

"No, not now," she said. "You're tired, and you're still a little drunk. You need sleep. You wanted me to dull the tension for a little while. This changes nothing that's happened in this town, George. The sun's coming up, and tomorrow is already here. Sleep now, George, and don't think any more. I'm glad you came to me, George...."

25

It was morning, and the sun came once again, scorching with its first rays. The town was shifting and stretching. Six o'clock. Seven o'clock. The business section began to stir. The flag on the central flagpole fluttered faintly against a warm morning breeze. Eight o'clock. The flag stopped fluttering, as though holding still now and waiting expectantly. To the south the river flowed east and now, beside it, at eight-ten, an Oldsmobile pulled to a stop. A moment later, a Ford convertible drew up beside it. The water of the river swept under the bridge, muddy and gurgling; and north, past the business section, within the walls of the gray stone courthouse, Al Jackson stood and looked out the barred windows of his cell and wondered why he was shivering when the heat had already returned almost full strength....

In the sheriff's office Doc Granger set his jaw and rubbed large hands over his wilted jacket. "I tell you, Grove, you've got real trouble in this town. Why don't you stop evading facts? Why don't you admit this has been pretty badly handled, right from the start, and—"

"I'll tell you just once, Doc. So long as you're in my office and I'm the sheriff of this county, you'll keep your mouth shut from talking that way."

"And I'll tell you something, Grove!" Doc replied loudly as the telephone began to ring, "you just try to keep me from it...."

And beside the river, Buggie helped Willy drape the white banner across the hood of the Oldsmobile. It read:

THERE'S A KILLER IN WILLOW CREEK

"It ain't good enough, damn it," Willy said, and Roger, standing silently beside Buggie's convertible, watched the way Willy was bristling with a growing self-importance. Buggie fixed his side of the banner to the Oldsmobile. "It's good enough, Willy."

"I hope you know what you're doing," Willy said.

"I know what I'm doing," Buggie said. "Are you ready now?"

"Let's go," Willy said tightly.

Willy climbed into the Oldsmobile. Roger started to get into the right side of Buggie's convertible.

"The other side," Buggie said to him. "It's going to look better if you're driving."

Roger got behind the wheel; ahead, Willy gunned the engine of the Oldsmobile several unnecessary times, and then wheeled the car onto the highway leading into Willow Creek. Roger followed in the Ford convertible, Buggie beside him.

"Slower!" Buggie yelled to Willy.

Hunching his shoulders grudgingly, Willy cut down his speed, and on they went along the highway.

At the south edge of town, a small man in a straw hat and thick glasses stopped on the sidewalk and stared at them.

Three blocks further, a black coupe pulled out from a side street, the two men in it—Curt Black and Bud Hinkle—nodding faintly to Willy and then to Buggie and Roger. The three cars, one behind the other, moved slowly toward the business district....

And George, once more in his own house, put down the telephone and stood there, brushing a hand across his forehead. Doc was getting nowhere at all with Grove Beaman. Somehow, George had expected that, and yet now that he knew the truth, he was still surprised.

He lifted the cup of black coffee he'd brought to the telephone and drank it, his hand trembling. He'd wasted a lot of time, he thought. He should have talked to Roger Cook by now. But he'd wanted to see Doc again. Then there'd been the drinks. And then... *Wasted?* he asked himself. No. He hadn't wasted time for himself. And he thought back to Amanda and leaving her only minutes ago. No, that hadn't been wasted time for him.

But nothing was accomplished yet. The cloud of violence was still moving on them.

He kept remembering that boy, Buggie, sitting there, actually telling him....

George shook his head, trying to make his brain function.

The boy had told him a lot, and he'd almost told him more, George was certain. He had said, "I could tell you more, as a matter of fact. I could—" And then the boy had stopped. What else *could* he have told him? George wondered.

George lifted the telephone. A few moments later he heard Mrs. John Cook answer.

"Alice," he said, "this is George. George Cary."

"Oh," Mrs. Cook said, and George could hear the coolness coming into her voice. "George, I haven't much time. Mrs. Boseley is honking for me outside right now. We girls in the sewing club are meeting this morning, you know. We don't all think like you, George. We may not be able to do much, we girls. But we're going to put all our strength together and do all we can in our own way to see that justice prevails and that that awful man in jail pays for the terrible thing he's done to poor, sweet Grace."

George closed his eyes, opened them. "Yes, Alice. I understand. But I want to speak to Roger. It's very important, Alice."

"Well," Mrs. Cook said, "he's not here, George. And I don't see what could be so very important that you'd want to talk to him. I told him, George, that I didn't approve of that editorial you wrote and that I wouldn't, if I were he, do anything at all that would make people think any of us in this family approved of what you wrote, George."

"Alice," George said quietly, "believe me—it is important that I talk to him. Do you know where he is?"

"No," Mrs. Cook said flatly, "I do not, George. Now I've got to be going."

George listened to her hanging up, and he replaced his telephone wearily. He stood there for a moment, then quickly put on his jacket, went outside, got into his car and drove toward the business section.

George sighted Roger just as the car procession, led by Willy in the Oldsmobile, passed the flagpole. The procession now was ten cars long, a slow-moving, snaking procession, creating no more sound than the throttled hum of vehicles in low gear.

George parked his own car and stared in amazement. People had come out from the shops now, and looked inquiringly at the unexpected caravan, and then, from between the parked cars, three boys stepped out and started walking behind the last car.

The cars moved on up the block as George got out of his car, and at the next intersection Willy made a slow, wide U-turn, then started retracing the block. There were twelve cars in all now, and seven boys moving along on foot.

At the intersection of the flagpole, Willy turned right, leading the growing caravan slowly down the street in the direction of George's newspaper shop.

Finally, recovering a little from his surprise, George moved forward. And just at that moment Buggie turned, catching sight of George. He smiled a little, then looked back to the car behind and nodded to Bud Hinkle. A rock sailed through the air and smashed through a front window of George's shop.

George stopped, eyes widening. A shout sounded from the boys trotting along, and then, a moment later, a second rock smashed another window. A third then, and finally a volley, with the shouting increasing in volume. Buggie looked back at George and waved politely.

Fred Mailer, from the drugstore, stepped to George's side. "You'd better get out of sight, George. I would, if I were you."

But George, not answering, moved forward. Willy, in the Oldsmobile, had now turned the next corner, around the hotel, and the head of the caravan was coming to a stop beside the sales pavilion. George, rounding the corner, saw Willy, head jutting forward, shoulders hunched, stride into the sale barn. Behind followed Buggie and Roger, then a growing swarm of people, coming now from everywhere.

Roger, George thought wildly. I've got to get to Roger! But the sales pavilion was packing now as the crowd shoved into the building, their voices echoing against the ceiling, mixing with the bawling of calves and heifers and the squealing of pigs. It took all the strength George had to plunge his way inside, and then he could not see Roger.

But Roger was there, standing on one of the board tiers of the amphitheater over the chute, standing beside Buggie, high enough to command a good view of the auctioneer's platform. Roger looked silently down at the show ring, watching a group of hogs moving aimlessly around the circular enclosure, grunting and snuffling. Then he moved his eyes to the platform where Willy, face dark, mouth grim, was speaking to the auctioneer.

The building was packed now with men, boys and women from off the streets, from out of the shops.

The auctioneer stepped back, and Willy came up to the counter facing the amphitheater, resting one hand flat against the wood before him, picking up and holding a gavel in the other. And Buggie, the excitement sweeping through him, looked through sharp, critical eyes as Willy stood there, commanding, threatening. Then Buggie glanced back toward the door. People were milling inside now, and the air was turning hotter, riper.

Willy, Buggie saw then, was watching the door, waiting, and then Willy's eyes switched, meeting Buggie's. Buggie smiled, and Willy looked around the amphitheater, sweat rolling down his face, glistening against the lights over the show ring.

"I guess you know there's a killer in town!" he bellowed. There was a sound of voices muttering.

And then Willy thundered, "I guess you know who he is and where he is and what he done!"

Again the muttering voices, like rolling thunder. Willy's chest heaved with his breathing in the tight, thick air.

"I guess you know what ought to happen to someone like that!"

It was not what he was saying, Buggie thought, feeling the excitement, nurturing it, it was the way he was saying it—using that hoarse, heavy voice, raking at the people with it, getting into their blood with it.

"He killed Grace, that's what he done!" Willy yelled, and he brought the gavel down with an angry crack.

"He did!" someone shouted.

"He raped Grace!" Willy said, cracking the gavel again.

"He did! He did!" a half dozen voices sounded.

"You know what we ought to do to someone like that!" Willy shouted, and brought the gavel down.

"You tell us, Willy," came the response; and Buggie, after the third crack of the gavel, stomped a foot, nodding quickly at Bud Hinkle and Curt Black to his right.

"I'll tell you what we ought to do to him," Willy yelled, cracking the gavel and getting in return an echoing thumping of feet, "we ought to hang him up!"

"Hang him up!" someone yelled, and Buggie thumped his foot down in unison with Hinkle and Black and a dozen others.

"Hang him up!" Willy repeated.

The gavel sounded once more, feet stomped. It was growing all through the room now.

The boom of Willy's voice, the shouted responses, the crack of the gavel, the thump of feet.

"Hang him up by the neck!" Willy yelled hoarsely.

"By the neck!" came the response, and then the pounding of feet became methodical, shaking the building.

Buggie could feel it growing, feel it in the air, coming through his nostrils and digging down deep to the pit of his stomach. He could see it, drink it in, the savageness of it with sweat rolling and eyes shining. Blood, he thought. They're thirsting for blood. And it's going to work, by God—just like those hogs running around, snuffling in the crap down there, they're snuffling for murder, racing blindly after an idiot, and it's going to happen, to happen....

Suddenly then, Buggie glanced to his right.

Roger was gone.

Buggie looked around swiftly. He got one glimpse of Roger moving through the crowd toward the door and disappearing. Buggie looked after him, then shrugged, smiling, and returned his attention to Willy on the platform, listening as the sound from the stomping, yelling mob around him increased....

George saw Roger leave but he could not move quickly enough. Roger was outside and trotting down the street before George got to the sidewalk. George got there in time only to see Roger turn the corner beside the hotel and go out of sight.

Roger ran diagonally across the street and down the alley, where he pushed in through the back door of the bank. A moment later he stepped into his father's office.

Mr. Cook looked up, frowning anxiously.

"Well, Roger."

"Do you know what's going on, Dad?" Roger said. His face had caught the dust of the road leading into town, and now it was streaked badly with sweat. His hair was tousled, and there was, Mr. Cook saw, a strange look in his eyes.

"Roger, yes, I do. It's a horrible thing, and I—" he stopped suddenly, peering at Roger more closely. "Son, I think I know what's bothering you. Someone told me you and Buggie were in that caravan. That's what's upset you, isn't it?"

"Dad," Roger said, "you don't understand. You've got to stop them!"

"Stop them?"

"They're at the sale barn. Pretty soon they're going to go over to the jail and drag that salesman out. They're going to hang him!"

"Son, listen—"

"You've got to stop them, don't you understand?"

"Son, I—well, look, I know how you feel, I think. But you see there just isn't anything I can do. Besides, I don't think they'll—"

Roger came across the room and gripped the chair in front of his father's desk with both hands. His face had paled to the color of white paper where the sweat had rolled it clean.

"Dad, the salesman had nothing to do with Grace dying. I was there when she died. Do you hear what I'm telling you?"

"Son," Mr. Cook said paling now, "you don't know what you're saying!"

"Oh, I know what I'm saying, all right. Buggie and I were there! In her room!"

"Roger," Mr. Cook said, struggling with his words, "what you're saying is preposterous!"

"Buggie and I, Dad! We were the ones up there, not the salesman. He came back to the hotel; but he was drunk, just like he said, and he didn't remember seeing us. Do you understand?"

"I don't understand anything," Mr. Cook said, his voice hoarse.

"Dad, Grace and I... we made love. Down the hall from her room, in Mrs. Hale's room. It wasn't what everybody thought. I made love with her, do you understand? And then when we got back into her room, Buggie got mad about it. He shoved Grace around and she fell and hit her head on the bureau. That's how she died. She wasn't raped, Dad. The salesman didn't kill her. Buggie pushed her and she fell down and she died. Don't you understand what I'm telling you?"

Mr. Cook stared at Roger. He didn't move. He didn't say anything.

"Dad, that isn't all," Roger said, his words pouring out now. "Everything that's happened since—that's been our fault. Mine and Buggie's. I didn't want to do it, but Buggie insisted and I was scared not to. All this— this was planned. Do you know what I mean? Everything. The little things and the big things, including that caravan. Buggie planned it, and I've been helping him. Will you help me now?"

Mr. Cook's head swung back and forth, his eyes dazed.

"It's got to be quick, Dad. Do you understand that? They'll kill an innocent man. You've got to go over there and stop them. Tell them what happened ... Tell them whose fault it really is. Will you do that?"

"This isn't true what you've been telling me," Mr. Cook said.

"It is true! Everything I've told you! And now you've got to go straighten it out before they kill that man!"

Again Mr. Cook's head was shaking back and forth.

"Dad, it's up to you. I wanted to tell Mother, only I couldn't. Now I've told you because you've always been able to do anything. You've got to do this and in a hurry. Do you hear me?"

"I can't do it—" Mr. Cook said in a breaking voice.

"You've got to! I've finally told you everything and now you've got to stop it, do you hear me?"

"Don't you understand that I can't?" Mr. Cook said wildly.

"Can't?"

"I can't, I can't!" Mr. Cook said, putting his hands up to his face, and suddenly his body seemed to go limp. "Years ago, maybe I could have. But I haven't got what it takes any more. I couldn't face them, to tell them what you've told me. Roger, I just can't!"

Roger stared down at him, then turned and walked out, slowly, unbelieving. He'd done everything now, telling his father. That was all he *could* do, and now his father was sitting in there, unable to move, unable to help him, unable to help the salesman. Oh God, Roger thought, it's over now, everything.

George, clinging only to the slight hope that Roger would tell him something, searched the street. The noise of that mob in the sales pavilion still echoed in his head, and the look on the faces he'd seen only minutes ago was stamped into his brain.

He walked slowly up and down the street, wiping a hand wearily across his eyes, turned a corner, and then saw Roger walking out of the bank. George ran forward.

The boy seemed stunned when George approached him.

"I've been looking for you all morning, Roger," George said.

Roger looked at him, nodded.

"Roger, do you hear me? Look at me, Roger."

"I'm looking at you, Mr. Cary," Roger said.

"Roger," George said, "I want to talk to you. I want to talk honestly with you. Is that all right with you, Roger?"

"I think," Roger said, looking at George, "they're going to hang that salesman today."

George nodded and took Roger's arm. "Just give me the chance to talk to you, Roger. Will you do that?"

Roger did not reply, but he allowed George to hold his arm and lead him down the block to George's parked automobile.

"Do you want to get in my car, Roger?"

Roger shrugged, got in, and George climbed in from the other side, behind the steering wheel.

"Now, Roger," George said, "listen to me. Your friend, Buggie—he came to see me. Did you know that?"

"No," Roger said listlessly.

"He told me that he and you had purposely incited this town. I know that much, Roger, because Buggie told me that."

Roger turned and looked at George with cold eyes. "Yes, I believe that. I didn't know about it. But I believe he told you, all right. Did he tell you it was his idea to ruin your equipment?"

"Yes, Roger, he did."

"Why didn't you hit the sonofabitch then?" Roger said. "Why didn't you kick his brains out?"

"This hasn't been your idea," George said, "I know that. This has been Buggie's work. You must hate him for that, Roger."

"He's a sonofabitch."

"Are you afraid of him, Roger?"

Roger took a breath. "No. I'm not."

"Then tell me just one thing, Roger. Why have you gone along with him?"

"It doesn't make any difference now."

"Yes, it does," George said. "You've got to believe that, Roger. There's a reason, isn't there? Buggie told me only part of the story, that you and he were purposely trying to set this town on fire. But he started to tell me something else, Roger, and then he didn't. It's the reason, the final reason, why you've gone along with him, isn't it?"

Roger looked at him silently, then said, "It doesn't matter now."

"Damn it, Roger, they're rioting inside that sales pavilion. What do you know, Roger? Don't hold anything back now."

"It's too late," Roger whispered.

George grasped the boy's arm. "No, now, Roger. Nothing's too late. Not yet. What else do you know, Roger? There is something, isn't there?"

"Yes," Roger said finally. "Buggie and I were in Grace's room. Buggie shoved her around a little, and she died—" His voice broke away.

George watched the boy steadily, examining him, hope crawling up once more inside him.

"Go ahead, Roger," he said quietly, "tell me exactly what happened."

And Roger, voice dull, hands limp in his lap, did....

26

In the sheriff's office, Doc stared angrily down at the courthouse lawn. "Will you simply tell me," he asked Sheriff Beaman, "what you're going to do?"

And the sheriff, sitting at his desk, said, "I'm doing all I can do. I've sent Doug over there."

"Will you tell me what the hell good sending Doug over there is going to do?" Doc asked.

"It'll be enough to stop them," Sheriff Beaman said.

Doc glanced at him, then looked out the window once again, down to the right. He could just see the corner of the jail wing. "Good Lord," he said, turning and pacing, "Doug isn't going to do any good, and you know it, Grove."

"Do you have any other suggestions?"

"Call the State Police, for God's sake!"

But then Doc stopped pacing and looked out the window again, out toward the business district.

"Never mind," he whispered. "Here they come!"

And almost at that same second, Doug Havery burst in the door, sweating, breathing hard.

"Grove, I couldn't do a thing. I didn't have a chance."

The sheriff was on his feet instantly.

"Get the .30-.30 and the shotgun out of the closet, Doug."

Doug did as he was ordered, and the sheriff took the shotgun.

"For God's sake," Doc said, "stop them, Grove!"

The sheriff and Doug Havery started quickly for the door. Doc followed, but Sheriff Beaman snapped, "Now stay here, Doc! It's bad enough as it is. Do you hear me?"

Then he was gone, and Doc returned to the window.

It was, he thought, like watching locusts swarm in, or grasshoppers, the way they had in the thirties. They moved on foot, in cars, on bicycles. They were small, large, thin, fat—a single solid moving mass; and, Doc thought, they have brought the smell of death with them.

Why the hell doesn't Grove get out there? He watched the mob reach the rim of the courthouse lawn, and still there was no Deputy Havery, no Sheriff Beaman.

Now he could see the leading, strutting figure of Willy Turner, marching ahead of the swarming oncomers.

"*Where is he?*" Doc whispered aloud, unbelieving, and now the mob was cluttering the entire front of the lawn, moving toward the back, toward the jail.

And then, finally, there appeared the figures of Sheriff Beaman and Doug Havery. Guns crooked in arms, they came out toward the crowd, moving into the right flank of it. Doc stared down, as though paralyzed, watching the sheriff move forward slowly, his deputy to the right a half dozen yards, moving in a line with him.

And then, through the raucous noise of hundreds of voices, Doc heard, "Git him!"

And four of them jumped on Doug Havery, knocking him to his knees, taking the .30-.30 rifle from his hands even before he had half raised it.

The mob moved forward, and Sheriff Beaman lifted his shotgun to his shoulder.

"Now stop there!" he yelled. "Every damned one of you!"

"Get out of the way, Sheriff!" someone yelled back.

"I mean it!" Sheriff Beaman shouted. "So help me I'll start shooting—"

And then someone, sneaking around him, had shoved him down and yanked the shotgun out of his hands.

"Now get out of here, Sheriff," a voice snapped. "We mean business!"

Doug Havery had climbed to his feet again, weaponless; and the sheriff, too, stood up and stepped back, empty hands at his sides. "What now, Grove?" Doug asked, watching the mob with quick inclusive eyes.

"We can't do anything," Sheriff Beaman said, a hard roughness in his voice. "I waited too long—"

Just then Sheriff Beaman saw Doc running out of the courthouse, sprinting straight for the mob. He saw Doc yank at the arm of a man in the mob, and he heard him yell, "Stop it! All of you!"

Sheriff Beaman was sharply aware of the futility of his own actions through watching Doc's; he saw the man Doc had grabbed whirl, strike out, and in the next second Doc had sat down in swift clumsiness.

Doc scrambled to his feet, but Sheriff Beaman hurried to him and put his hands on Doc's shoulders.

Doc shook his head wildly, the blood spilling from his nose. "Got to stop them!"

"You're not going to stop them!" Sheriff Beaman yelled. "You can't now, Doc!"

"My God!" Doc groaned.

Just then a shot rang out. Doug Havery, beside them now, said, "They're shooting the lock off his cell."

"Lord, Lord," Doc whispered.

Sheriff Beaman, face gray now, said, "Doc, I—"

"Get away from me," Doc swore softly. "Just get away from me, Grove."

By the time George had stopped his car beside the lawn of the courthouse, the mob had gotten Jackson out of his cell. They'd gotten him out and were dragging him across the lawn, swarming around him in a pack. As George looked, a foot kicked out through the movement of legs and arms, catching Jackson's left hip.

"Roger," George said, turning back to the boy, "you've got to do it! You're the only one who can!"

Roger, refusing to look at the mob, shook his head woodenly.

"Roger—" George said, then stopped to look back at the mob. There was a tree on the lawn, a tall oak just a dozen yards to the right of the front courthouse steps. They dragged Jackson there, and at the same moment a rope, looking like a wild snake, flew up and looped over a projecting limb. George looked at that rope, and then beyond, where he saw Doc on the steps, and higher up Sheriff Beaman.

George turned his head, searching the rim of the crowd until he saw Buggie Alstair, who stood casually beside his convertible across the lawn; he was still smiling, George noticed.

George turned back to Roger. "Now listen to me, Roger," he said, trying to control his voice. "You told me. I can't help. They're completely against me, don't you see that? I couldn't even get started, telling them what actually happened. Roger, you told your father. He couldn't help you. You're the one who can stop them. Don't you understand that?" But Roger did not say a word. He sat there, silently, face deathly white, hands gripped together, stone still.

And beside the tree trunk, Willy, eyes blazing with power and triumph, ordered, "Tie his goddamn hands. Make him stand up and take it. Here!"

He yanked the shivering Jackson to his feet.

"Let me get a swing at him!" somebody yelled in the crowd, and the mob surged forward.

Willy, sweeping out broad powerful hands, yelled, "Get back, damn it. We're handling this right. He's getting what's coming to him!"

"Please, God!" Jackson implored.

And Willy ordered, "Now loop it around his stinking neck."

"Roger," George insisted tensely, "you can't let it happen! You can stop it, son. I know you can. Don't you want to see this thing stopped?"

Willy, in a sudden burst of movement, kicked forward, catching Jackson in the groin. Jackson doubled instantly, dropping to his knees.

The crowd cheered. "Again, Willy!"

Then suddenly, before George realized the motion, Roger was out of the car and running forward across the courthouse lawn. George watched for an instant, then jumped out himself.

Bud Hinkle had brought a chair out from the courthouse and put it under the tree, and now Jackson was being lifted, struggling, onto it. And the rope, in a hangman's knot, was put around Jackson's neck, the play being pulled out of it slowly and surely.

Hurry, son, George prayed, locked now at the edge of the crowd, watching Roger fighting his way forward.

It was nearly impossible. They were like cattle, surging around the tree, making animal noises, and Roger tried futilely to claw his way through them. Finally, George saw, the boy switched direction and made his way to the courthouse steps, mounting them.

At last Roger had reached the top steps, and there he turned, facing the whole mob, in the center of which the salesman waited, white-faced, for someone to kick the chair out from under him.

"Stop it!" Roger yelled. "He didn't do it!"

"What are you doing?" someone beside him snarled, and reached for Roger. But Roger shoved the hand away, still yelling.

"He didn't do it! *We* did it!"

It seemed to George that Roger was simply yelling into a wild storm, yelling hopelessly and unheard, but the boy stayed at it until finally there came a booming voice from the edge of the crowd, a voice that sounded like Doc's.

"Listen to him!"

And now Willy had switched his head around, looking angrily in Roger's direction. He put a hand up and the crowd hushed slightly. He yelled, "What the hell are you trying to do, Cook?"

"Listen, everybody," Roger yelled. "Listen to me, please! The salesman didn't kill Grace! Buggie and I, we were up in her room, and—listen, you've got to listen to me!"

The voices pitched up around him again, a babble of voices. "Shut him up!" someone yelled.

"Listen to him!" came the booming voice again, and now George could see Doc Granger pushing through the temporarily diverted crowd.

"It's true what I'm telling you," Roger shouted. "Will you listen to me, please?"

"Go ahead then!" someone yelled. And Roger began to explain. He told the story in disjointed phrases, voice cracking. But he told it, the way it was exactly, and they seemed to listen—and then suddenly there was complete silence.

Roger stood there, body quivering, and George looked beyond, looked at Buggie poised beside his car.

Suddenly someone yelled, "Let that salesman down and put that other bastard up there!"

Two men grabbed Buggie as Doc Granger shoved his way up to where Roger was standing.

"Bring him over here!" Willy yelled, as Bud Hinkle removed the rope from the neck of a sagging Al Jackson.

Buggie was dragged forward; then Doc Granger shouted, "Hold it up!"

"Shut up, Doc!" Willy yelled. "We're going to hang this one up—"

"Willy," Doc boomed, "you've already shown well enough how dumb you are, haven't you?"

"Doc," Willy screamed, "if you want to make trouble, we'll give it to you—"

"Shut up, Willy!" Doc turned, starting to speak to Sheriff Beaman standing on the courthouse steps; but Sheriff Beaman had already motioned Doug Havery down into the crowd, where Doug took Buggie's arm as the two men who'd grabbed him let go.

"That kid's a killer!" Willy raged.

"Maybe he is," Doc answered. "But so are you, Willy! And so are the rest of you!" He faced the crowd, and Roger stepped back and rubbed a hand across his face.

"Every one of you would have killed today," Doc said, "and I feel sorry for you. Now somebody get that salesman over here to me so I can see if he's hurt, and all the rest of you go home, do you hear me? This is a rotten thing that happened in this town, and I think you know how rotten a thing it was. But before you go I want to say this—if any of you think you're much more innocent than that boy over there with Doug, or than Roger here, you're mistaken. You've all tried to kill today. Now go home, all of you, go home and feel ashamed and thank God that you were saved from committing a horrible, stupid crime."

There was a moment when nobody said a word or moved, and then there was a murmuring of voices, and finally the crowd was disbanded, and someone was helping Al Jackson walk toward Doc Granger....

27

George walked across the lawn and up the courthouse steps toward Sheriff Beaman, who seemed a peculiarly lonely figure in the half shadow, standing with hands at his sides. He looked at George almost blankly, then turned and motioned to Roger, who was still standing near Doc and the salesman.

"Over here, Roger."

Roger nodded silently and came over. They stood there, the three of them, until Doug Havery had led Buggie up the steps to where they waited.

"So now what?" Buggie said, smiling his fixed, sardonic smile.

Ignoring him, Sheriff Beaman called to Doc, "How is he, Doc?"

Doc turned from the salesman. "He'll be all right. I'm taking him over to my office."

Sheriff Beaman nodded, then turned once more to Buggie, his large shoulders sloping in weariness. "You're under arrest."

Buggie continued to smile, got out a cigarette, lit it, blew the smoke into the air.

"You kill me, Sheriff."

Sheriff Beaman turned to Roger. "The same goes for you, Roger."

Roger was silent.

"Both of you," Sheriff Beaman said, "into my office. George, I'd like you to come along."

Buggie, George saw, shrugged, flipped his cigarette away, and walked leisurely behind Sheriff Beaman, never looking at Roger.

Inside the sheriff's office, the four of them—Grove Beaman, George, Roger, Buggie—stood in the mid-morning heat. Sheriff Beaman sat down wearily behind his desk, placing his large, clasped hands on its surface. George stood near a corner. To Buggie and Roger, Sheriff Beaman said, "Sit down, please. Both of you."

Roger sat down on a straight wooden chair. Buggie said, "I'll stand if you don't mind." He leaned against a window sill.

Sheriff Beaman stared at his clasped hands for a moment, then looked up. His eyes were no longer empty. They were angry now.

"You're both of you under arrest, just like I said."

Buggie slouched a little more. "On what charge?"

"Murder, for you."

Buggie laughed. "Like I said, Sheriff, you kill me. You really do. Do you expect to make that stick?"

"I do," Sheriff Beaman said quietly.

"You're going to take Roger's word for it? How it happened? You think that's what really happened? Hell—"

"Roger was the one who spoke up. He probably was telling the truth, but we'll let a jury decide that." He turned to Roger. "If you hadn't withheld information, this would never have gotten started, Roger. Maybe the jury will decide you were an accomplice; maybe they'll take into consideration that you finally talked up. I don't know." Then he turned to Buggie. "You'll be charged with murder."

Buggie shook his head, the smile still on his lips. "How can you do it, Sheriff? How can you sit there and act like the big grown-up Boy Scout when five minutes ago you'd have seen that guy swing in the breeze by his neck, just like every other hick in this so-called town?"

"I think Doc Granger put it about right, out there," the sheriff said. "I think most of us are pretty guilty. I don't deny that. But there's going to be some justice done, just the same." He looked at Buggie, eyes black. "You pushed Grace around and killed her. You kicked off this riot. We're going to get as much payment out of you for that as we can."

Buggie shoved himself away from the sill, moving forward. "It figures! My God, it really does! A two-bit sheriff in a two-bit stinking town spieling off about justice! Is this what you call justice? Everybody alive in this dump is guilty of wanting to taste some blood, and you sit there and tell me Buggie Alstair is going to be the fall guy?"

Suddenly Sheriff Beaman had arisen and his right hand had snapped out and grabbed Buggie's T-shirt. He yanked the boy forward, into the desk edge, and the smile went out of Buggie's face.

"You've got it right, son," Sheriff Beaman whispered. "That's right. This is just a hick town. And I'm just a small hick-town sheriff. So this is the way we do things here. It figures, just like you say. So what the hell difference does it make if we don't do things the way they might do them somewhere else? We do things our own way. That's what you thought, isn't it?"

"Get your goddamn hand off me!" Buggie snapped. "I'm under arrest. You can't touch me!"

"Oh, but I can, son," the sheriff said, his voice still as quiet as a whisper. "I am touching you. I'm even going to rough you up a bit. Isn't that the way it goes? What the hell else did you expect in a dump town like this from a two-bit sheriff?"

George watched intently, watched the blood drain from Buggie's face.

"Lousy farmer cop."

"Right," Sheriff Beaman said softly, then struck Buggie across the right side of his face with a heavy flat hand, struck him so hard that Buggie tumbled backward, hands flying, slamming finally into the opposite wall.

Roger half rose, then sat down again. George wiped a hand across his mouth, looking at the white-faced Buggie. Blood oozed from a corner of the boy's mouth.

"Yeah," he hissed, eyes blazing. "It really figures, all right! It really does!"

Sheriff Beaman stood there, body rigid as steel, then he took a breath and called, "Doug, come in here!"

Doug Havery appeared, and Sheriff Beaman motioned shortly. "Get him into a cell."

Doug turned to Buggie as the boy pushed himself to his feet. "Come on."

George waited for the boy to answer, but this time he had nothing to say. Face white and grim, his body shaking with anger, he followed the deputy out the door.

Sheriff Beaman turned to Roger. "Go with Doug, Roger."

Roger nodded.

George watched Roger leave the room, a different looking Roger. He walked with an odd confidence, doubly odd, it seemed to George, because the boy was walking to a jail cell.

Then George and Sheriff Beaman were alone in the room. Sheriff Beaman reseated himself slowly, and he was once more staring at his clasped hands.

"That kid, that Buggie—" he said slowly.

George nodded. "I know."

And then finally, still watching his hands, Sheriff Beaman said, "The salesman. If that cigar in Grace's room was his ... How do you think it got there, George?"

"We'll never know, I guess," George said quietly, "unless Jackson can remember something more. I do think this. Jackson wasn't guilty, the way it turned out. But I think he could have been. I'd remember that, Grove."

Sheriff Beaman was silent for a long moment, then he looked up. "Go ahead, George. I think I'll sit here alone for a while and look inside myself and get good and sick. I'm sorry about it, George. The way I handled it."

George paused, then said, "We'll all get over it, Grove. In time we'll forget." But not too quickly, he hoped. Not too quickly....

George left, closing the door quietly behind him. He walked through the now quiet courthouse. And then he was outside, coming down the steps. He stopped as he saw Amanda White standing beside his car, alone there, across the scuffed litter of the lawn. And somehow, suddenly, all the loneliness, all the bitterness seemed to collapse, and he hurried across the grass to her.

THE END

WINNER TAKE ALL

— — —

James McKimmey

1

I was stretched out on the bed when the knock sounded at my door. I got up, annoyed and walked into the living room. I'd been doing nothing all day and the dull weariness had seeped in so deep it was an effort even to get up and open the door. Anyway, I was pretty sure it couldn't be anyone important. I knew almost nobody in San Francisco.

I switched on a lamp and squinted at my watch. Seven-ten. I ran a hand through my hair and opened the door. I looked at the man standing there in the hall. It was one helluva shock.

He was a bit over six feet. He weighed around one hundred and seventy-five pounds. He had a face that was not exactly handsome but reasonably clean-lined with a small nose and a rather broad forehead. He had blue eyes and short-clipped blond hair.

He looked exactly like I did.

He grinned. "Fascinating, isn't it?" One thing, he didn't smile the way I did. His was a sardonic, patronizing twist of the lips. "Mark Steele?" He spoke differently too—more precisely, and he gave a refined softening to the R in Mark. Sounded real elegant.

I looked at him. "Mark Steele, that's right."

He gestured at my room. "Do you mind?"

I opened the door all the way. He smiled and walked in. He surveyed the room for a moment, then touched a chair. "Mind?"

I shrugged.

He sat down, took out a pack of cigarettes from his jacket pocket. His suit looked expensive, tailor-made, and much more conservative than my own rather seedy outfit. Now he was examining me once again. "Absolutely fascinating," he said. "Your ears stick out a bit more. I can see the differences, a little. But still amazing, isn't it?"

"Amazing, all right, but so what?"

He laughed as though I'd just said something real witty. "Hard-shelled, aren't you?"

"Look, Mr.—"

"Byrd. Thomas Byrd." He offered his pack of cigarettes. I shook my head. "You don't smoke?" he asked.

"Not just this minute."

He laughed again. "All right. I'll explain, shall I?"

"It's up to you."

He crossed his legs, blowing smoke at the ceiling; he looked like the junior partner in a big stocks and bonds company.

"Yesterday," he said, "somebody addressed me as Mr. Steele. A Mr. Chickory, I believe, was his name."

"Who?"

"Mike, the bartender at a little pub on Green Street."

"Oh," I said. Mike, the bartender at the Green Lamp, was one of the few I knew even casually in this city. Lately I'd gone in there every evening.

"A girl named Dolly, I believe, also made the same mistake."

"Okay," I said. I knew Dolly, who also came in there every evening.

"The point is," he said, "I've been waiting for some time for this moment. I'm a rather egotistical fellow. I wanted to see how I looked from the other side—I've never been too ashamed of my facial delineations."

"All right," I said, stepping toward the door. "Now you've seen."

"You are a bitter fellow, aren't you?" he said smiling.

"Now, look—"

"I'm sorry. I apologize. I'm simply delighted, don't you see?"

"I'll make like a mirror some other time. Right now—"

"No, wait. Let me explain. I have another reason for coming here. I know something about you—"

"Which you got from Dolly," I said. You beat around the world the way I had been doing, and you wind up with a barmaid to talk to. It was a cold world when you kept moving.

He nodded. "Well, Dolly, yes."

"She didn't mention talking to you when I saw her last night. Neither did Mike."

He smiled, faintly this time. "I asked them not to."

"So," I said finally. "You found out something about me from Dolly."

"Yes. You're an engineer. But not the drafting-room variety. You like field work. You're transient in your profession. You'll go anywhere, if the job interests you. You've been in San Francisco about one week now. You just returned from Arabia. You're about to embark again, you haven't decided where."

I rubbed a hand along the side of my chin, glaring at him. For one thing, this résumé was all too accurate. For another, I didn't like the way he got it. You land in a strange city and you're lonely. You wish you could settle down and sit in front of a nice fireplace with someone nice sitting beside you. But you can't seem to make it. So you get a little drunk in a small bar and spill out the story of your life to a barmaid. Very touching.

Thomas Byrd went on: "You're thirty-four. You were in combat during World War II. Infantry. You got a battlefield commission and mustered out as a captain. You were wounded at Beek, Germany, and taken prisoner at Minden, escaping in three days. You won the Purple Heart, the Bronze Star with cluster—"

"Okay, okay."

"Since the war you've traveled as an engineer, but you've also gotten into other activities. There was a small sojourn in Red China, during which you had to fight your way back to the border. You got into some serious danger in Egypt, when you again had to fight your way out of—"

"So let's cut the history, shall we? I talk too much when I get drunk."

He smiled. "I don't see why you're reluctant to discuss a life that, to me, is highly satisfactory. You're a latter-day soldier of fortune, Mr. Steele. I admire that. You see, I sit here and look at you and realize I look just like you do. But that's the end of it. I'm no soldier of fortune. I'm—" He shrugged.

"So you're this and I'm that. Fine, Byrd. All very interesting. But—"

"Let me get to the real point," he interrupted. "I didn't learn quite all of that from your friend, Dolly."

"No?"

"No. It seems, Mr. Steele, that you and I are brothers."

I stared at him. "Brothers!"

"Indeed. Twin brothers."

"You're crazy."

"On the contrary. Do you care to listen?"

I sat down myself now.

"Took a little doing, tracing you down. Been working at it ever since I found out myself that I had a twin brother."

"Okay," I said. "Let's have it."

"Yes, of course. I'll try to make it brief. The Byrd family is quite prominent socially—has been for generations. This creates, as you might imagine, a rather restrictive attitude concerning conduct and such. Your father—my father too, as it turns out—was apparently something of a rebel. To the extent that he was virtually drummed out of the family when he married our mother. She, it seems, was not socially acceptable, which is in the Byrd clan quite enough against anyone."

I nodded, listening carefully but still not able to believe that I had a brother I never knew about before, much less the sort of family history Byrd was unwinding for me.

"All right," Byrd said. "Our father and his brother—Uncle Gosset Byrd—were the sole extenders of the Byrd family. And Uncle Gosset, though he never married himself, was quite set against the marriage of our father and mother. It seems Uncle, being the elder, had assumed a rather fatherly attitude, or perhaps you would call it a dictatorial attitude. At any rate, he fought the marriage tooth and nail."

"Which is all very interesting," I said, "but—"

"But does not get to the facts as they concern you and me. All right. Though Uncle, moving into total control of the family fortune when our grandparents died, disapproved of the marriage, he nevertheless was aware that one had to have an heir to carry on the Byrd tradition. When you and I were born he attempted to smash the marriage between our parents and gain control of the children—us. Do you follow?"

"I follow fine. So far I've learned something about Uncle Gosset."

"Quite true. That Uncle is an ass I agree. However, that is not the point. The point is that one day there was a severe fire—our parents' small home on the beach. Our father died in the fire. Our mother escaped— with one infant. She thought the other was dead. And in order to keep that child—you—out of the hands of Uncle Gosset whom she hated, she ran away, changed her name, and remarried—remarried a man named Steele, from which gentleman you got your last name."

He sounded convincing. I had known the man I called Father was not my real father. He'd been killed in a plane accident in Texas when I was ten. My mother died a year later. It was a series of orphanages after that. What Byrd was saying could be true.

"As for me," he said, "I did not, after all, perish. I was found by Uncle Gosset quite unharmed—this unknown to anyone else. Uncle did some fast thinking. He wanted an heir to the estate, and he wanted to be the sole controller of that particular destiny. So he smuggled me aboard a ship and sailed to Europe. When he returned a few weeks later, he fabricated the story that he'd found me in orphaned poverty over there, took pity and brought me home.

"I didn't find out about the story until very recently when Uncle, who is a hypochondriac, became ill and thought he was really going to die— then he told me what I've just told you. As it turned out, he was not close to dying at all, and will no doubt live to be a hundred and twenty. Regardless, having found out the story, I started checking on you. I traced you from Texas, to Chicago, into the Army. I found out you had recently been in Arabia, then that you had come here. Tracing was not too difficult at that, knowing your name. You have not left exactly a quiet trail. And so now three people know the facts of this rather bizarre story." He grinned and motioned with his cigarette. "And so here we are. How are you, brother?"

"Brother," I said, standing up, "I'm fine. I'm glad you bothered to look me up and tell me. It's all very interesting, but you know as well as I do, even though we're lookalikes we're strangers. And I'm not about to throw my arms around you and weep for joy, brother."

"No, brother," he said. "I didn't figure you would. I figured you would react just about the way you have."

"Well, then?"

"Well, then, I suspect you feel pretty much as I do. You've had one life, I've had another. Blood brothers, twins, whatever, after thirty-four years we are virtual strangers. So I have not looked you up simply to cement relationships with a long-lost brother. Among things I am not, brother Mark, is sentimental. I am, as a matter of fact, selfish. Consequently my motive for being here right now is selfish. I need help, and I've got a proposition to offer you."

What he said seemed reasonable—and if his proposition involved something to beef up my anemic bank account, I was ready to listen.

"What kind of proposition?" I asked.

"Financial. Are you interested in money?"

I smiled a little. At the moment I had a little over four hundred bucks left from the Arabian trip, and I was going to have to latch onto something new pretty quick. "Sure," I said. "Am I being cut into the family fortune?"

He smiled back. "If you were that kind of threat, I would never have looked you up and told you this story. Uncle has complete control of the estate, and he wouldn't send a cent your way."

"It figures," I said. "So what then?"

"I'll explain. I'm in trouble, brother Mark. Rather serious trouble. I've contacted you for a specific reason. I've considered the whole thing rather thoroughly and I think you can help me."

"Go on."

"A bit over a month ago I committed an indiscretion. I lost one hundred thousand dollars at roulette."

"That's a lot of indiscretion."

"I'm aware of that now. I should have been then. The point is, I still owe that money."

"If you're already in for one hundred G's, I don't see how I can do you much good."

"Let me explain. I'm—well, on the whole rather nicely fixed, as you might imagine. My wife, Clarise, and I have a good home in Los Angeles—Beverly Hills, to be exact, not far from Uncle Gosset's estate. I've never worked a day in my life, brother Mark. I suppose I'm what you might call a playboy. Rather disgusting to admit, but there it is."

I nodded. He looked it.

"My income, however, is doled out according to the conditions of a trust fund. I don't come into the principal until I'm thirty-five, which is eight months away. I do have some money, however, from my wife—"

"But not a hundred grand's worth."

He nodded. "That's the problem. And the people I owe it to want it *now*."

I shook my head. "Playboy or not, how did you get in for one hundred thousand?"

"For me," he said, "it was easy. I'm afraid I do things that way sometimes. You, apparently, talk to girls in bars when you've had a bit to drink, brother Mark—"

"Why don't you cut the brother bit?" I snapped. Somehow that now annoyed me. He did not seem like a brother, even if he looked like I did. And it made little difference to me that he was my brother—I had never needed a brother and particularly a brother like this one. To me he was just somebody named Thomas Byrd.

He nodded agreeably. "All right, Steele. I'm merely trying to explain. You have your habits, I have mine. And I try to reach the moon at times. Just to be doing it, you see? I regret these things later, when I wake up."

"I can imagine. Who took you this time?"

"A gentleman in Nevada—Las Vegas, to be exact."

I nodded. "I hear you can gamble a buck there."

"You can gamble a number of bucks. It's all very legal. But I'm afraid I went to the hinterlands this time. You see, they know me rather well in Las Vegas. I was rather, well, drunk this one evening. I wanted to see if I could make a quarter of a million dollars."

"Moon is right," I said.

"Yes. So—well, I kept running into limits wherever I went."

"You couldn't lose it fast enough, in other words."

"As it turned out, precisely. When the legal establishments wouldn't play my kind of stakes—I think they knew my condition and wanted to keep my business—I looked to the borders. It was a bit difficult to find what I was looking for. But I found it. And I really went for the moon. I—"

"You lost a hundred grand."

"Correct. In fact, I lost more than that. I lost the twenty thousand I had at hand and one hundred thousand of what I didn't have at hand. I gave a promissory note for that."

"Was the wheel honest?"

"I don't know. You see, the hell of it is that I'm really not a very good gambler. I do it a lot, but I don't know enough about it. At any rate, I lost it."

"Who did you lose it to?"

He shook his head. "I don't know."

"Look, Byrd—"

"It's true. I did the gambling in a kind of rambling ranch house outside Las Vegas. I was, as I said, fairly well boiled and consequently am fuzzy on some details—how I got there and so forth. I remember the place had a large red barn or stable, and some small cabins and this ranch house—quite a lush spot, on the whole. There was a horsy smell outside, I remember. And I vaguely remember the man who drove me out there. A large fellow with very broad shoulders—large hands and a very large head. I ran into him at one of the casinos on the strip in Las Vegas. He was just coming off work as a dealer or croupier or something, and said he knew where I could find what I wanted." He paused as though remembering the evening, smiling just a little sadly.

"Okay," I said. "And the rest?"

"Well, the rest is foggy. They had a craps table, a wheel and such set up in this big rustic room. The big fellow who took me out there ran the wheel. And there were three or four other people there—all dim in my memory now. There was one rather rotund fellow with black hair with a streak of white in it running back from the center of his forehead. I mean he looked fat, but the way he moved—like a cat—probably he wasn't fat but just built like a steel barrel. Tough-looking character. I never got anybody's name. The tough-looking fellow, the one built like a barrel, I've thought since could be the head man. But I wrote my I.O.U. out to Rancho Entertainments, Incorporated."

I shook my head. "How could you do it, Byrd? You go into a state where gambling is legal, where you can find all the legitimate businessmen you want in the industry, people who care about how they run their places, and you go running off to the country and start fooling around with a gaffed wheel. I know something about gambling, Byrd. It's tough enough when you're betting against an honest house. But when you do something like this—"

"I'm quite well aware, now, of what I did. You're quite right that it was foolish—especially since gambling is legal in Nevada and those people who own the legal gambling concessions do not want to see their own businesses endangered by illegal, and probably dishonest, operators. I know that. It also makes those illegal and dishonest operators especially dangerous, since they are not only opposing the law but other legitimate gamblers as well. But it's water over the dam, Steele, and I would rather not be moralized to about my actions."

I shrugged. "You were getting to a proposition."

"Yes. They gave me a deadline to pay off on what I owe them. It's nearly up. I've been contacted through subordinates of the man who really operates the venture, and they were quite explicit. As I told you, I don't have the money." He grinned wryly. "I will, of course, in time. But these people—"

"Let's have it, Byrd. Where do I fit in?"

"As I implied, brother Mark—pardon—Steele, I'm afraid you're everything I'm not. You've been around a good deal. I have a feeling you could be very rough if you had to. I think you know something about the sort of people I'm dealing with, right?"

"Maybe," I said.

"Yes. But on the other hand, I'm way out of my bounds. I'll be frank. I'm a coward. I've never had to be anything else in my life, because this is the first serious trouble I've been in that wasn't solved rather easily for me. I didn't go to war, due to a rather convenient ear condition. I've always had somebody else do what has been distasteful to me. That's what I'm trying to accomplish right now."

I didn't feel sorry for him, but I wondered how it might have turned out if he had been carried away by my mother and I had been found by Uncle Gosset. I didn't know. I did think that he was at least being honest. "I still don't see where I come in."

"Just this," he said. "Due to their quite dangerous position, these people wish to preserve their anonymity—which is the reason I don't even know the identity of the organization's head man. And I have been instructed to bring nobody else in—nobody at all."

"Well, then?"

"I would like you to take my place in dealing with them—as Thomas Byrd."

"You've been seeing too many movies, Byrd—"

"Look," he said, rising, becoming more intense. "It's dangerous, I'll admit. The people who contacted me—well, they made it clear there would be no hesitation about killing me if I do not come through with my payment. I mean that, Steele. They will unhesitatingly kill if crossed. Very bad for their business if it gets around that anybody has welshed on a debt and gotten away with it. But you could do it for me, don't you see? I can't! As I told you, I'm a coward. I want nothing more to do with these people. But you—"

I shook my head. "Hoods are hoods, Byrd. In the trade they call them crossroaders—I've been up against them in Cuba, and I know. You should have thought about what you were doing in the first place—"

"Damn it, brother Mark, don't moralize!"

"I told you," I said. "Cut the brother routine! Because brother or not, I couldn't care less. It's your mess. These people won't deal unless you can deal. And if you don't have money—"

"I've got sixty thousand, Steele," Byrd said, looking at me intently. "It makes a difference, doesn't it? It's not one hundred thousand, but it's sixty thousand. And that's a lot of money regardless. You can deal with that kind of money—if you know what you're doing. I don't. I'm certain you do. Am I right?"

I said nothing, but I was thinking hard.

"And how well you deal is your profit," he said.

"Meaning?"

"If you cut them below sixty thousand, you take the difference. In addition to that possibility, I'll give you, say three thousand as expenses. Anything you have left over of that, you keep."

I waited, still thinking it over. Three grand expenses and whatever I could whittle off the sixty thousand. I could use that kind of money.

"What do you say, Steele?"

"I don't know," I said. "I don't talk like you. And I've got a heavier build than you. I've been working for a living remember? We *could* be told apart, and you know it."

"It could still be done," he insisted.

I shrugged. "Maybe. Only you'd better send somebody else. Send your lawyer—"

"Steele, I told you they don't want anybody else but me in on it. But aside from that, if I did send somebody else they would *know* I was frightened of them. If they think I'm *not* frightened, there's a much better chance of dealing with them. And remember, I wasn't in that place too long that one night. They won't remember my looks too well. Especially if we do it the way I've planned."

"And how is that?"

"The deadline is in two days. In three days they'll start looking for me. Say I showed up in Reno in three days—not in Las Vegas, where I lost the money."

"Why Reno?"

"Because I'm not known in Reno. I never gamble there, and most of my crowd doesn't gamble there. The chance of your getting away with an impersonation of me in Reno is a good deal better than it would be in Las Vegas, where I've gambled a great deal. If I—or rather you in my identity—showed up in Reno and made no effort to get in touch with the people in Las Vegas, what would they think?"

"You're nuts, maybe."

"Or that I'm defiant, that I'm really not so worried. Steele, they would much rather have half of that money and leave me alive than none of it and see me dead. That makes sense, doesn't it?"

"Okay. But Reno is quite a few miles away from Vegas—"

"I know that. But they have a grapevine. That fellow who took me out to their ranch said he often worked back and forth between Vegas and Reno, and they'll have others who do that—to keep up their contacts. That also makes sense, doesn't it? They'll know you've checked into town—if you check in as Thomas Byrd. And they'll contact you. You can be certain of that. But since Reno is quite a distance from Las Vegas, the chances are they'll use somebody for the contact other than the people I was exposed to when I lost the money. That cuts down the chances of their discovering the fact that you have taken my place. Do you see? It's a good plan, and—"

"I still don't know, Byrd."

He studied me for a second. "If you cut it down to fifty thousand, you've got a ten-thousand-dollar profit. Plus expenses."

Ten grand, clear profit for a day or two of work. I looked at brother Thomas Byrd's face; it was still pale. His gambling friends were tough, I knew. I would be exchanging my safe identity for his dangerous one. But it wouldn't be the first time I'd stuck out my neck—for a price. And I was beginning to feel a faint and familiar pulse of excitement.

"I'll think about it," I said finally. "Leave your telephone number where you're staying. I'll call you."

He came over, offered his hand. I was again amazed by his looks; it was as though I were staring at a mirror. "Thanks," he said. "And—please don't mention to anyone I've been here, will you? I mean not just yet, until this thing is cleaned up. There's really no point in letting anyone else know what I've told you—being twins and all—is there? Not until this is over, anyway. I'm quite nervous about this, I assure you. The less people who know about us, the better chance it will have of coming off ... if you decide to do it, that is. Moreover, I wouldn't want my predicament to get back to my people at home in Beverly Hills. I know almost nobody here in San Francisco, of course, but you can't be too careful, can you?"

I didn't like him. He was, I was certain, warning me in a roundabout way that it wouldn't do me any good to go running to Uncle Gosset in the hopes of cashing in on my blood line. I wasn't going to. I knew that wouldn't work anyway. If Uncle had wanted to so bless me he could have tried to find me a long time ago. Besides, I didn't want any of it that way.

To hell with Uncle Gosset. But if I earned it taking Byrd's place, well, that was different.

"Okay," I told him abruptly. "Don't worry about me talking, and I'll let you know my decision sometime tonight."

2

I thought about it for an hour after he left, and suddenly felt in need of a drink and a little company. I put on my jacket and went down to the Green Street bar, the Green Lamp.

Dolly was there. She was a nice-looking blonde of twenty-one or -two. She had a dimple in her left cheek when she smiled. She had a body like you usually find only in your imagination. And she knew how to dress so you knew it wasn't imagination. She'd already had a couple of drinks, and she joined me at a back booth, sitting snug at my side.

She didn't mention Byrd. Neither did Mike. Mike just served the drinks. Dolly just sat tighter.

"Baby, you're lovely tonight," she told me.

"You've had an extra drink."

"I felt like an extra drink. And you're lovely. Am I lovely?"

"You're lovely too."

"You're not paying attention," she said, wriggling so that I would.

Any other time I would have, but my mind had drifted back to Thomas Byrd and the proposition he'd made.

"I've got a proposition on my mind," I explained to Dolly.

"Well, go ahead and try. This could be the night."

"Sounds like a movie I saw once."

"It's supposed to sound sexy. I'm no movie. I'm real."

"So I notice."

"Baby," she said.

But my mind was turning now. I was feeling that old urge for something new. It was the thing that had started in me years ago. It was why I couldn't stand still, always had to keep moving. Ten thousand, maybe. A lot of money. The unreality of a twin brother out of the past, of his proposition, became very real once again.

"Baby," Dolly said, "I'll just bet you're not even an engineer at all. You don't look like an engineer."

"What do I look like?"

"Not an engineer. What could you engineer, anyway?"

"You name it."

"How about me?"

I looked at her, my mind coming back to the present.

"Baby," she purred softly.

"Honey," I said disentangling myself, "I've got to beat it."

I stood up, and she looked up at me as though she couldn't believe it. "Weren't you going to walk me home?" she asked.

"Some other time, sweetheart."

"Some other time! Why—" I was halfway to the door when I realized she'd thrown her drink at me. It landed a foot to my right. I won't repeat what it was she said I couldn't engineer. She'd get over it, I knew.

I called Byrd that night. The next day we went over the details of his plan. By the following day I knew enough about brother Byrd's habits and background to be sure I could move in for him—as long as I didn't run into someone who knew him too well. I took five hundred cash of the expense money and bought two good suits, some shirts and ties.

At eleven-ten in the morning of the third day, I walked into the waiting room of the Ferry Building at the bottom of Market Street, outfitted as Byrd and I had planned the day before.

I wore a false blond mustache—not a conspicuous one, but a thin, neat upper lip of whiskers that had a startling effect in changing my looks. I also wore black-rimmed glasses with plain lenses, a shaggy tweed jacket and gray slacks. I'd topped things off with a short-brimmed hat that had been crushed at the crown in a pork-pie effect. It had all been Byrd's idea, and I was surprised to find how right he'd been when he said it took only a few reasonably conspicuous trimmings to make a man look entirely different.

Byrd had wanted the disguise at this point for a couple of reasons. He was worried about one of his friends accidentally showing up in San Francisco and spotting me as Byrd before I left. Since I would be impersonating him in Reno, he could not risk appearing to be in two places at the same time and so had decided to hole up in a cheap hotel in Sacramento, halfway between San Francisco and Reno. Since we'd decided to travel on the same train, to make sure that only one "Byrd" was traveling to Reno I would wear the disguise until it was time for him to get off. Then we'd switch—he'd go into Sacramento in my disguise and I'd go on to Reno as Thomas Byrd.

I spotted him on the far side of the waiting room, and I suddenly knew another reason why he wanted things done this way—it was a redhead. So wore a mink stole, and something knitted and form-fitting underneath. She was hanging onto Byrd's arm and looking at him in a way that made me wish we'd already carried out the identity switch. Byrd stood beside her, immaculately dressed in a good conservative gray suit, hatless and debonair, and I knew damn well the redhead was not his wife. Byrd, I figured, was not as worried about running into any of his friends from down south in Beverly Hills as he was about making a legitimate exit in front of the eyes of the redhead. If I'd gone on to Reno ahead of him and without disguise, he would have been forced to leave in disguise—to avoid being in two places at once—and thereby miss saying good-by to the redhead and risk getting her sore enough at him to stop the fun and games.

I bought a paperback and read until they blew the whistle for the ferry. The redhead, I saw, boarded the ferry with Byrd, and for the moment I could hope that since he and I would be switching places on the train, she might just come along with the package. It was a pleasant thought and kept me whistling to the other side of the bay and into the roomette I'd reserved, one car up from Byrd's. The redhead got right on the train with Byrd, but when the train started moving I saw her waving at Byrd's car from the platform. Well, you can't win 'em all.

I relaxed on the ride across the land legs, past Martinez, into the valley. Then on schedule a porter handed me the telegram Byrd had asked Mike Chickory, the Green Lamp bartender, to send. It was addressed to Joseph Weatherly, the name under which I'd gotten my train reservation and the name Byrd would use in Sacramento. Byrd had told Mike it was a gag on a friend of his. The wire said: *Emergency. Go to Sacramento at once. Edward.* I told the porter I was getting off at Sacramento.

As the train began to slow, I gave my bag to the porter and told him I wanted to stop in the washroom before getting off. I told him to leave the bag on the platform and gave him a tip. Then I went up the aisle, out of sight from him, and kept on walking into the next car.

When I stepped into Byrd's compartment, he was grinning broadly.

"So here's where I become Thomas Byrd." I said. "I can see why you're happy. The gunmen aren't waiting for you in Nevada. They're waiting for me."

"Think of the money you're going to earn," he said, fitting on the small mustache after I took it off my own upper lip. I took off the shaggy tweed coat, and he put that on. I gave him the glasses and hat, and in a moment he looked just as I had when I'd boarded the train. He was now officially Joseph Weatherly, ready to check into the Valley Hotel in Sacramento. And I had become Thomas Byrd. My own real identity had, for the moment, dissolved completely.

Byrd took a look at himself in a mirror then turned and grinned again and touched his hat. "Good luck, old man. I know you're going to do this perfectly."

"Yeah," I said. "How come you couldn't have talked the redhead into the ride?"

"I could have, my good fellow. I *could* have." I nodded.

"Thanks for nothing."

"Well," he said, "we never were too close, you and I, now were we?"

"No," I said, "and I've got a feeling we never will be."

He handed me an envelope and put out his hand. "Good luck, brother."

I ignored the hand. "Lots of luck to you, brother. And now I suggest you tail out of here before I call the whole thing off."

"Brother," Byrd said, "I'm gone."

He was. I opened the shade and watched him stride down the Sacramento platform in the hat, glasses, mustache and tweed coat, then climb into a taxi. I pulled down the shade and opened the envelope he'd handed me just before he left. It contained five checks, blank except for Byrd's signature. Four of the checks were for one bank in San Francisco; the account contained the balance of the expense money: $2,500. The fifth check was for a second bank, and that account contained the sixty thousand earmarked for the gamblers and whatever cut I could shave off in the bargaining.

I daydreamed for a moment about filling in my own name and cashing the one check for the full sixty thousand. Then I remembered what he'd told me when we were going over the details of the plan—that he had informed the bank with the $60,000 account not to accept my name as payee. They were also told not to accept the names of Mike or Dolly, or of anybody else that he had uncovered as my friends. And since I could count my friends on fingers of one hand, he had me really well covered. When I'd cinched this deal, he was to write a check to me for the amount of the cut I'd been able to get —and I had to depend on the fact that he would do it. I was not too nervous about it. If he failed, I would simply go after him. I was sure he wouldn't argue about it face to face.

In addition to the checks, there were a number of identification items: Byrd's driver's license, a country-club membership card, an old 4-F draft card.

I opened the valise he'd carried aboard. It contained the two expensive, severely conservative suits I'd bought in San Francisco. I put on one of them, a dark brown model. I looked at myself in the mirror, admiring the expensive look. I was no longer Mark Steele, self-styled wanderer and pincher of plump barmaids. I was now my brother, Thomas Byrd, paragon of wealth and expensive ribaldry.

I pushed a button. A moment later the curtain opened.

"Scotch and water, please, porter."

"Yes, *sir.* Mr. Byrd!"

I lit one of Byrd's brand of cigarettes and sat there waiting for the drink, grinning.

3

The train snaked over the high ridges of the Sierras, then picked up speed and rolled down to Reno; overhead the clouds were streaked with the yellows and reds and pinks of an approaching Nevada sunset. It was chilly in contrast to the valley heat when I got off the train and took a taxi to the Plateau Hotel, the rich structure Byrd told me he would use if he were ever to stop in Reno.

I registered as Thomas Byrd, giving my home address as Byrd's own address in Beverly Hills. The desk clerk was a woman, a rather raw-boned, ranchy type who nonetheless looked like she'd been gowned by Dior and made up by Perc Westmore. She gave me the treatment Byrd must have been accustomed to everywhere he went. I decided it was the good cloth I was wearing or the luggage of Byrd's or the fact that I was picking up one of their best suites. But then the woman said, "Are you, by any chance, a member of Mr. Gosset Byrd's family?"

I was a little surprised. "My uncle," I said.

She had perfectly white teeth, and I got them in all their splendor. "*Delighted* to have you with us, Mr. Byrd. Your uncle *always* stays with us!"

I hadn't expected that; I got the impression from Byrd that neither he nor any of his family traveled here. But then, I decided, maybe nobody in the family knew all the habits of Uncle Gosset. I only hoped that Reno was not Uncle's whim this week.

The cowboy-outfitted bellhop took me up to the second-floor suite, pulled drapes, slid drawers, opened closet doors, wiped the small bar, repeated my name through the procedure with great devotion and frequency, and at last stood fawning. I gave him four bucks more than Byrd probably would have, and he quivered. "Anything else, Mr. Byrd? Anything at all!"

The way he said it, I had the impression I could order a full-size band, magnums of imported champagne, and hordes of naked dancing girls by merely an arch of my aristocratic brow. But I settled for three fifths of good Scotch and set-ups. "Or maybe I should call room service," I said.

"No, *sir,* Mr. Byrd. I'll relay the order!"

He left doing a kind of buck and wing. I decided that in the future, whenever my spirits got low, I would simply check into the best hotel I could find, tell them my name was Byrd and slip the bellhop five bucks.

The liquor arrived, I showered, sent the brown suit down to be pressed and put on the gray suit. I mixed a drink and walked out to the veranda overlooking the pool.

It was too cold and too late for swimming, it seemed to me; but there was still one person down there, poised on the end of the diving board.

She was slimmer than Dolly, plumper than the high-fashion number who had seen Byrd off. She was a beautiful compromise, and I stood admiring the view as she performed a neat half-gainer.

The water barely rippled when she cut into it, and then she was swimming smooth and easy across the pool. She climbed out, stripped off the swimming cap, and shook loose a tumble of brunette hair. I got a full look at her face as she tossed her head back, touched her hair and looked straight up at me. It was no disappointment; the face went with the body.

I walked back inside and checked my watch. I'd been here a little over two hours. I wondered how fast the word got out, and if it *was* getting out. I decided I'd better get to work.

I rechecked my wallet where I'd placed Byrd's identification cards. I'd left my own stuff in my apartment in San Francisco. I took out the checks Byrd had signed and on some hotel stationary practiced Byrd's handwriting, as I had already done in my apartment in San Francisco. It didn't really matter to the banks; they would cash the checks as long as Byrd's signature was valid, and it was. But I didn't want to give anything away to the crossroaders who had taken Byrd for the hundred grand. I'd gotten Byrd's handwriting down now, well enough so that no one looking at the check without actually searching for the discrepancy would notice that the signature didn't match the rest of the writing—payee, date, amount and so forth.

I folded the checks once and placed them in the inside left pocket of my jacket. I didn't want to lose them—especially the one earmarked for the big amount. Then I looked over the card slots of the wallet again. I found, back of Byrd's cards, an overlooked club card I'd had in Arabia. I slipped it out and put it in the second drawer of the bureau.

I went downstairs. I skipped the casino of the hotel and walked across the bridge of the Truckee River to the heart of the Biggest Little City In The World.

Darkness had come, and the lights of the main drag blazed. People thronged the sidewalks, rushing from casino to casino. I'd heard that gambling had spread now to include nearly everybody, rich or modest; and I could see it. A pitman named Joe Kowalchuk, who'd worked for Harrah's Lake Tahoe Club, had told me there was an entirely new approach these days: everybody, it seemed, liked to gamble, and the better clubs were making it possible.

They would pick you up and transport you from two hundred miles away and give you a free drink and maybe a good dinner and even put you up in a good motel and then take you home again—all gratis, so you could bet your luck against their store, which was the pitman's jargon for casino.

But it was no longer just a ten- or twenty-dollar ante on the 21 table, or fifty bucks riding on the green double 0 for the bigger stakes. Now it was the big slot-machine business too—rows and rows of them, giving you an 80-20 payoff edge if your luck was good enough to pick the proper moment. With five dollars and good luck, you could go all weekend, and maybe go home a richer man.

You could feel the excitement of it. And that's why they came, to get some of that excitement, to take the ante, big or little, and pitch it against the house, to double it, triple it, multiply it a thousand times if they could. It was sticky and hot and grim in Sacramento. It was crowded and stifling in Chinatown, lonely for the oldster in the Mission, routine and empty for the widow in the Portola. But the lights were on in Reno. And the jackpots were cracking. The cards were rustling over the green of the 21 tables. And somebody was riding the hot dice on the craps table. The dealer snapped the tiny ball of the roulette wheel, and it was spinning around the rim, and somebody was going the long shot, a fiver on the single green 0. A waitress handed him a cold Tom Collins, compliments of the house, while he was waiting for fortune to come his way. The ball stopped. He won. Or he lost.

And if he won he would feel like a sultan, and if he lost he would try again, if he could afford it, and sometimes if he couldn't. This was the business of the city, and the good clubs handled it like any reputable business. You played the games legitimately, you were treated as though you were shopping at I. Magnin's in San Francisco. But it was a bad place for the grifters, the cons. There was a reputation to maintain here. If somebody lifted your wallet in this town, it was very tough indeed for the offender. Reno—it was as though a very large, high-class carnival had come to town and permanently taken over the heart of it....

I avoided the bigger, well-known clubs. There are, now and then, the small new ones—springing up, working out a length of probation, and invariably folding. But they last long enough to pick up some of the rim trade, the overflow. I didn't figure to find any of Byrd's gambling friends in the good clubs, but rather in one or another of the temporaries.

I picked a side-street den, the Yellow Tiger Club, where the slots were noticeably quiet. I plunked a few dimes and nickels in the machines as I wandered about, then fiddled with the 21 table. I won a few dollars, lost them back.

I walked to the cashier's window with one of the expense checks. I filled it out for one thousand dollars and handed it through the cage to a peroxide blonde with blue eye shadow. She looked at the check, then at me. I was rather conspicuous in this dive, with the Montgomery Street flannel. She checked that. She checked the pure silk of my dark blue tie.

"We'll have to verify this, of course, Mr. Byrd. Unless you've established yourself with us."

"I haven't. But I'm rather in a hurry." To my ears, I sounded just like Byrd.

"Well—" She paused, then pressed a buzzer. A moment later a tall, fair young man in a blue suit appeared. He had a brilliant smile, a completely engaging air, and eyes that made you trust him as far as you might a cornered rattlesnake. The girl explained my desire, and introduced me to Mr. Kris.

Young Mr. Kris gave me the same once-over the girl had. He smiled his brilliant smile. "You have credentials, Mr. Byrd?"

I showed him the cards.

"Yes, of course. We generally like to check through your bank, of course. It's too late today, but tomorrow morning—"

"The whole point, Mr. Kris," I said, "is that I gamble rather by instinct. I feel things. The stars look right tonight. I passed your little club here, and got the feeling. However—"

"Well of course, we try in every way we can to please. But—"

"Perhaps you might know my uncle from Beverly Hills?" I said. "Gosset Byrd?" I was ad libbing beyond the plans now, but I was feeling some of the Byrd jauntiness.

"Gosset Byrd," he breathed. "No, sir, I'm afraid not. But we're rather new. I—I'll tell you what, Mr. Byrd. We'll run this through just as quickly as we can. And—" He was actually rubbing his hands together. "How do you like to gamble, Mr. Byrd?"

"To win," I said, grinning.

He laughed the phoniest laugh I'd heard in years. "I mean, sir, the method."

"Well, to tell you the truth," I said, "I'm not really a very good gambler. I just like to do it. What's your limit on the roulette wheel?"

He told me. I shrugged a little.

"The whole thing is," I said, "I like the tension. The smaller the limit, the less the tension." I smiled at him, and at the same time congratulated myself on working into Byrd's characterization so quickly. He searched me over with those eyes, then returned the smile.

"I'll tell you what, sir. If you'll just leave your check with us, we'll certainly have it verified early tomorrow, but in the meantime—" He turned to the peroxide cashier. "Miss Gray, give Mr. Byrd twenty one-dollar roulette chips, please."

She stacked them, handed them out to me.

"Oh, well, now really," I said. "I'm not that strapped, old man."

"It's not that, sir," Kris said. "It's our pleasure. A gesture of the house. We'll be pleased to have your patronage. Was that Gosset Byrd, Mr. Byrd?"

"Gosset Byrd," I said, understanding better now how brother Thomas had fouled himself up with this kind of thing always going on around him. "And thank you."

"Just a little something for you to amuse yourself with this evening," he said. "To get the spin of the wheel, so to speak." He laughed again. "Where are you staying, sir?"

"The Plateau."

"Fine! And good luck, sir!"

I thanked him, then took my stack of chips to the roulette wheel. There was only one other player, a woman who wore a peasant skirt, a little-girl blouse and pale blond hair pulled back in a pony tail. From the back, she looked sixteen. When you saw her face ... forty-nine, if a day. She gave me a smile of invitation and put two chips down, the wheel spun, and the ball landed on a black twelve. She didn't look to see where it had landed. A shill.

I placed my chips on the board elaborately, then leaned back, eyes half-closed, expectantly. Young Mr. Kris was hovering off somewhere to my right, in the edge of darkness—as though ready to strike at anything that moved. I waited. The wheel dealer hesitated; I could tell by the way he'd snapped out of his semi-vegetable state that Kris had eyed him into special action. The man was bony and thin with clawlike hands. In fact, there was a desert-animal quality about all the personnel. He eyed my chip arrangement self-consciously.

"My special system," I told him.

He grinned weakly. "It's up to you, sir, but you've canceled yourself out with that arrangement." He laughed uneasily. "You come out even no matter how the ball rolls."

I laughed with him. "I'll be damned. I can't get rich that, way, can I?" I pulled off all the chips and played five on the double 0. I lost. I played five more on the double 0. I lost again. I put the last ten on the double 0. I lost the twenty bucks. I spread my hands, got up. I glanced at the banker; he was wiggling his eyebrows at Kris.

The young gentleman bounced over. He laughed. "No luck, sir?"

"I've lost the feeling somehow," I said. "Maybe it'll come back."

"I'm sure it will!" he said. He was talking to me like he would a child now. "You bet it will, sir!"

"I'll be back."

"Yes, sir! And we'll have your money ready, sir!"

"It's too bad you've got the short limit," I said, walking out, smiling at the cashier—the look of invitation in her blue-lidded eyes made me certain I could hear rattling again.

Outside, I took a grateful breath of clean Nevada air, then walked to the casino of the Plateau Hotel and found a seat at the bar. This was an extravagant place, unlike the small-time, tawdry air of the Yellow Tiger Club. I figured the wheels and the craps tables here were as legitimate as anywhere.

The gambling was to my back as I sat at the bar, and I could watch most of it in the mirror. Behind the mirror was the theater-restaurant where they played the name talent. Along the right angle of the bar were tables for the drinkers and a small stage for the bar entertainment.

At the bar, to my right by two seats, sat a large, overblown, gray-haired woman with a satin gown that looked as though a price tag might still be on it; she was loaded with costume ornaments, all very new, very shiny, very tasteless. She kept looking at the ringless third finger of her left hand, at the white band of skin just below the knuckle. She was drinking straight shots, and her face kept drooping; her eyes looked a little more moist by the minute.

To my left at the bar, three seats down, was a girl with black hair and a white gown cut so far down the front I couldn't see where the V ended. She had hair parted in the middle and pulled straight back, and this together with a slightly flat face made her look like something out of a Moslem harem. When she lifted her drink, the deep-cut gown created a noteworthy production.

Just beyond her, speaking loudly, was a couple: The girl wore shingled auburn hair, parted and combed like a man's. Her companion had identically colored hair, only his was long for a man's; it also looked shingled.

The fellow said, "It's just that I have both emotions, and I can't seem to keep them straight. Honest to God."

The girl said, "Honest to God, I know what you mean."

They stood up and staggered arm in arm for the elevators.

The flat-faced girl with the V-cut gown pushed her glass at the bartender. "They're going to get married, Joe. I heard them. Can you believe it?"

"I heard it too," Joe said, mixing her a new drink. "It's a strange world."

"I mean," she said, "who's got the ball? Do you know what I mean?"

"I know what you mean," Joe said.

I began watching, still through the mirror, a tall, broad-shouldered croupier working just back of me. He had a large head and large hands. I frowned, thinking back to that first conversation with brother Byrd. A man with a large head, large hands....

And then I remembered. One such had been the man who had driven Byrd to the ranch outside Las Vegas, where Byrd had lost his pile. But there were a lot of big men with large hands and large heads. I watched the croupier intently through the mirror, however.

He worked animatedly. He was pitching mostly at a small blonde with an expensively dressed executive-type, neither of whom seemed to know the game. He kept up a steady patter, reassuring the blond novice. She passed four times, in spite of her ignorance. The executive-type looked happy.

Then the croupier was relieved by a squat, balding gentleman who looked as though he might have been more at home behind a butcher counter. The big croupier walked across the casino and into the adjoining hotel coffee shop. If he was Byrd's contact from Las Vegas, I would—along with my pitch at the Yellow Tiger Club—have managed faster than I'd thought possible to palm myself off as Byrd and make my contact with his creditors.

I finished my drink and followed.

He was seated alone at a table, drinking a cup of coffee. Across the coffee shop I also saw the brunette from the pool. She met my eyes, and this time I was close enough to see hers were deep blue. She was dressed in a tasteful, silver-colored dress that made her tan seem even darker than it was. She was eating a sandwich, and continued to meet my stare. It reminded me I was hungry, in more ways than one.

I turned my back reluctantly and walked to the croupier's table, and he looked up at me with hard, gray eyes.

"Do you mind?" I asked, motioning at a chair. It was a touchy situation. If this was the boy who'd brought Byrd to the vultures outside Vegas, he should remember me—as Byrd. Especially with one hundred G's riding on my head. Still, even if he was the one, he saw a lot of people, day in and day out, working over a hot craps table here and in Vegas. So if he remembered brother Byrd's face at all, I was fairly certain he wouldn't remember it well enough to realize I was the twin brother instead of the real pigeon.

The croupier's eyes switched around the coffee shop, noting the empty tables. He shrugged. If he did remember Byrd's escapade with the wheel in that ranch outside Vegas, he was not giving it away.

I sat down, ordered a sandwich and decided to fire the gun and hope I hit something.

"My name's Thomas Byrd."

His eyes may have flickered then, but I couldn't be sure. He shrugged again. If he was the right guy and had me fixed now, he would remember, I was certain, that Byrd had been drunk that night—too drunk, possibly, to remember much about the people he'd met.

"Business good?" I asked.

"Sure." He put his elbows on the table. "What's on your mind? I'm off duty right now. Ten minutes. That's all. Tough grind if you can't relax for ten minutes."

"I know," I said. "Sorry to break it up. I just wondered what your limits are here?"

He looked pained that I would bring business to his table. "Limits." He shrugged. "We offer a good game."

"I'm sure," I said. "I just like to go for it at times."

"Go for it," he said, tasting his coffee. "Sure."

"It's a thing with me."

"It's a thing with everybody."

I ate my sandwich slowly. "Are there any other games around? You know what I mean?"

He looked at me with disdain. "Have you gone out and taken a look down the street, mister? We got a number of games in town."

I ignored the sarcasm. "I mean no-limit games."

He looked down at his coffee. "I work for the management. I'm very loyal to the management. We run a good table here. Try your luck, mister."

"I might, at that," I said.

"Be glad to oblige," he said, "when I'm on duty. I'm off duty right now."

"Sure," I said, "but if you happen to think of something, let me know, will you? I stay in the hotel. Thomas Byrd."

"I remember," he said. "You told me."

I nodded. "Thanks a lot."

I carried my sandwich to another table, figuring it had been a good try. Maybe I had done it, maybe I hadn't. If I had, the best I could do now would be to wait. Somebody would be in touch, and they probably would move fast.

The croupier finished his coffee in silence, then walked out. I looked across at the brunette. She was just finishing eating and met my stare again. She got up and paid her check and walked out to the casino. It was a pleasant action to watch. I paid my own check and followed.

She was at the bar where I'd been sitting. There was one empty stool beside her, and I decided I'd done enough work for the moment. I decided to relax a little.

I sat down beside her. She didn't look at me this time when I looked at her through the mirror behind the bar. The girl with the Moslem face and low-cut gown was still there. Behind me, the croupier had resumed his chatter. The female half of the auburn, shingle-haired pair was back at the bar, holding herself and a glass up limply.

"Poor Ansell," she told Joe the bartender.

"Where is he?" Joe asked her.

"He passed out in the closet. Honest to God."

"In the closet?" Joe asked.

The girl nodded. "Closets make him passionate." She sniffed. "They don't do a damned thing for me." Then she straightened suddenly, flashing a smile at a new arrival—a girl in a flouncing cocktail gown who wore heavy make-up over her obviously young face; from the chorus, I decided.

"Hello, honey!" the girl who'd been with Ansell said.

"Knock it off, Edna," the chorine said. "I'm in a stinking mood tonight. Go take it out on Ansell."

"He's passed out," Edna said. "Guess where?"

"In the stinking closet."

"How did you know?" Edna asked, hurt.

"I've got a closet."

"That two-timer!"

"Seltzer, Joe," the chorine said, grimacing at Edna. "Don't get jealous of me, Edna. Get jealous of closets. When are you and Ansell getting married?"

"Maybe tomorrow morning," Edna said.

"Wow!" the chorine said, shaking her head. "And quit fluttering at me, for God's sake! Ansell'll get jealous of you."

"All *right*," Edna said darkly. She tossed down her drink, then got off her stool with great effort. "I'm going to find a closet of my own. That'll make him mad as anything."

The V-cut shoved her glass at Joe. "It's like I say—who's got the ball, Joe?"

"The closet," Joe said.

The chorine downed her seltzer and flounced off. The bar was silent. A minute went by, two—the brunette owned some kind of marvelous perfume. I looked in the mirror and caught her eyes this time. She looked down at her drink.

"Well," I said finally, "it's a great life, isn't it?"

She looked up, meeting my eyes in the mirror, then started to laugh. "I've been trying to figure out what you were going to say," she said, turning and looking at me directly, "but I didn't think it would be that corny."

"I don't know," I said. "It's what people say when they don't know what else to say, isn't it?"

She nodded. "I guess it is."

"I saw you in the pool," I said.

"I know. I saw you when you came out on the balcony. That's why I went in again. I'm a great show-off. It was cold as hell."

"I can imagine. But thanks. It was a nice show."

She seemed pleased. There was something rather aloof and ladylike about her, yet there was also something warm coming through it. Very warm.

"Look," I said, "I'm going to be corny again—are you busy tonight?"

"With this drink."

"After that?"

She shrugged. "Who knows?"

"I've got an idea. Let's—"

Just then I was paged. A cowboy gave me a telephone number to call. I frowned. I had visions of Uncle Gosset. I turned to the brunette. "Look—"

"Linda," she finished. "Linda Amory."

"Wait for me a moment, will you, Linda?"

"I don't even know your name."

"Thomas Byrd."

"Well, now that we're old friends," she said, "maybe I will."

I hurried across the casino to the lobby and the telephones. I dialed the number. The young Mr. Kris of the Yellow Tiger Club rattled at me.

"We've got your money ready for you, Mr. Byrd!"

"Well," I said, "that's just fine, Mr. Kris."

"No trouble at all. We simply put in a call to your uncle in Beverly Hills, and while he seemed rather—uh—displeased with you, he did vouch for your check...."

I didn't hear the rest of it. I was closing my eyes, calling myself names. I may have made other mistakes so far, but this was one I knew I'd made. Byrd had stressed impressing his family, particularly Uncle Gosset, with good behavior. Now Uncle Gosset thought he was cashing a thousand bucks for gambling. Well, it was better, I thought, than Uncle Gosset thinking he was cashing a check for sixty grand.

"You've been very thoughtful, Mr. Kris," I said. "I'll be over."

I walked back through the lobby. Even from the casino I could see that Linda Amory had disappeared. I returned to the bar, swearing to myself. Everything was getting loused up. I finished my drink glumly, and when the bartender came back my way, I said, "The brunette, Joe. Do you know where she went?"

Joe shrugged. "She didn't say, sir." He wiped a glass, then bent forward. "I thought you had it made. This girl had been tried by every male in the place since she got here a week ago. She's very difficult to reach. I thought you'd done it."

"So did I Joe," I said mournfully.

"Another drink, sir?"

"No," I said sadly. "I'm going out and throw myself in the Truckee."

"I don't blame you," Joe said.

I walked sullenly back to the lobby, then stopped and stared at a young thing in a white dress sidling out of the souvenir shop. She had a big white teddy bear clutched in her pink little hands. She was blond—well, her hair was white or silver, and not because of age. This was a bottle job. She was barely twenty-one, wore a beautiful smile, and was as tanned as Linda—only the contrast, with the silver white hair, was greater. She walked with the most action I'd seen since I'd watched a belly dancer in Morocco.

I was right beside the elevators, and just then Linda stepped out, wearing a blue mink stole. I switched my eyes off the blonde, and Linda smiled at me and blinked her blue eyes.

"Ready?" she asked.

"Ready?" I said. Instantly I forgot about the blonde. "Well, ready, yes!"

"If we're going out," she said, "I thought I'd need something to keep me warm."

I nodded, feeling something I've heard described as weak knees. She slipped her arm through mine, and I cast an insolent glance back toward the casino. Five also-rans were watching as I swaggered with her to the door.

"Where to?" she asked.

"There's a little place down the street," I said. "I want to pick up a thousand bucks there."

"This is going to be a *lovely* evening," she said.

On the way, Linda asked me what I did for a living. I told her nothing. I asked her. She said she lived off her daddy, who owned a ranch the size of six counties in New Mexico; she'd gone to the University of Arizona in Tucson, got bored, and thereafter went where the whim blew her. I asked where she had been before she came here. Las Vegas, she said. I wondered suddenly if she and Byrd had ever run into each other and then decided, by the way she was acting toward me, they certainly hadn't—Vegas was a growing and crowded community, practically a suburb of Los Angeles these days. Perfectly reasonable that they had been there at the same time and never met.

Kris was all smiles and bows when we got to the Yellow Tiger Club. The place was even more deserted of paying customers than it had been before. I got my grand, pocketed it, and decided I liked the life of the rich.

"I want to game a bit," I told Linda. "Okay?"

"Sure."

"I'm not good," I said, "but I love it."

I took a seat at the 21 table, and Linda stood close behind, radiating that perfume of hers.

I put twenty bucks on the ante. I got a red jack and a nine. I asked for another card.

"You poor baby," Linda breathed behind me.

I busted. And the house took the shill's bet with a seventeen.

"I play it wild," I said. "No fun any other way."

"Mmmm," Linda said.

I lost a hundred bucks there. Young Kris hovered around the edges, smiling and rubbing his hands and rattling slowly and pleasurably.

"I think I'll try the dice," I said.

"You're masochistic," Linda said.

On the first roll I overshot the table, and as the dice fell on the floor I wondered if I were maybe overplaying it. "Sweetheart," Linda said, "why don't we go sit at some nice bar and talk? It would be ever so much cheaper."

"I've got the feeling tonight," I said. "The stars look right."

"Have you had your eyes checked recently?"

I blew two hundred there, and had fifty bucks' worth of chips left. "I've got it now," I said. "I can feel it."

Kris appeared from the darkness. "How is it going, Mr. Byrd?"

"Darling," Linda said, "you're bleeding and don't know it. Here." She took my fifty bucks' worth of chips. "I love to look innocent and coy, but sometimes—"

I stepped back and watched. It's always a pleasure to watch an expert at anything. I held her stole, and she flipped those dice like a retired sailor.

She played fast, making her bets with precision and confidence. When a hot craps player starts on a run, the crowd forms. And the bets start coming in from all around the table.

In ten minutes Linda had a crowd, and she was riding her luck like she'd been born with the bet-marked green felt for swaddling clothes. And I knew it had to be luck. The rattling Mr. Kris had no reason for letting her win, and I figured he couldn't risk a fix on the craps table. Even for the Yellow Tiger Club, shooting in loaded dice in a town like Reno would be like detonating his dump with ten tons of nitro. He might gaff his roulette wheel. His card-dealers might go flat ... because this was, I was certain, a flat store, a dishonest house. I figured agents, the con men of the gambling circuit, might crossroad with the house and take the suckers' profits; they might even handmuck, or sleight-of-hand, the cards. But load the dice I figured Mr. Kris wouldn't do, and so Linda kept going, hot and fast.

I heard the boxman whisper to the dealer on his right: "Man, check this six-and-eight," which was his word for the stacked build of Miss Linda Amory. I couldn't blame him. She looked great, and her playing matched her looks. I was jealous, however, because it wasn't only the boxman who was digging the six-and-eight, it was the entire room. All except the young Mr. Kris. His snake eyes were blazing because Linda had just taken him for three hundred clams.

"Okay," she said to me finally. "Turn the chips in, my little innocent. Let's get the hell out of here."

I gave her back her stole, and once more she looked demure and warm as a kitten. I cashed the chips, and young Mr. Kris made a final try. "Anything else, sir? I mean you mentioned limits, sir? I think perhaps something could be arranged. For you personally, I mean, sir. We couldn't do that for everyone, of course." He was eyeing Linda.

"Thanks anyway," I said to him. "But I've lost the feeling somehow. Later, perhaps."

We walked out, Linda nestled tight on my arm. "Let's," she said, "get back to civilization. Those folks are *way* out there."

I knew what she meant, but I knew if Byrd's Las Vegas gamblers had any connections in this town, they would have them with the management of a club like the Yellow Tiger Club.

We walked around and onto Virginia Street and stepped through the invisible "air" doors of Harrah's Club. This place, like the other legitimate houses, hummed with activity. We zigzagged our way through the casino and got two seats at the lounge bar, a large U-shaped affair. Linda ordered a stinger and I bought a *Kahlúa* rough.

"Now this," she said, "is legit. I feel at home."

I remembered her Las Vegas background, and she did indeed look at home. A male quartette led by a tall, easy singer, Kirby Stone, was on the lounge stage, and the quartette was funny. One of them was doing a take-off on Liberace. Linda roared, and I was beginning really to relax. So I was a marked goose now. So I'd been a target before in my life. I was enjoying the life of Mr. Thomas Byrd.

Linda had her connections from Vegas. A young executive of the club, Mark Curtis, dropped by and chatted and bought us another drink. Then Kirby Stone, the singer, finished his act and came down. And then a man I'd never seen before, a rather pudgy boy with rosy cheeks, and a little high, pushed through the crowd and exploded, "Byrd, old man! It's Tom Byrd, isn't it?"

I tensed, trying not to show it. It was another real test, and I hadn't been expecting it because I'd relaxed. I decided I couldn't make a habit of really relaxing until this was over. I hoped like hell this wasn't Byrd's best friend.

"Well," I said, "hello there."

"Tom Byrd!" the pudgy boy exploded again. "Sure it is! Don't you remember? The bash at the Beverly Hilton? Duck Wentworth?"

"Duck!" I said. "Of course. How are you, old man?"

"Great! Simply great!"

He pumped my hand, and some of my tension eased a little. He'd probably met Byrd just once. And apparently I was passing inspection. I introduced him to Linda, Curtis and Stone. He eyed Linda wickedly.

"Tell you the truth," Duckie boy said, "I saw you before. This evening—getting off the train, weren't you? Thought you were high-hatting me, old chum!"

"Really?" I said. And then I realized he'd said he'd seen me this evening. I'd gotten off the train late that afternoon. In the proper circles, I decided, afternoon was evening, evening was night. But now I was going to have to get rid of Duckie boy.

"What are you doing here, Duck?" I asked.

"Came up from Vegas. Got bored. You know how it is, old man. Saw all the shows. Got tired of it. Just decided to come up here. It's awfully good to see you!"

He was pretty ecstatic about it, and I decided brother Byrd must have been a few notches above him in the register—he looked like the self-made type, trying now to act like he'd had his loot from Mayflower days. I decided to do what I figured Byrd might do with him.

I wiped off the smile, turned it on again briefly in a patronizing way, then cooled my voice. "Really nice to see you again, old man. Delightful."

"Well, delightful for me too! Say, why don't we—"

"Sometime," I said archly, "we'll have to get together. Do you know? I mean that, old boy." And said it in a way to indicate I would drop dead before I'd lower myself to see him again. It upset him, I could see. His boy scout grin trembled.

I held out my hand. "Very delightful, ah ... Buck."

"Duck," he said miserably. "Yes, delightful, Tom. I—" He shrugged hopelessly, paid his compliments to the others and said to me, "Do call up, won't you?"

"I'll try," I said. "I'll try."

He was gone, and a few minutes later Linda and I were alone at the bar again. Her hand slid over mine. She swung around slightly, so that we were suddenly rubbing knees. I forgot about Duck Wentworth, I forgot everything but Linda.

"Darling," she said, "we could sit here all night, couldn't we?"

"We could," I agreed.

"Will we?" she asked.

I answered by taking her arm and walking her back to the hotel, into the elevator and then to my suite.

"Champagne?" I asked. "I can order it."

She was digging through the bar. She shook her head. "I'll switch to Scotch before I let anyone else come up here."

I was beginning to feel giddy. She hoisted herself up to the bar and lifted a bottle of Scotch, pouring a glass nearly full, giggling a little. "Here." Then she poured one of her own. She crossed her legs, swinging one a little. I switched on the radio and slow music drifted in. I watched that one moving, shapely calf. She checked the direction of my gaze. She lifted her eyebrows. "Like?"

I nodded. "Like, yes."

She stretched the leg forward, revealing the whole length of it. My throat got tight.

"Nice legs, no?" she asked.

"No," I said. "I mean, yes."

"Darling," she said. She slid easily off the bar and into me. "Darling— "

And then I saw it, just a fleeting sight of it. I looked over Linda's shoulder toward the glass doors to the balcony and swore silently to myself. I reached out a hand instantly and switched off the lights of the room.

4

"Darling," Linda whispered again, breathing hard.

I stepped away from her, and she kept coming; I had to step back again. "Honey, I'm sorry."

She stopped and stiffened as though I'd snapped a whip in front of her eyes. "Sorry!" she breathed.

"Honey, it's just—it's the time. It's two-thirty. I— "

She spun, picked up her stole, and marched to the door. I glanced once more toward the balcony.

"Why don't you go find yourself a closet or something?" Linda snapped.

I moved to her fast, caught her tightly and kissed her. She began responding again, then shoved backward.

"Damn you," she breathed. "Even from your balcony to the swimming pool I felt it. When you do that—"

I reached for her again, but she said, "Don't touch me! Don't even look at me any more! I start going to pieces and—"

She got a handkerchief out, dabbing at her eyes angrily. "It's another girl, isn't it? What time are you supposed to meet her? You're a louse, Byrd. I hate your guts!"

"Linda, listen—"

"Go to hell," she said.

"Linda, listen. Let me call you—"

"Call up a tree," she said. And then she was gone.

I stood there, still feeling her lips on mine, still feeling her body in my fingers....

I switched the lights on now, lit a cigarette with shaking hands, then edged over by the balcony doors. I opened them casually, letting the night air pour in. I walked forward toward the railing. Halfway there I spun, reached out and grabbed him.

I yanked him forward, and I could tell by the looseness of his body that he hadn't thought I'd seen him through those glass windows. I turned and shoved him back into my room. The surprise of it sent him flying across the rug, where he stumbled and went to his knees. I came after him, closing the doors behind me.

It was the croupier I'd talked to in the hotel coffee shop. He was big. Big hands. Big head. He crouched there like an ape, breath heaving in and out of his chest.

"I figured you for a lot of things," I said, "but not a peeper."

He swore, then came at me. I caught him flush on the jaw, but it was like hitting granite. There was the faintest grunt from him when he hit me, and then we were tumbling backward.

We rolled once, and I found one of those big hands pushing down on my throat. I snapped up my knees. He grunted again, and his hand came off my Adam's apple. I had only maybe eight inches for the punch, but I tried it anyway. Smashing his nose with my fist. He yelped a little, jerking back, and I was out from under him. But he'd got half to his knees now and he round-housed one heavy fist straight at my head. It hit my cheekbone, and I felt as though I'd been clubbed by a redwood tree. I lost heart momentarily, but then I thought about him crouching out there while Linda was showing off that beautiful leg, and something like a white flash exploded in my brain.

He never got straightened up entirely. He was straightening one minute, and I was going loose at the joints at the same time. But that flash of anger brought my knees steady again, and I short-jabbed him again, feinting from those huge fists every time they sailed at my face. I jabbed his nose for what seemed like ten dozen times. He was whimpering now, but he wouldn't quit. Then I got a clean shot at the very tip of his jaw. I put all I had into one looping right, and that crumpled him all the way.

He kind of melted down in the rug, jerked a couple of times, and then brought his head up, shaking it like a stubborn ox. I balanced him by touching one of his shoulders, brought my other hand back, setting my aim for his nose again.

"No," he whispered.

"Okay," I breathed. I straightened and stepped back. I couldn't have been happier. My right arm was about to fall off from all that punching. My head was still spinning from that one ham-handed blow on the side of' the face. I was damn near out of gas.

"Get up," I said.

He got up.

"Sit down on that chair over there."

He went over and sat down in the chair.

I got a towel from the bathroom, soaked it with cold water, came back in and tossed it to him. "You're a mess."

He cleaned himself up; that nose must have hurt him like hell. Tears kept coming in his eyes.

"And you're in real trouble, Byrd," he said eyes watering and hating me all at the same time.

"Not with you," I said.

"You're a smart bastard, aren't you?"

"Not always."

"You said it." He started to grin but that seemed to make his nose hurt. The smile faded, and he put the wet towel against his nose.

"Why don't you give it up," I said, "and go get that nose fixed?"

"Because I've got a job to do."

I got a bottle of Scotch from the bar and poured two glasses half full. "Here."

He may have hated me, but he wasn't about to refuse my Scotch. I drank with him. We skipped the toast. "So what's the job?" I asked him.

"You got a short memory, Byrd."

"You're talking in riddles," I said. "Maybe you're a little punchy—"

"Look," he said. "Knock it off."

"Which? Your head? I tried that. I'll try it again, if you want. You break into my room, make like a lousy peeping Tom out on the balcony, then get into a fight with me and wind up drinking my liquor. You're not telling me to do anything, friend."

"Who forgets a hundred G's?" he asked me. So I'd been right. He'd been the contact for Byrd in Vegas. I'd run smack into him, and I was obviously passing for Byrd.

But I only frowned at him, keeping up the act a little longer. "What about a hundred G's?"

"That's what Nicole wants to know."

And there I had it. The name of the big boy himself.

"Nicole?" I said.

"Maybe you've never heard of Nick Nicole?"

"Nicole," I said, again. "Oh. Oh, I've got it now. You were the connection in Vegas. Yeah. I remember now. Well, I have a habit of shooting off my face to the wrong people. I've done it again."

"So you have, pal. But Nick would have got to you regardless. You should have known that. Nick's got a lot of connections. Your deadline was up yesterday, pal."

Now, busted nose, crying eyes and all, he was happy. He was really happy.

"So how do you fit into the deal this time?"

"I've come to collect, pal."

I looked at him. I laughed at him. "The croupier has delusions."

"It's no joke, Byrd," he said tightly, holding that towel against his nose. "You make out the check, that's all, friend. No more, no less. Make it out to Nick Nicole."

"Let's put it this way," I said. "I didn't like your roulette then. I still don't. I think maybe I've been had."

The croupier started to speak, but I went on:

"Furthermore, Nicole's in no position to get that dough. How's he going to get it, I wonder? Complain to the Nevada Legislature? Take it up with the Governor? If Nicole runs a crooked game, that's his tough luck. He'll play hell getting anything."

"You're crazy, Byrd," the croupier whispered.

"Now get out of here," I said, "before I call the house dick and complain about the employees roughing up the paying guests."

His head wagged back and forth. "You don't know what you're doing, Byrd. You really don't. Don't you know that Nick—"

"Shut up," I snapped. "And beat it. I'm sick of looking at you."

Face paling, he got up, eyes blazing at me. He walked to the door. "Buddy," he said softly, "I feel for you. I honestly do. Your life, from this minute on, ain't worth a nickel. A lead nickel."

"Take off, cousin," I said.

He did, taking the towel with him. I walked over to the bar and poured another drink. My hand was shaking. It was from the effort of pounding on him, I figured. But somewhere, deep inside, I was not so sure.

I began to look at things the way Byrd had—and Byrd had been scared. He had, I figured, good reason to be.

I'd only pulled one of the small fry so far, and he would only be the start. I knew that. I'd counted on it. Besides, I couldn't be really sure about the croupier. He might have tried a check forge, although I doubted it. He didn't look to be the type to buck Nicole. And I purposely wanted to bang the croupier around. Nicole had been figuring Byrd for a scared pigeon. Now he would not be so certain, with his big-handed croupier pushed out of shape. Now he had some new respect for Byrd, which would increase my bargaining power when I finally did settle with him. It also meant, I realized, that Nicole would now send in his first string against me.

I felt a cold hollowness for a moment, wondering when they would come. Then I downed the Scotch and grabbed a little false courage.

What the hell, I told myself. I'd been in jams before, and this time there would be a fat payoff for me ... if I could just keep going. I had another drink and almost felt ready to take on the croupier all over again. My head was buzzing a little, and I tried to count the number of drinks I'd had over the evening. It was a wonder I'd won that fight at all.

I walked over to the couch with still another drink and lay back, taking my mind off the croupier and Nick Nicole. The memory of Linda Amory came back to my mind. I grabbed the telephone and asked for her room. She answered almost instantly. She hadn't gone to sleep. Maybe she was still thinking about me.

"Linda," I said, "it's me. It's I—"

She hung up.

I fell back on the couch, cursing that croupier. I stood up and paced. That didn't help. I stripped and took a cold shower. That didn't help. I went out on the balcony and breathed the cool Nevada air. Nothing helped. I went back inside, thinking that I should have pounded on that punk's nose for another ten minutes. I had another drink. I was, in fact, getting drunk. But who wouldn't?

5

The ringing of the telephone early the next morning clanged against my head. I reached out a foot, groaning, and kicked the receiver off the cradle. The murderous sound stopped. I lay there, mouth dry, hating the world. I could hear the chattering on the telephone as it lay on the floor. I let it chatter for a moment longer, then turned myself over and picked it up.

"Hello," I snapped.

It was Byrd.

"Where are you?" I asked.

"Sacramento, of course. Miserably holed up in this insufferable Valley Hotel. But look, old man—I just wanted to tell you an entourage of friends from Beverly Hills are heading over there. I telephoned home and my wife mentioned it. A wretched shame, but that's how it is. I don't think the impersonation will be entirely convincing with them. Perhaps you'd better stay out of sight."

It was a jolting reminder that I was working for Byrd. My own brother. And not, in reality, living his life. I'd changed my attitude, I realized, since I'd first met him in my apartment in San Francisco. I'd had a taste of his life and liked it. But Byrd was reminding me just how temporary it was. Byrd was the brother with the breaks. He was a part of an indolent, parasitic crowd. I remembered Duckie boy the night before, probably one of the scouts of the entourage Byrd was talking about. That guy had been on the rim of the sporty crowd, I judged, but he was still on the outside looking in. This morning all of them made me sick. I snapped at Byrd:

"What do you mean I'd better stay out of sight?"

"These people have known me all my life, you see. I just don't think you could pass inspection. They'll be there for just the day—"

"All right," I said. "So fine." My head was hammering like a rusty pile-driver. I decided to tell him about Kris of the Yellow Tiger Club telephoning Uncle Gosset.

He was silent for a moment after I'd told him, then said, "Well, it can't be helped. But did it work? The ruse to draw them in?"

"Yeah," I said. "Partially. I haven't written the big check yet." But I told him no more.

"You sound perturbed, old man."

"Look, Byrd," I said. "I'll talk to you again sometime."

"Old man," he said, "you're running the show, you know."

"So I am," I said and hung up.

I showered and shaved, and through the motions I tried to think. The contact had been made, once again, through the croupier. I'd beaten the croupier bloody. I'd made no effort with him to affect Byrd's fanciful chatter. Would they suspect anything? I didn't know, but they'd had only one exposure to Byrd and I didn't figure they would notice any difference—at least not from the croupier's description of me.

But that aside, I'd made them mad. I had a feeling Nicole wouldn't much like his man pushed around like that. But I counted on one thing: he liked money. Besides, it was the croupier's face which was mashed, not Nicole's.

I went back to bed and slept for a few more hours. When I woke up the second time, I was feeling reasonably human again. I put on a fresh shirt and ordered breakfast. The breakfast finished the hangover, and I lit a cigarette over coffee. I walked over and stretched out on the couch, and began to feel better about everything.

Then I remembered Byrd's call telling me to stay out of sight that day. I telephoned the desk. I told them I didn't want to be disturbed for any reason. I was out to everybody. Then I relapsed again on the couch. My mind quit turning for a moment. Then it started again.

I had the day and night to kill. I was locked up in one of the most elegant suites between the Rockies and the Sierras. I had a fifth of good Scotch left and the wherewithal to order more. I snapped on radio music. There was only one thing missing. I picked up the telephone and called Linda. I let it ring twenty-seven times. I hung up. I stood up, paced back and forth across the room twice, then suddenly walked out to the balcony.

She was down there—stretched out in all the glory of her smoothly curved beauty. I ran my eyes the length of her body; there was a noble quality about her figure as she lay there in that swimming suit. But there was also something intimate and profoundly inviting about it. I wanted her up here. I looked at her, remembering how she'd said, "Even from your balcony to the swimming pool I felt it..."

She looked up, straight at me. I smiled in what I hoped was my most winning manner. She didn't smile back. She stood up and walked over to the life guard. She stretched out beside him, chatting gayly. I glared at her. She looked up at me once more, then carefully leaned sideways and stroked Muscle's right biceps. I strode back into my suite.

I stretched out glumly. The warm feeling of contentment was gone. All I could think about now was the fact that soon Nicole would send someone else around. I wished it were over, that I'd already closed the deal and made it for ten extra grand. I could concentrate wholly on Linda then and....

A knock sounded on my door. I tensed. Nicole's man? Then I thought of Linda. I stood up and walked over to the balcony and searched the pool. She'd disappeared. The sweetheart, I thought. The baby doll. She's come up. She can't help herself....

I walked over and swung open the door. It wasn't Linda. It wasn't one of Nicole's hoods either. It was that gorgeous thing I'd seen coming out of the souvenir shop in the lobby the night before—the one who'd been carrying the big white teddy bear. She smiled, preening a little—this time she wore a pale yellow dress and from the look of her, I was pretty sure that was all.

"Tommy!" she said. "Don't you remember? I was sure it was little old you last night, only you trotted off with that real *cold* looking girl with the blue stole. Don't you remember, Tommy?"

I suddenly respected Byrd a notch more. This was obviously something out of his past.

"Why, sure!" I grinned. "Come in, honey."

That walk of hers was an unbelievable production. Once inside, she turned, blinking her eyes at me. "I'll bet you don't remember after all!"

"You'd lose the bet." I don't know, it was the way she looked at me, the way she stood there, running her fingers around the end of the sofa; maybe it was the frustrations of the last hours since Linda had stomped out. I walked over and kissed her. "You see?" I said. "I remember."

"Sweety," she said, "you've changed! You were so—well, kind of shy before."

"Well, now you know the real me," I said. I decided to play it light and cool all the way; I couldn't bluff through remembering a past I knew nothing about.

"Where was it, honey? Los Angeles? Galveston? Sioux City, Iowa?"

"Stinker," she said. Then she giggled. "Las Vegas. You remember!"

"Las Vegas," I said. "Of course! How have you been, ah—"

"Julie, smarty. See? You don't remember." She pouted her lips, and I proceeded to kiss them again. She didn't seem to mind at all.

"How could I forget?" I asked.

"Well," she said, "you were a little tipsy and all that. But I still thought—"

"Honey," I said, "let's forget the past. Let's use the present. What brings you?"

"You, honey doll," she said. "You were with that nasty old brunette last night. So I tried to call you this morning. But they said you were out or something. So I got the sweetest little old desk clerk to tell me your room number and, well, here I am!"

"You certainly are," I said. "How about a drink?"

"Sweety, it's only eleven-thirty. I never drink before noon."

I walked to the bar. "Honest?"

"Well, just a teeny one."

"Let's see—I've got Scotch. If you want something else—"

"Scotch is just fine," she said, giggling.

"How do you like it? It just slips my mind."

"You know."

I decided to try anyway. I poured it over ice, enough to anesthetize a bull.

"Sweety!" she said, grabbing the glass. "You remembered!"

I tried to blink my eyes back at her. It was no contest.

She put away that drink before I'd barely sipped mine. "Another?" I asked. The day was picking up.

"Honey, let's get out of here. Let's go some place. Let's do something."

"Well," I said, "there's plenty we could do right here—"

She came over to me and wrinkled her nose and chewed at my ear a little as she pushed against me. I was absolutely certain that dress was the end—it was all Julie after that. "Sweety," she said, "you're really an old flirt, aren't you?"

"That's me," I said. "Just an old flirt. Why don't we sit down, and—"

"Sweety," she said, pouting once more. I started to kiss her again, but she wriggled away, giggling. "You're so all sudden and everything. I liked you shy, kind of."

"Okay," I said, sighing. "I'll be shy."

"Take me for a ride," she said.

"Honey, I'd love to, but—"

"Sweety—?"

I decided to hell with Byrd and his friends. The way this girl looked, I would stand on my head and spin on a roulette wheel if she asked me.

"Sweety?" she asked again.

"Ride what? I don't have a car, honey."

"I've got the cutest little old car downstairs you ever did see."

Well, I put on my tie and jacket, and together we traipsed out to the hall. In deference to Byrd's call, I suggested we go down the back stairs. Nobody saw us—nobody but, of all people, Linda, who was standing at the edge of the casino, staring right at us.

She looked at me, she looked at Julie. She looked at me again. She killed me with that look, then tossed her chin up and marched off in the opposite direction. I felt kind of good about it, although I had to admit I would much rather have been with Linda than Julie....

Finally we were in Julie's cutest little old car you ever did see—a white Cadillac Eldorado convertible—whipping through Reno, and off towards the blue plateaus.

For the moment Linda faded from my mind. Julie was fleshier, but still well-proportioned. She drove, dress flipping up over dimpled knees. She drove like fury. Tires shrieked, whined, spun. She punched the throttle of that Eldorado like she was mad at it. I checked the speedometer as we took off for the mountains. Eighty-seven. She hit it harder. We were moving up now, swerving along what seemed to be a ninety-degree grade on a road that seemed no wider than a pencil line. We went up fast, and pretty soon there wasn't anything on my right but wide open space. I closed my eyes. "Honey," I said, "I just love thrills. But don't you think—"

"Isn't this the cutest little car you ever did see?" she said, and tromped that accelerator even harder.

The next time I opened my eyes, we'd wheeled onto the flat of a plateau. It looked like grazing land, although we were going too fast for me to focus. We dipped down again, almost careening out of control. Then, just in sight of a deserted-looking old ranch house, the car took a couple of peculiar jumps, then slowed. We rolled to a standstill.

"Oh, my goodness," Julie said, "we're out of gas."

"Honey," I said, "you didn't have to pull that on *me*."

She pointed a pretty finger at the gauge. It showed empty, all right. I motioned my hands. "Well, so, here we are."

"Sweetly," she said, "I'm sorry. I'm so forgetful about things."

I grinned. Byrd wanted me out of the way for a day. I was out of the way, all right. "Honey," I said, reaching for her, "never mind."

She was a nibbler, was what she was. She nibbled her way between my lower lip and my left ear, then she pulled away, gasping for air. "Sweety!" she said.

"Sweety!" I murmured in answer.

I reached for her again, but she'd hopped out of the car. "Let's look around."

I got out reluctantly.

"Maybe somebody in that house has got some gas," she said.

"It looks deserted."

"Let's try."

The only trouble with her was she was always moving. If you could hold her still for a minute....

We were up to the doorway of the house, which was in the middle of a rather typical barnyard—a barn in the rear, what looked like a chicken coop to the side and, way back, a windmill.

The door to the house, we discovered, was padlocked from the outside and the padlock was rusty.

"No gas," I said sighing. I took one of her hands and squeezed it. "Isn't that a bloody stinking shame?"

"Oh, look," she said excitedly, pointing over my shoulder. "A barn! I wonder if there's a hayloft in there?"

Now she was squeezing *my* hand, and we larruped across that barnyard like a pair of outsize pixies. Maybe, I thought, there was a proper setting here for Julie after all. We went in, blinking against the dark, and the next thing I knew, Julie was hanging around my neck, moulding herself against me, booting the door shut with her little yellow slipper.

"Oh, Sweety," she moaned.

Well, I've been taken, swindled, and conned a few times in my life. But I wasn't entirely naïve about this young nibbler. There was a little too much pattern so far. Julie had just showed up out of nowhere and at a very odd time, all things considered. She said she had seen me when I first noticed her, but how did she happen to know where I—as Byrd— was staying? And we had very conveniently run out of gas on a drive which had been Julie's own big idea. Now we were standing in the dark, Julie nibbling like a hungry squirrel. And I had the sobering feeling that I wasn't as enticing as all that. I had the feeling, as a matter of fact, that we weren't alone in that big dark barn. Before I could do anything about it, the bomb struck.

It struck right in the middle of a kiss, and for a foolish instant I thought it was the power of Julie's charms—because something was exploding inside my head like the incandescence of an atomic bomb. For that same foolish moment, I sighed at the reaction this kid could get out of a man. But I knew, as I started falling into that deep pool of blackness I'd always read about in the detective books, that it wasn't Julie who'd sent me there, but a hard and well-aimed blow squarely against the back of my head.

6

When I climbed my way out of that black pool and blinked my eyes at light, I listened to myself groan for a few seconds, then spent a couple of eternities working myself onto my stomach and getting a hand up to the back of my head. It came away sticky, and I'd felt a bump the size of a turkey egg.

I was still in the barn, and now it was lighted with a single bare bulb hanging directly over my head. I turned my head and looked around, off towards the right. Sure enough there was a hayloft. I switched my eyes down. There was a black Lincoln, vintage 1950. On its right front fender, seated with dimpled knees tucked up and circled with plump tanned arms, was Julie. She was smiling prettily at me.

To her left, leaning against the other front fender, was a short, thin man in a lightweight brown suit. He had light brown hair combed straight back and rimless glasses. He looked for all the world like a low-paid clerk, until I noticed his right hand, which was slowly twirling a sock with a rock or a steel ball in the toe—a sap, to be exact. With his left hand he removed his glasses and placed them neatly in his breast pocket.

To his left, lounging against the door Julie and I had come through, was a young gentleman in his early twenties. He was very neat—a good beige gabardine sport coat and tan slacks and a very clean, very white oxford shirt, tieless and open at the collar. He wore a pair of casual buckskin shoes and looked like an All-American college student with his carefully combed hair and broad, good-looking face. But his look somehow matched the look of the clerk-type holding the sap. For one thing, the boy carried a pistol loosely in his right hand. And it was in both their eyes—a vicious, sadistic look. I decided this was going to be a very bad afternoon.

I turned my eyes back to Julie; she was still smiling prettily at me. A very bad afternoon, I thought.

"Look," grinned the kid with the collegiate look, "he's twinkling."

The man who looked like a clerk said nothing, just stared at me and twirled his sap.

Julie pouted her lips. "Sweety," she purred.

One thing I will say: It may have been the sap, not Julie's charms, that sent me into a dream world; but the way she was sitting and the way I was lying ... well, at that moment I hated Julie's guts, but even with my head feeling like it had been busted open, I could still appreciate her.

The guy with the sap spoke now. Softly. Very correctly.

"Byrd, you're overdue. One hundred grand. That's all we want. You've had your fun with the croupier, now it's time to stop the games. How about it?"

I looked at him. I looked at the kid in the gabardine sport coat. I would just as soon have stuck my finger in the eye of a mad bull as cross these two, but I worked up my courage and said, "Go to hell."

The kid straightened. He walked over. He kicked me gently on the side of the head. He walked back again. He leaned against the door. He held his gun loosely in one hand. He kept smiling his winsome Jack Armstrong smile. I really didn't like that kid a whole lot.

"You see how it is, Byrd?" the clerk-type said.

"Sweety," Julie said, "give them their old money and then we can have some fun again. Freddie and Billy get ever so nasty if they can't have their old way."

I looked at her. I think she actually meant it! She rubbed her knees together gently. I turned my eyes away. This was pressure, all right.

"You can't beat it, Byrd," the clerk-type said. "Why try?"

"Freddie means that," the kid said.

I looked at the kid—Billy the Kid, no doubt. He whirled his gun neatly by the trigger guard like a good movie cowboy. I was getting nervous. I figured to earn the money but not die doing it.

"I haven't got it," I said. "That's the truth."

This time the clerk-type, the one called Freddie, straightened. He walked forward and stood over me. He walked around me. I closed my eyes. That ball inside the sock flicked my temple.

Freddie returned to the fender and leaned back. "We can keep it up all day, Byrd. And we're being gentle right now. Very gentle."

"It's the truth," I said. "I haven't got it."

The kid straightened again.

"I'll make a deal with you," I said in a hurry.

"Deal?" Freddie said.

"You can kill me," I said, "only I can't give you what I haven't got. You keep beating on me, I'll clam up on what I have got. I get stubborn."

"We know what to do with the stubborn ones," Freddie said. "We got a foolproof remedy."

I let my breath out. I sat up slowly and with great effort. "I just haven't got it," I said. "You think I'm lying, maybe. You're wrong. My money's sewed up. I can't touch a thing. You see?"

"We don't see a thing, friend," Freddie said. He tipped his head. The kid swaggered forward.

"But I'll make a deal," I said. "Twenty-five grand."

Billy the Kid stopped. Freddie stared at me. My hopes went up a little. "You must be nuts," Freddie said. My hopes collapsed.

"The game was rigged," I said, panicking a little now.

"You say," Freddie answered. "Right or wrong, we've got your I.O.U."

"Try to make it stick," I said, wondering at my own sanity.

"Just so it sticks with us, friend," Freddie said softly. "That's all that counts."

"I'll put it flat," I told him. "I've got fifty thousand bucks in the bank. I'll give it all to you and go begging. That's all I've got. I'm telling you the truth."

There was a much longer pause this time. The kid stood right over me but he didn't move. He was waiting. Freddie was thinking.

"You'd better try it out with Nicole," I said.

"Nicole wants a hundred grand," Freddie said.

"Why don't you check him?" I said. I said it as though I thought Freddie didn't have the brains to figure anything out by himself, but I had sense enough not to say it outright.

Freddie flushed a little. "He said one hundred grand."

"Nicole likes money," I said. "I'll give him some. Fifty G's. I don't have any more. I'll give you a check. I'll write it out for that amount. If I write it for more, it'll bounce. If you don't believe that, I'll try it for you now. Fifty G's. That's a lot of clams for an illegal operation." I looked up at the kid, back to Freddie. "I'm tired. The pressure's getting me. I don't like getting kicked around. Let's settle this and forget it."

Freddie still hesitated, then straightened once more. "Watch him, Billy," he said to the kid. "I'll check with Nicole."

He walked across the barn and picked up a five-gallon can of gasoline and carried it to the door.

Julie called after him, "You put in just the right amount, Freddie. We ran out right in front of the house. We didn't have to walk a step extra." Freddie disappeared and Julie giggled. She shifted her legs. I kept my eyes away from her.

I looked at the kid. He twirled his gun for me. Simple bastard, I thought.

"I'd come over and kiss your poor head, lamb," Julie warbled to me, "only Billy would be scared you'd grab me so he couldn't shoot at you if you tried to get away."

I nodded in wonderment. It was a genuine apology, I was certain. I wondered where shrewdness left off and dumbness began.

I listened to the Caddie roar away, and then there was nothing but silence and waiting. I looked up once at Julie. She preened for me. I looked away.

In what was perhaps a half hour but what seemed like six months, the clerkish Freddie came back in the door. His face looked grim. He'd put on his rimless glasses for the drive, but now he took them off and put them back in the breast pocket of the brown suit.

I tried to smile pleasantly, but my heart was sinking. "What did he say?"

"Write the check. Fifty G's. And make it snappy."

I got out the check quickly. I half bent over to cover the already existing signature. I had a pen in my jacket and I wrote that check out quickly. My hand shaking a little, but I did it.

I handed Freddie the check. His eyes brushed it. He got out the rimless glasses and put them on and went over it again. "Okay. This better be good. We found you once. We can find you again. Nicole wasn't happy, but he happens to like money. You're getting off easy, mister."

"Thanks," I said thinly.

"Billy?" Freddie said softly.

The kid stepped over and whacked me with the barrel of his gun. I opened my mouth and closed it, because I was pitching out once again and the barn was going around and around.

"Don't fool with Nicole again," Freddie said.

I swallowed, holding myself steady, with my knuckles pressed against the floor of the barn.

I knew Freddie was swinging his sap before it hit me again. I don't know whether or not I felt it. I was just sliding back into that familiar black pool....

I came to flat on my back on the floor, but there was something soft under my shoulders and head. Something equally as soft was moving over my forehead, over and over.

"Poor baby," I heard dimly. And then vision cleared and I rose from the black pool to look squarely into Julie's lovely face.

"You still here?" I managed.

"Why not?" she asked, stroking my forehead. "You're just the cutest old thing I've ever seen."

"Old is right," I said. "I feel like nine hundred and forty-seven."

"I'll bet you won't in a few minutes," she said. "I'll just bet you won't. I'll bet I can make you feel like fifteen."

"Doesn't it bother you?" I asked her. "I mean the fact that you got me sapped to hell and gone this way?"

"Sweety," she said, pouting, "that was just a little old thing I did for someone. It didn't mean anything. I *like* you!"

"Tell my head that," I said.

"Poor lamb," she said, stroking. "I can make it feel better. I can make everything feel better."

"How?" I complained.

"Let's go home, and I'll show you."

"Home?"

"Your hotel suite," she said, surprised. "Where else? I'm all tired out from driving. See, they took their car. My little old car is waiting outside. All filled with gas now. Okay, Sweety?"

All of a sudden the kicks and knocks I'd taken rammed back into my mind. I forgot about the fact that I'd pulled this deal off. I forgot that it was all over and that Julie was really like this, that all she wanted to do was go home and play house.

"I would just as soon take a cobra home," I snapped.

"Sweety," she complained, "you're not nice when you talk like that. And I don't like boys who aren't nice."

"I wish you'd stop stroking my splitting head," I said glumly.

She did. She got out from under it, in fact, and the back of my head dropped to the floor with a thump. I groaned. Then I sat up, with effort, and held my head between my own hands—they were not, I discovered, nearly as effective as hers had been.

But she was already at the door, and she stopped long enough to say, through pouting lips, "Sweety, you've gotten to be just a mean, nasty old thing." Then she swiveled out to the barnyard and disappeared.

All of a sudden I realized that my head on Julie's lap was where it should have been. I heard the roar of the Caddie's exhaust, staggered to my feet and weaved out the door. I yelled at her, waving frantically.

It was no use. Gone was Julie and that full, tanned body. Gone was the afternoon of house playing. Gone was the transportation back to town.

My God, Steele, I thought, sitting down by the side of that barn and holding my head with my own hands, you get more stupid by the hour....

7

I walked six miles to get to a road where it even looked like there might be traffic. In the next four hours, exactly four cars went by; and they seemed to speed up going by. I kept up a steady, if silent, diatribe against one Mark Steele. Late that afternoon, an ancient cattle truck ambled up and coughed to a stop. I was much obliged. I got back to Reno.

I came in through a side exit of the Plateau Hotel and took the stairway to my floor. I cleaned up, sent my suit down for pressing, then ordered a new supply of liquor. I poured a heavy jolt of Scotch, downed half of it, and when it hit bottom, I realized I hadn't eaten since breakfast. The hell with it, I decided. Maybe I could get drunk. Maybe....

The telephone rang, and I lifted it. It was Byrd again. "Old man, how is it going?"

"How do you think?" I snapped. "All things considered."

He laughed pleasantly. "Steele, you sound perpetually like a tiger. I merely called to say the scare is off. Those friends of mine——"

"They didn't make it," I finished. "They decided to fly to Hong Kong instead." There was something very irritating to me about the idle rich at that moment. To Byrd, the ten grand was peanuts. I'd just had my head kicked off for it.

"Mexico, as a matter of fact," he said. "However, that's over. And may I ask again—how are you doing, sport?"

"Sporty," I said.

"Any action?"

"Lots of action. A hell of a lot of action. But it's done, brother. They settled for fifty. Nick Nicole's the top man. He approved it. All I want now is to grab my cut and close this deal. Do you recall, by the way, a blonde from Vegas with a spectacular walk?"

"Dumb?"

"Like a fox. Only still dumb. You know?"

"Julie!"

"One of the collectors," I said.

He was laughing uproariously. "I should have gone myself. Julie!"

"She wasn't alone," I said grimly. "So how about settling this deal, huh?"

"Right," he said. "Of course, Steele."

"I feel like staying here for a while," I said, my mind turning to Linda. "Can you—"

"I get it," he said, and I could hear the grin in his voice. "Why, of course. I'll send you the money at the Plateau just as soon as this Nicole ships the I.O.U. to my home. A splendid job, brother Mark. Really splendid!"

My spirits had picked up. "Sorry I've been squawking at you, Byrd. It's been a strain."

"You've done a magnificent job, old fellow. I owe you my life!"

"Not your life. Just ten grand. So long, Byrd. Have a happy future."

"Thank you, Steele. And by the way, I'm continuing to take a few days' rest in this obscurity here. While you're there, just hold on as me, won't you? I mean I wouldn't want these chaps to reverse judgment and start going for the balance."

"Okay, Byrd."

"Don't spend it all on her, old man," he said.

"Who?"

"Julie, of course."

I put the telephone down. Julie. I had an idea Julie was on her way back to Las Vegas. And out of sight, Julie was out of mind.

Well, so the business was all over and all I had to do was wait for the ten grand from Byrd. I mused for a moment over whether or not he would come through with it as he'd promised. He'd certainly cut out of the gambling debt. Then, as I'd figured before, I decided he would. He was really in no position to argue about it. If he did, all I had to do was look him up personally and, if that didn't work, just give the pitch back to Nicole and they would be right on his trail for the balance of that one hundred G's.

I poured another drink, then walked to the balcony and looked down. Linda was not in sight. I telephoned the bar. Joe told me she was down there. Alone. Looking mad as a jilted bride. I grinned, hoping it was me she was thinking about. I put on the brown suit, admired myself in the mirror, and went downstairs.

I stopped at the desk and filled out one of Byrd's remaining checks for fifteen hundred dollars. I destroyed the two remaining blanks containing his signature. The hotel cashed the first check on the strength of Uncle Gosset. I put the bills in my wallet. Fifteen hundred, plus the thousand I'd cashed at the Yellow Tiger Club, which was nearly intact. And ten thousand more coming in. All for a few knocks on the head. Steele, I told myself, you're not so dumb after all.

And then I stopped short. I'd figured it all out very neatly, and it was all very perfect. But it was a feeling I suddenly had—a feeling that everything was too smooth.

I sat down right there, in one of the seats of the lobby, and thought about it. For some reason, all of a sudden, I had the feeling that I was not so smart at all. I had the feeling that somehow a lot of strings had been pulled and I'd been the puppet. But why? I asked myself. If anyone was pulling the strings, it had to be Byrd. But he'd gotten what he wanted, hadn't he?

I went back over everything once again, and decided it was Byrd's reaction on the phone that bothered me most. Somehow he hadn't sounded as relieved as he should have when I'd told him this caper was over. He'd only sounded excited, as though his mind was still working. But this was supposed to be all sewed up. Why didn't he go home now, and....

I remembered one of the last things he'd said: "... I'm continuing to take a few days' rest in this obscurity here. While you're there, just hold on as me, won't you? ..." The first time he'd called me, he'd whined considerably about being holed up in the Sacramento hotel. Now, when he had no apparent reason to stay there, he decided to hang on for a "rest."....

Then I was back thinking about Duckie boy who'd appeared at Harrah's. What was it Duckie boy had said? "I saw you before. This evening—getting off the train, weren't you?" I'd gotten off the train late that afternoon. Was it really Duckie's definition of evening? Or had Byrd himself gotten off an evening train? But what the hell, I wondered, would he have been doing in Reno? Well, it was easy enough to check that. Simply call the hotel in Sacramento and see if he was still there.

I got up and started for the telephone booths but on the way I looked at the bar. Linda was still there. I stopped, pulse speeding up a little. Steele, I told myself, quit when you're ahead. Stop dreaming up trouble. Relax. Check on Byrd later, if you still feel like it. If he's trying to pull something, you'll find it out soon enough anyway, and you can always deal with him then. Meantime ... Meantime, I set off for the bar at an even trot.

"Linda, honey," I said, climbing the stool next to hers. She started to get up, eyes sparking, but I put a hand on her bare tanned arm. She shivered a little, whispered, "Stinker," but didn't leave.

"I can explain everything," I said.

"So can I," she said, arching her eyebrows. "In one word. Julie."

I sighed. "You know her?"

"I've been in Las Vegas, remember? Julie is a legend." She finished her drink with one large gulp. "Give me another, Joe. Make it a double."

"Honey, give me a chance," I said. I shifted my left knee to touch her right one. She didn't move. I ran my hand lightly over hers on the bar. She moved her hand away, then put it back.

"I gave you a chance before. You blew it. Why don't you take off and let me be miserable by myself?"

My drink arrived. I'd asked for a double too. "Why be miserable, Linda? We could have fun together, no?"

"Yes," she said. "I mean, no. And stop rubbing knees with me."

"Do you mind?"

"That's not the point. Just stop it."

But she didn't move her knee away, and I didn't stop it.

"So explain," she said.

"Okay," I said. "It was an old gambling debt. I hadn't paid it. These people got mad about it. They sent Julie to bring me in to them. So I paid the debt. Now it's over."

"Some story."

"I got banged around, as a matter of fact. Feel the back of my head."

"I won't."

"Go ahead."

She did, without looking at me. She touched the goose egg and brought her hand away. "So I don't know what to believe. So all I know is you took off with Julie. So all I know is last night—"

"Honey, last night—" I looked up in the mirror, remembering the croupier. I noticed with satisfaction that he wasn't at the dice table. I decided not to try to tell Linda about the croupier.

"You just have to believe me, Linda."

"I don't believe you at all," she said. "You're a rat, Byrd. Leave me alone."

I looked at her carefully. Then I turned on my stool. "Okay," I said. "So long, Linda." I stood up.

"Don't."

I sat back down.

"I hate myself," she said, "but I can't help it." She finished her drink, then turned to look at me. She'd given in all the way, I could see; her eyes weren't hating me now. They were doing something else. "Darling, I— let's go somewhere, shall we?"

"Anywhere," I said.

"Where we were last night," she said, "before you so rudely interrupted?"

"Right," I said.

She nodded, eyes going soft. "My room. Four-twenty-three. Come up in twenty minutes. Don't bother to knock, darling."

She left, and a drink was placed in my hand. "Congratulations," Joe said. "It's on the house."

"Thanks, Joe."

"Don't mention it," Joe said happily. "We're all proud of you."

I finished the drink, then took the elevator to my floor. All of a sudden the bar seemed too public for my very private thoughts. I decided to have another drink in the privacy of my own room while I waited out those minutes and thought back to where Linda and I had left off. I walked along the corridor to my suite and went up ten feet with every step. I wasn't walking, I was floating. This was not a corridor. It was the surface of the rainbow. I was one thousand feet off the earth. I was sailing for the moon. All I had to do was flap my arms once and I'd be zooming out of the galaxy.

Somehow I dipped down from the clouds long enough to unlock my door, bend my rudder and glide in. It was dark now, and I reached for the switch; a switch that controlled from the wall the lamp near the sofa. I didn't make it. Something cracked me from the right, flat against the side of my head, cracked me so hard that I stumbled to my left, throwing up an arm and cleaning the bottles and glasses off the bar as I fell. I wound up on the floor, stunned, but realizing well enough that I was getting very tired of getting cracked on the head.

In the next second the switch snapped, and the lamp by the sofa came on. It was Freddie and Billy, my little barnyard friends.

8

Freddie stood to the side of the balcony door. He carefully removed his rimless glasses and placed them in that breast pocket. Billy the Kid was by the light switch. Freddie now was carrying the gun, equipped this time, I saw, with a silencer. The kid was twirling the sap.

I grazed my hand over the side of my head. "Look, we decided to quit this, remember?" I was getting sick of looking at these two faces. They didn't even bring Julie for me to look at this time.

Freddie spoke very carefully. "I thought you were nuts before, Byrd. Now I know it."

He put his left hand in his pocket, brought out what looked like a crumpled check and threw it at me.

"What's going on?" I asked.

"That's what Nicole wanted to know when he found out the check was rubber.”

“You’re crazy,” I said.

“Not us,” Freddie said. “You. You haven’t got a dime in that bank.”

There wasn’t any more confusion. I didn’t need to ask any more questions. I didn’t know why or exactly how, but what I’d only sensed a little while ago in the lobby was now perfectly clear. I’d been had. I silently called Byrd ten million varieties of dishonorable names, and all the while switched my eyes back and forth between Freddie and the kid.

It was bad. I knew that. Whatever the reason … I was the patsy, the pigeon, the mark.

I kept looking at the silencer on Freddie’s gun. Nicole had a position to uphold. The only way he could uphold it now was to gun me. A three-time loser strapped in the chair for killing the warden had more chance than I did. I was beyond arguments or deals. I was damned near beyond this mortal world.

For a moment I considered trying to tell them the truth—that I was not Mr. Thomas Byrd but his gullible twin brother, Mark Steele. I considered that for roughly a quarter of a second and then threw it out. In the first place, the expressions they wore were enough to convince me they wouldn’t give me half a chance to explain or believe me if I did. Moreover, I was damned if I was going to scream foul now. If I’d been fool enough to let Byrd pitch me into this spot, it was up to me to get off it without a big crying scene.

And then Freddie was saying, “Get up, Byrd. We’re going to take a little walk downstairs. Then we’re going to get a breath of fresh desert air—”

They didn’t want to muss up the hotel floor with my blood. They didn’t want to fuss the management by leaving around old bleeding corpses.

“Sure,” I said. “Sure. Okay.”

By that time I had my hand around an old-fashioned glass and was tossing it at the lamp. I didn’t think about it. I did it. I threw the glass, hoping I hadn’t lost my pitching arm, and at the same time I was rolling sideways.

The glass struck the lamp, smashing the shade and taking the bulb with it. A bullet was chunking into the floor at a point precisely where I had been.

I kept rolling until I hit a chair, and then I got half to my knees and threw the chair in the direction of the balcony doors. I must have hit Freddie, because he yelped like a bee-stung coyote.

Until then I’d never paid any attention to the marvelous sound proofing of the Plateau Hotel. The crashing, swearing, the pinging of a gun beneath the silencer; even the thud of the bullet as it embedded in the concrete below the floor—all of this was masterfully muted.

But now the kid was across the room, whirling his sap in long arcs, moving straight in the direction he'd seen me roll as the lamp was broken. The sap whistled by my ear once, then, on the next loop, clipped my right eyebrow. It was a grazing blow, but it bounced me back and I could feel the blood starting to stream. I judged the kid's approximate position, then grabbed for his arm. I got it and whirled him straight into the couch.

When I entered the Army, I'd been taught combat tactics by a gorilla sergeant name of Ducco. Ducco was a realist. He not only taught us how to fight hand-to-hand with the enemy, but also with anybody else who might be looking for trouble. The only time to fight with rules, he'd said, was in the ring; and he'd been doubtful about that. No such thing as a fair fight, he'd told us. You fight fair, you're a sucker; you might be even more than that—you might end up with a broken bladder or a busted groin. Don't ever fight fair in a brawl, he'd said. Fight to win.

I did not always go with Ducco's philosophy, but this time it wasn't just a matter of a broken bladder or a busted groin. This time it was a matter of my sorry life.

I ducked under that swinging sap of the kid's and punched one straight into him that would have lost me six rounds in a refereed fight. When he doubled with that, I grabbed for the approximate place where his right hand ought to have been. I got lucky and found it; I screwed his hand almost off its wrist until the sap bounced on the rug.

He was wild now, biting at me like an animal, trying to kick, gouge, punch, all at the same time. Maybe, I thought, he'd known Ducco too. I gave him Ducco's favorite then; I got just a little above him, cracked the back of his neck with the edge of a flat hand. I then turned my thoughts to Freddie.

Apparently Freddie was not the aggressive type in a free-for-all. I couldn't keep every movement straight in that dark room, but I was pretty sure he hadn't moved since he'd fired his gun. I turned the kid twelve degrees to my right, pointing his back straight at where Freddie ought to have been. I did it by yanking the kid straight toward me, twisting a little, and falling backward. At the same time, I got my legs doubled up between the kid and myself. Then I kicked straight out. The wind went out of the kid, and he went careening backward across the room, like a balloon with escaping air.

Freddie spooked, as I suspected he might. With that motion coming in his direction, he asked no questions. He fired the gun. I heard a sharp gasp from the kid, and then he was whimpering, "Leg ..."

I followed the kid, hopping over him before Freddie could sort things out. The gun went off again, but that slug wound up in the ceiling.

Freddie obviously figured to get out. He'd lost the support of his chum, Billy, and now he made a crazy, nervous dive towards the door. I got a foot in his way, which he hit and then sprawled to the floor. But he held onto that gun. I went after him again.

He'd slammed into the wall beside the door, and I slammed him there again, using the heel of one hand and grabbing for the gun with the other hand. I finally got hold of it, but by the barrel, and Freddie still held the butt—but his finger was obviously not on the trigger because he didn't fire again. I banged his head against the wall. The gun came away from his hand and he collapsed in a slow, senseless heap. The only sound after that was the steady, durable cursing of the kid.

I made my way to another lamp, switched it on, and surveyed the wreckage. Freddie was out cold. Billy was holding his right leg, cursing and glaring at me. I stood there for a moment, looking from one to the other, trying to clear my brain. Then I walked over and picked up the crumpled check, straightened it, and looked at it. I don't know why. It was the check I'd made out, all right. And I kept thinking of nothing but the double-crossing brother Byrd.

I slapped my things into a bag, including the other freshly-pressed suit, all the time keeping Freddie's gun ready in my right hand. I picked up the bag then and stood there, looking at the two. I could, I thought, put a bullet through each of their heads, but that obviously would bring repercussions. I decided Freddie was going to nap for a while. I decided Billy boy wasn't going to get anywhere too fast.

I walked out and down the hall, then realized for the first time that I was still bleeding from the cut in the eyebrow. Just then a man and a woman appeared in the corridor and came straight for me. I cut into the fire escape just in time and tried to wipe off a little of the blood with my handkerchief. It didn't help much.

I hurried on up to the fourth floor, paused, then trotted down the corridor, hoping for the best. I found four-twenty-three without meeting anyone else and walked in without knocking.

Up to that moment, I'd been cussing Byrd, but when I walked through Linda's door and closed it behind me, I realized that if it hadn't been for Byrd I would never have met her and I never would have stood there looking at her.

Her suite was the same as mine, except the bar was on the opposite side of the living room. She was sitting on one of the bar stools, facing away from me. There was a bottle of champagne in a bucket of ice. There was a frosted glass waiting on the bar for me. She had the other one in her hand, sipping from it. And I just stood and looked, even forgetting Freddie and Billy for that moment.

She turned around slowly, glass in hand, legs crossed. She looked just as she had in my suite when I'd seen the croupier on the balcony.

"You see?" she smiled. "Just like it was when we—" She stopped and paled a little under the tan. "*Darling,*" she whispered. "What—?"

She was off the stool and over to me. "Darling, you're hurt! What happened?" She led me to a chair, got the champagne bucket from the bar, disappeared, and returned with it filled with warm water. She also had a wash cloth, towels, and a small first-aid kit.

This girl was as nimble with her first aid as she was with a pair of dice. I closed my eyes, and she washed, swabbed and patched. Then she sat beside me on the arm of the chair, gripping her hands together and looking at me with large, worried eyes. I grinned at her and felt like a damn fool.

"Tell me," she said worriedly. "Tell me, Tom—"

"Mark." I wanted to straighten that out immediately. "Not Thomas Byrd. Mark Steele." And then I told her the story, quickly and briefly. I emphasized the fact, as I finished, that I owned neither the name nor the resources of my twin brother. I was, I emphasized, a drifter with only the smallest kind of financial fortunes coming my way, and sporadically at that. I gave her a chance to bow out quickly, if it was money she was interested in.

"Darling," she said. She circled my neck with her arms and kissed me. "It's *you,* darling. Nothing else."

I grinned at her, relieved.

"But what now?" she asked.

"Byrd," I said tightly.

"But can't we get away somewhere and—"

I shook my head, getting up. "Aside from squaring this with Byrd, I've got a pack of hoods on my back now. Nicole's hoods. I can't sit still now, and I can't run away and forget it."

"But if they knew you're not really Byrd—"

"How do I tell them now? This is beyond the ask-questions-first stage. It's a shoot-first-and-ask-later deal. Right now I'm probably the hottest target Nicole ever handed to his apes. I not only cut out with a hundred grand, but bruised three of his gunmen. I'm a walking bull's-eye."

"Darling," she said unreasonably, coming at me as I went toward the door, bag in hand, "wait a little and then—"

Her eyes were blue but they got black in the centers; she circled my neck again with her arms and I almost threw the suitcase down and locked the door. "Later, sweetheart. Will you wait?"

She nodded, tears sparkling in her eyes. "Be careful, Mark, I'll wait—"

I left and went down to the lobby. I hadn't been in Linda's room over fifteen minutes and doubted whether Nicole's pair in my room had had time to do anything but try to reorganize their jellied brains.

I paid my bill in full. I was once more the smiling, well-bred *bon vivant* of Beverly Hills; my cheek may have been bruised, there may have been a piece of tape over my right eye, but the desk clerk didn't seem to notice. I walked out, having been wished a fair ado, and half expecting to be cut down by a machine gun nosing out of that black 1950 Lincoln.

Nothing happened. I ignored a cab and walked across the Truckee and halfway down the main street, where I walked into a drugstore, collected change, and put in a call to Joseph Weatherly at the Valley Hotel in Sacramento. There was nobody, I was told, registered there by that name; there hadn't been during the past two days.

I'd known it would be like that. I thought back to Byrd's two telephone calls to me. Both had, obviously, been station-to-station, and so there had been no telephone operator announcement before I'd talked to him. Byrd could have called from anywhere.

I sat there in the booth, thinking about it. I had a good view of the street. I began to look with suspicion at everybody who walked by, at every car that rolled by. Byrd had set me up like a tin can on a fence post, and I damn well didn't like it.

I got up and walked to the doorway, looking up and down the street. Nicole's men were going to be after me, but I doubted if Nicole would use any of the three I'd already met and could recognize. He would, by now, be switching to the best talent he could hire; and none of the previous three would seem to qualify.

I took a cab to the airport; if there were any cars following my cab, I couldn't detect it. Maybe, I thought, Freddie was still napping and the kid was still lying there swearing. The thought pleased me.

I had no reservation, so I had to hope business was slow or that there would be a last-minute cancellation. I bought my ticket and asked for the first plane to San Francisco. I did it absently, my mind turning. I wanted to go home before I did anything else. I wanted to get back to my own apartment and pick up my own things. As long as I was walking around with only Thomas Byrd's identification, I was going to have a hard time proving to Nicole's boys who I really was, even if I had time enough to prove it before they emptied a gun into me.

"Leaving us already, Mr. Byrd?" the ticket clerk said. He was very polite and smiling about it.

I frowned at him. I hadn't even given him any name yet—and I hadn't intended to use Byrd's name but rather my own.

"Already?" I said.

"Let's see, it was just this afternoon that you came in, wasn't it, Mr. Byrd?"

"Oh," I said, wondering what the hell he was talking about, "this afternoon, yes—"

"... Yes, sir, Mr. Byrd," the clerk was saying, "we've got a cancellation on the next flight. That will leave in—twenty minutes."

My head was spinning as I walked away from the ticket clerk. I headed for a telephone booth, bumping squarely into a rather dignified-looking man in glasses who wore a dark gray suit and matching Homburg. He looked like a medical specialist or a banker; he carried a small black bag in his right hand and was heading for the small lunch counter.

"I beg your pardon," he said.

I begged his pardon in return, then got to the telephone booth. I made another call to Sacramento and this time gave my name as Lieutenant John Andrews of the Reno Police Department. I was calling the ticket manager at the Sacramento railroad station. I could get into trouble with that kind of impersonation, but it was nothing compared to the kind of trouble another impersonation had already gotten me into.

The ticket manager seemed impressed when the operator announced who I was. I told him I was looking for a Joseph Weatherly. I gave him a description. Tall, about one hundred seventy pounds, blond mustache, black-rimmed glasses, wearing, when last seen, a shaggy tweed sport coat.

The ticket manager checked. Then he reported happily that yes, such a man had purchased a ticket for Reno on the nineteenth, yesterday. He'd done so at late afternoon. The ticket clerk remembered the man well....

I thanked him and hung up. That boy at Harrah's—Duckie boy—he *had* seen Byrd, not me, because leaving Sacramento in the afternoon would have put Byrd in Reno in the evening. But what the hell had Byrd come to Reno for? What the hell *was* he doing, besides making me a walking target? I could see what he'd done so far. Gotten off at Sacramento, only instead of holing up in the Valley Hotel there, he'd gotten on another train, later, and come to Reno—getting off minus disguise, or maybe Duckie simply saw the back of him, which made better sense. At any rate, he'd undoubtedly made both calls to me right from Reno.

And now, a few minutes ago, the ticket clerk for the airlines had indicated that Byrd had just come into Reno this afternoon—by plane, this time. Maybe, I thought, I was going completely nuts. Maybe there were three other people who looked like I did. Maybe Byrd and I hadn't been twins but members of a set of quintuplets.

My flight was called and I hesitated. If Byrd had come in by train right after I had, he must have left again, then reappeared by plane. At the rate he was coming and going, I had no hopes of even remotely figuring out where he was right now. I decided to return to San Francisco, then start looking for him.

9

It was a short flight, but the time seemed endless. I smoked half a pack of cigarettes, alternately examining the country below, then the passengers. I was certain I hadn't been followed to the airport in Reno. I was reasonably certain nobody on this plane had anything to do with Nicole, except me. The dignified doctor-type or banker was forward, the one I'd bumped into; but he was the only one I remembered even seeing in Reno before we'd taken off.

Finally we were at International Airport.

I picked up a cab on the ramp and rode directly to my apartment house; I wanted first of all to re-establish myself as Mark Steele—not only as a possible protection against Nicole's men, but also for my state of mind. I'd grown to dislike even the name of brother Thomas Byrd during the past hours, and I was very sick of impersonating him.

It was evening now, and the apartment house was silent when I climbed the steps to the second floor. It wasn't the Plateau, but it was home; and even though I'd lived there but a few days, everything seemed suddenly more normal and natural.

I still had the apartment key on my key ring, and I unlocked the door and stepped in. I was surprised to find two lamps on in the living room. I decided I'd left them on when I left or the cleaning woman had forgotten to turn them off. I loosened my tie and dropped my bag on the sofa.

Then something else bothered me. There was a sound coming from the direction of the bedroom. I walked in. Lights were on in there too. And the sound was coming from the bathroom—the shower was on.

I looked at the bed. Draped out on the spread was a quilted robe that did not look like mine or even a man's, although it was large enough— I also saw a pile consisting of a girdle, nylon hose, panties and brassiere;

they damned well didn't belong to a man, and they sure as hell didn't belong to me. Just then the shower stopped running, the bathroom door, which had been slightly ajar, opened completely and I was confronted with the last sight I expected to see coming out of my bathroom.

She was a big girl. She was really big. She had big long legs and big hips and huge breasts; I could see all that because she was as bare as Mother Hubbard's cupboard. She gaped at me, towel in hand; her big eyes got bigger, and her mouth popped open, and I could see all those big teeth of hers. She wasn't really good-looking, but she was not bad-looking either. She was just so big. There was just so much of her.

I was surprised, I'll admit. But she was petrified. For three full seconds she stood there, just staring at me with wide eyes and open mouth and all the rest of that bare body, while the water dripped off her. She seemed made out of stone. And then finally I said, "Look, lady—"

Then she started screaming. She did honestly scream. She whooped. She hollered. It was a double cadenza in fortissimo. She yelled like a Texan at the Alamo. She brayed like a mule gone mad. She didn't move. She just stood there and bellowed.

Then she moved. She went by me like a charging bull. She didn't put the towel around her. She threw that straight up in the air. And she didn't stop that whooping. I watched her move with a kind of transfixed fascination. And it was a fascinating movement to watch. She didn't run. She pranced, the way some women do when they try to run. She ran right into the far wall of the living room. She bounced off that, wheeled and pranced again. I couldn't figure out what she was trying to do. My ears were beginning to sting with that howling of hers. Then she finally got to the telephone at the end of the sofa, and I realized she just couldn't see well.

Then I moved. I went across the room after her and slammed the telephone down, right out of her hand. I knew without understanding, that something was all fouled up, and I didn't want her braying that way at the cops, which was what I figured she was trying to do.

She stood there, right beside me, staring at me with those big nearsighted eyes of hers, but she didn't quit yelling. She wheeled again and pranced off for the bedroom, missed the room partially by bumping into the door frame, then found the opening and disappeared behind a slammed door. But she didn't stop that bellowing.

By that time the door leading to the hallway was being pounded, and people were shouting outside. I opened the door to the hall, and Mr. Henry Nidler, the superintendent, burst in, also yelling at the top of his voice.

"Mr. Nidler," I yelled back at him, "what the hell is going on?"

He seemed to realize who I was then, and he quit the yelling, although Leather Lungs in the bedroom didn't.

"Mr. Steele!" he said. "What are you doing here?"

"I'm beginning to wonder myself," I said. "Who in hell is that?" I motioned towards the bedroom.

"Miss Tyling, of course," he said. "We rented your apartment just as soon as you vacated."

That threw me. Vacated....

And then it all came to me. Byrd. Yesterday, the day we left, I'd gone from the apartment well ahead of train time. Byrd would have had enough time, before he went down to the Ferry Building, to come in and pose as me and check out. I'd only talked to Nidler, the superintendent, twice; he didn't know me well enough to detect the impersonation. But why would Byrd have done that?

I tried to regroup my scattered brain cells and decided to go along with it. "It's just that I forgot something, Mr. Nidler. So I had this key, and—"

"You found it, hey?"

"Yes, sir," I said, realizing that Byrd had claimed that he'd lost the key to the apartment.

"Well, you've scared Miss Tyling all to smithereens!"

We had to yell at each other because of the continued whooping in the bedroom.

"I'm sorry," I said, "I just didn't think you would have rented it so soon—"

Mr. Nidler rubbed his hands together, head swinging back and forth. There was a crowd gathered in the hall, heads sticking in the doorway.

"Try to explain to her," I told Nidler, and then I closed the door on those faces, explaining, "It's all right, folks. Miss Tyling's got the whooping cough."

Mr. Nidler went to work at the door, yelling through Miss Tyling's yelling. It took him what seemed hours, but then he seemed to get it through to her what had happened. The hooting finally stopped, but my ears continued to ring. Mr. Nidler gave a long sigh. Then the door opened a crack, and one of Miss Tyling's eyes peered out, this time behind one half of a pair of very large black-rimmed spectacles.

I smiled at her.

She slammed the door and started whooping again.

Mr. Nidler went at it all over again, and she finally quit once more. Again the door edged open, again an eye peered out, then two eyes. I tried a very faint smile, and she let out just one quack, then stopped. She kept staring at me.

"It's all right," Mr. Nidler kept telling her. "It's just Mr. Steele, the man who rented the apartment before. He didn't know you'd moved in."

And now the door leading to the hall was being pounded once more. Mr. Nidler danced across the room, tipping his head a little, slapping his right ear with his palm, as though he'd just been swimming and was trying to get the water out. It was that howling that had done it and I knew how he felt.

This time it was the police—obviously one of the tenants had called them in. "Oh, dear!" Mr. Nidler said. "Mr. Steele, will you—no, I'll explain to them. Mr. Steele, don't get her started again, will you, for pity sakes? My ears!" He started explaining to the cop in the hall, closing the door after him.

Miss Tyling was still gaping at me from the door. "I'm awfully sorry, Miss Tyling," I said. "It's all my fault." She edged the door open a bit more. She was, for God's sake, still nude. She realized that the instant I did. She opened her mouth again, and I put my hands over my ears, looking away. "*Please,* Miss Tyling!"

The door slammed shut, but she didn't start screaming again. I wanted to get out of there, but I didn't want to leave without what I'd come for: my identification. I'd put my cards in the back of the top bureau drawer, and I didn't know whether or not Byrd had found them. I walked over to the bedroom door and knocked lightly.

"Yes?" she squeaked.

"Miss Tyling, I know I've caused you a lot of trouble, but there was something I forgot and—"

"It was all a mistake, wasn't it, Mr. Steele?" she called back.

"Yes, Miss Tyling," I said. "It sure was."

"You're not—" She stopped, and I heard the quivering in her voice.

"No, ma'am," I said. "I certainly am not!"

There was a pause, then finally she said, "Just a moment, Mr. Steele."

The bedlam had ceased in the hall, and now it was all quiet in the bedroom. Time went by. Five minutes. Ten minutes. Fifteen minutes. I couldn't figure out what she was doing.

Finally she opened the door and stepped out, wearing the bathrobe I'd seen on the bed. She also wore a smile, and she was completely madeup, hair combed, lips lipsticked, cheeks rouged and powdered. She smiled that smile at me and she had the whitest smile I'd ever seen—it would have been a beautiful smile if her teeth had been smaller. As it was there was a kind of horsy quality about the whole effect. She blinked her lashes at me from behind those big black spectacles.

"I'm ever so sorry, Mr. Steele, but you can just imagine! Well, I mean—!" This time she laughed, and there wasn't, I discovered, so very much difference between her laughing and her whoops of fear. It was all very unsettling.

"Imagine," she said, "just walking out and seeing a man—well, I just never —" She laughed again, and my ears stung. "Wait until the girls at the office hear about this! They'll just never in the world believe it! You see, I'm a secretary at the Arwell Tool Products out on Bayshore...." She went on. She was a runner-on, I realized. She whooped, you couldn't stop her. She talked, you couldn't stop her.

"And so you're Mr. Steele!" she said, laughing and saying it as though she'd heard all about me, which she hadn't. I was getting nervous.

"Miss Tyling," I said, "it's just that I forgot a couple of cards and—"

"Why, of course," she said, those big white teeth gleaming at me. She held her robe coyly at the neck, and that was something that this girl shouldn't have done—act coy. She was just too big. Standing closer to her now, I realized just how big she was. She was at least two inches taller than I was, and I felt kind of skinny and washed out by comparison. Her face glowed with health, and I would have bet ten thousand dollars there wasn't one filling in any of those big white teeth. "Can I help you, Mr. Steele? But first, wouldn't you like a drink or something?" She tittered, and it was like a fog horn blowing in a wind tunnel.

"Really, no, Miss Tyling," I said. "It's just—"

"I've got a whole bottle of rye!" she said, grinning wickedly. "Just waiting—"

"The cards," I told her. "If I could just look for them."

"Why, of course, Mr. Steele! Maybe then you'd like a drink." She giggled and I shook my head a little. "Where-ever do you suppose you left them?"

"In the bedroom, I think—"

"In the bedroom!" She giggled again, those eyes flashing brilliantly at me from behind the lenses of her glasses.

"If you don't mind," I said, motioning towards the bedroom.

"Of course not!" she whooped. I hurried into the bedroom, and could tell by the trembling of the floor that she was right behind me.

"The top bureau drawer," I said, moving towards it.

She jumped ahead of me, almost knocking me down. "Let me!" She outweighed me too. And there wasn't anything too soft about her. Just big.

She opened that drawer, pulled up a handful of lingerie, went into another war whoop, stuffed it back, then began searching. "No," she said, "but maybe you'd better try, Mr. Steele. We'll both look."

I stuck my hand in that drawer and searched for where the cards ought to have been. They weren't there. She bumped hands with me in the process, and I realized that she'd moved right next to me. "I'm afraid not," I said.

Then her robe opened at the neck as the result of her taking her hand away from it, producing a rather gigantic falling out effect. I averted my eyes. Miss Tyling whooped again, only this time it was laughter, and I realized she now had hold of one of my hands.

"Miss Tyling—" I began. I was really getting nervous. "Really, Miss Tyling—"

I tried to turn and move away, only she'd let the bathrobe go completely now and was hanging onto my hand like a drowning swimmer. I accidentally stepped on her robe, tripped, and I really don't know what happened then. She fell into me, whooping away, wrestling with me, shouting, "Why, Mr. Steele!" Whooping again. And the next thing I knew I'd been thrown on the bed. "Why, Mr. Steele!" she yelled once again. "Whatever are you doing!"

I wasn't doing a damn thing, except getting thrown around the room like a sack of potatoes. She was all flying robe and natural accessories. I tried to crawl off the bed. "Look, Miss Tyling—" But she'd gotten to me again, and we were all scrambled up and I suddenly realized that she had a hammer-lock on me. I did a half roll to the right and got out of it.

"Why, Mr. *Steele*," she was yelling, flinging herself at me again. "What are you trying to do!"

I was trying to get to the door, was what I was doing. The croupier and Freddie and Billy the Kid were nothing compared to Miss Tyling. This was really dangerous. She'd gotten both arms around my middle now, and was squeezing the breath right out of me.

"You just stop, Mr. Steele!" she yelled.

Stop what? I wasn't doing anything but turning purple.

She eased up for just a moment, regrouping herself, and I did the only thing I could do. I made a dive straight off the bed and took off for the door.

"Mr. Steele!" she hooted, thundering after me, "you're just a devil, aren't you?" She roared with laughter. I grabbed my bag and went out the door to the hall and down the steps to the street. I didn't stop until I'd gotten to the end of the block.

I was sweating and my hands were trembling. I half expected her to come hurtling out of the apartment house and down the street after me, but she didn't. I lit a cigarette, trying to hold the match steady. I let my nerves calm a little, then walked down the street towards the Green Lamp. I noticed a cab parked a few doors down from my former apartment house, but I paid no attention. I was wondering what in hell Byrd was trying to pull?

I was still wondering when I got to the Green Lamp, because Mike promptly greeted me by saying, "Why, hello there, Mr. Byrd. Back again?"

I walked over to the bar. "Take another look, Mike. I realize the resemblance is—"

But he interrupted. "Hey, Dolly. Mr. Byrd's back!"

"Tommy!" Dolly exclaimed, coming towards me.

Okay, I figured. The resemblance was closer than I'd thought. But I didn't talk like him, didn't act like him and was heavier. I was also getting sick and tired of being called by his name. "Never mind about Byrd," I said. "This is Mark Steele."

Dolly blinked her lashes at me. "Tommy, what are you going on about? Mike, I'll bet Tommy's a little drunk. I'm a little drunk too, Tommy. Let's have a drink, shall we?"

"This is pretty funny," I said. "A real gag. See how I'm laughing?"

"Tommy," Dolly said, "you're playing a game, aren't you? Tommy's playing a game, Mike."

"You're a card, Mr. Byrd," Mike said.

"I know," I said. "I know. I'm a cut-up. I am also Mark Steele. Did you folks ever hear of a Mark Steele, engineer, just back from Arabia? Look, I just want to know one thing. Has Thomas Byrd been in here—?"

"Tommy," Dolly laughed. "What a riot! What kind of a game is it? Mike, Tommy wants to know if he's been in here?"

Mike grinned. "Sure, Mr. Byrd. You've been in here. You're here right now."

I tried to make up my mind whether to reach over and bust him or call a doctor for him. I decided to be patient. Maybe they'd both been drinking.

"Look," I said, "games I love. Charades, kick the can, checkers, you name it. But not just this moment. Right now I want to get across one small point. I'm Mark Steele—"

"He's Mark Steele!" Dolly said happily. "That's the game, Mike. He wants to play Who Am I! Who Am I, Mike?"

"Let's see. Greta Garbo?"

Dolly giggled. "And Mike is Frank Sinatra. Tommy's Mark Steele. And I'm Greta Garbo."

I walked out of there and stood on the street, thinking how unfunny this was. I couldn't figure out exactly what was going on, but Byrd had apparently had his hand in here too. He'd talked Dolly and Mike—or hired them—into that routine. But exactly why?

So far it looked as though he'd done everything he could to eliminate the identity of Mark Steele. And he'd done a pretty good job of it. Dolly said I was Byrd. Mike said I was Byrd. And they were the only two I'd gotten to know in this city. I hadn't been able to find those identification cards of mine. Byrd had gotten those, and done so very simply by reversing things and palming himself off as me. Moreover, I figured he might not stop there. He knew my background pretty well, and he had my identification. He could go right on being me, and in the process wipe out my ability to identify myself. But *why?*

The only one who could answer that was brother Thomas Byrd himself, and I was going to find him and get it out of him if I had to go to Tibet to do it. If he figured to leave me holding the bag for one hundred G's and skip completely, he was crazy. If Nicole's boys had made good the ride on the desert, it might have worked. Still, I didn't figure that was all of it. Byrd had a fortune coming up in eight months through inheritance—he wouldn't permanently skip with that kind of money coming in. So what the hell was he doing?

Well, brother Byrd had the answer, and I was going after him. But where was he now? I remembered that redhead he'd brought along to the train when we'd left San Francisco. Maybe she could help. But I didn't even know her name.

Somehow, I doubted he'd be in San Francisco. And I didn't figure he was still in Reno either. Not with Nicole's crowd there. The most logical place, it seemed to me, was his home. Los Angeles—Beverly Hills, to be exact. It was so obvious, maybe he would figure nobody would think of it. I made up my mind. It would keep me moving and I had to stay ahead of Nicole's hired guns. I would make the trip down the coast and maybe net my very odd pigeon. All I had to do was stay alive in the meantime.

I saw a cab approaching, thought briefly about trying further to establish my own identity. Then I thought about Nicole's crowd somewhere just back of me. I wanted to get to Byrd and I decided I'd better do it while I was still breathing. I flagged the cab down, remembering briefly that other cab I'd seen close to my former apartment house. I stepped back instinctively. Nick Nicole, I was thinking. One of his hoods in the approaching cab....

But as it slowed, I could see there was nobody inside but the cabbie. I got in fast and said, "Southern Pacific Station."

As we cruised towards downtown San Francisco, I looked back. There was the same brand of cab behind us, but I couldn't tell if it was following. San Francisco is a big city. There are a lot of cabs that look alike in it and....

When I reached the station, I was beginning to feel very damned tired. I'd been knocked around most of the day, and that wrestling match with Miss Tyling had just about finished me. I got a bedroom on the Lark for Los Angeles. I got it in my own name. An hour later, after a huge steak, I crawled into my berth and went out.

I slept instantly but I had nightmares. I kept dreaming about Linda Amory sitting on that bar in my suite at the Plateau. She would hold up that nylon-sheathed leg, and the minute she would, somebody would sap me just over my right ear. That repeated a couple of dozen times. And then the scene shifted.

Julie was nibbling on the lobe of my right ear now, and I was sitting on the floor of that barn. Julie was asking to go up to my room, and this time I said all right. We rode in her Cadillac, only instead of roads we were driving over pink clouds. And instead of my hotel suite, it turned out to be a gigantic bedroom with a bed the size of an ordinary living room. I went to the window and looked out at Freddie and Billy the Kid and the croupier all standing down in what looked to be a courtyard. They waved at me happily. I held up my hands like a boxer who had won the fight and waved back at them. Then I looked at Julie in the bed, a sheet pulled up to her chin, smiling at me. I walked over and kissed her, only when I looked at her up close it wasn't Julie, it was Linda.

"Darling," she said, and I put my arms around her and it wasn't Linda any more, it was Miss Tyling. I made a dive for the door and Miss Tyling tackled me. I kept crawling and struggling but it wasn't any use. She had her arms around me, squeezing, and I was gasping for breath, running out of air fast....

I woke up, certain I was choking to death, and sweating like I'd just done the mile in four minutes. I got up and shook my head. I looked at my watch. It was five after six and we were just pulling out of Santa Barbara.

I washed and shaved, then walked to the dining car and ordered black coffee and breakfast. A large breakfast. Despite the steak the night before, I was starved. After all, I'd just wrestled with Miss Tyling.

Sipping at the black coffee, waiting for the food, I tried to think. Everything now seemed confused and unreasonable, but I was certain that as far as brother Thomas Byrd was concerned, there was nothing confused or unreasonable about it at all.

My breakfast arrived, and I put the thoughts out of my mind. I always hated to think before breakfast. I was going to enjoy this food....

I didn't. I was one quarter through when two people came into the dining car. The first was a dignified looking man in glasses who wore a dark suit and matching Homburg; he carried a small black bag in his right hand. My mouth went dry, and my appetite diminished suddenly. Reno airport. The plane, Now here....

He sat down at a table at the opposite end of the car, his back to me. He had never looked at me once, not since I'd bumped squarely into him at Reno. I studied his back, the carefully brushed, graying hair exposed when he removed the Homburg. He looked precisely like the medical specialist or the banker I'd thought about when I'd first seen him. Nicole's man? He didn't look that part but....

I thought back to the moment when I'd come out of my apartment house, running from the eager Miss Tyling. I'd seen a cab parked down the block, and the same kind of cab had been behind mine when I rode to the station in San Francisco.

But if he was Nicole's man, why hadn't he acted before? He'd had a dozen chances to gun me down and hadn't. He was merely around—Reno, the airplane, this train, and he never so much as looked at me. Maybe it was a coincidence, I told myself, but I was far from convinced.

The second person was moving in my direction. He wore a blue sport coat and gray slacks and a gray sport shirt buttoned at the throat. It wasn't so much what he wore, though, it was what he carried under his arm—a Santa Barbara newspaper. He sat down at my table, nodded politely to me, wrote out his order, then opened the paper. Something caught his eyes on the back page, and he lifted the paper, pointing the front page straight at me.

It was like aiming a double-barreled shotgun and firing both chambers point-blank in my face.

Staring directly out of that newspaper was Thomas Byrd—it was like looking at a picture of myself.

I looked at the picture of Thomas Byrd; I looked at the picture next to it and the caption beneath it: *Gosset Byrd.* I read the headlines and the sub-heads and a part of the news story. Gosset Byrd was dead. Murdered, in fact. He'd been murdered yesterday at about the time he'd had a meeting with his nephew, Thomas Byrd. Thomas Byrd had, however, disappeared. There had been an argument over gambling and money, Thomas Byrd's wife had admitted. She did not know where her husband was....

10

The man across from me brought the paper down, turned it around, glanced absently at that front page, then folded it as his breakfast arrived. He grinned at me. "Beautiful day, isn't it?" he said.

"It really is," I said, paying my check. "Absolutely beautiful."

I left, certain a thousand pairs of eyes were on me. I visualized that smiling man with the newspaper jumping up the minute I walked out of the dining car, grabbing the conductor and pointing wildly at the picture of Byrd. I visualized the train being brought to a thundering stop at the next station and police charging aboard. But nothing like that happened, and I was back in my compartment.

There I looked at my face in the mirror. I'd owned that face for thirty-four years now. I was suddenly very damned irritated that Thomas Byrd had the nerve to own one like it. Then I sat down, trying to shake my brain clear. All right, so I looked like twin brother Byrd. But that was the end of it. I wasn't brother Byrd, and I could prove it to the police. My fingerprints certainly weren't Byrd's, and my fingerprints were on record. Driver's license, passport, Army—a half dozen places those prints had been put on record. Was Byrd completely stupid?

It was pretty clear now what he was trying to do. He'd simply worked out a very precise scheme to use me as a mark. My mind whirled back over everything that had happened so far. Byrd arriving in Reno. Byrd leaving Reno. Byrd returning to Reno. He'd worked it out very smoothly. Leaving San Francisco openly in the first place, then getting on that train to Reno from Sacramento. Even calling that one time to tell me to stay out of sight for the day because friends of his were expecting to arrive in Reno, friends who, aside from the chance appearance of Duckie boy, never appeared. Stupid?

Not stupid, but very well planned.

I'd been out of sight for the day, yesterday, to everyone but Julie, Freddie and his chum, Billy. And Byrd had taken over then. As Thomas Byrd himself. With my being out of the way, he could do that. Which explained why that ticket agent at the Reno airport had said he'd seen me earlier that day—as Byrd. I could see, now, what Byrd had planned and how he'd done it.

I'd left the trail as Thomas Byrd into Reno. Yesterday morning, when Byrd told me to stay out of sight, he picked that trail up. As Thomas Byrd. He'd gone out in full view to the Reno airport and taken a plane home to Beverly Hills—the flight, I figured, would take about two and a half hours. There he'd killed Uncle Gosset. Then he'd taken a plane back to Reno. All very obviously. Then he'd told me on the telephone to go right on playing his part. Because after that last telephone call to me, he'd disappeared and I was left holding the bag.

Nicole's boys, Byrd figured, would get to me just as soon as they found out that the check was no good. Nicole's boys, Byrd figured, would knock me off and leave me on some stretch of wasteland while the desert buzzards circled. What then? Thomas Byrd, wanted for the murder of his uncle, would be found dead on the desert. But the corpse would be me, complete with Byrd's identification. The investigation would prove Byrd, murderer of his uncle, had been in trouble with illegal gamblers and threatened with death by them. So dead he would be, and you can't prosecute a dead man for murder.

And Byrd would have it made. The only live people who knew about him having a twin brother, it appeared, were Mike and Dolly, whom he'd obviously paid off to keep quiet. I figured if they would accept a pay-off, then they would also be the kind who would be around later trying to shake Byrd down to go on keeping quiet. Byrd must have thought of that, and I had a chilly feeling that he had the same kind of plans for them that he'd had for Uncle Gosset, who was the only other person who knew about Byrd's twin brother, and who was now dead. With Uncle out of the way, and no doubt Mike and Dolly to follow, Byrd could simply go on living as me, Mark Steele, go right on his happy way. Neat—except one thing had gone wrong in his plans: I was still alive.

My forehead was beaded with sweat as I thought how it would have been if Freddie and Billy had made it and taken me on that run into the desert. I thought about how Byrd had cold-bloodedly rigged this thing, and how every minute he'd been smiling at me and chattering away he'd been thinking of how well everything was going to work out when I'd been pumped full of slugs.

I wiped at the sweat and tried to think exactly why he'd bumped Uncle Gosset. I tried to remember everything my eyes had brushed over in that news story. I'd seen something about Byrd's wife claiming that Byrd and Uncle Gosset had been arguing over Byrd's gambling and mishandling of money. So there was the obvious motive. Very obvious. Like everything else had been made perfectly obvious. There would be no doubt about pinning the murder on the corpse which was supposed to have been found in Nevada and identified as Thomas Byrd—me.

But what had Byrd's whole motive been? Maybe pretty much what the police already thought—but maybe with something added: money. If Uncle died, who got the money? Byrd? Only Byrd had killed his uncle, and Byrd couldn't collect in the gas chamber. And he couldn't collect if he was found dead on the desert. So if Byrd was going to go in life as me, Mark Steele, who would get Uncle's money then? Byrd's wife?

No doubt. Byrd wouldn't give up a fortune just for the pleasure of killing Uncle Gosset. He had a lot more in it than that. I was certain what he had in it was money.

So he had to have help. And the only one, it seemed to me, who could help was his wife. I couldn't be sure of that but it seemed reasonable. And so I was, I thought, traveling in the right direction by heading for his home in Beverly Hills. If anybody had a contact with Byrd now, wherever he was, it should be his wife....

Just then I heard someone in the corridor. I looked up just in time to see the man in the Homburg hat go past the curtain I'd left slightly open. I was getting spooky. But why not? I'd gotten away from Nicole's boys temporarily, but they were after me, I knew. And how about Byrd? He'd expected me to be gunned by now, but he would know from police reports—which would start coming in now that they had discovered Uncle Gosset dead—that I'd been seen in Reno, seen taking a plane to San Francisco, seen appearing at my old apartment, and the rest of it as the police trailed along somewhere behind me figuring me to be Byrd. Even though I'd used my own name in San Francisco, I still met Byrd's description.

I wondered how far the police were behind me right now. I wondered how far behind me everybody was, including Nicole's hoods, or maybe even Thomas Byrd himself—the only way Byrd's plans were going to work out now would be if I were dead—as he'd originally planned it. Otherwise I might establish my real identity with the police and Byrd would be left to take the rap for killing his uncle.

At that moment I began to wish the police had already caught up with me. I could clear the whole thing with them right now. But they hadn't caught up with me and they weren't available on this train. And so I wasn't going to clear up anything until I got to them or they got to me. Which meant I had to live that long. If I were gunned in the meantime, Byrd still won his gamble.

I stood up and walked to the curtain, holding it aside just in time to see the man with the Homburg enter a compartment at the other end of the car. I stepped back inside my own room and thought about it. Nicole's man? If so, I couldn't even get to the conductor for help if the man wanted to stop me.

I opened my bag and took out the gun Freddie had owned, the gun I'd taken away from him in my room. I shoved the barrel between my shirt and belt, buttoned my jacket, and walked down the corridor. I hesitated only a moment outside the compartment, then pushed the curtain aside and stepped in.

He'd taken the Homburg off, and his hair was brushed neatly. He seemed neatly brushed all over; the suit was immaculate and expensive; his face was very close-shaven and faintly talcumed. His hands were white and the trimmed nails were glossed from buffing. He looked at me, and his glasses—framed over the tops, rimless below —were polished to such a high luster that they sparkled against the light coming in from the window, sparkled so much I could not define his eyes behind the lenses.

"Yes?" he said. His voice was impersonal, though softly polite. He didn't move a muscle, only looked at me from behind those sparkling lenses. He rested his trim hands gently on his knees, his black bag resting just beside him. If the occasionally spectacled Freddie had looked deceivingly like a cheap clerk, this gentleman looked like the president of the corporation who paid his salary. And I still didn't know if the look was, as with Freddie, one of deceit. I held my own right hand just in front of my buttoned jacket and asked, "What does Nicole mean to you?"

I don't know just what I hoped to get in the way of reaction. His facial expression didn't change. I couldn't see any perceptible change in his eyes because of those polished glasses.

"Nicole?" he said softly. "Nicole? No, nothing, I'm afraid."

"You never heard of him?"

He lifted the trim hands slightly, dropped them back on his knees. "Not that I recall. Of course—"

"Let's not fool around any more," I said angrily.

"Fool around? I'm afraid there's some mistake."

"No mistake, friend. You come from Nicole."

He wagged his head ever so slightly. "I wish to be polite, but your tone is rather abusive." He lifted a hand, moving it toward the buzzer that would summon the porter.

"No," I said. I didn't want him ringing in the porter, then the conductor, to have me kicked out of his compartment where I couldn't see what he was going to do next. I wanted the advantage of having him alone and in front of me where I could watch him every minute until I had straight who he really was.

He kept the hand in midair, then lowered it again.

"You are threatening, sir?"

"I'm just telling you not to ring the buzzer."

He smiled very slightly. "This is all very confusing, I'm afraid."

"What's your name?" I asked.

He brought his hands away from his knees, brought them back and put them gently on the seat on either side of him.

"Craywell," he said. "Joseph T. Craywell."

"All right, Craywell," I said, "if you don't work for Nicole, who then?"

He motioned with those hands, by simply turning them palms up. "I'm with Horn, Jones and Craywell, an investment house. I work, of course, for myself. I'm afraid you've made some mistake in identity."

"I don't think I have," I snapped. "I think you have."

This time he'd tipped his head slightly, so that I saw past his lenses. His eyes were a cold, pale gray. Once again his left hand was moving for that buzzer.

"I told you," I warned. His hand stopped, returned. The other hand still rested, palm up on the seat cushion.

"I'm afraid," he said, "you've made an error. If you'll allow me to show you—"

Now the right hand was moving inside his jacket, and this time it didn't move slowly.

"Hold it!" I snapped, and pulled the gun from under my jacket.

He froze, staring at that gun, lenses sparkling.

"Bring your hand out slowly." If I'd made a mistake, there was going to be hell to pay later. But I was no fast-draw artist, which he would be if he was Nicole's man. I had to have the gun out and on him to get at least an even break.

He removed his hand from inside his jacket slowly. He kept watching my gun. "Is this robbery, sir?"

"No. "

"I was merely going to show you my identification."

"Okay. Open your jacket. Slowly."

He did as he was ordered.

"Hold it out. Both sides." He used his left hand to turn one side out, then the other. He was wearing no shoulder holster, and the jacket was too flat to hold a gun in an inner pocket.

"All right," I said, "let's see the identification."

He drew out a wallet with that left hand, shook it open, revealing a series of cards held in a plastic file.

"Toss it over."

He did. I glanced at the cards. *Joseph T. Craywell. Horn, Jones and Craywell.* They all looked legitimate and they all backed up his statement.

I tossed the wallet back to him.

"You got on at Reno," I said.

"I had business in Reno."

"You flew to San Francisco, then got on this same train with me. Why?"

"I had a short business call to make in San Francisco." He smiled a little. "Is it so unusual to have business in three cities—Reno, San Francisco, Los Angeles—"

I was beginning to believe that maybe he was who he said he was. Still, I'd been so certain that Nicole would never have let me—or rather Byrd—get away. Maybe Nicole had planned merely to send a man to Beverly Hills to stake out Byrd's house....

And just at that moment I realized his right hand had moved farther to the right, had snaked towards that black bag, had inched up to the handle of that black bag. Now I saw that hand fly into action.

It was the fastest human motion I'd ever seen, like the flick of a cat's paw. The bag was flying open and the hand was dipping inside, but I had already moved. I used my right toe. I kicked straight out, aiming at that flash of moving hand. I struck the target just as the hand came out with a snub-nosed .38 caliber revolver. The revolver flew across the seat and bounced onto the floor. Craywell grunted slightly but didn't seem to change expression. He raised the hand slightly, then started lowering it once more.

"You're not that foolish," I told him.

He pulled the hand away.

"Shove the bag across the seat, away from you," I said.

He did. I moved to pick up the revolver. It was loaded. I looked in the bag and saw an odd-looking kind of pistol, also a .38, but long-barreled. It was clamped into the bottom of the case, and that barrel was nearly the length of the case. There were two telescopic sights clamped to the lid of the case. There were several boxes of ammunition. I looked at him once more, at the neat, polished, brushed look of him. He must have been the best-dressed, most respectable-looking gunman in the business.

"Just how does this tie in with the investment business?" I asked.

He smiled slightly. "You have quick reflexes, Mr.— " He motioned with his hands. "I'm afraid I'm not sure of your real name. You're not Thomas Byrd, however, are you?"

"You know that?" I asked.

"I suspected it," he said. "For several reasons. Starting when you gave the croupier a rather severe beating."

"The croupier is a lousy fighter."

"I acknowledge that as a possibility. But this is not true with the other two emissaries we sent to deal with you. Your actions seemed to belie those of a man of Byrd's background. A gentleman like Thomas Byrd would, I think, have trouble with even our croupier, not to mention the skilled professionals you left in a rather deplorable state in your hotel suite."

"So Nicole figured I wasn't Byrd? Then why—"

"Not Nicole. Nicole has good judgment about finances. He's quite a solid earner all around but he is no judge of people. I'm giving you my own impressions. I had a short talk with Julie. Her impressions of you led me to think I was working in the correct direction. Moreover, you left a card in your bureau. I have it—"

He got it out of his wallet, and I saw it was the card I'd forgotten in my wallet, then removed and put in the bureau in the hotel suite.

"Let's see—Mark Steele, is that correct? Is that your real name?"

I saw no reason to deny it. I wanted very much, in fact, to confirm it. "That's right," I said.

He nodded, smiling a little, as though pleased he'd been right in his assumptions.

"So all right," I said, "you see how it stands now. You and Nicole are after the wrong pigeon. Thomas Byrd is your man, and I'm not Thomas Byrd."

"So it seems," he smiled. "But apparently there is a rather amazing similarity in looks. Blood possibly?"

"Possibly," I said. "Twins, to be exact."

"Yes," he said softly. "But the point is you made a very great effort to convince us you were Byrd—"

"I did," I said. "Until a few days ago, I'd never heard of brother Byrd. He looked me up for this job. I was supposed to bring the payoff down to fifty grand for him, which I did, and keep ten. Sixty G's was all he had, he told me. The mistake I made was believing that Byrd had money banked to cover that check I gave your boys."

"Ah, yes. We all believed that, didn't we?"

"At least," I said, "we understand each other now. So the big impersonation is over. When we pull into L.A., I'm going to make sure it's over. I'm getting a little sick of being a patsy for brother Byrd. Particularly—"

"Particularly," he finished, "in the light of the newest developments—the death of his uncle?"

"You know about that?"

"I knew about it last night when I telephoned Nicole—the news had just been released on the radio."

"Then you know what I'm going to do in Los Angeles?"

"And what is that?"

"Turn you over to the Los Angeles police, for one thing. Give them the full story, for another. And get my own identification straight with them."

He nodded agreeably, glasses sparkling, hands resting easily on his knees. "I think not," he said.

"You think not? You think wrong, friend."

"I'll show you something." He reached into the left-hand inner pocket of his jacket and drew out a telegram. He held it out toward me. I took it and read it, switching my eyes back and forth between Craywell and the telegram: FOUND OUT ABOUT SUBJECT'S INTEREST IN GIRL NAMED LINDA AMORY. MAY BE LEVERAGE. DO YOU ADVISE PICKING UP?

"Nicole, as you see, thought she might be useful," Craywell, or whatever the hell his name was, said. "I thought so too. I advised picking her up. She has been, by now."

I tried to keep my voice calm. "Useful for what?"

"To begin with, to prevent you turning me over to the L.A. police." He smiled contentedly.

"That's to begin with," I said.

"To begin with," he repeated.

I paused, then said, "So I keep your artillery and tell you to take off the minute we hit Los Angeles. You're out of it then."

He laughed this time, quietly and gently. "I have a feeling you're rather attached to this girl."

"You could be wrong."

"True. But that's easy to find out."

"Like how?"

"Like getting funny with us. You see, I always work as carefully as I can. In addition to wiring Nicole to pick up the girl, I also wired him that if I didn't check with him by telephone every twelve hours ... well, he should then go ahead with the girl. Nicole's quite astute about business affairs, but he is also dogmatic about certain things. Unpaid debts, for example. About such matters, he has a tendency to become emotional."

"Meaning?"

"Meaning if he can't get satisfaction any other way, he'll get it out of the girl."

My mouth felt dry. I held the gun, but I was powerless. If they just hadn't picked Linda up ... It was no use crying about it. They had.

"You see how it is," he said gently.

"You want out, free and clear," I said. "Is that it?"

"I can settle for better than that, Steele, and you know it."

"Better?" I said.

He nodded. "I have a job to do, you see. My time is valuable, you'll have to understand that. I'm not one of Nicole's hired thugs, you know. I work for him only in special cases for quite a substantial fee. I don't like to waste time, and I don't like to lose a good fee."

"So?"

"So I don't intend to pull out of this job, and there isn't much you can do about it. I intend to find Byrd."

"Find him then!"

"While you run off to the police and tell them the particulars of this case?" He shook his head sorrowfully. "No, I'm afraid not."

He smiled, drew his hands lightly over his knees, then grasped them together.

"Byrd double-crossed you, you say," he went on. "All right. You promptly left Reno by air. I thought you might do that. I was waiting when you got to the Reno airport. You then went to San Francisco, where you disappeared into an apartment house. You then went to a bar. You then took a compartment in this train. What are you doing, Mr. Steele? I'll tell you. You're after Byrd, right? You appear to me to be the kind who dislikes being double-crossed, particularly when the double-cross involves additional complications. The check bounced, and you risked reprisal from our friend, Mr. Nicole. Now there are further complications. Byrd's uncle has been murdered. Obviously that was planned to implicate you as Byrd, correct? But only if you ended up dead."

It was the same reasoning I'd used, and I couldn't argue with it. But I said, "You're going nowhere."

"Ah, but I am," he said. "I'm going after Byrd, right behind you."

"Behind me?"

"How else?" He crossed his legs now. He seemed to ooze charm. "You see, I believe looking for Byrd by myself would be a tiresome and difficult endeavor. Obviously he has committed murder. Obviously he doesn't want to be found. He has surely worked this out for reasons other than simply committing a murder. I don't believe he did have the money necessary to meet his obligation with us. But I believe he might have worked out some method of obtaining money as the result of the murder he has committed. Is that not logical?"

"Maybe it is," I said. Again he was thinking as I had.

"All right. I would much rather leave the labor of finding Mr. Byrd to someone else, yourself, for example. The police are hard at it right now. But you have diverted them, and I suspect they are trailing after you, not Byrd. Which means that as long as they don't find you, they probably won't find Byrd. And I would rather they did not find Byrd before I do, since it's obvious that would make collection most difficult. So that leaves it up to you to reach Byrd first, does it not?"

"What if I can't find him?"

He shrugged. "I'm a businessman too, Mr. Steele. I like my profit. I never like to lose a fee. I don't intend to in this case. If you don't find Byrd that means I don't find him either. I might have to settle for you, in that case."

"You're crazy!" I said.

"That's the one thing I'm not, Mr. Steele. I could have been a number of things in this world. I'm well educated. I have a taste for culture and have developed that taste. But I ... chose this—"

"Why?" I broke in.

He smiled at me. The gentle, polite, charming smile. He was poised, correct, cultivated. "I like killing, Mr. Steele. And I like the rewards it pays me."

Kris, in that Yellow Tiger Club, had reminded me of a rattlesnake. I think I would have preferred a dozen rattlesnakes to this one....

"But," he said, "I'm not crazy, Mr. Steele. Indeed, I'm not." He shifted a little. "Look at it this way. You want to find Byrd because he tried to arrange your death. On the other hand, I'm sure Byrd would like very much to know where you are—because until you're dead, he is in, shall we say, a rather awkward situation. I'm sure he would like very much to see you dead and quickly, Mr. Steele. I believe sooner or later your path and his must cross. I wish to be there when that happens."

I stared at him grimly. "You said you might have to settle for me—"

"True," he nodded. "My fee will be paid if Byrd is eliminated. I think you would suffice, so long as your identity remains that of Byrd. Byrd will never refute it. It will suffice for Nicole because he does not have my verification of your real identity. However, my fee is proportionately higher if I am able to get a substantial amount of money in place of what amounts to a simple revenge killing. This lacks the excitement of my specialty, but I always lean towards money. So, you see? I wish to get to Mr. Byrd, simply because I believe he may, under duress, pay this overdue obligation; and I don't believe you're capable of that."

The train rolled down the coast. Outside, white-crested breakers of the Pacific were moving into the sand of the beach towns north of Malibu. The sun was up now and the sky was blue. It was a beautiful day in Southern California. And I'd had it. I'd really had it. I kept thinking of Linda, of the blue eyes and tanned body. But I thought, too, of how the physical desire had shifted to something deeper the last time I'd seen her.

Now Nicole had her....

Craywell was watching me behind his sparkling glasses. "You may as well put the gun away, Mr. Steele. You must surely be tired of holding it on me, and guns pointed in my direction do make me nervous."

He was right. Holding the gun on him was pointless now. I slid it back between my shirt and belt. He reached over and picked up the snub-nosed .38 and returned it to the black case, then snapped down the lid.

I had one last thought before I left him—I could skip looking for Byrd and go straight for Nicole, convince him that I was not Byrd and get Linda out of this, maybe along with my own life. But I threw that out. Getting to Nicole by myself would be almost impossible. I might be gunned on sight by one of the others of his organization. I had a feeling Craywell was the smartest of them, smart enough not to have shot me on sight. But in the long run, I was certain, he was also the most dangerous.

No, there was only one way for me to go now—to Byrd, if I could find him. I also wanted him for some special, personal reasons. He'd cold-bloodedly set me up for a skinful of bullets. Moreover, until I got to him and restored my own identity, Craywell would not be off my back. And since that was the case, until I got Craywell diverted to the right man, Linda would be in ugly trouble up to her pretty neck. I *had* to get to brother Thomas Byrd.

"We'll be arriving pretty soon," Craywell said to me. "I will, of course, expect your co-operation. I'll be following you, and I would advise that you not try to lose me. It would be very simple for me to place a telephone call to Nicole at any time relative to the disposition of the girl."

"What if I'm picked up by the cops?" I said.

He smiled at me. "I think that would be very unwise of you, Mr. Steele. I wouldn't recommend that you make an error like that, not if you really care about your girl."

"Any other orders?" I snapped bitterly.

He shook his head pleasantly. "No. And now, if you don't mind, Mr. Steele—"

I returned to my own compartment, congratulating myself on the beautiful way I'd handled everything; if I'd been in trouble before, it was nothing to the way things were now. We were rolling into Los Angeles, and I tried to calm myself. I was still brother Thomas Byrd, whether I liked it or not, whether I cared to keep up the impersonation or not. I was brother Thomas Byrd on the run, because all I had were his identification cards, because if any trail was being picked up by the cops, it was my trail. No doubt several reports had been picked up by now. They had surely traced my flight to San Francisco. I'd used my own name when I bought this compartment, but they would be working on descriptions ... and if they did get to me, well, Craywell had made it clear what would happen to Linda. I had no good reason to doubt him.

The train was slowing now, moving into the unloading tracks of Union Station. I kept the gun under my jacket. I checked the mirror. The gun didn't show. Then I picked up my bag and moved into the aisle. The porter reached for the bag, but I wouldn't give it to him; I didn't want to wait for baggage distribution in the station. I looked down the aisle. Craywell had appeared, looking like the successful banker or surgeon, carrying his little black case. He didn't look at me, just smiled faintly at some inner joke; I knew what the joke was—me.

11

I checked the platform. People were swarming off the train and I moved with them, searching. I couldn't see anyone that looked like a cop. I took a breath and kept moving into the ramp, a long, concrete tunnel with smaller wings leading to the various trains. I looked down the length of the main ramp. Then I saw them—a duet, dressed in business suits, snap-brim hats and looking very much like cops.

I looked to my left; Craywell was moving along briskly. I edged over and bumped into him, looking at the same time at the ramp leading to a loading Las Vegas streamliner. I thought of Linda again. I looked up ahead at those cops. And at the same time I had nearly upset Craywell by bumping into him.

"I beg your pardon," I said. Then, whispering, I added, "Carry my bag up."

I couldn't see his eyes behind those lenses, and I didn't wait to get his response. I simply turned abruptly and headed down the ramp to the Las Vegas train.

On the platform there was a trio of young men who had obviously been up all night and were seeing someone off. It was a role I'd hoped to get into myself when I'd given the bag to Craywell—in order to keep those cops at the head of the ramp concentrating on incoming passengers instead of people who were merely saying good-by to the departing. The trio was waving at a couple inside the train, a young man and a woman. The man was grinning foolishly and was obviously drunk. He held up a bottle, motioning with it at the three men on the platform. The woman, a blowzy looking redhead, took the bottle from him and drank from it. She had an eye tooth missing. The trio on the platform cheered. They were also laughing. One of them was laughing so hard tears were rolling down his cheeks. Then he started singing, "Here comes the bride …"

"Good luck, Harry!" one of the trio shouted.

Harry grinned stupidly, then slowly disappeared under the window. A moment later, he pulled himself up to look out again, still grinning. The blowzy redhead kissed him and drank from the bottle again.

"By God," one of the trio whooped, "he'll do it. He'll sure as hell do it!"

"Good old Harry," one of them said. "What a great marriage!"

I decided to be an actor again. "Why," I said, "that's Harry!"

They looked at me. "You know Harry?"

"Do I know Harry! Old Harry?"

Much laughter. "Harry's getting married!"

"Married!" I said.

"To the ugliest waitress of the dirtiest, stinkingest bar we could find on Main Street."

"You're kidding!" I said. "Hey, Harry!" I was waving at him too. Harry tried to wave back, only he disappeared under the window again. The blowzy redhead pulled him up by the back of his collar.

"Wait'll he comes to and finds that next to him!" one of the trio shouted.

"Wait'll his pappy finds out!" another yelled.

The redhead was still guzzling out of that bottle; she was, indeed, a sight. The trio was roaring again. And then the train was pulling out. Harry disappeared once more, then came up again with the assistance of the bride-to-be. He waved happily.

"Good luck, Harry!" I shouted. I was thinking what a great sense of humor this trio had. One of them put his arm around my shoulder. "Good luck, Harry! Good old Harry!" I yelled. We were all arms over shoulders now, heading back down the ramp. One of them again started singing, "Here comes the bride …" and I joined him. We were one hell of a quartet. We sang all the way to the main ramp. The cops were still there, I saw. I stayed right with the trio, arm in arm with them, singing my lungs out. We went by the plainclothes cops. They wouldn't bother us, I knew, but at any second one of L.A.'s uniformed cops would.

I disengaged myself in the lobby and took off fast, listening to them calling after me. I got out of sight and into the washroom. I could still hear that singing echoing through the place.

I stood beside a long row of wash basins, thinking about what to do next, when I saw one of the plainclothes cops coming in. I unloosened my tie, turned on a faucet, and ducked my head down, splashing water onto my face. When I finally came up for air, he was gone.

I walked back to the lobby. Craywell was not in sight, and I called him a few choice names. He had me sewed up so tight he could do almost anything he wanted, and I had to go along.

I rounded the corner and looked down the length of that waiting room—no Craywell. There was a newsstand just to my left. I stepped in and bought three late newspapers, looking at Byrd's picture on the front page of all three. I checked the clerk's eyes when I gave her the change. She smiled brightly. I left and walked down that part of the lobby to the opposite end, then turned right and found Craywell. He was sitting in a telephone booth—making his twelve-hour check with Nicole. It was just ten o'clock now.

My bag was resting outside the booth. I walked over and picked it up, listening to the booth open as I walked away. I walked away fast, figuring I'd make it as unpleasant as possible for Craywell to follow me. It was small balm, however. I felt as though ten thousand eyes were on me—and every pair belonged to a cop. I kept thinking about Linda. I kept thinking about Byrd. I was getting awfully anxious to get to Mr. Thomas Byrd.

Nobody stopped me. I kept on walking, right out of the station. I walked up the street to Sunset Boulevard and paced it as fast as I could. I could picture Craywell puffing behind me. It was a pleasure to think I was inconveniencing him even slightly. Then I turned right and headed into one of the toughest-looking neighborhoods I'd seen since I'd been at the edge of the Casbah.

I found a dive called City Hotel. The lobby was little more than the stairwell. There was a registration desk in the middle of it, and a door opened into the adjoining bar where a juke box thumped away with Latin-American music. I still had my shirt loose at the collar, but I knew I was conspicuous in the expensive suit. I was eyed by the short, extraordinarily fat, black-eyed woman at the desk. I was eyed by the kid who lounged at the doorway to the bar, a loosely built, skinny kid of eighteen or nineteen with a dark face and great quantities of greased black hair combed back at the temples and ducktailed in the rear. Despite the variance of weight distribution between them, they looked like mother and son; and I would have bet my citizenship that either would have knifed the other for a few bucks.

It looked like a good place, though, to cool out until dark. I didn't feel like walking around in daylight with a picture that looked just like I did blazed across every front page of every newspaper in town—and it pleased me to know Craywell would have to stick around this area too. I looked back and saw him puffing along the street, lugging his black case. He would have looked comic to me, if I hadn't known better.

I glanced at the dark bar on the other side of the doorway and approached the woman behind the desk. "Room, please," I said.

Her black eyes looked me over. The kid with the greased hair looked me over. The woman didn't answer.

"Have you got a room?" I asked. "I thought this was a hotel."

"Why, mister?" she asked.

"Why? What difference does it make?"

She looked over my good suit and shrugged. "Ten dollars."

I frowned at her. "Ten bucks? For a room here?"

"Take it or leave it. Ten dollars. In advance."

I got out my wallet and gave her the ten, and I could see both her eyes and those of the ducktail switch hungrily to that wallet. I'd forgotten about having that big sheaf of bills in there. I put down another ten bucks. "I need some liquor. Bourbon. Bonded."

She kept looking at me, but motioned one of her chubby hands at the ducktail. "Son, get the man a bottle of bourbon. Bonded, Miguel."

She pushed a dirty register pad at me. I signed my name as John Parcell.

"Okay," I said. "I don't want to be disturbed for any reason."

"This isn't the Biltmore, you know."

"I noticed that."

"You want service here, you got to pay for it." I handed her another five bucks.

"You won't be disturbed," she said.

Miguel came back with a fifth of bourbon. He handed it to me. "How about the change?" I said.

"We ain't got no bottle sales here. You got to pay bar prices. You get it cheap for ten bucks."

I felt like a big neon sign had been hung on my forehead and was flashing off and on with the word, sucker. I had one thing going for me, though. I'd thrown a little money around, and I figured money was the god here. I knew they were suspicious of me, and I couldn't be sure whether I was convincing them that I simply wanted to throw a quiet drunk away from my own neighborhood. But I was fairly certain they wouldn't deal with the police before they tried to deal with me, no matter what they thought I was doing here. I was also pretty certain they didn't read English; but I couldn't be sure, especially about Miguel, who might have been a product of the L.A. public schools. Whether or not they would find the stories on Byrd in the papers and nail me with them was a chance I had to take.

I carried the bottle of bourbon and my bag upstairs, along with the key that Miguel's kindly old mother had given me. The room looked straight into a brick wall. The shade was up, but it was still as dark as a moonless night. I didn't turn on the light. I figured my eyes would get used to the gloom, and I was afraid I'd never stay if I saw it in the full light. I wondered how Craywell was doing. It was the first really happy thought I'd had for hours.

I took my jacket off and hung it on a chair. I took the wallet out of the inner pocket and put it on the top of the bureau, where I could see it. In a joint like this I figured I ought to watch it every second. I reconsidered. I took the money out of the wallet and put it under the pillow on the bed. I removed the gun from my belt and put that under the pillow too. Then I sat down on the edge of the bed with a bottle. There were a couple of glasses by the sink in a corner, but the grime on them discouraged me. I drank from the bottle, one long drink, then lay back. I liked Scotch, but drunks generally don't use Scotch. At least it was good bourbon. I had another drink. It eased the tension. I relaxed slightly for the first time since I'd seen Craywell and that newspaper picture of Byrd on the train.

I looked at my watch. It was just eleven o'clock. I had to kill some long hours until dark. But so did Craywell, and I hoped he was miserable.

Motionless like this, I let my mind turn to Byrd. Good old brother Thomas Byrd. I thought what a cold, sadistic sonofabitch he was. I wondered how the same blood could flow in my veins as his. I wondered where he was right now. I was after him, but I knew very well he wanted me too. I simply wanted to nail him, to get to him and stop him and hand his own miserable identity back to him. I would have liked very much to clip him a few times, wipe off that sardonic smile of his. But that would be kid stuff, and nothing compared to what the talented Mr. Craywell had waiting for him.

No, I wanted to get to him to take the heat off and get Linda out of this mess and go back to the slap-happy life of Mark Steele. Byrd, like a vulture, was after only one thing—to see me dead.

I closed my eyes and tried to visualize him. Where was he? Holed up somewhere? Maybe a room just like this one? Lying on his back on a cheap bed, one drink under his belt, just waiting for a break? Waiting for me to stumble onto him so he could finish off what Nicole's pals hadn't done yet?

Or was he on my trail somewhere, not far behind? I tensed a little, thinking of that. But then I remembered Craywell downstairs. Craywell was the enemy too, but in a way he was protection. If Byrd was just behind, and he tried getting to me in this hotel, Craywell was waiting too. Craywell would nail him.

But I didn't figure Byrd going at it in that way. He was too smart. He would know Nicole's thugs were right behind me. He would know the police were right behind me too. And it would be, he would figure, too difficult to get in between and knock me off. Better, he might figure, to count on my evading the police. Better to count on my coming after him.

That, I was sure, was what he was doing. Waiting for me. Like a hunter who has stuck the ripened carcass of the pig up in the tree and is waiting for twilight and that one good moment to shoot the leopard between the spots when he finally goes for the bait.

Except instead of the ripe pig for bait, he would be counting on my so-called brain—on my working things out in my head. I was going after him, and he wanted me to so he could kill me. He wouldn't, I figured, make finding him any harder than he had to. But he did have to stay out of the hands of the police. So where was he?

He had to have an accomplice in this, and the only accomplice who could be worth anything to him—because she was going to get Uncle Gosset's money—was his wife. His wife, I figured, would have to stay home under police orders until this was cleared up. Consequently brother Byrd ought to be home too. Home in Beverly Hills, just a taxi drive away from where I was lying right now. It was so deceptively obvious that the police might have relaxed and loosened up a little and made it possible for Byrd to have gotten in there, even if they had the house fairly well covered. I thought of him there, sitting, lying down, whatever he was doing, but waiting—waiting for brother Mark to come in to be killed....

There was a knock on my door. I'd been in here ten minutes, I'd told the landlady I didn't want to be disturbed for any reason and paid her five bucks for the privilege; now somebody was knocking on the door.

I walked over, turned the key in the lock, then stepped back to the bed, near the pillow where I could get to the gun. "Okay," I said. "Come in."

12

The door opened, and a young girl with long, coal-black hair came in. She shut the door behind her. She was perhaps sixteen. She wore a black satin dress and heavy make-up. She was bare-legged, and she wore patent leather slippers. Her face had the same similarity of features that Miguel and his mother shared.

"You wanted me?" she asked.

What a sweet, lovable old family this was, I thought. What a grand, old-fashioned household. Just folks. "No, honey," I said. "I'm afraid not."

"I thought you did."

"You were wrong."

"Well," she said, crossing the room, "now that I'm here, maybe you've changed your mind."

"Actually, no."

"Why not?"

"It would take much too long to tell you, sweetheart." Her eyes flashed a little. She brought her jaw up a fraction. "You're the loser."

"I suppose I am," I said, trying to get sadness into my voice, but getting, I was sure, pity instead. "Why don't you go back and play with your friends in the sandbox? You're a little young for this."

"Go to hell, mister," she snapped, "and stay there!"

She flounced out of the room, and I relocked the door. I thought of the Plateau Hotel and compared it with this one. I thought of Linda, even Julie, and compared them to the one who'd just bounced out of the room. It was amazing how fast a man could slip when he got in with the wrong people. But it wasn't funny.

The appearance of the girl left me feeling a little old and tired and sick of humanity. I was thinking of Linda again, my nerves were beginning to go raw. If I didn't pull this thing off....

I had another drink, a short one, and stretched out on the bed with the newspapers. I read more carefully the stories of Uncle Gosset's murder, but didn't learn much more except that Byrd was the only suspect. His wife had an unbreakable alibi. There were pictures of her—a considerable dish.

I quit reading then and turned everything out of my mind. I can do that sometimes in moments of extreme tension. It's a kind of suspended state. The tension is there waiting, ready to resume when the trigger is moved a hair. But in the meantime I can usually manage to blank out.

I slept hours, flat on my back. I woke up once and checked my watch. It was four o'clock. Then I went back to sleep. The next time I woke up it wasn't just gloomy in that room, it was absolutely dark.

I couldn't see a thing. Yet, suddenly, I knew somebody else was in that room. I knew, somewhere in that unconsciousness of sleep, there had been a sound that woke me up—the turning of the key in the lock, the careful steps across the floor.

I heard the faintest creak—over by the bureau. I came off the bed fast, but not fast enough. I slammed into a chair instead of whoever was in there.

I smelled the sweet scent of cheap hair oil, grabbed to my right, caught hold of some cloth, then lost it. There was a banging of feet across the room, then the door was open and I caught just a glimpse of Miguel winging it out of there on the double. I listened to his steps moving downstairs, a door slamming, then nothing. I knew it would be useless to go after him in the maze of an unfamiliar neighborhood.

I went over and kicked the door shut. I picked up the key from the floor, where Miguel had pushed it when he'd inserted his own key from the other side, and relocked the door, wondering what good it would do.

I turned the light on and checked the bureau. The wallet was gone. I checked my watch. Six-thirty. I walked over and reknotted my tie. I put on my jacket, put my money in an inner pocket, then reinserted the gun in my belt and buttoned the jacket. I picked up my bag, and just then the key in the door fell out again, the lock clicked, and the door opened.

Mother appeared this time.

"What I like about it here," I said, "is the wonderful service. I didn't want to be disturbed, and I paid five bucks to prove it. This has been Grand Central ever since I got in here "

"What are you really doing here?" she asked.

"Not to be impolite," I said, picking up my bag, "but I repeat I don't think that's any of your business."

"You didn't want Maria," she said.

I stared at her. I'd thought it was at least Maria's own initiative, but her mother had sent her. Sweet, lovable old mom.

"You bought a bottle, but you're not drunk." She peered at the bottle, saw it was only slightly dented. "You didn't drink hardly any of it. What are you doing here?"

"I told you twice before. I don't think it's any of your business."

"You're in trouble, aren't you?"

"You're wasting your time. I'm checking out."

"I can call the police."

I examined her eyes. Apparently no one had yet read the newspapers. But Miguel had picked up my wallet. The wallet had those cards of Byrd's in it. Miguel didn't get my money, but he got something that would bring down the entire L.A. police department in a minute if he told them the name that was on those cards. I figured Mom didn't know about

Miguel's heist. She'd be using it on me if she did. This was really one of the sweetest little families I'd ever met.

"Why would you call the police?" I asked.

"You could tell me, I think. Maybe they could too, after I call them."

"So what do you want?"

"Money," she said honestly.

"So I give you money. So you call the police anyway."

"You maybe need a place to come back to. You maybe come back here. You're okay here. Safe. I like steady customers."

I took enough time to make it look like I was considering it. "How much?" I said finally.

"One hundred."

"Call the police."

"Fifty."

"I'll give you twenty, mom. Okay? And don't cross me up. You do, and I'll come back and—"

"Don't worry." She held out her hand.

I knew, of course, she was as honest as the day was long. I pulled a twenty out of the pocket and placed it in her palm. "Good-by, mother. This has been just like home."

With Miguel holding that wallet, I wanted out fast. I glanced in that dark bar as I walked through the so-called lobby. I saw Craywell there. He was the sorriest looking gunman in the world at that moment. He no longer looked so pressed and polished. Some of the dirt of the neighborhood seemed to have rubbed off on him during the past seven and a half hours.

I hurried to the street and took the first cab in sight, an old broken-down job manned by a hackie who was asleep when I came up.

He straightened and opened the door for me, and I gave him Byrd's Beverly Hills address. I leaned back. Craywell, I knew, would be following.

We traveled out Santa Monica Boulevard, looped into the rich boulevard of Beverly Hills, and the cab slowed. I spotted Byrd's house. There was a patrol car in front. I said, "Go on to the next block. I'll get off there."

He shrugged and drove on, stopped, and I got out and paid him. He rolled on, the cab rattling like a truck loaded with tin cans. I looked back to see a similar looking cab roll to the curb—Craywell. There was nobody behind him. The street was silent as death. The modern mansions lay back of their green lawns, looking like high-toned mausoleums.

I decided I wasn't going to walk down the block and go past that patrol car and knock on Byrd's door. I certainly wasn't going to do that, but I was going to get into that house and have a chat with brother Byrd.

I walked down the street, passed Craywell's cab without glancing in his direction, then cut up the north side of Byrd's block.

I walked casually, bag in hand, wishing now I'd taken time to check it. I decided to check it now—behind an ageing palm halfway down the block.

Then I took off. I ran low and zigzagged. I scrambled, climbed, jumped and crawled my way to the center of that block where Byrd's house was. Then I was climbing over the louvered redwood fence, and dropping just beside a kidney-shaped swimming pool. I saw how Byrd could have made it in despite the police patrol.

The pool wasn't just a backyard pool, it was a hotel-sized number. Light slanted across it from a broad window across a terrace between the pool and the house. Everything was expensive and cultivated and very modern: stone and wood and glass. I went across the terrace fast and came up to the broad window. I stood at the very edge of it and looked in.

The blond dish I'd seen pictured in the newspaper was sitting there. She had a drink in one hand, gazing at a television set. It made a real heart-warming picture, so homelike, so American; that room alone with its decorating and furnishings would have set back the average, middle-class worker for more than he'd be able to pay even if the installments lasted to his ninety-ninth birthday. But it was the illusion of everyday created by the advertising agencies and the home magazines, the illusion carried around in the average middle-class mind as being typical, regardless of the fact that it was strictly rich.

I tried the sliding glass door. It was unlocked. I stood there, frozen for a second, wondering if I had been right about Thomas Byrd being here. The scene was so peaceful I found it hard to believe that my murdering brother was anywhere around. There was, I decided, only one way to find out.

I slid the glass door open in one motion, stepped inside, reached for the cord controlling the drapes, yanked them shut behind me, and stood looking at Mrs. Thomas Byrd. So this, I thought, was what brother Byrd came home to. I decided to try her first reaction.

"Baby," I said in my best Byrd voice, "papa's come home."

I'd done it all very fast, and she just sat there, drink in hand, looking at me while the television went on across the room. She was a sleek thing, clothed in a stylishly simple white dress. Her hair was not phony-looking blond, although that color could have been and probably was carefully fashioned too.

She was about thirty, I judged. Slim but proportioned. She had rather high cheekbones and good facial structure all around. She also had lovely brown eyes, and full, sensual lips.

She didn't scream. She didn't get up and run for the door. She didn't drop her drink. She didn't do anything but just sit there and look at me with mild and controlled surprise.

Then she was getting up, placing her drink down in the same motion; she was coming across the room, a swift movement that was nevertheless graceful. I didn't know what she was going to do now—finally start screaming, start clawing at my face, pull a knife from her handsome bosom and stab me with it. What she did was the last thing I expected.

She circled my neck and put her face up and kissed me hard.

"Tommy, darling," she breathed finally, "what are you doing here?"

Well, pleasant as it all was, I'd really had enough of it. The gag was going much too far. If it went any further it was likely to kill me.

She stood there looking at me, and I'll admit the physical attraction went the distance between us. She stepped forward one step, and I stepped backward one step. She was taking me off guard, and I didn't like that.

"Darling," she said, "what are you talking about?"

I sighed. I tried to keep my mind on Linda—which shouldn't have been difficult, but at the moment was.

"Look," I said, "why keep it up in the privacy of the house? Why—"

I thought cop instantly. I had figured they would have staked out this house from outside, but not inside—maybe, I thought, they had bugged it. Maybe this girl knew that. My eyes grazed the pictures, the lamps, everything. There were dozens of places a mike could be hidden.

"Darling," she said, "what happened? It's been so horrible, with the police and everything. You didn't ... Uncle Gosset—"

"Sweetheart," I said, stepping forward, "you've got to believe in me."

If there was a flicker, the slightest change in expression in her eyes, I couldn't detect it. She was a marvelous actress. She was also radiating a lot of current. I walked straight to her and put my arms around her, more certain every minute that I'd been wrong about Byrd deciding to come home. "Honey," I said, "I just couldn't stay away."

"Darling—" she said, and once again we were all wrapped up together.

I put my lips against her ear. "So let's quit acting, shall we? Where's Byrd?"

She was breathing hard, leaning into me, kissing me along the neck. A really good actress, all right, but I was certain she was enjoying herself too.

"You know, don't you?" I whispered.

"Yes," she whispered back.

"Where, baby?" I asked, holding her tighter. "Where is he?"

"Right behind you, darling."

13

I turned and looked at Byrd ten feet away from me. He looked a little less formal this time. He wore slacks and an open-collared white shirt. He was smiling, although there was no humor in his eyes. He was also holding a gun in his right hand, pointing it at my middle.

"Move away from him, Clarise," he said.

Clarise did, and Byrd said to me, "You did come, didn't you?"

"I surely did."

"I thought you might."

"I thought you'd think I might."

"I'm glad," Byrd said, a nasty look on his face. "I'm truly glad, Steele."

"I know," I said. "I can see it in your eyes." I spoke quietly, he spoke quietly, and all the time I was trying to figure out how to jump him.

Byrd moved forward toward me. I thought of the gun in my belt. I measured him. He motioned with his gun. "Your hands, Steele. Put them up in the air, as high as you can. Quickly!"

I did. I'd measured him. He looked desperate about this. Jumping him, I figured, was going to be about as easy as a triple somersault off a low board.

He was three feet away now, two feet. I kept watching his gun and his eyes. I wanted to see some relaxation, some hint of opportunity. I didn't find it. He snapped my jacket open and removed the gun from my belt with surprising speed.

Clarise took my gun from him and held it gingerly. She was watching me, and I swear that first charge we'd generated was still going.

"Get some rope from the workshop," he told her. "There's some clothesline there. And put the gun away in there."

She nodded and disappeared.

He stepped back and turned a black armless chair around.

"Over here," he said. "Sit down and put your arms behind you."

"You act like you know what you're doing."

"I do," he answered, "now that you've been thoughtful enough to come right into my house." He motioned the gun. "Hurry up, Steele."

I sat down facing the chair back and put my hands behind me. Clarise had returned now with the clothesline.

"Tie his hands," Byrd snapped. "Tie them tightly!"

She did. She wrapped that rope around my wrists, around my thumbs, and interlaced it back and forth a dozen times. Then she tightened it up and knotted it. I tried to hold my wrists apart a little to provide slack when the job was done. It didn't work. I was tied, but good.

"Now," Byrd said, moving around and approaching me from behind, "search him, Clarise. Carefully."

She began the search, and I felt the muzzle of Byrd's gun go against the back of my head. I hoped his trigger finger was steady. I looked at Clarise's eyes as she searched me slowly and thoroughly. She kept watching me, her hands moving. It might even have been good fun if there weren't a gun pushed against the base of my skull.

"You're being pretty careful, aren't you, Byrd?" I asked.

"I think I should be," he said coldly. "You should have been dead a day ago. You aren't. I'm going to continue to be careful, Steele. I wouldn't try anything at all, if I were you."

I sat there, not talking any more, wondering what in the hell I *could* try, even if I'd lost interest in living.

"Nothing," Clarise said finally. She stepped away, and Byrd came around and surveyed me impersonally. I meant nothing to him, twin brother or not.

"Why did you knock off Uncle Gosset?" I asked finally.

His eyes brushed mine, as though it were impertinent and unimportant for me to know anything. But he said, "I told you he held the strings to the family fortune. He was going to stop my share of the income."

I nodded. I'd figured it fairly accurately. I don't know that I felt any better for knowing that. As a matter of fact it didn't seem to help anything at all.

"You were really busted, after all?" I said.

Now he was behind me again, testing the rope around my wrists. "Precisely. On relative terms, anyway."

"And that's why Uncle Gosset okayed that check the Yellow Tiger people in Reno called him about? It was all relative?"

"A thousand dollars," Byrd said, "was a drop in the bucket to what Uncle controlled—and he wouldn't have put family relationships on public display by failing to authorize an amount like that. Not Uncle."

"So you wore the disguise from Sacramento to Reno, then flew home as yourself and let Uncle have it ... all to save your piece of the income."

It was really a dull conversation—no heart in it either way.

"Stand up," he said.

I did, moving backward away from the chair. "Clarise," he said, "you drive the Chrysler over to Rexford Drive and Elevado. Wait there."

She left, and Byrd motioned toward a door. "That way. Go exactly where I tell you. Move as fast as I tell you. Don't make a sound, do you understand? I'll kill you if you do anything to resist me."

Well, he was calling the signals. I couldn't see my way clear now to argue with him about anything. We moved through the house, out through a breezeway, past the pool, and onto the grounds of the estate behind Byrd's. I heard the exhaust of a car as it left Byrd's garage, and I thought about the patrol car I'd seen in front. They weren't going to help me now. I looked back and saw another cruiser moving slowly down the street on the opposite side of the block, but Byrd stopped me, that gun hard in my back, until it disappeared. We moved on, Byrd guiding, whispering his orders tensely. We stuck to the dark spots, hedges, trees, moving along now with surprising speed. My wrists hurt like hell. Clarise had laced them like an expert.

Then we were arriving at an intersection and I saw the Chrysler waiting. Byrd put me in the front seat beside Clarise, then got in the back seat and replaced the muzzle of that gun at the back of my head. I wouldn't have felt right without it.

Clarise drove carefully. West into Santa Monica. Byrd balanced that gun against my head. I sat still and did nothing. I shifted my eyes once and noted, in the light of passing neon, that Clarise had lovely legs. Then I stopped that. Byrd was very tense and I had the ridiculous thought that anything could set him off, including the direction of my eyes which he could not even see. I just didn't want him to start yanking that trigger.

"Police check the car?" Byrd asked Clarise from the back seat.

"They ran a flashlight over the back seat. That's all. They looked kind of sleepy."

"They didn't follow you?"

"No." She said it so positively that I was certain she was right.

We swung north then, and a few minutes later the car was wheeling down into a drive that led to a beach house. Clarise put the car in a garage, while Byrd kept that damned muzzle pressed against the back of my head. I was directed into the house.

Once more Byrd put me into a chair, then walked away where he could get a good front view of me. The house seemed to be composed mostly of a huge living room: there were beams and nets hanging on one wall and rustic rattan furniture. One whole side of the room was made of window panes, and it looked out to a stretch of private beach. Darkness had come, but I could see the phosphorescence of the waves as they rolled in.

Byrd, for the first time, seemed compelled to explain the house: "Private retreat of ours. Practically nobody outside the family knows about it. Clarise didn't, of course, tell the police about it. She will tomorrow." That sudden, nasty smile on his face told me nothing except that things were now rolling along well for him, poorly for me.

Then he straightened a little, tense and businesslike once more. "I don't think we'd better waste any more time, Clarise. Take the gun now, will you?" He was as polite as could be.

Clarise took the gun and held it on me. Byrd's eyes thinned a fraction, as though his mind was spinning, working out the last detail of whatever it was he was planning to do. Then he walked over to a small writing desk and got out pen and paper, watching me carefully between movements. Byrd's pen scratched away, and finally he held up the paper he'd been writing on, silently read what he'd written, smiled a little, then placed it back on the table. "Very touching, if I do say so."

For the first time Clarise's poise seemed to crack a little. I could see it mostly in her eyes, hear it faintly in her voice when she said, "Don't be sardonic just now, Tom. Just don't be that now."

"Sorry, my dear." He stood up. He looked at me. "Well, Clarise, the longer we put it off—"

She actually shuddered now. I thought how he'd made so many plans, each one scheduled to work under any given circumstance. They could not have been absolutely certain I would appear at their house, but Byrd must have figured that was the best possibility. He'd made plans for it if I did. I had....

"Razor blade, I think," he said, taking the gun from her and holding it on me. "Yes, I think I'm right about that. It's what I would actually do."

"Get it, my dear," he said.

She shuddered once more.

She disappeared. She returned. She held a double-edged razor blade between her fingers. I felt myself sweating. I was indeed sweating. Sweat was pouring down my face. It got in my eyes.

"Will you ?" he began, looking at her.

"No," she whispered. "Oh, no."

He smiled understandingly. He gave her the gun again in exchange for the razor blade. He walked around in back of me.

I found that I was breathing hard now, and I really couldn't help it. Byrd was silent for a moment, then he said, "I think the cord marks will have disappeared by morning, don't you, Clarise?"

"Don't talk," she said. "Just don't talk any more! Just—"

She was really shaken now, and it was getting to me. He gripped one of my tied wrists. He gripped it with unbelievable strength. I started to struggle, but he had hold of me with the kind of grip a drowning man clamps on someone trying to save him.

Through his teeth, I heard, "Mustn't cut the tendons or ..."

14

I felt the razor blade bite my wrist. I must have half screamed, but I don't know if the sound got out. I tried to bite it off between my teeth just as the door swung open. Clarise spun, and behind me Byrd gave a short curse. I could hear, gratefully, the faint clink of the blade as it dropped to the floor.

I had never supposed that I would be happy to see the face of Craywell, but I truly was at that moment.

He carried his black case in his left hand, the snub-nosed .38 in the other.

"*Shoot*, Clarise!" Byrd ordered.

But she didn't. She seemed stunned. She held the gun in her hand, but it was tilted down a little. I doubt if she would have hit Craywell once if she'd emptied the whole gun at him.

Craywell smiled a little. "I'm an expert at this, Mrs. Byrd. I'm quite capable of placing a bullet directly in your heart before you so much as tip your gun. I would drop that gun, if I were you. Quickly."

She did. Craywell stepped into the room and placed his case on a table. He picked up the gun Clarise had dropped. He smiled at me. "I see, Mr. Steele, that you did discover your elusive brother."

"Yeah," I said, "I really did. Byrd, meet Mr. Craywell, emissary royal of Mr. Nick Nicole."

Byrd stepped past me towards Craywell. "Look," he said, "I—"

"Far enough," Craywell said. "I would remain right there, Mr. Byrd."

Byrd stopped, seeming to quiver all over.

Craywell smiled.

"Listen to me—" Byrd began again.

"I think we've listened to you quite long enough," Craywell said.

"I'll pay you, don't you see?" Byrd said, voice rising.

"A promise you have made previously," Craywell said, "and taken very lightly, it appears."

"I didn't have it," Byrd said. "Don't you see that? I didn't have it!"

"Have you got it now, Mr. Byrd?" Craywell asked gently.

Byrd was breathing hard now. "I will. Soon! But this has to be done!"

"What has to be done, Mr. Byrd?"

Byrd waved at me. "Steele, that's the answer!" he said. "The whole answer! You know he's my twin? Well, nobody outside this room does! Look, this note—" He grabbed up the paper he'd written on earlier and waved it at Craywell. "Suicide note," he went on. "Written by me, explaining the argument I got into with my uncle, explaining why I murdered him, explaining how my conscience has driven me to take my own life—"

"Do you honestly think you can get away with this?" Craywell asked Byrd.

"Of course! Wrists cut. He's discovered dead tomorrow. Clarise will identify the body. I will disappear from sight. Then Clarise will assume my trust fund—which my uncle would have stopped, but cannot stop now."

"And how soon is this trust fund paid?" Craywell asked. "Immediately?"

"No," Byrd said. "But the insurance, you see?"

"Insurance?"

"I carry a life insurance policy of one hundred thousand dollars. My wife is the beneficiary. You'll get the entire sum. It can be done, don't you see? I carry Steele's identification. I'll leave the country. Rejoin Clarise somewhere abroad, as Steele—" He stopped talking, watching Craywell with hopeful eyes.

I watched Craywell too. Because if I had felt a small return of hope when he came in that door and prevented Byrd from sawing my wrists completely, I lost it now. Craywell was no friend of mine, nor of anybody else, except momentarily of those who hired him or those who could do him some good. I watched Craywell's eyes, and saw the gleam in them. He was a sadist, I was certain, and I knew now that he was contemplating a double pleasure instead of just one. He was going to get the full fee for his services by collecting the one hundred thousand, and he was going to see somebody die. It was going to be one of the happiest days in Craywell's life.

He motioned with his gun. "All right," he said to Byrd finally. "And this time we will not be gentle if you fail to meet the obligation."

I licked my lips and said, "You'd better listen to me first, Craywell."

Craywell's eyebrows went up, then down. "I'm afraid you're in a very poor bargaining position, Mr. Steele."

"Am I?" I asked. "Think about it, Craywell. You heard Byrd's plan. How does it sound?"

"Very practical," Craywell said, smiling just a little.

"As practical as it would be if Byrd actually died instead of me?"

"Instead of you, Mr. Steele?"

"There's no room for error that way," I said. "The way Byrd has it, I wind up a suicide as Byrd. Clarise identifies the body. Is that enough, Craywell? Do you think any insurance company is going to pay off on that? How far do you think they're going to check it, Craywell? Take Clarise's word alone? Or how about fingerprints? I hear they fingerprint even corpses."

Byrd was really fidgeting now. "Surely you're not going to listen to him," he said to Craywell. "He's desperate and—"

"How about others who know brother Byrd?" I said, talking to Craywell and ignoring Byrd. "You think they wouldn't recognize the switch, even if I am dead? I'm heavier in build. I've got two scars from the war—"

"Closed coffin!" Byrd shouted. "Clarise will demand it!"

"And speaking of Clarise," I said, trying to keep my voice reasonably calm and convincing. "Clarise?"

She looked at me, and I felt that faint vibration coming on stronger.

"Let's just look at it from your angle, Clarise. I don't want to die. I really don't. So let's say Byrd will meet you abroad later, as Mark Steele. So will I, Clarise. You've got a choice, did you realize that?"

I studied her reaction carefully, studied it hard in the short time I had. I wondered how deep her love, if any, was for Byrd. I wondered if their relationship had gone all the way downhill. She had *all* the money now.

"I'll play ball, Clarise," I said. "Indeed I will. I don't think it's any chore to play ball with you—"

Byrd was coming at me now, but Craywell jerked his gun, and his voice though still quiet, was like the snap of a whip. "I wouldn't, if I were you, Mr. Byrd. I would stop and stand still right where you are. I'm enjoying Mr. Steele's monologue."

"How about it, Clarise?" I said. "I know a fine place to meet in Europe. On the French border of Spain. There's a hotel there that serves the finest wine—" She was looking at Byrd now. Examining him. With a cold disdain, I saw. My spirits rose slightly.

"And money, Clarise—don't you think I could handle that better than Byrd? I'm reliable, Clarise. My word is good. I'm also faithful about other things. Ask Byrd about a certain redhead in San Francisco. He hasn't lost money just gambling, honey. Ask him about a blonde in Las Vegas."

Byrd was about to lunge at me again. His wife had a pinched, white look. I glanced at Craywell—there was immense satisfaction on his face; he'd never enjoyed himself more, I knew, watching the scales tip back and forth, with only a matter of a life at stake.

"You hold the cards, Clarise," I said. "One of us is going to die, regardless. And the money is all yours. You make the choice. But remember you have to live with the choice. I'll promise you one thing. If you get tired of me I won't bother you. I'm independent. Byrd won't be. You'll have him hanging around your neck for the rest of your life for that trust fund—"

"Shut him up!" Byrd yelled at Craywell. Craywell merely smiled.

Then Clarise moved. She walked around and back of me, and I knew she was picking up that razor blade. Byrd stared at her, terrified in his fascination. Craywell watched her intently. I felt her hand close around my wrist, and my forehead beaded with sweat all over again.

Then she began cutting, and the rope fell off my wrists. I grinned. I stood up and checked my right wrist. Byrd had only nicked it. I turned and looked at Clarise. Her eyes had a wild look now. She moved to me, lifted her face, and I kissed her. It seemed the least I could do after what she'd just done.

She held that blade between her fingertips and stared at Byrd with a half smile on her lips, a chilling look in her eyes.

"Tell him to come over here and sit down," she told Craywell.

Byrd's jaw was working up and down, and I didn't blame him. She had murder written all over her face. Every pain of that marriage, every hurt she'd taken—and I imagined Byrd had given her plenty—was now ready to be repaid by the slash of a razor blade across a wrist, and she was ready and willing to do it herself.

Craywell smiled delightedly. "The lady's decision," he said, "is also mine, Mr. Byrd. You'd better go over there and sit down."

Byrd stared at Craywell, then at his wife, in utter disbelief. I felt a kind of disbelief myself. I'd talked my way out of it, but I'd held no real hope. And it had mostly been just talk. I had no intention of meeting Clarise on the Spanish border or anywhere else. I didn't really believe that the insurance company would fingerprint a corpse that they had no reason to suspect wasn't as advertised; they didn't know about me, after all, and would doubtlessly have paid off on my corpse as readily as on Byrd's. My plan, though, must have seemed safer to Craywell, least likely to cheat him of his fee—and that was what really did it for me.

Now the pendulum had swung the full arc, and Byrd's wife was running my blood cold by that look on her face.

"Mr. Byrd?" Craywell said.

"No!" Byrd gasped, crouching a little. *"No!"*

"You really have no choice, Mr. Byrd," Craywell said.

I suppose during that moment when nobody said a word, when nobody moved, there was the passage of no more time than perhaps one or two seconds; but it seemed much longer than that. It seemed as though everyone in the room had become waxworks dummies, no longer molded of flesh and blood but of some permanent stuff, to be preserved in that pose eternally.

Craywell stood across the room near the doorway, gun in hand, staring at Byrd with a viciously pleasurable smile on his mouth; Byrd was still half crouched, eyes brilliant, hands slightly spread on either side of him; I still stood by that chair where I'd almost died, just a step from Byrd's wife; and she still held that razor blade between slim fingers, a look of pleasure derived of revenge and the excitement of what she was about to do showing in her eyes and on her mouth.

And then Byrd broke the entire scene by whirling and leaping for the door leading to the beach. He crashed through it, glass splintering as the lock gave and those paned doors slammed open, and dashed onto the sand.

The sand slowed him, and he seemed to be trying to run through heavy mud, a painfully slow running, as though in a nightmare.

Yet the whole action had occurred much faster than it appeared; the entire tension of the moment had speeded up senses so that the movement of Byrd only seemed much slower than it must have been.

And I knew, without looking, that Craywell was bringing up his gun, aiming carefully at that bobbing foot-heavy figure moving across the sand in the light pouring out through the crashed-open doorway.

And I also knew what I would do. I'd served Byrd up on a platter. But regardless of the fact that only a few moments ago Byrd would have gladly sliced my wrists, I could not allow him to be cut down by the man I had, in effect, brought to him. My own movement seemed as slow as brother Byrd's, but I knew it was fast, as fast as anything I'd ever done in my life.

That chair beside me was in my hands, and I was throwing it across the room at Craywell.

Craywell grunted as it banged into him, and I followed the chair, running a few steps, then leaping the rest of the distance. The gun had flipped out of his hand, and he was going for it, but without the gun actually in his hands it was no contest. I was on him, using both fists in a fast trio of blows, the last one, with my right hand catching him directly on the tip of his chin. His head bounced back against the floor, and he was out.

I got up on the run, scooped up his snub-nosed .38 and went for the outside and the beach.

There was a wall on either side of the beach strip, and Byrd was trying to climb the right-hand one. I aimed carefully and knocked out a piece of concrete just to the right of his clutching hands.

He dropped and ran the opposite way. Behind me I heard wood splintering and feet pounding across the floor, but I didn't look around. I aimed carefully again and skipped a bullet into the sand just in front of the running Byrd.

He stopped, tripping, then picked himself up. He'd never looked at me; undoubtedly he thought I was Craywell, enjoying himself. He hesitated only a minute, then headed straight into the ocean.

He obviously didn't know what he was doing. He fought with those waves, struggling with flying hands and feet, coughing and spluttering. A good breaker spun him head over heels once, and now I realized that there were two men in the room, one on each side of me.

They wore light suits and snap-brim hats. I handed one of them the gun I'd taken from Craywell. Out of the corners of my eyes, I saw a blue-suited cop take Byrd's wife to the edge of the stone porch leading to the beach. She wasn't struggling; there was a look of resigned defeat in her eyes. She was watching the struggling Byrd.

"Byrd?" one of the cops asked me.

"Out there," I said.

Then Clarise spoke, spoke with a tone compounded of dullness and a kind of crazy jubilation: "He can't swim."

I took off my jacket and kicked off my shoes. "Hold it," the cop on my right said. I went into the water anyway.

Byrd didn't fight me when I got to him; he'd taken in too much water. I pulled him back to the beach and stretched him out. He was a pathetic sight. Clarise must have thought so too, because she was laughing a little now, a queer unnerving laugh.

The cop on my right said, "I'm Sergeant Pohl. Do you want to tell me what's been going on?"

"Sure," I said. "I'll tell you the whole thing, only it'll take some time—"

Then I remembered. I twisted my wrist, looking at my watch. It was nine-twenty. Nicole still had Linda. Craywell was supposed to call in at ten. If he didn't....

15

There wasn't time to explain in detail; but I hit the highlights fast, and the cops listened. I developed a sudden and new respect for them. I'd caused them a hell of a lot of confusion. They had mixed up the trail of Byrd with mine all the way, so much so that they had been certain Byrd was not hiding out at home because they had picked up my trail in San Francisco.

It was only when Miguel, of mother's old-fashioned hotel, had dipped into my stolen wallet and come up with Byrd's cards that they got the right scent—Miguel had finally heard a news dispatch on Byrd and had gone in hoping for a reward. The cops had traced me through the cab driver who'd taken me out to Beverly Hills, and then had trailed Byrd's Chrysler to the beach house.

They didn't seem to hold any grudges against me, and when I explained why I hadn't gone to them for help, they seemed a little annoyed but understood my reasons.

And they listened to my explanation of what was going to happen to Linda if Craywell didn't get in his ten o'clock call to Nicole in Las Vegas. But that wasn't helping Linda.

We went to work on Craywell, but it was like trying to warm your hands on dry ice. Sergeant Pohl tried it all ways, polite, tough, every way in the book. But Craywell was not budging. He refused to make the call, and it was going to be chop-chop for Linda if he didn't. I felt sick. It was five minutes before ten, and Craywell still was not tumbling.

Then, as we were ringed around Craywell in that beach house, with Byrd and Clarise paddied away, Sergeant Pohl hit a nerve with Craywell: "Look at it this way, Craywell—you don't report in to Nicole, Nicole does in the girl. What good is that to you?"

Craywell, not even sweating slightly, shrugged. "What good is it either way? Dead or alive. Nicole knocks her off, not me."

"But then what?" Pohl said. "Nicole doesn't get your phone call, so he knocks the girl off, but he also figures something is wrong. Check?"

"You have a brilliant mind, sergeant," Craywell said. "Why don't you tell me?"

"I'll tell you this. Nicole takes off. He hides and who's going to find him then? Us? Not likely. He's all safe, all hidden away. And you take it alone then. You're an accessory to murder. You're mixed up in an illegal gambling racket. Your past gets to be an open book ... How about that? You take the whole thing all by yourself, and Nicole gets out."

You could see the flicker in Craywell's eyes. Sergeant Pohl straightened, wiped his brow, and said casually, "Is that how you want it, Craywell? Or do you want to call Nicole now and report in and tell him everything's fine so we can go get him? It's up to you, Craywell."

Craywell got his handkerchief from his breast pocket and wiped his hands gently and said, "I'll call Nicole."

A few minutes after Craywell made his call, I was speeding in a patrol car to the airport. We couldn't be sure just what Craywell had managed to tell Nicole and what he hadn't. The conversation had sounded right, but we couldn't be certain that Craywell, in some fashion, had not alerted Nicole.

The Vegas cops met me at the Las Vegas airport, and in minutes we were whipping into the desert. The cops, on the whole, were happy. They had wanted Craywell for a long time. Now they had him, as sure as they had Byrd along with Clarise. Now there was a chance of getting Nicole, who had really put his head in the noose when he'd picked up Linda.

But I was only worried about Linda. I'd remembered Byrd's description of the ranch-type place where he'd done the gambling. The cops, who hadn't before been able to pinpoint his place, had singled out a location that met the description. I'd also remembered Byrd's description of the guy he'd thought to be the head man—toughlooking, built like a barrel, with a streak of white running back from his forehead. That matched the cop's description of Nicole. And now we were heading for that ranch.

But we didn't know if Nicole would be there, or if he'd taken Linda some place else—*If* she were still alive. My hands were sweating, and even the cool night air of the desert didn't help.

The place was on a small country road. The cop in charge spread his men out in a large fan, and we went in, on the predetermined minute, toward the lights of the main house.

There was no apparent movement anywhere. Three large cars were parked in front of the house, a low, rambling structure looking ghostly in the moonlight. To the side of the house I saw a row of small cabins. There was also a detached garage, very large, and on the opposite side of the house from the cabins was a stable. I could smell the horses. It was pretty much the way Byrd had described the place.

I went in behind two cops, who ordered me to stay behind them. Linda. Where was she? Or was she here at all? If she were alive ... My throat got tight, and I refused to think about that any more.

I just went in behind the cops, closer and closer, tensing more every second, until I finally heard the whistle. Then there was the pounding of feet as cops hit the long porch of the house, and I started running in too.

I heard perhaps half a dozen shots, and saw one very large, very big-headed figure run straight out of the house and tumble onto the turf outside—the croupier, I decided.

The two cops ahead of me motioned for me to drop, and they went on ahead. I did as they ordered, because I had begun to respect these boys a good deal. After all, they were specialists. It was a good thing I did drop because a bullet whined over my head just then—just about, I figured, where I'd been standing.

I looked ahead, trying to see how it was going, hoping like hell they were getting Linda out. The cabins lay to my left, and the cops were methodically kicking in the doors. The stable was off to my right, and as the night breeze blew against my face, carrying that horsy smell, I detected something else mixed with it—something familiar, very familiar, a scent I could never forget: Linda's perfume!

The next second I saw a flash of dress and then the outline of Linda as she was being pulled, a hand clamped over her mouth, by a man shaped like a barrel. I caught the glint of a white streak in his hair in the moonlight, and then I was going after them as they headed for the stable.

Most of the cops had hit the house from the front and the cabin side, and all of them had entered now. Nicole, I figured, had taken Linda out a back-terrace window. It was only a short run to the stable, and I yelled for help. But guns were popping inside now and nobody heard me. I went after them alone.

I realized by the time I got to the stable doors that I had no gun. But the pull towards Linda was too strong to go back or wait for help.

I bounced into the stable on the dead run, figuring Nicole hadn't seen me follow. Moonlight coming in through the stable windows revealed him dragging her along between the stalls. His back was to me.

I went after him, sprinting hard, hoping to hit him before he saw me. I didn't make it. He'd just kicked open a stall gate when I dived for him, and I never touched him.

I surprised him, though, and he let go of Linda. She started screaming—from sudden relief and hope, I guess—when she saw me, and threw herself at me just as I got to my feet. I pulled her back, both of us stumbling against another stall gate. It all happened in two, maybe three seconds.

I had a live, breathing Linda on my hands; but Nicole had whirled around in front of that open stall, standing in front of a big black, saddled stallion, gun in hand, all set to chop us down.

We couldn't do a thing about it, I knew, and I even realized with a strange detachment what he'd planned to do—take off on that horse, with Linda for protection, get out in the desert where the cops couldn't follow him in their cars, then threaten to kill Linda if they didn't stay off his tail and give him a chance to escape.

Well, I wasn't going to stop him, but he was going to have to shoot my hands off Linda before I gave her up. And that was what I was waiting for in that brief second it took Nicole to focus and put the gun on me and fire the first shot.

The shot sounded like ten cannons going off in that stable, and I waited to go down. Only I realized the first bullet he'd snapped off had pounded into the wood rail beside me. I clutched Linda tighter, getting myself in front of her. As Nicole started to get off the next shot, that stallion behind him in the stall, reacting to the first shot, reared up, flared its nostrils, let out a terrible whinny and slammed forward.

Nicole got it in the back, and it wasn't pretty. He went down like a broken rag doll, and the stallion finished him when it bolted straight forward and then around for the open door leading to the desert.

Suddenly it was very quiet in that stable. I held Linda's face gently, so she couldn't look at the battered form on the stable floor, feeling her tears turn my hands wet, and then the cops were coming into the stable....

And so I had Linda once more in my arms, only this time it was different. It had been just fun and games before, now it was more than that. About a lifetime more, I figured.

THE END

9 781944 520281